Joanna Briscoe's first novel, *Mothers and Other Lovers*, won the Betty Trask Award, and has been translated into several languages. She has had short stories published in several anthologies, including *Revenge*, and has written features for many publications, including the *Guardian*, *Observer*, *Sunday Times* and *Vogue*. Joanna Briscoe lives in London.

Skin

JOANNA BRISCOE

PHŒNIX

A PHOENIX PAPERBACK

First published in Great Britain
by Phoenix House in 1997
This paperback edition published in 1998 by Phoenix,
a division of Orion Books Ltd,
Orion House, 5 Upper St Martin's Lane,
London WC2H 9EA

A CIP catalogue record for this book
is available from the British Library.

ISBN: 0 75380 164 7

Printed and bound in Great Britain by
The Guernsey Press Co. Ltd,
Guernsey, Channel Islands

FOR HOLLY BRISCOE

Many thanks to: Kathleen Anderson, Carole Blake, Luigi Bonomi, Carol Briscoe, Frank Briscoe, Sylvia Brownrigg, Stephanie Calman, Anne Cassidy, Eleanor Clarke, Tony Dixon, Lisa Eveleigh, Peter Grimsdale, Erika Guha, Tania Guha, Susan Hochman, The MacDowell Colony, Maggie McKernan, Tejina Mangat, Kathrin Perutz, Kate Saunders, the Society of Authors and the Betty Trask bequest, Poppy Strachan.

ONE

I have very pale skin, very red lips. The lips are a fleshy cushion of pink, but I colour them dark scarlet. The skin is naturally pale, that prized magnolia of lovers, the skin of fairy tales and calves, and it is dusted with Shiseido, a white powder. The journalists have always talked about my skin.

Today I'm walking through the Jardin du Luxembourg on my own. It's April, there's a sore yellow light teasing the shadows between the trees, and young English nannies push babies along the paths and stop at the sandpit.

The shaded section soothes me. I must protect my face from the divings of sunlight because I am using Retin-A, a vitamin A-based cream that sheds layers of skin like sheaves of paper. If the sun reaches my face, it will burn. So I use sun block all over, that gives me a greased sheen when I first step out, but which is later absorbed, and will protect me from second-degree burning. I am Adèle Meier, something of a celebrity, and I must protect my skin. The Retin-A plumps and dissolves the surface wrinkles, and makes me only faintly sore. It comes in a harmless little tube, with just a touch of the medicinal about it so that beyond the acidic, my skin exudes the rosy-pink smell of cosmetics.

As I walk around, I can observe who looks at me and who doesn't. Today I'm wearing a closely fitting dress coat over a long skirt. The coat falls just above my knees and its darts are stiff as whale bones at my waist. My waist is very slim: I've kept it that way. My new shoes, little pumps in a raised black brocade, please me when I look down at my feet: their tippy-toe neatness.

'Could you tell me the time?' someone asked.

I told him, but he didn't look at me afterwards. He was quite young, early thirties, and handsome, dressed in the manner of Parisian men all century. But his gaze didn't linger after I had consulted my watch.

'Adèle Meier.'

I heard my name quite distinctly, and yet perhaps the words were broken into the syllables of suggestion through the trees, as a group of people passed, and walked on. They had English accents. The British don't recognise me so often. Sometimes they do, and then they are very courteous, because they are pleased with themselves for having recognised someone whose reputation originates elsewhere.

There was another, younger man looking at me, standing by the statues beyond the trees. He seemed fleetingly familiar: perhaps he lives in the neighbourhood, or perhaps he is simply representative of a type, those young men with hurt chiselled faces and big eyebrows. When I turned, his eyes appeared to be following me, though it was difficult to be certain through the dances of blindness in the tree paths. I looked at him directly, and he turned and walked away, feigning insouciance.

I have begun to wonder recently, to wonder seriously, whether men still find me quite so attractive. You can barely see the fading of beauty in yourself, and ageing comes in fits and starts, a clear period in which you appear to be ageless, a sweet unfrowning passage of time granted as a reprieve; and then one morning you wake up and dry lines are etched in a new pattern of frowns and crannies, the fine boundaries of new worlds delineated by a cartographer, as if my forehead were lines of black ink, blocks of blue and green. It all happens in the space of a night.

So recently I saw a dryness across my forehead, more a surface crazing of the skin than the deeper explorations of wrinkles. I project one image into the mirror, onto the camera, before I see myself, and the reflection, perhaps, obligingly melts into the shape of that illusion. It is possible that a new dulling has taken place that I have failed to see. This wasn't meant to happen. I sort of imagined, without ever consciously addressing it, that I might stay a girl for ever.

A few days later I saw with all certainty in the morning light that the recent dryness had cast a dullness across my skin and settled into a permanent tarnish. So slight, not so much the dropping of a petal as a curling of its edge, but still I pulled at the flesh and ran my finger back and forth across the dryness, grinding my forehead and the bridge of my nose across my sleeve to see the dust of my skin nest there, my face laid to waste.

I walked out later in the afternoon along the boulevard Saint Michel. I veered away to go to Félix Potin – get myself bread, some lamb's lettuce – and to the library to do some work. It is so stifling sometimes at home, myself a stuffed pigeon overlooking the roofs of Paris, the Jardin du Luxembourg. But outside, I could see the loss of bloom reflected in shop windows, glancing to one side as I drifted along the boulevard. This is a woman who is beautiful, in whom beauty is a precise description, not the approximation of a term that is bandied about and applied to mere prettiness. *Ugliness* is as closely related to beauty as prettiness, prettiness possessing only the power to please, not the simultaneous ability to excite and disturb that is beauty's own province.

The woman is forty-something but she could perhaps be thirty-seven, thirty-eight. She is one of those people who might belong to another era, to the forties, or, at times, the fifties. It is the skin that makes her so remarkable, the milky creamy substance of it. The bones in their dives and lines and proportions are the sculpture underneath, the chance of their classical arrangement the basis of her beauty.

I see her now. I see that my beauty does not please everyone. They say I am like a spring ghost; they say I'm like a geisha. The journalists call me stunning, kittenish, vampiric.

The library was hot. Nevertheless, I needed to be there to research some facts about women in broadcasting for a television debate. Since I stopped my *Loulou* books, my work has taken on a life of its own. No longer the slave of one contract, I am free to dip and taste.

I noticed a student sitting in the library. He was youthful, but there was an ugliness about him, a coarseness of the mouth composed of over-large lips or a slackness of expression. His T-shirt was loosely tucked into his blue jeans but spilled out over his belt at the back. He was tall, and he shifted in his chair, wrapping his feet around each other until they sickled and exposed the muddied white tracks of his sneakers.

I moved silently through the aisles. I didn't look straight at him, but he swam like a dot in my consciousness as mentally I trailed him. The loose lips worked in silent concentration, mouthing fragments of his essay. He frowned, and the sun lit the ends of his eyelashes, turning them fair.

I brushed against him as I walked by the row of desks. Drifts of sweat nestled in patches around him in the still warmth from the window. There were other young men on other tables, ones with sharper haircuts or finer profiles, a clump of them from the university, but I was drawn to this one. I walked back along the aisle and jolted his elbow in passing. He looked up at me with slight irritation, but I had already passed, and he probably stared at my back.

4

This time his sweat was sharper: the smell of three days of underarm on close-weave cotton. I imagined, briefly, his student's life, his grubby union cards and note pads, his inevitable cringing paranoias and frequent erections in his lodgings. Perhaps there was some fresh-bosomed first year he dreamed of. I saw a girl, white and moley and virginal, studying the microfiche, and thought that perhaps he would like to have sex with such a girl, this very girl perhaps, glove his penis in untried flesh to prove something to himself.

I walked back again. The boy had become conscious of my meandering along the aisle, and was fidgety and aware. I stared at him. Young thing! He stared back momentarily, the eyes blankly pale, hormonal, then dropped his gaze. The sun washed out his lashes again, and he closed his large lips firmly and returned to his essay.

I flicked my nails across some spines in the Italian section. My nails made a clackety sound as I trailed them over the books. They are long and polished, today a coffee coral. I paused and looked at the boy, narrowing my eyes to identify him against the sun. He was there, the mouth loosening again, the dispersed concentration regathering.

Returning through the central aisle unobserved by him, I loitered near the pale virgin and the microfiche until the sun had baked the back of the student's head into perfect stillness. Little darlings, they can't help themselves, just can't help their young groins twitching when certain women pass them by. The movements of paper and insects were the only sounds that edged the silence.

He was quite attractive in the gauche, white-limbed manner of arrogant boydom. I wanted to stroke, briefly, the section of his lower back where the T-shirt spilled out over the jeans, or tuck it in for him, padding the sun-warmed base of his spine. I wanted him to want me, momentarily, strain for me, his groin straining and thrusting.

I stood in the sunlight, then walked slowly by the row of

desks, bathed in sun, in sinuous unconcern.

'You are looking a little hot,' I murmured.

He glanced up from his desk by the window, made a sound.

I smiled at him slightly.

He breathed out through his nose in acknowledgement of my comment, and returned to his essay.

I moved nearer the window, swivelled, bent at the waist, and looked at the traffic in the street below.

'I am sure . . . I'm sure there are things we'd all prefer to do on a day like this,' I said to him. 'The sun's so hot . . . look at the gleam on the foliage! I'll walk out there in a moment, and buy a new dress.'

He looked down at his work.

'Do you like what I'm wearing now?' I said to him teasingly.

'Yes,' he said. He looked down at his essay.

I stared down at his head. His hair baked and gathered electricity in the sun.

He looked up at me after a while, his pen held above his essay.

I turned to face him, smiled at him. I stretched. The sun from the window was on my arms.

'Well,' I said.

I moved away and began to look at book titles. His eyes followed me. His mouth was slack again. I was wearing a white gauzy dress with a little cropped black jacket, a little velvet jacket with three-quarter-length sleeves, like theatre wear.

He almost smiled at me, a chunky grimace, then shifted, the jean-clad legs rearranging themselves, and returned to his essay.

'What a shy thing,' I murmured, leaning over his desk again. The sweat mixed with the straw flat scent of his hair. Afternoon stubble dotted his skin. His hands were large but sweet skinned. He was ordinary.

'I'm used to a little . . . ' I rearranged a stray page.

6

'Are you studying?' he said eventually.

'You think I'm a student?'

'No, but . . . '

I smiled at him. 'I'm conducting some empirical and theoretical research on women in broadcasting. What does that mean to you?'

'*Hein,*' he shrugged, that French boy's noncommittal grunt.

I laughed. 'I must leave you,' I said.

'No, you . . . ' he said.

'You want me to stay and talk to you?'

'OK.'

I raised an eyebrow at him.

'Yes.'

'Well, what shall we talk about?'

He was silent.

'Does the sunlight make you a little bit horny?'

He raised his head violently, his mouth slack and jutting like a suckling animal pulled from the nipple.

'It makes me feel like a cat,' I said, 'like a cat purring and arching its fur in the warmth.'

I walked away. Let him follow me. Let him prove that I'm irresistible still.

I caught sight of myself in the glass door leading into the dark stairwell.

Oh God. Oh sweet fucker. I have big weals in my forehead, the lines around my eyes grooved deeper with a smile still held. There is a roughness of age where I picture a moving bloom. And I had been playing like a kitten, feeling my slimness only, imagining youth, reflecting myself back in the boy's face, the bird of youth. A sob of despair at the back of my throat. I had been warding off truth with a double bluff: I feel old, so that is my insurance against old age; I fear my face is ageing, so the fear is the thing, not the ageing, and my friends will laughingly tell me so. Now I see age like I've never seen before: I have passed into a different phase of it. A frozen, granular fall of realisation. This is not how I feel. I do not look how I feel. This is not me. The despair of this, etched into that web of lines, the cruel ghosts of laughter and coquetry preserved in mockery. To mock me: how dare you think glory, old woman. *Old woman.*

So I had to try it out. I went back to the youth. I stumbled back. I passed him, whispered a rush of tangled sweetnesses into his ear.

'*À bientôt,*' I called out to him.

I walked slowly towards a side exit.

He would follow me. My heart thumped. He hadn't recognised me. The young usually don't. Certainly not young men.

'Closing,' called a librarian. 'Library closed in quarter of an hour.'

He hadn't followed me yet. My heart battered the pause. I waited for a minute, two minutes. The sounds of people packing up their bags, returning books, gurgled like water above me. I waited, and into the clatter he emerged. He was hesitant, playing cool.

I smiled at him. I looked like a kitten again.

I walked ahead, down the stairs and out into the street. He followed me. A boom of heat and traffic swallowed us, and then settled, bird sounds through the fumes, the traffic pumping quietly like my blood, and this boy, a slack-limbed stranger beside me, our limbs moving together.

And then we saw the other boy, the one who must live in my neighbourhood, because I think now that I have noticed him before, before the day in the park. The boy, my neighbour or my strange little observer, now stands out in all clarity watching me, with his dark eyebrows and air of concentration; then his figure bends in the traffic fumes, a mirage in lines of heat, and he walks away on the shaded half of the street. He seems to recognise me. Whether as Adèle Meier or as a resident of the Cinquième, I don't know.

*

8

He saw me with the student from the library. He saw a woman step onto the street with fine ankles bony in strappy shoes, her wide netty skirt white wings over her legs. The bones and pearls of the crotch beneath it in his imagination only.

Her nose is emphatic: large but defined, a demanding nose over a mouth that has an upper lip bigger than the lower (this is unusual), so it is sexual and vulnerable at once. Those bruised upper lips do not form the pout that a dominant lower lip creates by pushing the top lip from beneath. The larger upper lip makes it look as if it had been hit a few days earlier; it holds the mouth a fraction open over the teeth. The nose imperious; the mouth a sexual area. What is unexpected are her eyes, apricot-green pool water, bruises on the pale skin. They should be grey or grey-blue on that colouring. The eyes have scattered themselves on the surrounding skin, in ghosts of freckles, the after-image of the colours spilled out on the paleness. You can't look at that echo of darkness – it draws you in too far.

The young man of the Cinquième saw the beautiful woman with a boy younger even than himself. They stepped out of the library together into the throttle of blaring May sunshine on the street, the boy with his slack mouth and thumping heart giving the impression of a wet-jawed dog, trailing half a step behind her onto the shaded half of the street to escape the sunlight.

'What's your name?' he said.

'Adèle.'

Rogue heat in May.

'Yours?'

'Thierry.' The name a Gallic grunt.

'Oh I like French boys' names,' I murmured, but I was concentrating on the mirage ahead, the dust and fumes on metal, and his chattering buzzed by my ear. I remembered,

9

momentarily, being a child, and the bugs in the air, and the big bully boys walking back on the same road from school.

We reached my apartment building. I hesitated. Thierry pushed in through the door. He suddenly grinned at me proprietorially as if I would escape. The faint smell of animal sweat rose in the cool of the lobby.

'Jean-Pierre, how are you?' I asked the concierge.

'Well, thank you. How is Madame? Any more problems with the pigeons?'

'Are you offering to come and shoot them for me, Jean-Pierre? Isn't he just so kind?' I turned to the youth. 'He makes sure my flowers are delivered, he bullies unwanteds away, and now he's offering to come up with his shotgun and deal with the vermin! Are you going by the Post Office later, J-P? I have a little package . . . Oh, fabuloso! I think I'll go out later and pick you some roses myself from the Jardins; with my own hands. This is, this is *. . . Thierry*, the son of a friend of mine.'

I turned away. The supremely ordinary youth followed me into the elevator, though I didn't bid him. He shuffled his feet in his chewing-gum white sneakers. We stood in the elevator cage. Madame Tabet, the cantankerous old bitch from the fifth floor, stared at me accusingly. She always looks at me as though I'm a prostitute, even if I'm dressed in a long winter coat. Even if I cover myself like an Arab wife.

The cage rattled up through the floors.

Mme Tabet got out. We rode a further storey. The elevator cage shook like a dog at the sixth floor. The boy got out with his loping dog legwork and waited patiently for instructions. I imagined someone whipping him like a cur, and he would like it. I imagined palming his sap-pale penis.

Pigeons tocked along my windowsill and stabbed the flower boxes. Their excrement had turned the surface white; spurts of white and grey lightened the lower panes. We were high up there, over the gardens, the roofs. Over to the right, far up the boulevard and into the river, is Notre Dame. I think I can hear it sometimes, mixed with the Panthéon, on the wind. Little Esmeralda danced on her mat. There was a feather on my carpet.

The photo of me with Mebarak Husni the Algerian activist caught fire on its glass. The sunlight ate a hole out of it, a disc of invisibility, but as I moved, my face appeared, its features emerging as if in a developing tray, the lines darkening. I look like a little girl sometimes, the lines under the eyes the worries of youth; the little monkey lines even babies are born with.

Thierry, the boy, stood near the kitchen. I ran him a glass of water. The sunlight quartered my desk and its piles of paper. It painted the bed. I paddled through it onto the mattress.

He drank his water. He stood with his feet planted apart and wetted his whole mouth.

He walked towards me. He grinned shyly, but he was more confident now.

'How are you?' he grunted.

'How am I? The same as I was an hour ago, when you first saw me in the library.'

'Oh,' he said. He smiled awkwardly. He was one of those slightly scruffy youths of a pale straw colour whose attraction lies in their lust. His penis will be shifting in his underpants now, moving for me.

Seconds went by.

'Well, what can I say?' I said to him. 'You look very appealing, standing there like that in the sun. What do you think of my apartment?'

He looked around. 'There's so much stuff!' he said.

'Yes. Well, what do you think of it?'

'Pretty.'

'Do you recognise the woman in the photos on the wall over there?'

'It's . . . You.'

'Yes, but I look different in a couple of them, don't I? Photography almost always results in some strange metamorphosis. Television more so.'

He shifted towards my bed and sat precariously on the edge of my mattress. I lay against the wall end without moving.

On the bed was a pink satin eiderdown, a shimmering upholstered coverlet from a Joan Crawford movie glowing with early Technicolor. It was punched and rucked: I had been sweating the night before, because I was worrying, and in the morning I'd kicked it into a roll on the side of the bed. My slip and my salmon silk kimono lay twisted in its folds. A pubic hair clung to the sheet; it became buried under the boy's jeaned leg.

'Well,' he said. He looked at his big metal watch. 'My tutorial's starting now.'

'Go, then,' I said. The pigeons clawed the window boxes.

'Oh,' he said. 'I want to stay with you.'

'Oh,' I said. 'Why do you want to stay with me?'

'Because you're . . .'

'Because I'm what?' I stayed still and looked him in the eye.

'Pretty.'

'Am I? Thank you.'

He extended a large hand and kneaded my ankle. His blunt boy's nails were almost as large as the ball of my ankle.

I lay back. He continued to knead my ankle, caressing the tendons around the bone.

'Press the foot,' I said.

He moved his thumb inside my shoe to my sole and rubbed the flesh, rolling it, pressing into the instep. I breathed out through my nose; I lay back further, gazing at the ceiling without focus, and he rubbed my foot and I absorbed the soporific pain of it, the foot a quiescent object in his grasp.

He raised my leg and slipped my shoe off and brushed my toe with a sodden butterfly kiss so I shivered with the dart of wetness, his lips covering the nub. I extended my foot and sank it deeper into his mouth, until he bathed the toe in saliva, his tongue flapping and circling, its tip tickling the bridge of skin between my toes.

The bells, the Panthéon bells, or perhaps it was the bells of Notre Dame, rang in discs of sound beyond the boulevard.

There is a donkey harnessed to a tourist cart outside the Notre Dame, a bucket hangs below his penis to catch his urine. He stands there with his passive gaze all day while tourists point at him, and the plastic bucket deals with his functions.

The young man moved his mouth up my ankle and nibbled the side of my calf. He has learnt a few things in the short period of his sexual flowering. His lips moved up my leg; he shifted on the bed, bending over me, exposing the area of back above his jeans that curved into a dip, a warm hollow of spine and down.

'Come closer,' I said.

He moved his body further up the bed. I inserted my nails into the little space beneath his belt. I scratched his skin. I ran my fingertips over the ridges at the base of his spine and crept, backwards and forwards, backwards and forwards, towards the root of his ass. I edged into that plateau, that blank pale inch before the buttocks divide and rise; I probed and withdrew.

He issued a muted moan. His Adam's apple loosened.

I lay against the pillow again. The sun was now a bright triangle where his foot dug into the sheet. A section of his hair flopped in a slow arc against my thigh. I lay back; I did nothing. He looked faintly disconcerted. He leant over me and took my legs in his large hands and moulded them. I clearly excite him more than the pale virgin, though he could have gorged new routes into her. He could have made an indelible mark on her with his penis; her first lover in some college room strewn with posters and discarded bottles.

I lay back. The springy cloth of my skirt floated up about his hands. He worked silently, emitting the top notes of grunts as he felt my thighs in steady explorations. I lay back, and my chin faced him, the white skin of my neck exposed to his vision. He ran his middle finger up my inner thigh, circling and pulling his fingertip back down my leg. I moaned. He pushed further. The tip of his finger moved in that little hollow of my thigh below the vulva with an electric moth lingering. I jerked minutely.

'But you see, Thierry,' I said, 'women need to be talked to.'

'Eh?' He looked up.

'Seduction is psychological, don't you think?'

'Oh, yes,' he said. 'Lift your . . . please . . . so I can . . . '

'But, Thierry, my sweetness, what did I just say to you?'

'You're gorgeous,' he muttered into my skirt.

'I suppose that you sexually liberated "young people" are not so given to simple talk.'

I ran my fingernails through the back of the head that now nuzzled my crotch area. He nibbled through my skirt, his large lips rucking the material and dragging at it, guzzling and blowing warmth, pulling it against my panties beneath. I moaned; my thighs moved without me, pushing into his mouth.

My hips rose involuntarily, and he rubbed his mouth harder against my pubic bone, sucking a stain of sodden ridges in the tulle of my skirt, working there, biting and trembling and not rising. The friction of the layers rubbed together scattered grains of sensation through my genitals, fragments mounting to a point of heat.

I murmured to him, sending him signals. I scratched his scalp harder, shaking his head in an echo of his jerks.

He dropped my skirt like a gnawed bone, lifted its fabrics in a crown above his head, and dipped his mouth on my thigh. The pigeons tapped more lightly on some outer skin of hearing.

*

I can see now that he wants me. His mouth on my panties. He doesn't dare rise above the waist and kiss my lips. He buries himself down there, a shy and horny little stag.

He must work harder. I sent him flickers of encouragement. He has never touched my breasts; they have softened and pointed. I am aware of my new age in every angle, for all my slimness. I have to know. Only to see, to tease and prick the surface.

His arm, splayed forward like an animal drinking or bowing at a fountain, was pale and gold-haired, a perfectly formed male forearm. His fingers flexed and balled as he moved his lips over my pubic mound. I tickled the spaces of soft boy skin between the fingers, and he looked at me, and I smiled at him.

'Thierry, you can't be accustomed to visiting unknown women's bedrooms,' I murmured.

'No,' he said. A grunt.

'We must teach you some *boudoir* manners, don't you think? Sex is not just genitals, is it?'

He sat up with rumpled hair. He looked at me out of sly eyes. These boys are so arrogant, even the shy ones. It's in their smile, the way they feel no need to grease the wheels of social convention. It is the birthright of their gender. They breathe, they eat, they exist.

His hand encased the span of my ankle. His foot rested thoughtlessly on some antique glass beads on the floor, little moons of glass on a string that I bought once in the market and love.

'Men are so very strange,' I said. 'They think women want sex in a void. They think ... that sex is about flesh and movement and possession, and they forget that seduction occurs in the mind. Caress my heart, Thierry.'

He moved his mouth. He shifted his jeaned leg still further up the bed, and briefly embraced me, stroking my chest and my breasts through my dress.

'Oh, Thierry . . . ' I said with a quick laugh.

His hand slid over my shoulder, and he tried to unzip my dress from behind.

'No,' I said.

He stopped. He hesitated. He pulled off his T-shirt. The flat pale hairs of his head were echoed in darker gold on his chest; his torso was tight and precisely grooved where it met his belt and tapered to his penis. The area between his neck and the balls of his shoulders was a fan of tendons. The sweat smelt fresher.

'I don't want to undress, Thierry. Clothes are a frame, don't you think? I'm in an ivory silk frame.'

'Just your dress,' he said.

'What do you think of the picture I've conjured up for you?' I said. 'Do you like it?'

'You are pretty,' he said, each word a monotone nudging the loose expanse of his lower lip.

I arched my back. He lightly fingered the tips of my breasts through the silk.

'A little harder please,' I said.

My neck arched backwards. He flicked his fingers over my nipples, the silk echoing the sensation in its grain. A spasm rippled through my thighs.

I breathed out. The friction on my nipples fanned nerves in my forehead. My vagina was congesting. I breathed deeply.

'In a minute, you must go,' I said.

He shrugged. He sat there.

'Oh, you want to stay, do you?'

'I want to touch your soft flesh.'

'Do you, Thierry?'

He stroked my shoulders, my breasts.

'Which section of my soft flesh is it that appeals to you, precisely?'

'Your – ' he stopped.

'Let me try to guess, shall I? Where would a young man such

as Thierry like to touch a woman he desires?'

'On all your beautiful flesh,' he said.

I moaned.

I heard the elevator rattle from subterranean depths.

'I said that you had better go,' I whispered. 'But first, touch me where you . . . '

He caressed my breasts swiftly, harder, in a valedictory caress, his shoulders now sweating in urgency, and he grunted, and shifted on the bed to ease his aching penis, pressing his crotch hard down in the mattress. His hands travelled downwards. He encased my thigh. I darted my tongue across his flesh.

'Tell me, tell me where you're touching me,' I said. 'Tell me *as* you touch me.'

'The top of your leg . . . your thigh.'

'A little harder.'

He moved slightly. He lay, his hip hooked to mine, the swell of his penis pressing on the mattress, and he shook and arched, and held my shoulders, nuzzled my neck, rotating in small circles on the mattress while his hand wandered over my crotch. He sucked my neck. I suddenly pressed my nails hard into his back, grasped his buttocks in their jeans and squeezed them, my nails pressing into the denim. I dug harder, and he jerked his head up. I pulled his head back towards me and grabbed a clump of his hair, grinding him into my neck, his mouth open. He bit me. I breathed faster. I moved my hip against his crotch, pressing hard. He ground his body into me.

He inched his hand upwards and fumbled for his zipper.

'No,' I said languorously, 'I really don't feel like being penetrated, Thierry.'

He moaned, grunted. He dropped his hand. He grabbed my waist and rubbed himself harder against my hip, the seams of his zipper bunching my skirt, while his hand travelled over my thighs, plucking at the hems of my panties. He ventured a fingertip into the mound of pubic hair.

17

'Not in there, Thierry,' I said lazily. 'It's very sacred, don't you agree? Only – poets – are permitted in there. Only those who speak poetry. It's a very private place.'

He was beyond speech. He muttered something, grunted into my neck, sucked and bit; he caressed the lips of my vulva through the cloth of my panties, their exact damp shape, tugging the cloth over the hair, fingering the wet hollows in a frenzy, and as the heat mounted, and my body rose, with no pigeons, no sound, no time, he rubbed himself into me and bit my shoulder, and I moaned high as he yelped a deep male cry, and as I lay afterwards in a haze of sweat, a strand of my hair curved over the bite on my shoulder, mahogany against blood. The dark brown glinted in a bed of fresh red. I breathed fast, my body light, and then he left.

I rested on the bed, and the shadow and rose of early evening fluctuated as I lay, now in a bath of grey light, now in a bath of pink, and the pigeons had softened, and I breathed deeply and steadily, alone. What is the sadness – their *tristesse* is more accurate – that hits you when you're alone after orgasm? You are more alone than you will ever be in your life. Laurence used to leave me in this state, wet and beached, and stranded. The loneliness slams you in the throat and you know then, like no other time, that you are born alone, you live with someone, and you die alone.

I slipped into another dress. The dancer's dress, or the theatre dress, slipped over my hips as I unzipped it – as Thierry had not been permitted to do – and collapsed on the floor. It died without me. I saw my breasts. I tied a scarf round my neck.

The afternoon had paled, the shadows in my building already dark stains of cold in the corridors. The carpeting in the common areas with its absurd crested monogram soaks up the gloomy overhead lighting that burns all day even in summer.

It's a clanking old edifice – a ship, a hotel – breeding cockroaches in the hot-water pipes, pigeons on the balconies. A faint fug of urine emanates from the old ladies' apartments; the young couples leave bicycles in the corridors and bribe the concierges; there is a highly sexually motivated janitor called Saâd whose libidinous expectations revolt me. It's a tank of an apartment building, but being French, its solidity is scrawled over with curlicues of latticework, shutters, baroque curves. There's the obligatory courtyard. There's the steep grey roof.

I have some problems with the concierges. When I arrived here I made out I was some American businessman's wife, a Euro Mrs Nobody here for the shopping. Since then they've figured out that I'm sometimes on their television, but their behaviour remains atrocious. I don't understand men. Marie-Pierre, the little junior, is sweet and helpful; Jean-Pierre understands the role of the concierge; but the other two, those surly bulldogs with their Pigalle features and greasy pants, make my life as difficult as they possibly can in some perverse expression of their misogyny, while Monsieur Rouillier, the head gardien, has been put on this earth only to torment me. To lose my Fed Ex packages. To refuse to bring up my flowers. To ignore my simplest requests.

This evening one of the bulldogs, Alain or Aziz, was on duty. They shuffle, half snigger, when I approach the lobby. I have reported them repeatedly to M Rouillier, but since he is even more execrable, he does nothing, and manages to offend me still further. The inefficiency of these people drives me into a frenzy.

I had applied cream, fresh Retin-A. For some reason it made me feel sore: my skin was probably rubbed and therefore vulnerable. I stepped into the false lights of the lobby.

'There was a bike . . . ' I said to the concierge.

He said nothing. He greeted me with his blank and insolent stare.

'There was a bike with a package expected this afternoon,' I said.

He stared back at me.

'I will spell it out for you,' I said patiently. 'I am asking you whether you have signed for a package in my absence and whether I may now collect it.'

'Can't sign for packages,' he said.

'Listen, Aziz . . . André? We have had this discussion many times, haven't we? Many times. I have long established that the porters can sign for my parcels – as indeed J-P frequently manages to. Do you expect me to be at home all day? To wait around for stupid bikes?'

'Don't know, Ma'am,' he said. He refused to look at me.

The other one rounded the corner, his twin *voyou* of motor mechanic mien. Alone, they are taciturn. Together, they incite each other to greater displays of misogynist aggression.

'Well, from now on,' I said, 'I would ask you please to sign for any parcel that arrives for me. Permission granted. I give you power of attorney, Alain!'

'Haven't got the time,' he said.

His friend's mouth twitched.

'Oh, pardon me, boys. I momentarily forgot that you have this demanding – high-stress profession,' I said.

The second one lounged against the wall of the *loge*. He spat into an ashtray.

'We're not your servants,' he said.

'What?'

'We can't do *everything* you want us to do.'

'It would be a full-time job!' muttered the greasier one.

'You'd better get your fucking acts together, or I'll report you,' I said.

One of them shrugged.

'We're not paid to cart up your roses, Ma'am.'

'Look, you stupid pricks,' I said. 'I . . . Go and jerk off in the boiler room, why don't you?'

'Whoah!' said the rattier one.

'Do what you're fucking paid to do, or shut the hell up,' I

shouted at them as I left the building.

They erupted into laughter. Such men are rapists.

Out on the street, the day was gauzier. Away from the bright stark shadows of the lobby, I breathed. I walked away, toward Montparnasse. Strange, there in the shadows – something. I'm not sure if the boy, the boy from the Cinquième, is around, or whether it's other boys I glimpse, or whether it's in my mind only.

I walked towards the cemetery, that curious Montparnasse back yard of dogs and mausolea. The light was threaded with the grey dots of dusk and traffic. People were heading down the boulevard du Montparnasse in swathes and dribbles to dine at La Coupole or Le Dôme. There was a birthday celebration at La Coupole, all yellow and green light swimming behind the glass front like a postcard-bright Lautrec, its old-fashioned waiters veering between the banks of flowers, the lobsters and crabs. I could see the waiters gathering round a cake.

I detected a movement to my side. A flash, two, three. There was a photographer, with the battered equipment and jacket of the professional, standing on the boulevard, waiting for someone else outside La Coupole. I stared momentarily, and he caught me again. He saw a woman who looked familiar, though he may not have known who she was – Adèle Meier, celebrity; Adèle Meier, novelist, creator of an erotic archetype, incarnation of Loulou; Adèle Meier, well-known feminist, disputed beauty – but whose screen image was dishevelled, knocked out of kilter by a sordid interlude with a stranger.

'Cut it out!' I shouted at him.

He looked up at me.

'Do not invade women's privacy, jerk.'

The woman, her planes and angles and the pigmentations of her skin translated into infinitesimal grains of silver bromide, looked tarnished. Her hair flopped to one side with the slow movement of residual hair spray, and the notable whiteness of her skin, the whiteness that journalists like to talk about, was pricked with pink under the powder; and her clothes had become rumpled since they were last dry-cleaned. Her kitten-ish delicacy was abused. The geisha precision of her beauty was blurred.

I hurried up along the boulevard towards Les Invalides to escape that man and his molesting flash gun.

I caught a cab back to boulevard Saint Michel. I couldn't bear to confront the oil-stained inhabitants of the *loge*: the idea made me feel sore and stripped. They might report it to the press that Adèle Meier brings boys young enough to be her sons back to her room for an afternoon of fucking. One small tawdry exploit blown up across the pages of a national gossip rag on a dull day or bedded as a noxious little diary story in one of the broadsheets.

I would collect my nightwear, my underwear, the pages of my book, and put myself into the Montalembert. I would go to sleep for a few days. The Retin-A was sore.

I knew there would be another damn pigeon feather on the floor. They are vermin: fat grey rats on wings.

The taxi stopped. Further up the boulevard, away from my apartment building, the same boy. He turned and stared down the street. All traces of the other boy, Thierry, were gone: except, as I walked, my panties were stiff with dried saliva. The sensation was both sore and pleasing against my crotch. My little shadow, with his hurt bushed eyebrows, was there again. He is there, somewhere, perhaps two days in every week. He must be a student.

I smiled at him faintly, or perhaps only in my mind, and I turned away and paid the cab driver.

The boy seemed to disappear. He can disappear into shadows and between moving cars; he's thin and wears over-washed navies or perhaps faded dark sea-greens. And then he suddenly appeared quite near me on the street. He must have seen her, Adèle Meier, close up. He must have imbibed her presence momentarily.

Fame emanates a signal that changes a room or a mood. The frequencies are different. Fame sketches a nimbus. It carries the frisson of a civet-heavy perfume, or of sexual anticipation, or of a promise that all things are possible. All things are possible for *you*, *you*. The feeling fame gives you, it washes out the colours of other people, and their colour floods to you. You absorb it and then reflect it back anew. They have the power, that moment, to become anything they wish.

I have never been able to get it into my head that I am famous in the way that other people are famous, as if some childhood dream of finding flower fairies or being able to fly had at some stage become reality. A cartoon-coloured reality.

The boy must have sensed it as he walked by. He walked away from the cab, on the building-lined edge of the sidewalk; he must have been aware of the woman's presence.

As she moved towards the front door of the building, he walked past her, speeding along the street as if embarrassed to be caught by her. He must have glimpsed her in close proximity, the details of her skin even, under the street light.

'Sorry,' he said. He almost bumped into her.

She raised an eyebrow.

'Sorry for being in your way,' he said.

He backed off up the street. He was thin. His chinos, held up by a brown leather belt, dipped over his stomach. His dark hair curved away from his scalp, arched, and then fell downwards over his forehead.

'No problem,' I said.

'Well I . . . ' He edged slowly away, padding backwards to indicate that he was leaving. He seemed to want to speak still.

'I would never want to bother you,' he said.

'Now I'm sure you wouldn't,' I said. My voice emerged low and quiet; I feared the sallies of André and Aziz.

'Well, bye, then,' he said. He was staring.

'The phantom of the Cinquième disappears,' I said.

He blushed.

His mouth carried that intensity which makes every facial expression other than a smile appear serious, so that his smile, when it came, was an abrupt radiance in contrast.

'I won't . . . ' he began.

I raised an eyebrow. I returned his gaze. I felt amusement play around my mouth.

'. . . I'll go now,' he said.

He set off up the street.

'How many times – how many times have you caught sight of me this last month?' I called out to him.

A ripple of anxiety crossed his features.

I looked at him. I looked him up and down, as though he were a recalcitrant child.

'I only like to see you because . . . '

'Because . . . '

'. . . Your face,' he said.

I looked at the sky.

'It reminds me of . . . you know, that Camille Claudel in the Musée Rodin.' He said it with effort and embarrassment. He closed his lips firmly.

'Well, I don't mind little spies if they are clean and well mannered,' I said.

I waved to him without looking at him again.

'Goodbye,' I said. I walked into the building.

In the end, in America, I had my network spot and they cancelled it. They said I was 'difficult'. Women are always called 'difficult' if they have a brain, if they open their mouths.

My face is changing. Now when I smile, the vertical lines

beside my mouth echo the movement as though in mimicry. Soon my whole face will be crazed and my eyelids plump like a dog's, my jaw line a blurred angle.

I rested my face in my hands under the bathroom spotlights, and the flesh travelled upwards and made Oriental puffs of my eyes. The flesh is barely rooted, you know; it can be loosened, it can travel – once there, now here. I plucked at it, pulling it away from my cheekbone until it hurt. How loose and pliable it is!

I could have sobbed. I pressed a nail into my flesh to punish myself. I remember my actress's face, my Kobal portrait face, sculpture tight.

There is a solution to this. Even the forehead migrates. This little freckle can move one fifth of a forehead upwards with just a prod of the fingertip. It is quite flexible, the man said. (A tiny, tiny shot of toxin, botulin, just a prick like a butterfly bite below the skin, will paralyse the movement of the facial muscles so you no longer frown. The frown line loses its anchor and smoothes out.)

The doctor, appraising me professionally, said I am beautiful, too beautiful ever to injure.

The smell of that place, the disinfectant just nudging into the book-lined, couch-lined sanctuary where he told me that I am, of course, beautiful, that natural beauty needs to be handled with eggshell care.

There is a solution. The thought keeps buzzing around my head with the lightness and persistence of an insect, brushing me at intervals with a cold wing of nausea. God, but it's sickness. The insect thought threads my dreams at night. Its flavours are the cool bile of illness, of disinfectant and pain.

Only nine or ten millimetres.

Perhaps ten years would drain away into the pillow. Just a little little blood and clear brown fluid, dribbling a tiny country-shaped stain on the pillow case. Other women's seepage – the years they lived – the ghosts of other maps on the cambric of the pillow.

TWO

I used to love this man. I loved him so much, perhaps a little part of me came to Europe to be nearer him. Surely grains of skin, human dust, migrate in eddies and we breathe them in, so even the essence of our neighbours tints our bloodstreams, their breath and splinters of their hair forming motes of our organic matter.

Therefore, Laurence Mahon is a part of me. His essence is carried towards me in a sluice of European humanity. He's a segment of one cell of me. The same European sun shines on us. Oh, Laurence. He lives in London now, only two hundred miles away, and in the country at weekends. He will emerge from the illusion at some future date, but in the meantime, may he enjoy his English squire act. May he sire heirs. And may he remember his wild rich dreams with me.

Nine years ago I came to Paris because it's the most beautiful city in the world; I came, perhaps, because a secret strand of my mind twitched with that irrational hope – reason beyond reason – that is the final motivation for change.

You work it all out methodically, your lists of pros and cons, your hesitations and justifications, and then your perfect package of an idea stays on the shelf, and it's only that wild final impulse – the half-promise of an accidental meeting, or some fevered artistic delusion – that ignites the lifeblood of the hypothesis and puts you, in a dream state, on a plane.

The kick-start of madness for me was the memory of Laurence's smell, and the thought that I would be nearer it. I was simply used to it. It was as if I needed it to function properly, in the air or on my clothes. When we were first lovers, I was like a hound baying after one scent, a junkie after the white heights of an addiction. But I was calmer then. It was a calm addiction.

He smelled of sweet animal – the imagined scent of lion sweat, or dog, soap beyond that. He's quite beautiful, Laurence Mahon, tall, his face has a strong structure, but there are uglinesses too, in the over-largeness of his nose, his hair's ridged pelt. I liked the mixture. I was absorbed by the vagaries of his attractions.

He made love with me as though I were shellfish, had only pink flesh to be tweaked. He traced latticework over me. I was all flesh, contracting and bleeding juices at a touch. Then when he had turned me into membrane, I would take hours to close up and grow normal skin again. I was vulnerable to air, and grit and temperature, vulnerable to memory. I needed hours to recover, sometimes weeks, like a woman who has had her face lifted and who must lie in secret silence, no air currents, no life, only a daze of soreness, amazed that someone could do that to her body.

I didn't know it could be like that, that love was a condition you lived with in your limbs and thoughts, like illness. I knew Laurence and I would be together for the rest of our lives – if there was anything I knew it was that. And yet it was not so simple.

My own apartment here in Paris is a nest of old silks and brocades. When I first moved to this city, I lived in hotels, and with an old friend, who is no longer a friend. The hotels were like serviced balm. The apartment building is a hive of vicious old tricoteuses and yuppie couplings. But through the balustrades of the French windows, there is a Dufy painted on my square of sky: filigree, roofs like sails, dogs trotting by below in ink-lined delicacy.

When I was a child in an Austrian small town, then a teenager in a Virginian nowhere, I was circumscribed by suburbia. New York City was a far-off foreign land, and Paris was a film set of carousels and hunchbacks, and in my suburban wanderings, I never even dreamed that I would one day live by the Jardin du Luxembourg, on a long boulevard between Montparnasse and the Île de la Cité.

I had a sudden image of Laurence today as I stepped out onto the street. What if he were walking there, by chance, in the shadow of the buildings on the boulevard Saint Michel? Sometimes he comes here from England. He might be walking along the street in one of his dumb expensive jackets, those superlative jackets he wears for work, walking along the streets of Paris on business, and just as I step out for my daily constitutional or into the depths of a cab, there, he sees me, glimpses his lovely Adèle. She's the same, the exact same, like a ghost, the precise template for the memory that presses against the inner lids of his eyes, so that he sees the image of her at odd moments in flashes of membrane orange when he's looking aside and least expecting it. Does he remember her skin smell? Does he know that she still, to this very day, wants to press her lips against his and taste just a little of his saliva; that she would like to rest her head against his shoulder, and be comforted, not tired any more?

Fantasy can grip you in the daytime more fiercely than at night, and as I stepped towards the waiting car, I thought that Laurence would really be there. I felt a tinge of surprise as the driver opened the front door for me into a street of strangers, and I climbed into the car unseen. The loneliness of the strangers on the street coated me all day.

'Pleased to meet you, Madame,' said the driver.

'Thank you,' I said. 'Can we go the long way? Can you take me round the park? I need to breathe for a little while.'

I give speeches in France, and Americans turn up. There are ten thousand Americans living in Paris; they think that the river fogs alone will infect their bloodstreams with divine afflatus.

We exiles become professional 'personalities': paid-up eccentrics. We can burst the cultural corsets that restrain the natives. When I am written about here, it's as if every facet of my personality springs from the fact of being not French. They think I am a German for being Austrian. They write about me as if I'm some delectable freak.

I was still in the grip of Laurence. When you love someone, it's like bereavement when they're not there. Your mind hurts as if it's cut flesh. With a sensation close to panic, I start to realise that he might go on occupying a living part of my mind, like an active mould or culture, for years and years, until I'm too old and too stupefied to feel any more.

When I went to see the doctor, he said that younger skin was easier to work with, that my skin still had its quota of collagen. It was relatively elastic. It would settle itself quite easily.

How remarkable that you can do that. By chance, by luck, I live in this century, the only time in history in which it is possible to reverse the physical signs of ageing. It's so beautiful, so complete, just the simplest of solutions. How remarkable it is. You can correct your vision with plastic discs; you can correct your ageing with scalpels.

It took me a long time to go and see Dr Kreitzman. When your subconscious is searching you absorb the information, so I know who they go to in Paris. I heard his name and read it without really registering it, and then I heard it again. He is particularly respected for his face work.

I felt so bad, you see.

You go in for your nip and tuck, and then you're out again, and you have this youthful return, this new confidence and freshness of cheek, and no one can quite identify what has happened.

'You look so well,' they always say. 'Have you had your hair cut?' they ask. 'Have you been on vacation? Have you lost weight?'

I was very excited when I first let myself think about this. I played with it delightfully, knowing it was an impossibility for me, a naughty conundrum – candy, cocaine, posing in a porn magazine. It was pink, then, and clean.

Dr Kreitzman was cool and professional, as though my tentative thought was entirely reasonable. 'Yes, of course, it's all perfectly feasible – quite standard,' he said. We had a pleasant consultation.

When our talk was drawing to a close I nearly cried. The relief was like exhaustion preceding the certainty of sleep. I wanted to lay my head on the table in defeat and gratitude.

When I got out of the cab and sat at the table to give my speech, I could see the audience looking up at Adèle Meier as the journalists portray her, pre-cast in the image of her reputation, and yet with that shock of difference in the flesh. She has the whitest skin I have ever seen, they think.

When she entered, an alertness stirred in the room. Her eyes alighted on individual members of the audience. She sat there in her beautiful clothes, the clothes of one to whom dressing is an art; and yet she gave off just a momentary impression of dishevelment, as though she were a girl who had rifled an old clothes box, the effect being at once child-like and sexual.

'Good evening,' she said.

The audience shifted.

She wore a lollipop coloured dress from the mid-forties. The neck was squared off and low cut. Her hair fell to frame one of her cheeks, and her lips were dives of dark red.

'I guess I've been invited here tonight to talk about my career . . . '

She had the voice of a grown child. It was illusory and mesmeric, shifting down-scale sporadically to the whispered vibrations of more womanly knowledge. She never raised the tones. People were lulled. They listened to her as though they were fed by her.

'But a career to me is an odd concept . . . ' she said. 'The idea of a structured personal odyssey, it's an artificial frame placed over the living, shifting thing that's your whole life.

'However . . . Well, in the beginning I thought I was going to be an actress. I had never acted, and then when I was in my teens I was in a play of *Snow White.*'

The audience murmured. A young man watched her from near the back of the hall. He watched her intensely. Her delicacy, her bleached-out skin, imbued her with a tear-washed, rabbity flavour. The darker hair was a contrast. The voice was mellifluous and almost robotic. As he watched her, his eyes were very focused.

'They thought I would be right because they thought I sounded European, and so should Snow White, *Schneewittchen,* you know, as though she stepped out of Grimm and emerged a sexual American teenager.

'It was the sixties, and in America, the mores of the fifties spilled over into the next decade. So this little play was slightly scandalous in my little town in Virginia.'

The candy-coated monotony of her voice rose. The boy from the Cinquième moved at the back of the hall.

'I did other things,' said Adèle Meier. 'People periscope that time. They forget that actually it was a decade before I published anything, and another two years before *Loulou* became international.'

'What was the secret of Loulou?' someone asked from the audience.

'What was the secret of Loulou? That she was what people are in their dreams. That was the secret.'

'Who was Loulou based on?'

'No one, everyone,' she said.

'Was she you?'

'*Madame Bovary, c'est moi.* She's as much me as she is you. Only the jacket pictures are me.'

The *Loulou* books with their notorious covers were stacked on a rack behind the table. Elliptical images of the author herself, the flared monochrome outlines of the body's details a tribute to the surrealists in their abstract eroticism, were synonymous in the public's mind with Loulou. The lesser-known, later books had a more prominent position at the front of the rack.

'Loulou does things that women wished they dared to do. They want to be Loulou, in the same way as they want to be Holly Golightly and Scarlett O'Hara – and Madonna or whoever it may be now. That is, they want a great deal of attention but they don't want to be the victims of men. Loulou has very exotic sex and manipulates men and says what most women only dare to think in their secret minds. And she becomes vulnerable and love-sick as well, but she tries to work it out.

'Women, you see, want to be more daring: they don't want a man carrying them off on a charger, they want permission to mount it themselves. They want a shot in the arm of absolute daring, pure, essential fearlessness – sexual wildness. And my Loulou did that, she was a naughty heroine.'

What they don't understand, the sweet spectators who pay to hear me speak then pay to carry away a signed copy, is that the vein runs out. You have to be a chameleon in art as in mass media. When Loulou arrived, it was the seventies and she was extraordinary. At the same time, something rose from her like a thought bubble of possibility and fizzed in people's minds, and inspired them. I'm happy that I did that for people, made certain women realise.

Loulou is bewitching to this day, but some of her activities have entered the realms of the commonplace. I grew beyond Loulou. I love her but despair over her like a child I once knew. She brings me royalties.

Sitting near the side of the room was a girl who was too thin. Her mouth had developed the simian prominence of the anorexic. Wisps of hair had loosened from a ponytail hanging by her face and she had a nervous prettiness. I kept glancing at her as I spoke, because in each fleeting glimpse she was Melina. It was only the standard aspect of the emaciated that created the resemblance, but as she passed me in a roll of faces, the blurred split second of recognition was unsettling: the features were almost those of Laurence's lovely little daughter.

I don't know where Melina lives, or whether she exists any more. She's probably incarcerated in a white-walled clinic getting high, high as an angel on starvation.

'The photos became as famous as the titles of the books . . . ' said someone in the audience. 'What did you think of that?'

'I think they're beautiful photos,' I said, as I have said hundreds – many hundreds – of times before. 'They became erotic archetypes, and who am I to object to that?'

'But did you mind your . . . body being used in that way?'

'No, because it was never oppressive. I think they're beautiful,' I said simply.

The audience murmured.

Suddenly, again, I saw the boy from the Cinquième. Clearly, then, he is some species of fan. I realised that I might have been aware of his presence all along, but his habits make it difficult to ascertain whether he is there, or it's a shadow of him, superimposed on certain corners of Paris, or an expectation of him, watching. It was the eyebrows I noticed, their largeness and earnestness. He stood with his hands in the pockets of a dark blue-grey raincoat, standing weighted on one leg with the nonchalant lolling posture essential to students.

I knew he would linger and talk to me, attempt to be inconspicuous in the milling straggle who always hang about for their capsule of conversation and their signed copy.

He didn't. He left with a girl, a leggy blushy someone from the university. I signed copies, and I talked, and the publisher's car took me back home.

I had given myself another name when I made the appointment with Dr Kreitzman. I was soothed by him, so soothed by him, but afterwards his consultation room twisted in my mind and became the locus of my nightmares. I woke with the remembered smell of expensive wool carpet and disinfectant on my night clothes each morning, as if I had visited the room during hours I'd forgotten about. The worry rocked and pitched distantly during the day, but it was contained; after midnight, it swelled, and broke over me in the early hours, and as the sun stained my bed in the morning, I woke to a scattered, nonspecific dread.

I used to campaign, with Helen Kaufman and the others, against the beauty industry.

I wrapped a scarf over my head and caught a cab there for my next appointment. I was nervous this time because details were beginning to frighten me. I always went right out of my way, to be beside the river. Around the Quai Voltaire there was a honking gridlock. The cars along the Quai snarled with the bridge filter, and we were motionless for whole blocks of time. The gas rising through the windows made me nauseous. Its blue fumes pumped to the pulse of the engine. So I nearly went home. I thought that otherwise I might throw up in the back of the cab, you see.

I arrived outside the building. How many little chunks of flesh have come out of that door? The offcuts must be disposed of somewhere. I suddenly felt as though I wanted to protect the people that had happened to. They were walking unknown to me around Paris. What was once a piece of your cheek, soaped and moisturised and stroked by lovers, is later a slop of discarded flesh in an incinerator bag. Look at that little section, just in front of your ear, honey and mobile in your childhood photos. Wouldn't you have been shocked, blankly uncomprehending, if you had been told then that one day it wouldn't be with you any more, that you would give away that centimetre strip of your face like the unwanted baby in a litter?

There was the pure wool carpet: I could smell it. I breathed through my mouth so I wouldn't catch strands of disinfectant beyond it and topple into nausea.

'How are you today?' said Dr Kreitzman. He was American. He sounded East Coast. He had dark brown eyes.

'Sit down – please,' he said. He sat at his desk and leaned back against his chair. 'It's been raining during the night,' he said. He took a fountain pen and rolled it between his thumb and forefinger, as though spanning his own penis.

'I can smell the rain in the air,' I said.

'Then you have a better nose than I do. And you do have a beautiful nose, if I may say that. With that touch of poetry that rhinoplasty just never quite matches.' He smiled.

'Women have a better sense of smell than men.' My voice was thin. 'It's the oestrogen levels.'

'Then women are superior creatures biologically as well as aesthetically,' he said swiftly. 'Ms Lee, I think maybe you're not quite at ease today. Can my secretary bring you a coffee?'

'Yes, thank you.'

I thought I might cry. I had finally made the appointment. At the initial consultation, the doctor appeared to be quite accustomed to nerves. We had talked in buffered abstracts; he couched his terms in flattery and professionalism, rarely euphemism, as though it were a phase of life we were discussing, or the toile for a new fitting, or our son's relatively pleasing progress at grade school. A trickle of relief suffused me as he talked, and he looked at me coolly, this was the most normal of things, and his appraisal of my classical proportions was that of an expert, a master craftsman or sculptor.

But today I thought I might cry. I would have liked another cosy consultation with Dr Kreitzman, have the shrink come visit me at the manicurist, but we needed to start to talk in specific terms.

The clinic was set in a discreet street at the western end of the Fifteenth. Cars stopped periodically in the passageway, their engines ticking over, their doors shutting. The reception area led to other practices, and to Dr Kreitzman's own consultation rooms. Possibly there was another entrance to that inner chamber. There must have been a more discreet doorway for the wounded to emerge with their flesh newly shifted.

'We make the coffee the real way for our American ladies,' Dr Kreitzman said. 'The French think they have it cornered.'

He looked at me. I suspected that he recognised me. The idea made me cold.

I couldn't say anything. I could not speak. I just remembered love then, out of context, all the people I had loved. On the walls, modernist watercolours alternated with photographic portraits: an ice-cold study of Dietrich, the profile of Grace Kelly: the mechanics of perfection mathematically proven. A couple of lesser-known Hoppers hung behind him.

I was wearing a suit, black, narrow-skirted and small-shouldered: I wanted to appear professional. My heart fluttered like a bird inside the jacket. In another room, swabs were used and discarded. Only the smell of disinfectant – or was it imaginary? – hinted at something else.

'Please don't be anxious, Ms Lee,' said Dr Kreitzman. 'Really, there's nothing to worry about. Absolutely nothing. Procedures these days are very simple, very straightforward.' His voice possessed a calm male timbre oiled by testosterone and professionalism.

'How long would it . . . ?'

'A couple of nights there. Couple of weeks staying in at home.'

'There?'

'I use private rooms at the hospital. We do just some of our smaller work here. Lips, collagen therapy.'

'Oh.' My mouth was dry. The taste of bile.

He leaned forward. The coffee arrived. I averted my face from the secretary. Blood and disinfectant make a strange marriage, hot human frankness with a barrier of artifice.

His skin was tan, just falling to fat. Perhaps he should have it pulled away from its roots, that face, and redraped.

'Well,' he said calmly. He took the lid off his pen. 'As I recall I said to you when you came to see me last time, you have a very fine natural bone structure. Bone structure like that supports the face for some time.'

'Thank you,' I said.

His voice was like a burble in my veins, beyond my ears. He was calm, calm.

He chatted now. He wanted to put me at my ease. 'Women come up to me – here, at parties – they say, "What can you do for me, Dr Kreitzman?" They want to know that I can do something for them. Some of them, I have to tell them – "Nothing, I'm sorry, I cannot do anything for you." Some of them are simply too old, or, truly – the procedure wouldn't help them. They have to have something worth helping in the first place. I try to balance the sum of their features, that's all.'

He had the slightly plump, gym-trained expansiveness of the wealthy. His hair was pulled back from his face and bunched in a small, faintly laughable ponytail, in the fashion of M Lagerfeld. He wielded the minutiae of his profession with consummate confidence.

'I don't know . . . ' I said. I looked out of the window. A sadness bothered me that day.

'As I explained, we'd actually have to do very little,' said Dr Kreitzman.

On how many familiar faces with unfamiliar names have these hands worked alchemy?

He would smell of aftershave, of clean male.

'I like to work with natural beauty most of all,' he said. 'That's the most rewarding aspect of my work. Not touching it, but maintaining it. Returning it to its true state.'

His phone dribbled sound discreetly. He dealt with the call.

He spoke to me again. 'People I meet, they talk to me, asking me questions, but really they're asking me about themselves – will I be there for them when they need me? I could tell them right then how much I could do for them, whatever age they are: I can more or less predict how the gravity of age will fall and what I'll be able to do when the time is right.

'With you I'll need to do very little. The problem areas are very small.'

How much blood? How much sickness, because this is what I chose to do?

'I think if we fixed a date, a little while from now, then you could come and see me again if you have any more questions. I'll always be here for you. Now, and whenever you need me afterwards. There will be as much individual care as you need.'

'But I don't – know right now . . . ' I said.

His voice was lower. A velvet voice. Velvet beef. He watched me with his dark brown eyes. He soothed me like a girl.

'Let me see,' he said. He stood up. His suit was black, pressed. A shirt with a little collar, buttoned up. No tie.

'Excuse me. You don't mind?'

He placed his hand on my forehead, turning me slightly towards the natural light from the window. His warm dry hand pulled back my hair professionally. He placed a mirror, on a long stalk, at just the right height, in front of me.

'Now you see,' he said. 'The rejuvenation process sorts out these little areas.' He pulled my hair gently back from my forehead. It was cool. It whispered, then firmed. He skimmed over my jaw line.

'This,' he said, lifting the skin around my chin. 'This,' he placed his finger tips on my temples and pulled upwards. 'All of that will be gently lifted. Does that feel good to you?'

I nodded.

I wanted him to touch me more. My forehead was cool where he held back my hair. A car engine started up in the street below.

'What about here?' I said. I touched the area around my mouth.

'That looks fine to me. The naso-labial fold is quite soft, nothing to worry about. We could give you a light chemical peel around the mouth if you wish. The whole face will be refreshed by a general lift.'

He ran a finger down my hairline, by my ear. It tickled. 'We'll lift gently from here. We would not touch any of your features, unless, of course, there's anything you want to ask me about. I'd suggest just a lift, and we'd do the eyes at the same time.'

'Would I definitely . . . look more youthful?' I asked him.

'No question,' he said. 'Eight to ten years. Sometimes it can be more, sometimes a little less.'

He looked at me, there were little lines, little blubbery rings below his round dark eyes like the Italian-Americans I used to know in New York. I wondered what went on in his mind, and whether he had feelings like I have, and what he thought about as women's blood lay in smears on his latex surgical gloves.

He was silent.

'Will it hurt?' I said. My throat was painful.

'A little. Really very little. A little discomfort. I can see you have some questions you'd still like to ask, Miss Lee, and that's fine. So I suggest – You and I are going to meet again in a couple of weeks. We're going to drink some coffee together and you're going to bring me all those little worries – please don't forget your questions, write them down for me – and we're going to talk about them. Hey, I don't want frown lines spoiling that face – that poetic face you have. There's nothing to worry about. It's very simple now.'

I left the clinic, I caught a cab, and then I saw him again, the young phantom of the Cinquième. I saw him on my way back when I was nearly at home, just as he emerged from the Sorbonne. This time, I think it was by chance.

He looked shocked when he saw me. I had stopped the cab to take a walk back to my apartment and air the disinfectant, the carpet. I let the scarf blow away from my head to flutter freely around my neck, and he appeared on the place de la Sorbonne.

'Hello,' he said.

'The coincidences of life,' I said.

'How are you?' he said quietly.

'Well. Thank you.'

'I was at your speech.'

'I know.'

He looked up at me. 'Did you see me there?'

'Did you like it?' I asked.

'Oh, yes. It was . . . It was great.'

'Have you read the books?'

'Well. I didn't know you had written until then. I've been reading *Loulou*.'

I smiled at him slightly. The wind tugged at my scarf.

'Shall we go and sit down in a café?' he said.

'Oh, not today,' I said. 'Sometime, perhaps.'

'Please. I'd like to buy you coffee. I want to ask you – about Loulou.'

'No, I feel bad today. You should read beyond Loulou. I look terrible.'

'*You*! You could never look terrible,' he said.

'Just quickly, then,' I said.

We sat side by side on a plastic-covered banquette facing the traffic circulating the Luxembourg, and I thought, idly, that he was like a young priapic boy, with the golden musculature of a little Greek bowing his arrows high into blue skies on cliffs above seas.

But of course he was nothing like that. He was brown-haired and city-coloured; not golden. He was nervous with me. Beyond that, his nerves belied a deeper strand of assurance, the arrogance of youth in possession of certain intellectual powers.

'What would you like to drink?' he asked. His voice was lower and more resonant than his frame would suggest.

'A petite crème.'

The boy called a waiter over. Cars were honking in circles, in the circuits of sound and engines with which the French feel so at home.

'I'm happy to meet you, Mlle Meier,' he said.

Mlle! The boy called me Mademoiselle as though I were in possession of peachy youth.

'Eric.' He held out his hand, formally, though he sat beside me. The jewelly liquors stained the shadows above the *zinc* with colour.

'I like French boys' names,' I said, and there was an echo to it, as though I had said it before, some place.

'Adèle,' I said.

'Adèle Meier,' he said.

'Did you know that before?'

'No, my moth– someone told me.'

'Oh?'

'I used to think, when I saw you around, that maybe you were an actress.'

'Or a sculpture?' I murmured.

His skin darkened below faint afternoon stubble.

'But that Camille Claudel – ' he said. He looked embarrassed again. 'You should see it.'

Laurence – the rough waves of his head, his dark off-centre eyes – ought to have been sitting here. He has never sat here with me, in a café off the Jardin du Luxembourg with the traffic pressing close to the window and some kind of admirer on the banquette.

'Do you go to the university?' I asked him idly.

'No, I study photography,' he said. 'At college.'

His voice had shades in its depths, tree roots.

'Oh,' I said.

'Yes.'

'I imagined you to be a university student,' I said. 'You look as though you've emerged from the groves of academe.' I focused on him. I wanted to forget the surgeon. 'You look like a classics student . . . perhaps a student of eighteenth-century French literature. But no – I guess you could be a photographer after all, a young man with a Nikon and a big flash gun. Or a reporter in a raincoat, in a movie from the fifties, a very serious young man with a pencil and a Hasselblad. Like Tintin. You need a Milou dog under the table. You need a quiff! You must never wear beaten-up brown leather jackets with camera-stuffed pockets.'

'All right, I'll remember that . . . ' He hesitated.

'Do that,' I said. I turned idly to the waiter. The waiters have small moustaches and large white napkins in Paris. They do it for the tourists; they do it to secure larger tips.

'Can I – Could I – photograph you?' said the boy.

I was silent.

'I'd really love to,' he said.

I looked at the synthetic liquors.

'Perhaps. But only if you can do it well,' I said. 'I don't have very much time.'

'We have to photograph some models on the place de la Concorde. As a news item. There's some stunt . . . ' he said.

'When?'

'Wednesday morning. So perhaps I could set up your portrait afterwards.'

'But you can't photograph me straight after a crowd of – models,' I said.

'Why not?'

He waved to someone out of the window. She had dark eyebrows, like his, but severe and neat. She flashed a smile, a hemline, Parisian chic encapsulated on thin legs.

He carried the afterglow of his smile when he returned his attention to me.

'Is she one of them?' I asked.

'One of whom?'

'A model.'

'Oh, no! That's Lucie, from the university.'

Lucie, she of the university, a designer waif, may trip on down the boulevard spilling flashes of grins like Coca-Cola youth, and this boy may find his blood stirring at the sight of her through the window, and then return, his gaze still caught in the waif's mesh, to me.

'I've had my portrait taken lots of times,' I said. 'If you do it, it has to nearly match up. It has to be good, or we'll be wasting our time. Won't we?'

If you're called Lucie, with a swing of dark hair, aged twenty-one, you can do absolutely anything. You can convince anyone.

The young actresses today have their full little mouths, they have sticky-out ears with hair stringing down fore and aft;

they have petal complexions and small curved asses in jeans. They are like heavily sedated fauns. The glorious Ms Winona Ryder; Ms Uma Thurman; the Mlle Paradis with her distortion of a bee-sting; the new breed of French hussies with their long hair and their languid sex and their ugly boyfriends.

Youth can do anything. They don't realise it. They think they are ugly. Yet all those tiresome little insecurities are coated with an absolute assumption of sexual power. The fleeting spots of hormones, the blotches of youthful rabbit colds (cause for little *moues* and frettings) are mere floaters on the vision that can never destroy the glow of fresh elastic collagen, of a bobbing walk, bright brownness.

Youth can do absolutely anything. They don't realise this at the time though their movements suggest otherwise. They are blessed with peaches, with pouts and petals, little ephebes, little Übermenschen.

I think I'm going to kill a little part of me, just a little little strip. Something is, perhaps, going to be performed on my flesh: a ritual, like sex. Did you know you can choose to remould your body with a knife? If drugs can alter the mind, men trained to it can sculpt the body.

This is the body of Adèle Meier, after all. Once she was very famous.

THREE

And so I tried to work at home. I had an interview and a meeting with a production company with an idea for a pilot. I only wrote two pages; actually, one and two thirds. The boy from my neighbourhood, Eric, was due to visit me.

He said later that he had been watching me for three months; in the parks and on the boulevard, in the 'Champion' supermarket on the rue de Seine. He must have been lonely.

When he had first seen Madame Meier, in the Luxembourg, the dappled light on the tree paths was like an old granular film; he was absorbed in the effect, and then he saw her walking by the statues.

He thought she looked overexposed; her skin seemed too fine for the daylight, as though it would flake on contact with air. She was walking through the circle of statues in a tentative fashion, avoiding the sun. She was strange, illusory: he couldn't contain her in one look.

It was only later that he thought her at all beautiful. That day he found her strangeness an irritant: the whiteness of her skin, the dark red stained mouth, as though she had wandered off a film set, the contrasts too abrupt for French daylight. The beauty was masked by a shock of oddity.

Approaching the building on the boulevard Saint Michel to

compose Adèle Meier's portrait, Eric stopped and lingered because he was nervous at the thought that this brick tank enclosed the woman, her own air and flesh contained by these grandiose blank walls.

The old women in the foyer looked moneyed. Eric felt conspicuous, yet charged.

He wore a faded sailor scarf, holding back the section of hair that lopped over his forehead. He had tied it as a bandana against the dust and the heat of the place de la Concorde, and combined with his stubble, with his jeans, his cargo of reflectors and lenses, he seemed to personify every *branché* young photographer who carries a Leica and clubs with models. He instinctively knew that Adèle Meier might prefer his more classic incarnation, but he had thundered away from his morning's work in a rush of sweat and equipment.

'I've come to see Madame Meier,' he told the concierge.

There was a stirring of awareness in the *loge*.

A second concierge raised his eyebrows slightly at the first. He held Eric's gaze for a moment.

'Sixth floor, turn right,' he said.

Eric lugged his equipment into the lift. He caught his finger in the legs of his tripod, creating a swollen ridge of flesh.

The corridors were illuminated by a dark yellow stain of light. Eric hesitated and rang Adèle Meier's doorbell. A uniformed caretaker was lingering outside. He scrutinised the photographer, then disappeared into the further shadows of the corridor. Adèle Meier's door remained closed. Eric waited. He rang again.

He heard noises from inside the apartment. He waited, leaning against the corridor wall.

He heard her in the hall. Eventually she opened the door, and he was surprised by her appearance, as he had been when he first saw her; by the disparity between the mental image that he had recently nurtured and unknowingly distorted and the reality that was now presented to him. She was wearing

46

impenetrable sunglasses; she stood in the half-light of her entrance hall like a ghost in black shades. She was beautiful still, but her hair had ratted into strands as though she were breakfasting amid egg and coffee steam and had not yet set it in the more formal sequence of waves that graced the streets. She wore leggings and a white T-shirt, and her head looked slightly too big for her body, as is common with famous people.

She smiled at him. She held out her hand, as if they had just met. Her touch was light; he could feel the little bones of her hand.

'You know, I never let journalists up here?' she said.

Eric nodded.

She paused. She was not quite focused. Her presence seemed to be drifting, crumbled with the remains of sleep. But behind the sunglasses, she seemed vulnerable, as though he could hurt her.

'Come in,' she said.

'I've got a lot of equpment with me,' he said.

'I'm so sorry. I can't be photographed today,' said Adèle.

Eric's face tensed.

'But – '

She was silent.

'Well, I thought you – '

'You could set it up today. Come in. Don't stand here. Saâd the janitor will try to get you into the basement.'

Eric felt as though he were visiting the headmistress, who had turned seductress, who led him into the library, which had become a brothel.

The apartment only dawned on him slowly. He thought, in the first moment, that this was the home of a mad person. The grandeur of its dark woods, its thumping thirties plasterwork, projected that hushed gloom necessary to all notions of taste, yet its shadowy opulence was stuffed and draped as if from the Arab markets. Synthetic swathes of cloth in pink and lemon yellow and baby blue were draped over low tables and picture frames. Those same materials, the candied artifice beloved of sari manufacturers and amateur dramatists and little girls, were propped in shimmering falls as makeshift curtains or partitions. Shocking pink netting sprang from a light, as though her bedroom, glimpsed from the hall, was the dressing room of a third rank ballerina or a pantomime angel. Plastic roses and lilies stood in vases, and there were poppies everywhere, cloth and plastic poppies, and twenties poppy prints on silk. There was a preference for jewel colours and pink. Bags – baby doll, satin, twenties tote – were piled up near the door. Notes and books and gloves, strands of material – ribbons and scarves – lay in piles on the floor, on furniture, sliding over chairs. He glimpsed the bathroom: a dressing-up box, a choke of lipsticks and hair ornaments. He caught sight of other rooms in shots of intense colour. There was a little day room with a computer.

Two stuffed toys – mouse and rabbit – sat either side of a swirling pearlised vase from the fifties. Eric had an uneasy feeling that if he looked, in the gloom of some corner, he might find dolls. The face of Adèle Meier looked down at him from the wall, impromptu snaps and photographic portraits – the brief sunshine of smiles and crowds; the expertise of light and shadow in monochrome liquid. She was right: her portrait had been taken by some superlative photographers.

'We can set it up,' she repeated. 'You'll need at least a couple of hours to experiment with lighting, won't you? They normally do.'

'That's right,' said Eric.

'Yes,' said Adèle. She turned to him. There was a softness to her. 'I had a hard night. I couldn't sleep. So I – '

'Nor could I,' said Eric. He looked up at her. His stubble was dark.

'And why was that?'

'Oh I . . . ' He tailed off. 'Perhaps I drank too much coffee.'

'With me?'

'Yes. With you'

She turned to him and smiled. Her smile colour-washed her skin, and her eyes formed a kitten slant.

'Today, Eric,' she said, ' – and see, I do remember your name – and you look not remotely related to M Tintin – today you have adopted the guise of a young man who goes out with a model and gets himself featured in *Elle* magazine! It's quite interesting – you look completely different. You've forgotten the little round sunglasses . . . you need a couple more hours' stubble to complete the picture. As long as I never see a cracked brown paparazzo jacket in your closet.

'Anyway, today's not right for taking my portrait. I don't feel my best at all. I hope you understand?'

She looked at him. She drifted still behind a skin of sleep, a little shaky. She swayed, and she was all softness and subdued yawns.

'I'm inviting you to tea,' she said. 'You must be hot and dusty after photographing – these models. Aren't you?'

Eric was silent.

'They worry me, these models,' said Adèle. 'They're too thin. They remind me of Melina, my daughter, my stepdaughter; her thinness is an illness. My poor lovely girl.'

'They're too thin when you meet them in the flesh,' said Eric. 'It's just that the camera – coats them. With more substance.'

'It's as though they're unreal. As though they're not women.'

'I know,' said Eric. He paused. 'Are you – Are you married, then?' he said.

'No,' said Adèle. She looked at him with pink-lined morning eyes, though it was mid-afternoon. She looked slightly sad. 'But my – husband, Laurence, or Laurie some people call him, but not me, had a daughter, Melina. She's very lovely, but they kept having to take her to hospital, because she was too thin.'

'So you are married?'

'My ex-husband, really.'

49

The feeling of steam was still in the air. She smiled at him, and he felt she was kind, like his mother, like the good fairy in a movie. Her face was as he had remembered, with occasional blurrings of the recalled image, human scents of breath or skin suffusing it, so the familiar tugged against what was unfamiliar, and she gave off a confusion of notions. Her face dived from width at the cheeks to a smaller pointed chin, so it was all heart-shaped, her face.

'You'd like to have tea before you disappear again into the shadows?'

'I won't disappear. I was going to photograph you,' said Eric.

'Clever snapper in your stubble and bandana incarnation, how could I forget?'

'I – ' He shrugged.

'I just can't . . . '

She closed her mouth, sealing a yawn with a fraction of a burp. 'You see . . . Eric, it would be great if you could have tea instead, afternoon tea, the way they have it in England – you won't have experienced that in France.'

He remained silent. He looked at her. The stubble shadowed his chin and made him seem moody.

'Perhaps I can make it up to you in some way,' she said. 'I'd like to.'

The equipment preyed long-legged about her. She flinched minutely. This was a lens accustomed to framing long-limbed nymphic undulations dressed in wisps of cloth from some designer's *atelier*, thighs attached to rosy behinds just so. They would be called 'Hélène', 'Nikki', 'Lili'. He probably got to fuck some of them. He would flirt with them, banter youthful cool, cigarette insults, in a manner far more fluent than the one he adopted with her.

She touched his sleeve briefly. 'I want you to be happy in my apartment. How can I make you – happy – when the arrangement of your features is this serious? Your smile is so rare . . . How can I make it appear more often?'

He smiled. His mouth twitched self-consciously.

'I'd like it if you were happy here. Jean-Pierre will fetch us cakes if he's on duty now. I'll tip him. Don't be angry with me that I'm not feeling one hundred per cent, Eric . . . '

She looked at the floor.

'My heart used to be so pretty.' She laughed. 'I shouldn't say . . . '

'I'm sure it is pretty,' he said.

'But now it has small scars on it. *He bit my pretty red heart in two!* My heart was very comely before he mauled it – small and neat, ticking nimbly.'

'Who? You mean – your husband?'

'The same man,' she said dismissively. 'You men are so cruel. You hurt us.'

Eric was silent.

'I wish I could photograph it,' he said at last.

'How adorable. How worrisome!'

Afternoon pigeons fluttered and twitched on the windowsill. She moved around the apartment making English tea, picking up stray objects, pieces of paper.

'Where is – he?' asked Eric.

'In another country, and besides . . . Anyway, he's in England. In a cottagelet with a roof of corn. He probably reads Shakespeare at bedtime now. He used to watch *Peyton Place*.'

'What did he – '

'He hurt me. What else? Eternal story. You might play it out yourself one day. You may up and leave Lucille-l'érudite. One day you might think you love that farouche faun glow; and the very next her every murmured word, the very patterns of her breathing, send you into convulsions of irritation, and the next day you stop calling. Just stop calling. She lies in bed and cries for a year, her little hooves curled up to her body.'

'Lucie, you mean? But she's just my friend,' he said.

'Do you have a girlfriend?'

'Not really.'

The concierge brought up cakes and refused a tip. Adèle poured tea. Afternoon light slanted and lingered by the window, leaving the inner section of the apartment indistinct, so the sugar pink and plastic elements receded in shadow and the grandiose aspect grew dominant in the half-light. The curtains, gauze-lined brocade, were draped in theatrical curves, falling from the ceiling with a midway hitch to pool, over-long, on the floor. Discreet off-centre candelabra, sconces, islands of paper clutter, gleamed in the thin afternoon light. The ornate fire-surround loomed large. Necklaces and crystals that hung on the walls and from light fittings glinted slowly. The sound of traffic circulating the Luxembourg was a faint sea boom.

'You'll have to photograph me another time, if you don't mind, Eric,' said Adèle.

'OK,' he replied. 'I think I know how I'd like to light you.'

'Do you?'

He had grey eyes. Not a smudged amalgam of blue and brown, but a pure clean wool grey. He looked intense, despite the bandana, the jeans. Adèle studied his torso briefly. Their eyes met for a moment.

'You're a stranger, but it feels as if you knew me before,' said Adèle. 'Kind of like you knew me a long time ago. Perhaps when I was a girl.'

She skimmed his sleeve with the tips of her nails as she set a cup in front of him.

'I read *Loulou*,' he said.

'Oh,' said Adèle.

'But I think of Loulou as you anyway.'

'I haven't written a word about her for six years,' said Adèle.

'I know,' said Eric. 'But there are those cover portraits. I think they're very great photographs.'

'If you were a woman, I think you'd think – secretly – that Loulou was you. You know, I feel a kind of huge responsibility

52

towards all those girl readers; I feel as though I love them a bit, still, because they *were* Loulou, and so I feel protective towards them and wonder how they grew up. And she was them. I like that, because it's vital, it's so vital that women don't mould themselves into men's vision of what they should be. Would you like some more tea?'

'No, thanks.'

'Are you all right, Eric? Is there anything I can get for you?'

'I'm fine. I'd just like to photograph you.'

'You will. Let's do it in a few weeks.'

'Highlight the mouth, the upper lip,' he said.

A little crest marked Adèle's upper lip, the tiniest ridge of flesh running vertically from the point at which the two arches of her Cupid's bow curved to meet. Her father had remarked on it when she was very young. Adèle's palimpsest.

'You can do anything with light,' said Eric. 'Like paint. I could make your upper lip fill a picture completely, highlight its curves and that little line that –'

'Don't scrutinise me!' said Adèle, recoiling. 'Photograph me another time.'

'I'm sorry,' said Eric. He stalled. 'I didn't mean to –'

'I know you didn't. Yes, I know. But you'd better leave. I have to work.'

He looked upset.

'It's OK,' she said. She smiled at him. The kitten again.

He smiled back.

'I really think I should do some work.'

She leant over and touched his head gently. She reached towards him as he left and kissed him on the cheek, just once, as his mother would.

So – Laurence bit my apple-red heart and crunched into it with his careless male appetite. It used to work quietly and politely before I met him.

They all think that my face is for public consumption, all of them. They believe that rough masculinity is their licence. The statues in the Luxembourg are all female, round-breasted Victorian idylls, domey draped warriors, and I will walk there, in the bower, in its clean sexless cool until I am leached.

That son of the Cinquième, Eric, commented on my lip – *your crest, Adela* – and what gives him the right?

This morning, before Eric came, I knew that Laurence had been here in Paris, and I tried to push it out of my mind. My friend, Helen, saw his name in the *Washington Post*. A French story he had written. So he must have been here, recently, studying the international architects – Japanese, British – whose work changes the face of Paris and becomes symbolic of all that is Gallic itself. Of course Laurence must come here as much as anywhere else to write his terse macho reports, his steely analyses of arcane trends. But he really cannot write well, and he should stick to building buildings.

When I first met Laurence, in New York City, my face was still cut out of hearts. The skull was finely balanced with my features, the head feline and precisely placed on the neck. If there was anything people loved about me in my life, it was my facial skin. It was soap white, it was like liquid. The magnolia was tinged with the faintest pulsing of life, the blood a warm suggestion you could feel but barely see.

Laurence used to say that our relationship had gone rotten. He said that we could never repair it because there were areas that were crawling with mould. Then we would go to bed for the day and night.

He was like that. He said brutal things. His brutality always co-existed with a certain refinement, as though he were a big striding behemoth one moment and a ruffle-clad British actor the next. He was an architect when I met him; later, he wrote about buildings, to siphon off his wilder notions, and I helped him, because he was such a terrible writer.

We lived together, he and I, and then Melina. He made me think that anything I wanted in my life, I could have. He had that ability.

Once – actually twice – I've seen him here recently. The former was arranged; the latter, the chance meeting, had been so projected, shot from every angle in my mind, that I almost failed to recognise it when it happened. A part-formed image of Laurence buzzed like a bad signal most days in some back recess of my brain, and so the surge of recognition on seeing this man with his brown hair and thickening torso was automatically rejected, and I walked on, and there he really was, turning from a newsstand on the place Saint Sulpice and walking towards me like any *boulevardier*.

Paris was mobile with leafery and shadow that day. The Seine flowed by its crust of buildings. He walked towards me carrying a newspaper – a *Herald Tribune*. I remember – in the sun, in the painted weather. It was June. He didn't see me at first. As he walked towards me his gait shot a memory at me: the times when we were a couple and he would anticipate the moment of my passing through the Sheep Meadow on my way home from lecturing Wednesday afternoons. I'd see him come to meet me on the walkway. He'd have taken a chance that I'd be there at that time, and the sight of him still surprised me, and he'd turn and we'd travel home together.

He was beside me. In the confusion of reality stepping loud and fleshed from an old tired fantasy, I was dumb.

'Adèle?' he said.

I was caught like an animal. I was embarrassed.

'Adèle, sweetheart. Adèle! God. How are you?' He looked embarrassed, defensive.

'Laurence.'

He wrapped his arms around me, his *Herald Tribune* pinned

to my back. We hugged. His shirt was rumpled against my chin. His chest seemed shockingly large, a wall of hard flesh. I breathed him, and I remembered, of course, that was it, this was how he was. We pulled apart.

'I'm surprised to run into you,' he said.

'I live here.'

'But I haven't seen you for so long.'

'I know. Yes, I know,' I said. 'We haven't, have we?'

We were silent. Then the moment began to disperse. I tried to say something. There was awkwardness or indifference. The sight of him made a deep cut in me, infected me with pain and howling frustration. It was cross-grained and urgent. I wanted to contain him, to eat him.

'You're looking well,' he said finally.

'You always say that,' I said. 'It's a *dull* thing to say . . . '

'I try my best,' he said in a monotone.

'Oh, don't do your put-upon act,' I flared up.

He stood there. He said nothing. He looked endearing, older. I wanted to cling to him. I did nothing. I watched time slice into seconds. I could sense it visibly, ticking. I hadn't meant to be horrible. I just didn't know what to say to him; he angered me.

'Well . . . ' he said.

'You know . . . I miss you,' I said.

'I miss you, too,' he said. 'But you know that.'

'Are we always just going to say this to each other?' I looked up at him. 'When we bump into each other three times a decade?'

We caught each other's eye. And I knew that colour, that blink, the mind behind it, so intimately, just as I knew the smell of flesh through his shirt and his minute tics and the growl of a syllable caught in his throat before he delivered it. Just as I knew the name of his great-aunt he had never seen and what books he read when he was a boy, and what his mouth felt like on my breast.

I looked down and the street broke into lines because I was going to cry, because he was going to walk away, and I was going to wish that I had made that moment retrievable. And I knew that two years later I would still be moulding it into an infinite variety of different outcomes.

A touch on my shoulder, near my neck. His voice by my temple. I felt his breath. 'This isn't a good idea.'

And this time, he hasn't come to see me. He didn't bother. He arrived at Charles de Gaulle, he shuttled into town on the RER, he booked into a hotel. We used to make love in the Montalembert, night after morning.

I have to see Dr Kreitzman. I want to run as far away as possible from him, ignore his secretary's letters, write off the complimentary consultations. I want to run to him. Hatred comes at me in the mornings. It takes the form of daggers with blades like butcher's knives. I wake up to daggers, speeding at my body, all at once like swarming bee stings. I roll and shift in half-sleep to shake them off, but they come at me, they slice at me as if it's me who's plunging them, but the hand is invisible, and I weave through skeins of half-sleep, like a baby just born, to protect myself. Then other people say they wake to the daggers too. Mimi, and once little Melina said it. 'Oh, kitchen knives. In the morning,' she said, and I worried about her. My existence is draining away because I spill hours of grey half-life between sleep and wake.

When Helen had told me that Laurence was here, I was in a daze, and I managed to subdue the memory, to entertain that boy Eric, though I could not be photographed.

But I know that during the next few days I won't be able to stand it because Laurence might still be in town. I feel cool for hours, long marble reaches of time in which I work and potter and he can't touch me. He can't penetrate the life that I've created for myself in Paris, because it's established now.

Then he can. He can pinch me from the Montalembert. He sends out bees into the calm weather to bite me with stings.

I feel protected now – cold and strong – but later I'll be amazed at the absence of messages on my answering machine. I'll mentally retch. He can still do this to me. He can put me in a prison of old failures. He can drain my confidence with one act of neutrality, like bleeding a calf.

Dr Kreitzman's nurse took a blood sample. She made a scraping on my hand, to see how efficiently my flesh heals. It formed a light scab by the evening.

I can't write any more, you see. The fat fountain pen – Laurence's old Parker Duofold – shunts frogs and pips of ink. The computer screen glows like a sick migraine. What they don't realise is that I've stretched the canvas in my brain so far, it's blank and only blank. When I sit down to write, it slips and fades into that grey-white shade of hospital walls, the grain a pigskin-dotted fake. I stretch it further. I grind against it. I make cups of coffee.

There's more to be said in this life than the expression of liberty through a character called Loulou. I tried to convey it later, but I got marketed as a slim volume. Loulou's gotten dated, like Gidget, like the zipless fuck, and in any case, she no longer makes natural appearances in my mind: she has to be dredged up, a simulacrum of a free spirit, for periodic commercial use.

It was the work she generated, the persona she span me, that made me a public entity. They made a movie of *Loulou*. On television, I spoke, I read, they filmed me. They sold that television film in eleven countries, and so it went on, and I was asked to comment, in print, on camera, and different offshoots would be born, little infants which looked nothing like my original creation, and so it went on.

The pen scratches hairs; I shake it; it burps pools of black Encre Waterman.

I'm so very tired. He might well be round the corner this very minute, charming someone, and I'm so tired, and he does that to me. He drains me. One tap from him (he is here; here's his name in a newspaper) and my energy spills out: the colour drains away from me into a pool on the floor, leaving me in reverse-image. When we were first splitting up, I used to go to bed in the day. I tried to sleep it off.

I'm so tired. I want to sleep. This tiredness is like a nervous twitch thrumming through my body, a chamber of sleeplessness inside me, so I shake with near fearfulness a lot of the day. Oh, Laurence, come back to me. Come back to me. I need you. Don't you realise, you fucker?

I hate him too. I want him nowhere near me ever again. It's the only choice I can make. I want him to die, so he can stop pinching my flesh, snaring my brain awake when it should be asleep. I would be very pleased if I read he'd died, and could go to the funeral to take a look at his girlfriends.

I wake up in the mornings, tearful, exhausted, like a hag. He cheerfully eats his bowel-healthy breakfast he has ordered at the Montalembert, food that only he would procure in this land of low roughage, and then he transmits his copy by modem.

Dr Kreitzman is like a friend. It's the idea of Dr Kreitzman that reassures me. He has performed thousands of rhytidectomies. It is a routine procedure for the Doctor. He has a cool professional air about him, that clean skin smell of Mommy's boys – not to be touched, though he enjoys his fucking. The aftershave is on top, the clinical smell a flat middle suggestion. His voice is low and leatherette as he wields the battery of technical terms at his command. It's a proven procedure. It's fourth generation in the States now.

I want to hurt myself to stop Laurence hurting me. I once went to get a permanent when he had threatened to leave me – I needed to have something done to me – and the hairdressers tangled my hair, could barely unravel it from the curlers, and the pain was what I needed or deserved, and my eyes sprang with tears. I started crying, and they were all horrified because they thought it was their prodding and tearing that had made me so upset, no matter how much I told them that it was not their fault.

Dr Kreitzman will not only give me pain, he will soothe me. He will give me just the right, nice little amount of pain. 'Nip and tuck' it is called. First he pierces me with a shoot of discomfort which will balance and nullify Laurence's pain, and then he tucks. He tucks me, smoothes me over in bed, pulls the sheets up, straightens them. He tucks me in. He kisses my forehead goodnight with botulin. He tucks me in. With kindness.

Laurence hurt me all over again, that lacquer day on the place St Sulpice, and I think I've taken a long time to get over it.

It frightens me.

On the way to Dr Kreitzman's, I was calmer. It was as though I was attending a business meeting: I dressed for the appointment and for Dr Kreitzman. Some of my clothes are said to carry a forties air. I wore a long skirt in light stone grosgrain, a nipped-in jacket with minimal brocade detailing near the cuffs. My waist has always been small. My skin is very pale against my clothes. They say I look forties; they say my cosmetic contrasts are Oriental. Deep red mouth. White skin. Darker hair, the eyebrows dark and emphatic.

I was slightly late. The liveliness that delay injects into events made me happier – the cab driver told to speed, the leap, column of skirt, rush of professional pressure.

There was a sign: DR M. L. KREITZMAN. Three other doctors. They pretend it's a house. In truth it's a clinic, a small hospital. I had a misfortune. Someone left the waiting room with a plaster cast over her nose. A normal face, and in the middle of it, like a military tower spank in the middle of a field, a white plaster mould. A dome stuck to flesh. She looked at me momentarily with the blank eyes of a blackbird, and I had to meet her gaze: we passed each other with blankness and awareness.

The receptionist must display discretion.

'Yes, Dr Kreitzman is expecting you,' she said with a hush and a slight smile, casual and inscrutable. Do they think that I and my ilk are just vain, or pitiful, or rich, or lucky, or about to be conned? She led me to the waiting room from which the rhinoplasty patient had emerged. Dr Kreitzman was expecting me, yet he kept me waiting.

I started to feel nauseous, queasy with nerves. Nurses chatted in passing. The building was tall and narrow, perhaps five floors. The waiting room was full of dour furniture, alternating with spindle: ugly ugly and French elegance. Who do they think they are damn well fooling? Oh, I see, I seem to have stumbled into someone's sitting room – it must be a very elegant town house replete with taste and old money. I am supposed to be lulled as I flick through magazines and wait for Dr Kreitzman to tell me how much of my face I need to have cut off.

The Turkish bath hallway shrieks hospital, hospital, and the waiting room mutters fake, its brass standard lamps with their ugly growths – leaves and animals' heads protruding – the floor-to-ceiling drapes, the shutters, oh such soft fat sofas. No more than by this am I duped by rhinoplasty – the retroussé button tips, the too-narrow bridges and strange wasted ghosts of after-flesh below where the nostrils now sprout. Pretty amputations beloved of sixties actresses. Perhaps the human eye will be fooled, but not the shady area of the subconscious that houses suspicion.

The pure wool carpet – charcoal navy – in Dr Kreitzman's

rooms, and then I swear that that man smells of operations. It's anaesthetic, or it's disinfectant, or something a little sweeter. I smelled it as he took my hand, and the warm dry firmness reminded me of Laurence, or of men as a species.

'How are you today?' said Dr Kreitzman.

'Fine, I'm fine,' I said.

We sat and an assistant made us coffee.

'One of my patients, she took ten years to decide,' said Dr Kreitzman. His voice was low. I had to focus on him to absorb his speech. 'Some of them take eight – mulling it over. They know there's a need, but it's not yet as urgent as it might be later, so they think about it with a little time to spare.'

'They get used to it?'

'I guess so. But some nerves are natural. Don't worry.'

I have seen the advertisements in the back of *Vogue*. Young women's torsos, their breasts soft upright mounds. They look air brushed, or computer generated; they smile at me. Cosmetic surgery is so simple: it is morphing, it is an egg. The rounded clean lines are nothing to do with blood. I don't even know how they do it.

Dr Kreitzman was calm. He draped a layer of new skin over my nausea. When ageing comes, it is a shock like when you lose a person you love. It's very sudden, the realisation more abrupt than the fact. I was always a pretty girl, though I thought I looked strange as a child. I was one of those girls who moved through her life protected by prettiness: it was like a patron, it would have selected me from the children's home, though I was never certain of it at the time; I was aware of my own foreignness. Then later my features became larger and more defined. They said that I was very beautiful, or that I was strange, possessing a spectral quality that was arresting and disturbing. I still project a younger image of myself into the mirror and enact it to the world, my looks my amulet, and then a glimpsed jowl in repose or a spray of fine lines makes my heart beat suddenly with the truth and the horror of it. I never had the ability to cope with this. Plain girls know all the tricks of compensation.

'Procedures are very straightforward now,' said Dr Kreitzman. 'I like to space it out a little, take things slowly. It's gentler that way. Most surgeons will do the whole shebang, but I like to put a little time into things, get the results.'

'Will the results be good? Guaranteed. I mean . . . ' I said. My voice was not my own. It changes when I'm with Dr Kreitzman.

'You can't put a cast-iron guarantee on anything except a new stove,' said Dr Kreitzman. 'But my results are good. Would you like more coffee?'

'No. Thanks.'

'You've come to me at just the right time – you're very perceptive about what little changes need to be done – and the full face lift will give you a very clear, youthful appearance. Without any doubt. You'll get a definite rejuvenation from the eyes, especially the upper lids. No problem there. And we'd just do a straightforward lift. We can book you in week after next.'

The nausea pumped out of its seal.

Dr Kreitzman folded his hands together. His cuffs were pristine, starched and bright white, his skin tan with dark hairs.

I was nearer to sickness than I had been.

Laurence had looked at me protectively on the place St Sulpice. There was softness in the way he looked at me. I think it was because his look contained pity, or relief, subliminal relief that I was now more containable and therefore less an object of desire. His sexual lust for me was, at the end, my principal possession.

I focused on Dr Kreitzman. His ridiculous sculptures had been shifted around. They did not convince me. Art as influenced by a Sunday colour magazine.

'You'll stay over a couple of nights,' he said. 'Will that fit into your schedule?'

'Yes,' I said. 'I guess . . . Are you sure that it's so soon?'

'I beg your pardon?'

'Uh. Do I – I mean. You definitely – want, can do it the week after next?'

'I made a reservation for you some weeks ago, provisionally, Miss Lee. When we had a consultation. You remember – we discussed possible times for your stay?'

'Yes. I – When? When would I . . . Would I be under . . . ?'

'Anaesthetic? I like to work with sedation, and then a local anaesthetic. We'll give you a pre-med, you'll be quite happy.'

I was silent.

'No nerves,' he said briskly.

The phone rang.

My head felt light. There were no pigeons here. It is usually the pigeons that make me nauseated, their fat grease flesh and feathers.

'You sure you won't have some coffee, Miss Lee?'

I shook my head. 'Thank you. No.'

'Shall we go over the rest of your questions? Your blood tests, by the way – ' he picked out a sheet of paper from a pile on his desk, 'were fine. Cholesterol fine, sugar levels etcetera, etcetera. Cardiologist's report normal. Quite healthy. Fine job.'

'Thank you.'

'I can see that you know how to look after yourself.'

'Thank you.'

'So we'll just finish here.' He looked down at his desk. His chin plumped in concentration. His hands as they padded over the papers on his desk were large, clean, hair-covered.

Will they soon be inside my flesh, flush with my skin like a lover, whatever it is he has to do? Will I let him do that to me?

I am so scared. I am so scared. I cannot believe I am sitting here. The blood in my brain forms frozen blocks between Dr Kreitzman's passages of speech. My scalp contracts with realisation – in glimpses – of what this is, why I am here, and I have to breathe very deeply. And then my mind shuts down again, and Dr Kreitzman is merely lulling. He is a blessed relief.

Glimpsed truth prickles: it is an icy pulsing, it vibrates with a drilling sound. It makes your heart thump wildly for seconds, and then the knowledge cuts out. This is an everyday event, after all. It's no big deal.

'So,' said Dr Kreitzman. 'You'll be fine. I'm looking forward to working with you. We'll get a really pleasing result here, because you have all the ingredients – beauty is all your own – and there's just a bit of tidying up to be done. So we won't achieve anything dramatic.' His voice was soothing.

'No,' I said.

'You've come to me at just the right time. The older we get, the less elastic the skin becomes, but there's plenty of collagen there still – I can almost see it! Elastic – you know, we'll just do a little restorative work. A tiny bit of lipo on the chin; eyes, face. It's very special for me to work with someone like you, not the – ' he shook his hand towards the window – 'jowled wives in from Vanves.'

'Some people look too . . . stiff.'

'Stretched?'

'Yes.'

'Some people have a poor aesthetic sense.'

'But why?'

He shrugged. 'Look at their clothes. A mystery. Some patients want every little bit pulled back. I'll do as they wish, but really . . . only so much juice in an orange. But – ' He looked at his watch, his cuff retracting, chrome on hairy skin. 'I like to think I subtly embrace. I don't draw attention, it's, as I said, it's restoration. Simplest things are best.' His voice was low.

I nodded.

'OK.'

He took a pen.

'Miss Lee, I will book you in for Tuesday after next. You come to the hospital at nine a.m. or a little before, and you eat and drink nothing from the preceding midnight. My nurse, Mlle Martin, will explain everything else.'

'Yes,' I said.

'This is an important choice in your life, and you need to be happy about it. When you're at home, think it over, and don't forget I'm here to answer all your questions. OK, Miss Lee? So I'll look forward to seeing you Tuesday. I love the suits you wear, by the way.'

I walked from there to Fouquet's, avenue des Champs-Elysées. I drank tisane. My Paris is so beautiful, but Haussmann cut huge swathes through it, and the tourists infest it.

FOUR

I was tired. I was so tired, I was sick.

My apartment is large. I padded round it in my little Moroccan slippers, their hard camel soles denting the pile of the carpet. I was still myself. It was me. It was me. My feet made velvet imprints on the Esfahan rug, and the flesh on my face was still soft.

The slippers were a gift from my step-daughter Melina, my ill little ward who one day brought me some satin slippers covered in birds and palms from a souk near the Atlas Mountains. She gave them to me, and we kissed each other. I wonder whether she buys pots pourris now for other women in Laurence's life. Probably, but I think we had a love, Melina and I. I would give her suspender belts, chemises by Rosy, and her father disapproved and was embarrassed by it. Melina kept having to go back to the hospital because she starved her body, and finally Laurence refused to visit her in his conviction that it didn't help her, so I visited the clinic alone.

It was a light cold day, the day of the operation. There was a mist so slight it was like myopia, the finest blur to the roof of the Invalides. The gold of its dome looked faintly tarnished. Even the pigeon in the cool early morning was not repulsive; it didn't choke me with its feathers and its tocking, alone as it was, pecking my seeds. It was like a creature flown in from the woodlands of fable, it was animated and it lived.

My apartment, then, is sizeable. The living space runs thirty metres. Its windows stripe the walls, their minute balconies balustraded, so in high autumn they are the striations of baroque grandeur, but on dozy summer afternoons they are the stock architecture of any Luberon farm house. They are tall and narrow, they open like a door – French windows, precisely – and the drapes balloon to spinnakers, and then snare in gusts from the Luxembourg. The wall sconces that are not wired hold gelatine-pink candles, and there above the day bed is my girl picture. I'm a little European *Mädchen* in it, a *Mäderl*. The American girlhood was yet to come. My face is a fat heart on a slender stalk. Braids looped back on themselves and tied. Did I know then the number of words my hand would write? Did I know how much sex I would have? Did I know what would happen to me? There is no knowingness in that look, just the stoical passivity of childhood – accept a biscuit, a slap on the face – just torten and heart shapes, and eyes big berries.

The bell rang ten minutes too early. I grabbed my bag and I felt newly hungry as I moved. The cab carried me to the hospital. It tangled with the manual workers' traffic, as I knew it would, so I had left early, and still the breezes by the bridges were fresh from the Seine, the traffic fumes a distinct layer that had not yet permeated, and I was calm, calm. I breathed the river breezes. I was so tired, I sleepwalked through that limbo between water and traffic. I was still free to choose. I hadn't made a decision; I was airy and drunk on trampled-down nerves. I could get there, if I wished to, and decide to leave.

My throat was dry from lack of water. I was blank, then the tiredness spilled over me, knocking my head against the cab window. My face, its pores and slackness, pressed against the surface. It was preserved, like an extinct species flared beneath a layer of glass. So I could still leave. I could run free from the hospital with my night bag, bare-legged like a girl across the

Pont de l'Alma and it would still be me, I'd be me.

Thérèse Raquin used to lie in a garden along the river at Vernon, upstream to the west, and she who had pretended to be demure let the monsters come upon her. She seduced beasts in her head by the Seine.

I could buy a little house in St-Germain-en-Laye. It would have ornate railings enclosing its garden, peeping drapes, a piano. My bed would be stayed with Egyptian cottons, eau de Nil and white, narrow ivory ribboning laced through the pillow edges. Young men could visit me there, each one with something to leave behind – his virginity, his sadness his T-shirt – in the house of Adèle Meier. They'd take me pony riding in the woods of St-Germain. I could stroll about like one of those half-lesbian courtesans promenading the Bois de Boulogne –Liane de Pougy known for her profile and her pearls, or her girlfriend Mlle Flossie – with a duenna to look after me, a rich man for rare sex, and a scattering of male admirers from the *banlieues*.

The cab chugged outside l'Hôpital des Cevennes. My fingers were shaking with that old grainy slew of nerves as I found change in my purse to pay the driver. Someone walked past me on the street. She was a normal person. A nurse came to meet me at the reception. She greeted me. Am I a sick person or Madame L. booked in for a facial at the beauticians? I am this morning's face lift patient. That is all. This is to her as switching on the computer is to me, though for her the daily routine may carry an edge of faint scorn towards the punter.

Dr Kreitzman was not to be seen. He's too important. He sits, no doubt, in his dressing room before coming out to conduct his symphony, since the approximation to art and the appreciation of his art are his only concerns. Not for him the comforting of silly matrons who come to him for his skills.

The hospital was clinical and discreet. Nurses slipped between corridors and partitions. It seemed underpopulated, but it was still early in the day.

'Good morning. How are you?' said the nurse.

'I'm feeling fine,' I said.

'Shall I show you to your room, Miss Lee?' said the nurse.

'Yes. Thank you,' I said.

The room was very small. It was covered in textured wallpaper printed with abstract splashes of pastel, and above the bed was a fake canvas Fragonard reproduction. The bedspread, pulled tight over the bolster, was a pink-orange shade more vivid than its peach pastel echoes in the wallpaper. This was the bolster that would support my head with its freshly shifted flesh. I put my bag down on the bedcover. My heart thumped faintness through my head. A paper gown lay folded on a chair in the bathroom; a bottle of acetate was provided for the removal of nail polish, and scent-free cleanser for the removal of cosmetics. I was to clean my face and prepare it for cutting. I threw up with a series of heavy heaves into the toilet.

I rang for a nurse. I hid my face. I told her they would have to cancel the operation.

I didn't run long-limbed across the Pont de l'Alma after all. I slid into a Mercedes from the cab rank, and I could taste vomit as I told the driver where to go. I scraped away a remnant of dried vomit with my nail from the corner of my mouth, and held my head down, loose on its stem – I was so tired and hungry – and the cab shunted me back home. I slept most of the day, and the daggers started appearing early evening.

My days . . . *mes jours*, to be sure . . . are like this: I try, very hard, I think, to paint a new life for myself. This period of time seems to be like a second adolescence, a compound of despair and illogical springing hope that is highly reminiscent of that strange time lag between the end of high school and the start of real life or for me the interim between *Snow White* and my adult career.

These are my days: I'm woken up, sometimes to the daggers speeding at me like flies, propelled in the early morning by my own ghost hand or by a punch of self-hatred or a jolt of humiliation less palpable. It's like remembered embarrassment which hits you without warning in the street and causes a jerk of the head and jaw, and you utter a groan through the teeth to shake it off. I don't know why the daggers come, and I twist and sweat away from them in my half-sleep and fight off a fresh swarming just before I wake. Do I hate myself so much? Or was there someone else?

My days: I appear in studio discussions broadcast here during the early evening, or on the later night slots, which are preferable. Journalists from Holland and Belgium come to interview me; the French and American media peg their interviews on concrete happenings, publications, then use me predictably and regularly as a commentator. They clearly think I can be relied upon to be 'controversial', 'eccentric'. Last year, my publishers in the States and here in France simultaneously released new editions of the *Loulou* books, those same infamous monochrome images passed through a slight tint – silver, rose – and redesigned with new typefaces, new borders, so they look quite groovy, as Melina would say. I have a contract for a new novel, to be delivered this year.

I have barely started it. I have written two folders' worth of notes. I'm onto my third folder, making a fresh start with a chock-full stack of paper, and dividers in sugar-paper solutions of lime and chalk blue, like the covers of the books you used in high school, the folder an intricate baroque design. This inertia haunts me. I pick at it. There are too many projects, worrying away at the stretch of time that should be inviolate.

I have no lover just now. One day, in graceful middle age, I may meet a man who is not Laurence, whose brain cells and body smells mesh and move in counterpoint to my own, but right now Paris is a vast and elegant desert.

So I walk a lot. It wraps me in a lonely but dreamy solitude that drip feeds me a species of hope. I keep a tube of total sunblock right in front of my bathroom mirror, to remind me, and I dab it on; sometimes it mixes with my powder and I have to re-smooth the paste, and then I take my bag and I walk through the Luxembourg, along rue de Fleurus, or Jacob, Visconti. To the river.

I know I'm waiting for my new life to unfold. My life has ended. I see daggers. There's not very much left of me. Depression is like the weather – the weather in my head is a dark grey cloud, a thick blur too solid for storminess.

And yet sometimes I sense budding, the elastic hormones of youth bulbing through the cracks. I feel as though there are amorphous but serendipitous signs that my reputation is remoulding itself. The line between has-been and legend is very fine. If you analyse any career, there's a largely unnoticed ebb in activity before one graduates from mutable celebrity to fixed reputation.

After leaving the hospital I went to bed, essentially, for five days. My skin flopped and dragged when I got up in the evenings like an old basset hound's. I do not want to become a silken monster for men to pet. I stroked myself.

Laurence used to stroke my cheek in the exact same spot, very gently, as we lay there. If I had had that area pulled back, would that have meant that Laurence had once stroked a spot one centimetre closer to my ear, or is it the underlying muscle and bone that count in the annals of memory?

He used to stroke me just so, his fingertip exploring and then fading as we lay talking. Other times, he'd suddenly decide to undo my bra, when I didn't expect it, in the day time. My breasts were naked, pale and chill, and he cupped them with warmth and teased the flesh, pinching the nubs and then moaning minutely as he moved downwards to suck on my nipples. He said they were small pink sea shells, girl's nipples. The sensation of his mouth against the puckered nubs fanned and funnelled downwards.

Very soon after he met me, Laurence informed me that he 'fancied' me. He said this casually in a loud British accent. I thought the manner of his announcement was outrageous, and I didn't go to bed with him for some months. When I did, I experienced addiction.

I was rescheduled. They fitted me into a slot.

'Quite normal,' Dr Kreitzman said. He was cold, unemotional about the subject. He lifted his pen and put me into his appointment book. 'My ladies suffer from nerves. You'll be just fine.'

It was recommended that I stay the night before, so I arrived by cab in that quiet interlude when the restaurants are full and a cab can speed unhindered along the underpass by the Quai d'Orsay. It was quite dark then. It felt as though I were going out to Roissy to catch the shuttle to Britain.

The hospital lighting was more subdued than in the first glare of the morning, a sole receptionist on evening duty, a small delay for the nurse to take me to my room.

I followed the nurse upstairs. The room was situated on a corner of the building. This time, the wallpaper's abstract markings were printed in shades of blue instead of peach, the bedspread a corresponding powder violet. The windows, double-glazed and small and metal-framed, were designed to open only with discouraging effort. They looked out on the back of the hospital, away from the traffic, where staff cars were parked in a courtyard bordered by a row of large square garbage cans. I could not look at those cans. The flues and ventilators of the heating system were stacked in a repeating pattern of grids and concrete blocks and metal fixtures, the metal now weather-browned. There was an extension of merged red brickage, dull concrete, grilles. There is something sinister about walls, bricky thumps of solidity: you don't know what's going on behind them. Steam, or smoke, was drifting from one of the grilles, low down, near the car wheels, and I thought of the obvious, I thought of Dachau, of blood, of brick, and I was ashamed of myself, and quivered involuntarily and violently. It was industrial and clinical. Where would human fluids be drained? Blood seemed inappropriate.

There was no paper gown on a chair. There were towels, and cleansers, to prepare the body for the surgeon. There was a telephone by the bed: 'O' for Reception, like a hotel.

I lay in bed and thought of the Hotel Montalembert. When Laurence and I came to Europe from New York for work, we used to ring for room service and for television guides and cabs at the Montalembert, staying there just because we liked it, or because of sex, or some semi-self-conscious brand of fun in which we had to do spontaneous things to be romantic. This was a hotel we had found that was nearly faultless in its ability to provide pleasure. We explored it as though it was a new home and we were children grubbing in corners and making houses under tables, tents of sheets. We took the service elevator to the staff areas a couple of times, late evening, and looked in unlocked cleaning cupboards, filched piles of fresh towels on a trolley in case we needed them. We took them back up the service elevator to our room. I sometimes wandered into the kitchen. The chefs got to know me, and we chatted at eleven at night while Laurence stayed in the room, and I would, strangely, delay pleasure, to taste it better; I sampled icing or petits fours they had made, and they gave me fresh fruit, and all the while I knew I would shortly be having sex. I gave them a couple of copies of my books, and they had to pretend they'd read them.

It was home from home. We had our favourite rooms, high up in the Montalembert.

The staff saved the new batches of bathrobes for me, because they knew I liked them fluffy and polythene-wrapped. They put in extra shampoo and soaps so I could take them. We wore the bathrobes over our underwear, the clinical to enhance the sensual. Laurence's underwear was nothing. Underpants sometimes. I wore robes over my basques and bras.

When I was in France for work, and Laurence came with me, we took the nights into the mornings, playing about. It was as though we drew one over the other, the late hours of the night dragged over the early hours of the morning in a semi-opaque blind so they merged into one sleepwalking span of time in which we were beyond tiredness, or we incorporated it into the mechanics of our daily lives, and had to catnap or take long slugs of sleep. Then Laurence would leave before me and call me from New York in the early evening, to say he had slept fifteen hours and missed an assignment.

The hotel was joke Paris, Maurice Chevalier luxury in the sunshine, our overheated bolthole in the winter. Our brothel. Our own steam bath.

I look back at this time, and of course, it's a jewel box, the memory sews events into a satin soft box. I can only remember the harsher realities – menstrual cramps, times when we had nothing to say to each other, unexpected sexual failures or simple boredom – when I force myself to focus on how it might actually be if we were about to meet up. Memories of love are the most intransigent of all, like candy-coloured tracts of childhood – your Momma brushed your hair for you and you were a foundling fairy.

Now, I'm in this small boxed room, dry heated, its pastel hues there to combat the dull flavour of vent and function, and I could cry so badly. I mustn't. It would be dry crying, and then in the early hours it would turn wet, and they would have problems performing blepharoplasty on me, my eyelids pink and swollen to cut into, and then dark cherry rimmed and bulbous after they had been operated upon with the scalpel. I am alone, and no one in this world knows what I am about to do. No one except Dr Kreitzman and his assistant surgeon and an anaesthetist and a few anonymous nurses and administrators, to whom I am a fake name and a patient number. Laurence doesn't know that strips of flesh his tongue tip has met are about to be parted from me, for the sake of my appearance.

The Montalembert was so over-padded, bolstered and stuffed with wadded bedding, we unravelled pillows from the undersheets and heaved them across armchairs. I walked to the bathroom in the terry robe, and it made me feel girl-like, the robe falling just below my knees, my legs beneath it pinny and barefoot. I could see myself as he saw me – I knew he was watching me. I closed the door and made myself a scented haven without Laurence. The steam of a shower bent strands into kiss curls along my hairline. The bathmats at the Montalembert were bright and hard from laundry service. I sat on the mat after my shower and stroked my legs with body cream. As I rubbed the length of my calves, I felt the mat on the floor pressing against my labia, places Laurence would soon touch. I felt delicate, sea-like. I was almost complacent with the calm of sexual certainty, and then a swell of nerves or lust (the surge through the stomach indistinguishable) would take me. Laurence was out there, just behind a door. This excited me so much, the idea of it, and threatened me as it excited me. I ran cream over my face with my fingertips in the bathroom. My skin was scented, plumped out and absorbent. I looked at myself in the mirror, looking myself in the eye as though I was another person, my pupils in duplicate through the steam, and walked out into the room.

At l' Hôpital des Cevennes, they gave me a light sleeping pill. My nerves floated above me and settled themselves. I could see ganglia and blood spots drifting and ticking above my vision, behind a different skin, and I shifted into a chemical feathered sleep.

In the morning, early, my mouth was dry and foul tasting. I couldn't drink: I sucked a weak little spring of saliva from inside my cheeks. Somehow they had rearranged the room. Someone had left me a new pile of towels; the paper gown was now in place. I thought that maybe I remembered that someone had come in earlier.

It was half past eight in the morning. I urinated. It came from me, me now, my own body in its natural state. I looked at my thighs on the toilet seat, with their dimples, puckerings, and smooth sections. I wiped my eyes with the cleanser and cotton pads provided, since all make-up must be removed. My lashes looked shiny and individual and my eyebrows stood out in relief from my skin. Bald doll face, patchy red with too much cleansing. It was hard for me to confront the hospital staff without make-up.

He was going to pull my face open and sew it back.

A nurse knocked on the door.

'The nurses will be ready for you soon,' she said. She smiled into my eyes. 'You can slip into the gown when you're ready. No jewellery or underwear.' She glanced at my nails.

'Thank you,' I said.

Walking along the corridor, I realised the hospital was not so small, that it stretched back in a double 'L'. There were probably several operations going on today, the theatre booked for the removal of cancerous tumors and for nose jobs. I was not the only one. I had a robe over the paper gown – white like the Montalembert's – and Melina's slippers, gaudy reds and palm greens against the contrast of the white. The nurse led me to an elevator at the end of a corridor.

Downstairs they made me wait in a small room by myself. It was cold in there. I was alone in the paper gown, and I was chilled.

'The doctor is coming in to see you now,' they said, and Dr

Kreitzman came into the room wearing a plain suit. He was brisk and didn't really look at me as he had before: his glance was briefer and matter of fact.

'Good morning, Miss Lee,' he said. 'How are you?'

'Fine, thank you, Doctor,' I said. I don't know why I said 'Doctor'. It sounded like a person in a movie.

Dr Kreitzman was carrying a briefcase and a larger, metal box bag. 'I'd like to take your photographs now, if you can sit just here,' he said.

I hesitated, briefly confused. I thought he recognised me.

'This is for the records,' he said. 'So we can record the improvements.'

I felt naked under the white light of the flash, a criminal – ugly, criminal for being ugly. I was a skinned heifer. I was acutely embarrassed to look this way in front of Dr Kreitzman. He takes the woman with her jowls and her eye bags, and then he gets rid of them, and then later he photographs her with her new taut youth. I recoiled. He had seen me only with curving red lips and mascara.

He barely looked at me.

I felt nauseated with dread, yet the tiniest part of me ticked with anticipation. I was to surrender to Dr Kreitzman. I would surrender all will and he would invade me and mutilate me. It was my punishment. A little hidden section of my mind wanted him to make a pass at me before he cut me. I swallowed it. I looked at his hand. I was granting it permission to slice me. I had already made a payment with my AMEX card.

Dr Kreitzman repositioned me to draw lines on my face. I felt the cold liquid of the pen as it traced a track past my ears, down by my mouth, over my laughter lines, my eyelids and under my chin. The pen pulled the skin of my cheeks as it was pressed.

'You need to sign this for me, just here and here,' said Dr Kreitzman.

'What is it?'

'This is a description of what we will be doing today – face, neck and eyes. And this is just for your consent.'

The consent form seemed less reassuring, its tone and choice of language differing from Dr Kreitzman's in his consultation rooms. 'Cosmetic surgery is not an exact science,' it said. 'Beyond surgery, the healing process is not entirely predictable.' I signed it. The signature was shaky and hardly like my own.

I needed water. I felt suddenly nauseous again, the nausea that segues into black-out. I swayed. There was no blood in my face. My skin was cold and wet with nausea. I wanted Laurence. I wanted him to stride into this room carrying his trench coat and briefcase and take me by the hand and drive me home.

I cried, very slightly, while Dr Kreitzman put away his camera. He didn't notice.

'Miss Lee, thank you. The nurse will come and help you now, and – we'll meet up later.'

He left, and then a different nurse came into the room.

'Good morning,' she said. 'How are you feeling today?'

'Good,' I said. My voice was barely audible.

'You'll be fine,' she said. 'If you could follow me, please, Miss Lee. Dr Horiot will come and see you.'

'Who?'

'Dr Horiot is the anaesthetist working with Dr Kreitzman today.'

I followed the nurse along the underground corridor. My nerves were like a fever. This was the chamber reserved for my punishment.

The basement was painted purple and white. It was cold down there. The floor was tiled. Metal doors led to other rooms: 'Clean Zone – Theatre Clothing Must Be Worn', 'Preparation Room', 'Recovery Room'. Somewhere, I heard the sound of air conditioning, or heating systems blowing. In a further room, the nurses helped me onto a type of tray, a bed-size metal pallet lying on a trolley. They secured my hair with small elastic bands.

'This will make you feel calm and relaxed, if you could just turn over,' said the nurse.

My nerves swarmed and bubbled in my head. I felt as I had as a child. I did as she said, and the nurse inserted a needle in my buttock. I winced. She wiped the punctured skin.

I lay on the trolley, and two nurses wheeled me into a room off the operating theatre. Dr Kreitzman was there, in a mask and overalls, talking to the anaesthetist. He didn't look at me. I wanted him to look up. I studied his back and his thighs in his suit, and I wanted him to look at me and smile at me. Then I remembered I had purple lines drawn down my face. I rested my head on one side.

The pictures of women with their eggshell skin in the advertisements in the back of magazines for cosmetic surgery are smooth and complete. They don't tell you about all this, about the gauges and steel pumps and rubber tubes, about the blood. There was a smell of disinfectant; people were there with paper masks over their mouths.

I went into hospital for my looks.

I watched Dr Kreitzman's broad back in his surgical gown. I was naked under a blanket.

The anaesthetist came and put a needle in a vein in my hand. It hurt for a moment.

A small tube led from the patient's mouth to protect the airway. The surgeon and his team wore shoe covers and theatre hats and gowns, and chatted through their face masks. Dr Kreitzman asked the nurse to select a symphony, which she inserted in the CD player at a very low volume.

They prepared themselves. The nurses made small talk with Dr Kreitzman, displaying careful deference. They referred to him as 'Dr Kreitzman' at all times.

Oxygen pipes led from the ceiling. Sinks lined one wall. There was a faint, regular beep.

The patient lay on the bed with her head to one side and the tube leading from her mouth. The anaesthetist calibrated his monitors.

Dr Kreitzman pulled on his surgical gloves. The latex compressed the hair on his arms. His chair was pulled near the patient, while a nurse laid out the sterilised tools.

'She's a bit pale!' said the anaesthetist.

Dr Kreitzman focused on the patient. He shifted her head around and pulled a few stray strands of hair from her ear.

'She's all right,' said Dr Kreitzman.

The patient's hair was scraped into sections, the bunches secured with small elastic bands, like a poodle or a small girl. Her mouth lolled open.

Her head was placed on a circular pillow, a ring of hard sponge. She lay on a thick blue cotton sheet, which was stiff with washing, but retained faint stains from former use. She was motionless. The operating lights were very bright on her skin and on the purple lines indicating where the surgeon would cut.

Her chest was slightly mottled and baggy, exposed above the blanket. Her arms were placed on arm rests, and her legs were positioned on a pillow. Clips were attached with tapes on her chest and arms. There was a yellow bag attached to a bin behind her head. 'Clinical Waste – For Incineration Only' was printed on it.

The doctor's face mask was pulled on. His hair was covered by a blue surgical cap, and a light was clipped to his forehead. Only his eyes were visible, dark brown and focused on the body in front of him.

The nurses had prepared the swabs and would note on a board how many were used, in case one should be left accidentally inside the patient's body. The surgical instruments were laid out on a cloth, newly sterilised after other people's operations. There were sutures, blades, bulldogs, skin hooks, a throat pack. Bandages were stacked on trays. A bowl sat beside them, filled with liquid.

Dr Kreitzman focused on the rhytidectomy patient.

'Did you do the mouth, Dr Kreitzman?' asked a nurse.

'No, it's hers,' said Dr Kreitzman.

The anaesthetist was chewing gum and routinely unravelling a black rubber tube. He punched more keys on the bank of monitors.

The nurse unwrapped syringes, and they were filled with local anaesthetic, and with saline, containing adrenaline, to lift up the skin and facilitate dissection.

Dr Kreitzman pinched the patient's face softly, feeling the flesh of the cheeks and chin to ascertain its elasticity and measure the pouches of fat that had travelled downwards with the ageing process.

Then Dr Kreitzman pierced the facial flesh with a syringe. The woman lifted her arm minutely. He injected fluid along the lines he had drawn on the face. He inserted the needle gently, then he worked more swiftly. He used a second syringe. A string of blood beads decorated areas of her facial skin.

The monitor bleeped, constant and low, in the background. The anaesthetist glanced occasionally at the patient.

The patient on the bed looked like a baby merged with a middle-aged woman. Her mouth dragged open, the breathing unconscious. Her arms were loose and defenceless, appearing fatter and whiter. The nurses and doctor shifted the weight of her body for optimum working conditions, and she flopped, heavily, on the bed. Her head lolled, her mouth was loose around the tube, and her eyes were slightly opened to reveal a slit of white.

The surgeon felt her face again. He seemed to caress the flesh as he sized it up. Then very slowly he inserted his scalpel. His dark eyes were focused on the woman's flesh. With a fine scalpel he incised the right eyelid. Very delicately, he drew it along the flesh. The patient groaned, faintly but deeply, like a cow in a distant field. She lifted her arm to her face. The nurse pinned it back down.

'Just relax,' said the nurse.

Blood sprang to the cut, and the nurse dabbed it. The surgeon wiped his scalpel and inserted it once more, on the pre-drawn line beneath the incision, and dragged the scalpel slowly along a curved line. The delicate flesh sprang to embrace the blade as it cut. The patient murmured. The surgeon's breath was heavy and concentrated behind his mask. An elliptical section of flesh was then cut slowly from the eyelid. It resisted and stretched as he pulled. Blood drifted from the lid into the patient's eye, and the nurse wiped it away. A bead of it leaked and pooled in the inner corner of her nose.

With small surgical forceps, the surgeon removed a string of fat from the patient's eyelid. This was shining yellow and lumpy in texture. His hand movements were delicate and precise, but he had to pull the fat hard. It stretched as he removed it from the eyelid, clinging to its original location.

Using a very fine thread, the surgeon inserted a needle into the skin and made a row of small discreet stitches. The wound swelled and quickly began to turn purple.

Then Dr Kreitzman made an incision below the lower eyelid. He cut away the skin and cut out the pouches of fat that had collected beneath the woman's eyes over the years and now needed to be removed. The fat was injected with more local anaesthetic, the area beneath it cauterised. He repeated the procedure on the other eye.

He breathed hard. He wiped his scalpel, and he stroked the area above the patient's ear before making an incision. The areas that had been injected were now swollen and marbled. Nurses chatted in a side room. One of them wheeled in a table with a new pile of cloths.

Between operating on the eyes and the face, the nurses and doctor made jokes about patients.

The white areas were now turning yellow on the patient's face. There were red patches among the purple pen marks. The hair stuck out in its little bunches.

The nurse unrolled some thin paper, which was cut and placed over the nose area and forehead of the patient. Swabs were placed in her ear holes.

The surgeon held the scalpel just above the patient's head and then carefully positioned it. Very slowly, he cut in front of the ear. The flesh split into red lips and revealed itself. The woman's blood spread. She pulled her hand up. The nurse held it down. She moaned and reached for her face again. The nurse pinned it down quite hard.

'Relax. Relax. What's her name?' she said.

Dr Kreitzman rested his scalpel on the patient's face. He shrugged slightly.

'It's false. Another Smith-Dupont-Martin. American.'

'You don't know the first name? Calm down,' she said to the patient. 'Relax, darling. Just relax.'

'No. She's someone . . . Some American with an accent – looks like someone. Uppity.'

Dr Kreitzman cut around the front of the woman's ear, following its outline, around the tragus and above, into the hairline. The scalp was tougher, areas of sensitivity on the face varying according to their clusters of nerve endings. He pressed hard, his breathing faster. A surgeon must cut deeper into the scalp to prevent death of the hair follicles. Blood danced around the roots of the hair. It pooled in the ear, soaking the swab, and running down the neck. The nurses swabbed it silently, and passed instruments to Dr Kreitzman.

Then Dr Kreitzman inserted forceps, resembling large tweezers, attached to an electric current. He pressed on a foot pedal, and a beep sounded. He cut behind the ear.

The nurse held the ear. Dr Kreitzman began to remove the

facial flesh from the patient. The nurse held up the edge of the flesh while the surgeon cut into the face. It resisted. It was hard to cut away the skin, naturally attached to the muscles and bones beneath. He cut delicately at first, tensing the scalpel against the fibre that kept the facial flesh in place. He cut in small insistent movements. Blood flowed steadily.

Then he began to cut with scissors. White strands of tough connective tissue glued the skin and muscle. This had to be incised, the facial flesh then separated from the muscle beneath. Once Dr Kreitzman had dug himself a workable pouch of cheek flesh, the nurse held the flesh flap open for him with forceps to enable him to work more efficiently.

'I did my first ever theatre work for you, Dr Kreitzman,' said one of the nurses.

Dr Kreitzman nodded.

He worked faster. This was the 'undermining' process of the full SMAS facelift. The flesh was strong and resistant. He had to work the scissors hard. He returned to the scalpel and chipped away at the white connective tissue, jabbing and tearing. The human flesh does not pull away like chicken skin. It is attached firmly to its roots. It needs to be cut and sliced away with some effort.

Dr Kreitzman thrust a scalpel backwards and forwards, harder and faster. He held his breath, then breathed hard. It required strength and concentration. He became heated, jabbing and thrusting. The skin started coming away. The nurse still kept it raised. By now the theatre lights shone through the loosened skin, making a golden bloody glow. It was like a cave or cavern, the flesh of her cheek a loose pocket above her face.

The nurse constantly wiped the area. The shape of the scalpel and scissors pressed against the inside wall of the separated flesh so the scissors' movements could be seen from the outside.

Dr Kreitzman inserted his hand into the patient's face and

pressed and punched until his fingertips reached right down to the edge of the woman's mouth. He tore away at the last resistance. The scissors cut further down the inside of the face, bypassing the mouth and reaching the neck. Their outline was visible. They made a click click click audible from inside the woman's neck. The facial skin was now separated from the underlying muscle.

It lay slack and rumpled. The nurse then raised the skin several inches above the patient's muscle and bone so that areas of excessive bleeding could be cauterised. There was a hiss and a smell of burning flesh as the bleeding muscles inside the patient's face were sealed with an electric current, the area that was burnt forming a speck of grey. Sometimes a strand of smoke emerged from inside the woman's face.

Dr Kreitzman's fingers spread inside the flesh. His whole hand fitted inside the woman's cheek, like a glove. The peeled cheek was held open with a wide steel instrument with a light attached to it, so the surgeon could light the face from inside. The muscle sheet was gristly and lunar. Dr Kreitzman pinched areas of her muscle together and sewed them with sutures to tighten the underlying muscle system.

The patient's cheek was now loose. It flopped over her ear, unattached, rooted only at the mouth, nose and eyes. Dr Kreitzman inserted his hand again. There was a film of blood on his right glove.

He cut further behind the ear and into the hairline, where the flesh came away more easily. Under the skin, the face's pitted surface of muscle and blood resembled another fine, bloody face; part smooth, part marbled; yellow with a crazing of blood.

'The skin's OK,' said Dr Kreitzman.

'It's good skin,' replied a nurse.

With her face half-attached, the patient suddenly jolted as if in pain.

'Shh, shhh,' said the nurse. 'Keep still, darling. You're fine.'

The patient breathed sharply through her nose. The anaesthetist made some adjustments.

Dr Kreitzman dabbed right inside the face, so the whole swab emerged soaked red. He then cut into the fatty area beneath the chin and suctioned the excess fat. The fat was broken up with a cannula and vacuumed out. By now, only the patient's ear was intact on the side of her face, an island of ear on muscled and exposed flesh, all the skin around the ear peeled away like an orange.

The doctor pulled the loose facial flesh and the flesh of the head and neck up over the ear itself, so both edges met there, as he decided the amount that should be cut off. Blood had stained the pillow beneath.

Then, using his skill and judgement, Dr Kreitzman cut away a section of the patient's face, perfectly following the outline of the ear. As he cut, an ear-shaped template of flesh flopped onto the pillow. It hung from behind the woman's ear. He cut more away. Another strand hung from the bottom of the ear, like a long earring of flesh. He cut it off, and the nurse dropped the woman's flesh on a cloth on the table as she passed the doctor a needle holder. Later, the scissors were placed casually upon it, then it was gathered with other waste and thrown away into the incinerator bag. Groups of several flaps hanging together, like wind chimes, stuck to her neck. The doctor cut them off in one section, and finally removed a long strip of flesh from around the ear.

A portion of her scalp was cut away where it was no longer needed. A triangle of the scalp was removed and thrown away; it nestled, a piece of flesh with long hair growing from it, on some tissues in the incinerator bag.

The new flesh seams were stapled on the head and above the ear. The stapler made a hard clicking sound along the skull, and rucked the flesh seam.

The surgeon was handed a needle holder containing thread, then he sewed the new edging of flesh flush with the ear, using precise small stitching, as far inside the seam of the flesh as possible.

So the woman's flesh was separated, pulled up, redraped, and reattached, stretched more tightly than before.

There were gleaming metal staples nestling among the patient's hair, and small knots of black thread on her ears and eyelids. The patient's eyelids had swollen fast and become bulbous, to embrace the stitches placed there. Her whole eye area was now purple and raised and bruising.

A thick flap of scalp lay on the cloth on the table. A whole area of the original scalp and face was now missing, the flesh pulled and joined to its new location. The last sections of flesh were thrown away.

A plastic tube was inserted in a hole in the area behind the neck that remained open, and threaded into the face, its outline snaking along below the skin. This drain, to siphon off fluids and reduce bruising, was stapled in place, a length of it protruding from the neck. The nurse fixed the drain to a pump and pressed it. Bloody fluid was suctioned out through the opaque white plastic tubing.

A gauze strip was laid over the wounded flesh.

The process was repeated on the other side of the face.

The anaesthetist sat and read a novel. Swabs were counted and marked off on the board. The nurse wiped the instruments used to cut the woman's face.

The bleeding was more extensive on the left side of the face. Sometimes the doctor had to wipe the excess pieces of blood or flesh from his tools onto his hand, or his gown or a tissue. He wiped little pieces of her face onto his sleeve.

There was an outburst of chatter at lunch time. There were jokes about one of the nurses, and how she liked pain-au-chocolat.

A new section of the woman's face nestled with the waste paper and thread in the bag for incineration.

Her skin was now yellow and purple, crazed with a thin

layer of blood. Blood matted the roots of her hair.

The bleeding was quite extensive. The surgeon worked swiftly on the second side, his movements rougher and faster as he progressed, inserting the instruments hard inside her face, thrusting and teasing to separate the flesh.

Gauze was placed over the patient's wounds. She began to show signs of consciousness. Bandages were swiftly wound around her head. The doctor and nurses swaddled her in a mass of cotton wool over the bandage, and covered this with more bandage, a thick wedge of material sealed with a final length of plaster under the chin and over the scalp.

Only her mouth, nose and eyes were visible, her head surrounded by a large muff of bandages that made it appear twice its size, like a white furry hood. Her head was lifted and placed on a protective pillow so she could not turn and damage it. The patient moved slightly and tried to touch her face. The nurses wheeled her out into the recovery room.

FIVE

A decade had seeped into the pillow in discreet stains of human fluid. A little blood was ringed by clear exudate, so that it formed flared orange circles. Patches of wet blood spread beneath the patient's neck, the areas that had dried in the air turned madder. The inflammatory response had begun, the blood cells now rushing to the injuries sustained to flood the damage. The woman's facial skin had been excised from the underlying muscle blanket, lifted and repositioned further up the face.

So when I woke, my skin was as it had been, ten years before, when it had been tighter and had not succumbed to gravity.

At that time, ten years ago, I felt my life was rarefied, that it had accelerated to a peak that made me uneasy, as though I breathed thin air and might fall, or as though God might punish me for believing it. It was only me. It was only Adèle after all, a poor girl. I was not even an American. I watched that section of my life and could not quite absorb it, except in condensed moments – it was afterwards, when it thinned out, that I finally realised what it had been.

We lived in Gramercy Park in Manhattan then. I lived with Laurence Mahon in an apartment building on the east side of the park itself. The architectural firm of which Laurence was a partner flourished under the construction boom that had come with the eighties. There was a feeling of resurgence in the city, as if it had now entered a new phase, sluiced with white spanking light, and high rises, and Laurence would draw up plans that chunked the sky.

'You are Mr Bauhaus – in another life you came from Dessau,' I said to him.

'You have the most simplistic vision of what I do,' said Laurence. 'Shall I build a building just for you? How you'd design it. All curlicues and Gothic turrets. Gilded bloody frippery like the monstrosity we live in.'

We had argued for three and a half months over where to live in Manhattan. It had become our epic, our point of reference. Every day was a battle in the larger war we waged over a territory of a few square miles, yet secretly we were both prepared to concede, prolonging the struggle only for its enjoyment, for the heated triumph of calling up with fresh proof of the inferiority of the other's favoured location – minutely falling property prices, rumours of cockroach infestation, suspected nouveau riche tendencies. Laurence had all the advantages of his profession: he would call while I was working, interrupting me to inform me of alarming new zoning laws on Bethune Street, or to purposely dazzle me with details of a survey conducted by his firm that proved the majority of buildings between Prince and Spring on Broadway were suffering from secondary subsidence. I could rarely distinguish his bogus reports from his real findings, he presented both with such serious and detailed information.

Then I attacked him from a social standpoint, with vaguer weapons, casting matter-of-fact aspersions on the pseudo-bohemians and sad losers, the psychiatrists and students, who lived on the Upper West Side, pretending to be something they were not. These observations were incorporated into general conversation, through the Park or shopping, during an apparent moratorium.

So we bought a co-op in the apartment building on Gramercy Park as a grudging and battle-scarred compromise, and eventually we loved it, and it became homey like nowhere else had ever been, though Laurence maintained his architect's despair over it, calling it a terracotta-clad wedding cake, 'Meier's Neuschwanstein.'

Loulou lived in there, people thought. People always wanted to talk about Loulou, and who she was, and what would happen to her. Sometimes they'd come up to me in Rizzoli's, or look at me from a table across the way in a neighbourhood restaurant, and seem to want to speak. In the locked garden at Gramercy Park, they always left me alone.

Our girl Melina ran about the garden. She tried to sneak in Laurence's dogs, but dogs were forbidden, and some local custodian of propriety inevitably made her return them. And then she'd come inside, and there would be Laurence and I, and we all stayed in together, and the Park seemed cut off from the rest of Manhattan, a little urban island.

It was spring – 9 April, cool – in New York City when I had met the English man, Laurence Mahon, for the first time. Later, our meeting became the stuff of household legend, and for many years he used to tell me the story of the 88th Street apartment and the girl on Fifth Avenue, because I would ask him to tell it again and again like a bedtime story. And some nights I'd tell him what I'd thought of him in the Russian Tea Room. I always remembered how I first perceived him, and the subtle discrepancies between my initial impression of him and my later knowledge.

I had been taken by my room-mate Mimi Ceccato to her friends Mary's and Chris's apartment on West 88th Street. They were slightly older than us. They had rented this big apartment in a brownstone on the Upper West Side with chipped marble hallways and strange shaped bathrooms. I thought it was exciting. There were wooden floors and stalky chrome lamps, they served piles of brown rice and cooked pineapple, candles bobbing in water on the table, and people were noisy and high, elevated in that tall-ceilinged apartment looking out over Columbus Avenue.

There were about ten of us. The candles rocked and made light quiver on faces. There was a lacquer plate full of hash cookies. A man had brought his guitar. Mimi winked at me from across the table. I hardly knew anyone there; I talked to the man next to me, and I wanted to giggle because Mimi was watching me. We were younger than the others in the room, and we flirted and we attempted to be serious, but we became increasingly childish in our awareness of each other.

I listened to the man next to me, an attorney with a beard, and then I looked up and Laurence was there, sitting beside a woman with dark hair cut like a boy's. Something he had said was making people laugh. His British accent jumped out at me.

I saw him in an indistinct row of faces. I was drowsy with wine. I scarred salad leaves with a fork, making tracks on their surfaces. There was a babble around me; I was warm and tired. He saw me as he looked up during a pause, we focused on each other for the first time, and he smiled at me.

That was the first time I saw him. How strange, no arrow points, no erotic charge. How strange, not to know that your mind and your flesh will merge with that person's for half your life, and there they are, sitting there like anybody else.

The night was blurred behind smoke and wine. I was aware of him then, of someone with a British accent. I could distinguish the faces at the other end of the table. His wife Carolyn was sitting beside him. She was from the west coast, but she looked like a French boy. She was pretty in a strained thin way, with fleeting smiles and jolting movements and shadows under the eyes. She wore a black polo neck and silver hoops. Laurence was large and expansive beside her, his gestures verging on the clumsy. He had wavy nearly-black hair, and a large frame. He wore a white T-shirt that night, the tautness of his chest visible through the cotton as he leaned over. People were laughing as he became more damning and more explicit, avoiding censure by delivering his claims as understatements in his calm English accent.

The attorney was plucking a guitar at my end of the table, the sound discordant with the music from the record player. Mimi and I kept smiling at each other as if we knew something, as if we shared jokes and were waiting to discuss them, and I toyed with leaves and I drank red wine until my head was swaying and fermented, and I had an awareness that the man was there. I turned to his end of the table, and caught a delayed impression of him glancing at me.

We stayed there late, and his presence was a mere strand of warmth at the end of the room, tangible but unseen.

A long discussion began at his end of the table about going over to a drug store on Amsterdam Avenue to buy more cigarettes, and who would go, and how long it would take.

'Do *you* want to come?' Laurence turned to me suddenly across the table. It was the first time he spoke to me.

'Me?'

'Yes.' He nodded. We looked at each other directly.

I glanced at his wife, but she was talking.

'I think it's a little cold out there,' I said.

'Well, I'll get you a jacket.' He stood up. 'I'll rifle through Mary's coat hooks and find you one. Come on.' He gestured. I stood up.

He went towards the hall, and he returned. I walked over to him. I was a little unsteady. We met by the door.

'Here you are,' he said. He held out an old fur coat. I laughed slightly. 'You won't be cold now,' he said.

'I should go,' I said.

'Why should you go?' he asked in a factual manner.

I hesitated.

'Is someone waiting for you?'

'Yes.'

'All right,' he said, and he left with his crowd from the end of the table, and Mimi and I went home shortly afterwards.

Laurence said later that he had first noticed his Adèle at the beginning of the evening, before she looked up. She wore a close-fitting black crêpe dress, and he noticed her waist in the dress when she sat back, how narrow it was, how it tensed and straightened with the tempo of her conversation.

He returned to his friends, then he glanced at her again later in the meal. He thought she looked endearing and faintly strange in the black dress with her markedly pale skin. He imagined everyone else at the table would be looking at her more than they were. He kept glancing at her in gaps between conversation just because he thought she was attractive.

Later, he began to find her presence distracting. She talked to another man for a long time, and then to a woman; she chatted and she laughed, but he imagined he detected something fragile and resistant about her.

She had not noticed Laurence. People were becoming drunk. Laurence decided that she had a young married look, the look of a woman who has married in her early twenties and whose autonomy is buffered by the financial security of a husband. He strained to look at her hand. There was dark blue polish on her nails. She wore no wedding ring.

She looked at him for the first time then, and he smiled, they smiled at each other, and then she was absorbed back into her group. He wanted to address a comment to her across the table. He had rarely been lost for words in his life, but the woman's after-image hung like an icon in the corner of his vision, just feet away, her detached ease bothering him. He wanted to talk to her. He glanced at her waist again. They suddenly caught each other's eye again. Her mouth opened, her top lip almost smiling, but she turned away from him and began to talk to a woman beside her.

By the door, he saw her properly. He saw translucent blue-grey shadows under her eyes. The milky skin was just as fine up close, but there were faint ghosts of freckles beneath the powder. She looked like a kitten, a cat in black crêpe, Laurence thought.

Later, at home, Laurence suddenly remembered. He thought that perhaps he had seen her before. The memory moved him, but it was not so much a flash of recognition as a delayed and wilful welding of two images to create a pleasing new myth. He remembered, some years before, he had seen a girl waiting for the bus on Fifth Avenue. They were both up near the eighties, waiting at a stop, the air swollen with uncertain drizzle, that gnatty dark green feeling under the trees which canopy out from Central Park over the sidewalk. Laurence stood back, nearer the railings under the trees, to observe her unnoticed, because she was so satisfying to look at, so very precise in her high heels and sheer stockings and neat chic schoolgirl's dark blue raincoat, belted round the waist, like a young but polished French Mademoiselle. She had brown hair tied back and caught under her collar, and a small petal of a face, a straight nose and light brown eyes, and she was perfection. She was just perfect. So neat and independent and impatient and sexy-legged. Laurence watched her move from bus stop to sidewalk, to nearer the trees (he had to pace back to the stop), to the sidewalk again, clicking her heel on the step, peering crossly but still elegantly up Fifth Avenue. Then suddenly she gave up, and hailed a cab, her arm raised in its neat dark blue sleeve, leg disappearing, her mouth forming words in the glassy darkness of the cab, and the bus took still another ten minutes, and Laurence carried her in his mind as it began to rain and the bus trundled home in the dusk.

It was her again. He was reflecting after the supper, and he formulated this idea, his heart ticking at the image. The same

96

unimpeachable self-containment. The perfection of the petal face with its browns and whites. The impact of recognition, real or imaginary, blanked out the prototype, and gave him licence to be forever certain that he had seen her before.

Then Laurence Mahon wanted to see Adèle Meier again. It was the vaguest game in his head, a consciously unrealistic notion, as he began cutting along 57th Street to work, the days he remembered, or during the afternoons on the way to appointments and after late lunches, armed with only a nominal thought that he might see her because he had overheard her talking to the friend she had arrived with about the many virtues of the Russian Tea Room.

He tended to such flights of fantasy, to abstractions that contrasted with the rigours of his work and his manner. He flirted with extremes and absorbed them, so there was something tense and sprung about him. He was given to such sudden conviction.

He took the 57th Street route erratically for three weeks, and then one Friday afternoon she was there.

She was sitting in a booth on the far side of the Tea Room, surrounded by a group of women. Laurence stood in the doorway. A rich mesh of laughter rose from a table in the back section, as though a teenage girls' gathering was in full swing, or a debutantes' tea party had turned unruly. It was exclusive, female. Laurence hesitated by the door.

He looked through the red and gold gloom of the Tea Room. He had never been there before. The four women at the table were somehow surreal as though they were ornaments on a Christmas tree, suspended there in the dull light. They were of a similar age, well dressed and talkative. To Laurence, they looked vaguely fifties, all of them, as though they lived in the Barbizon and only met men in groups. They seemed to start several conversations at once, intermittently laughing as they lolled against the backs of the seats. Words such as 'patriarchy' were interleaved with amusement. Laurence sat down at a table in the front section and took out some work. He looked up at them very occasionally. He felt as though he was spying on Adèle Meier. He thought her obviously good-looking, and yet there was something ornate and dissonant about her he could not place, and that disappeared as he tried to define it. She was wearing a white chiffon headscarf and a blue dress that seemed to be composed of layers of the same material, more suited to a boudoir than a midtown afternoon, oddly incongruous with the volume of laughter that reached him at his table. Her make-up was noticeable even through the fog of low red lighting. He had savoured her lazily, emblematically, like a doll or a richly flavoured token of liberty, so now when he glanced at her she seemed known, prefigured, like an image from a picture.

Suddenly, she saw him. She looked up and waved at him with a smile of uncertain recognition. Laurence smiled back, feigning surprise. She beckoned him with a twitch of the head, so he gathered up his papers and walked over to the back of the room.

'A very good afternoon to *you*,' said Laurence, exaggerating his accent for her benefit.

'It's you again,' she said. The edges of her mouth arched with their own independent movement as she smiled. She looked younger than she had in the apartment, a very young woman made up with reds and whites.

She slipped spontaneously along the bench. There was just room on the padded red seat beside her.

'Sit here,' she said.

He sat. He was slightly nervous. He was suddenly aware of the white chiffon and female scents, the warmth and movement of a human next to him, the laughter subdued now he was there. He continued to pretend surprise a little longer than necessary, but Adèle seemed unbothered by his presence.

'I met this man,' she said to her friends, 'at a dinner party uptown. He was surrounded by heinous drunks. His name is . . . What is your name?'

'Laurence.'

'Laurence. I hardly met him,' said Adèle. 'But I remember him. He should stay for some coffee, shouldn't he?'

'Thank you,' said Laurence. 'So graciously put.'

He sounded more abrupt than he meant to. He looked faintly embarrassed. He ordered tea with lemon. The conversation resumed in a generalised babble.

'I can't quite work out,' said Laurence in a low voice to Adèle, 'if this is *dames* of the camellias time, or a gang of feminist militants.'

There were snorts of laughter and irritated looks in his direction.

'This is my group of friends,' said Adèle, trying to subdue amusement. 'We meet on Friday afternoons sometimes, when we want to slack off work.'

'How bad of you.'

'But lovely. Utterly pleasing.' She turned to him. 'We come to the Tea Room and have blinis and so forth and talk about men.'

'So I'm allowed to join you and talk about men?'

'If you have anything to say.'

'You could have introduced me as Laura, your softly spoken but strangely hulking new friend.'

'What are you doing here?' she suddenly asked.

'I – I walked past. I decided to work in here. Here you were.'

She caught her breath, as if about to speak.

'I'm glad you did, then,' she said.

There were small silences between the talk and laughter at the table, as the others half listened to their conversation.

'Did you,' said Laurence, turning to Adèle after a moment and resting his chin on his hand so his voice was low and directed only at her, 'did you once wait at a bus stop on Fifth Avenue, and then give up and catch a taxi?' he said. 'I mean, a few years ago?'

'Oh, sure,' she said. 'I give up waiting for the damn buses all the time.' She stretched over the table for the menu. 'It bankrupts me.'

'On Fifth, in about the upper seventies?'

'Oh, yes. At some point. Lots of times. Why are you asking me?'

'Oh, nothing . . . Once. Maybe – six years ago, I think I saw you. I saw a woman, she looked like you, and she was wearing a dark blue coat I think. Have you got one?'

'Of course,' said Adèle. 'Two at least. More black ones.'

'And she – you – disappeared into a taxi, and I never saw her, you, again, until – a few weeks ago.'

'And why do you remember her, this woman?'

'Because she was so lovely,' said Laurence, in matter-of-fact tones.

Adèle opened her mouth, and then said nothing. She looked to one side momentarily before returning her gaze to him. He was drinking tea, unconcerned.

They were silent. 'So you are telling me,' she said suspiciously, 'that this is the third time we're supposed to have run into each other in this city of half a dozen million when we don't even know each other?'

'It must be,' said Laurence. He looked at his watch; he stood up and lifted his briefcase from under the table clumsily and with strenuous effort. 'Odd, isn't it? So can I see you again?' he said casually.

She hesitated. 'By your law of averages we'll bump into each other around the middle of next week.'

'We – we'll invite you and your friend round for supper,' he said.

For years before I met Laurence, I had a number of boyfriends.

I didn't meet Laurence, after all, until I was twenty-six and had lived in New York City for nearly a decade. The relationships fell into one another, the dates and lovers interleaved and overlaid so for a few years at the beginning of the seventies, when I was in my early twenties, I felt drunk or hung-over all the time, drunk on an excess of men, but I made the sex rare, I would not have sex with all of these men, so I could keep awake and inviolate in the day. I had a resistance, a fastidiousness. Sometimes the smell of different men's semen on my underwear in the wash basket made me feel nauseous. It differed subtly. I could tell it apart, like breeds of fish roe. I would feel nauseous then, after all the pleasure they had given me, sickened by the dregs they didn't know they left behind, and throw my panties into the laundry with too much detergent.

And when I was a girl, I had thought that men were a thing apart, refined and strange like truffle pigs or war heroes. My father left our home for another woman nine months after we left Austria for America, so Uncles Stefan and Ed, our Virginian uncles, were the only adult males ever to tower and stoop through our house.

It was men I thought of, not boys. At twelve, thirteen, fourteen, my features were too womanly and defined; I looked strange, I felt quite ugly, even as I thought I was somehow spectacular. Older men glanced at me; boys did not, moved as they were by tip-tilt noses and palomino ponytails. So mentally I seduced men. I was their lover. They took me with all their hard flesh, their alien men scents. Then when I was fifteen, sixteen, boys would come round to our house begging like calves. My friends and I had this power. We knew we had this power; for a few years, five or seven years, we were omnipotent. We believed with simple assurance that we could seduce anyone if we wanted to, and yet still I felt physically inadequate: it was merely a subliminal knowledge of the terrible power of youth, and virginity, a gift in fumbling hands. There were fat old businessmen in the town, men in sports jackets and winter coats who walked between car and parking lot with their keys and their maps and briefcases, their pictures of their kiddies, and you could turn them into mad bulls.

I didn't sleep with these men. I just talked to them.

Such allure is about the satisfaction of a pre-formed dream, a hunger for illusion. It's all subliminal, a murmur of a suggestion, a voice that holds the disturbed vibrato of promise. Something sweet and dull and faraway.

If you offer them peachy girls, they will bite with their big horses' teeth. I could exercise a mesmeric force over them, get them addicted. I could smell their longings. I didn't know if men loved me or if they hated me, but I knew that my youth and sex was a trap as soft as milk curd. They came towards me and they sank. Even the boys I half loved succumbed to a feeble softening, their limbs and minds like watered bread.

There was something about my childhood that was sad in the way that stained carpets are sad in the sunlight, the tawdry claustrophobia of the immigrant illuminated by the glassy expanse of the New World. My shame was not underpinned by pride, but by a sorrow about my family that I could hardly express, my family with their hopes and unknown griefs, their scrubby lawn.

The house we lived in when we arrived in America from Austria was a small square: garage, dog bald garden, extension in the roof. I slept there, under the roof, with my sister. The house was dominated by dark wood, rubbed to a shiny grime by hands and cooking steam, all kitchen nooks and plated glass on a small and cluttered scale. My parents kept our clothes, place mats, tablecloths, until they were thin with wear. It was usually dark in our house. We could have had a bright square vista of elm tree, hose-pipe, shivering foliage across the street, but some old European gloom had to fall across the rooms like a decorative choice, unaired corners, spotted enamel pots, grey-brown dust drifts in the light bars through the blinds, all imported to a lower-middle income stretch of suburban America, the vapid new vowels of the high school as iconoclastic as breezes and open windows.

It was as if we were all ashamed of each other and for each other, the lack of cohesion and jumbled inertia of our existence a secret rotting in the back yard. We barely knew each other. We were not cohesive, yet we were exclusive, keeping our rituals to ourselves. I liked to walk out into the light outside the house and tap along in my socks and high heels, and breathe the trees, breathe the light blue air and the regular neighbours.

It was Papa who called me Adèle, like a French girl. My name was Adelaide Anna Christa Meier, for my grandmother Adelheid, but Papa called me Adèle. It was like my birthday, April fourth, like my Papa, part of me.

He always said we would go to America. He had lived in Virginia for two years when he was a boy. His mother was from North Carolina. His brother Stefan returned to the States after high school, there was a great-uncle who ran a paper store, and a myth floated through our family that one day we would emigrate. I, who had been to Vienna once, and never beyond, would one day become an Austrian in another country. An American Adèle.

We moved from Leibnitz, a small town near Graz in south Austria, when I was fourteen and spoke a little more than gymnasium English, and my breasts were composed of swollen nipples and my features too large, and I was Papa's favourite, I loved Karli like a pet, and Mammi had begun to cast an eye over my body.

We moved to Chesapeake, a small town in the south-eastern corner of Virginia where the rivers empty into the great bay and then into the Atlantic beyond.

The plains and suburbs, the highways grading to the ocean, had an ease to them after the mountains and speckled streets of Styria. It was as if land were water, and endless. Meiers before us had emigrated to that Tidewater area of Virginia, so there were the uncles, and the great uncle, and scattered half-relations who spoke no German. The town of Chesapeake grew with us. It was brand spanking new: all sprawl and malls and vacant lots, stretched beside swamp land. The noise of the construction workers lined our route to school. Around us, the land was complacent with historical awareness.

I thought people would perceive me as a Catholic girl, touched by God, a confection of frills and head bands. A marzipan girl indeed. But we were shabby with austerity, and volatile with too much discipline. Our schoolteacher father drilled us in verbs, scales, manners, the concerns of the provincial autodidact. He lost his grip on us in America.

I was the youngest for a very long time. Karli was a late-born sprout. He was my own baby when he arrived, my head to stroke, my body to hold, as though I were the youngest still and had been given a doll. Kathrin, the sister above me, was quiet and placid as a lake. She played her musical instruments, she went on diets, she absorbed our father's litany of rules, though she had sly boyfriends. She damped down speech in the manner of our mother, just as John, the oldest, was reedy and silent. Silence dominated our household.

'*You* are the verbal one,' said my father to me. 'Adèle, talk to me.'

And I talked to him.

My Papa: upright but not tall, handsome, dark, the spine ruler-straight. He had studied a decade for his Ph.D. in the evenings, then it slipped from him in the wake of his women.

'Do you think I will go to college?' I asked him.

'Oh, yes. Without any doubt. If you work hard every day – never slack. No slack. You have the mind. The verbal facility. Then when you graduate with honours we'll let off the cannons, float balloons. We'll make the church bells ring for you. Won't we?'

'Yes, Papa.'

'Surprise me, Adèle,' he said.

I was my Papa's favourite. I was Adèle-Adela. I was the little mouse, the Mauserl. He filled us with the terror of his rules, and the fear of his voice, but beyond all that, beyond our tears and our nerves, he favoured me. He was consumed with anger towards me, then he was amused by me.

'You are my special daughter,' he said. 'Adela.'

I was a rich girl, therefore. I was a rich, rich girl. I could do what I wanted. I could lie on my own Chinese carpet and kick, extending my legs to the sky to look at them, lengthened by a heel, smoothed by hose, and pretend I was a child in lace collars and patent leather Mary-Janes, wrapped in scent. In my head I was spoiled and vain and rich. I was cross and charming and I had servants.

'Adelaide behaves badly,' my mother said. 'Kathrin behaves.'

'Kati is a fat and monosyllabic bore,' I murmured to my father, in my head only, wanting to impress him with my vocabulary. He looked at me. He looked into my eyes momentarily, his strange apricot-green-brown irises almost the same shade as my own. My mouth twitched. Then I wandered out into the street to escape, and the neighbours looked at me because I wore high heels with old dresses.

I had a group of friends. They did things for me. They bought things for me, and I kissed them, I kissed the girls and I kissed the boys. And I became a baton twirler, even though they thought I had a Hitler accent in the beginning, even though I was a strange pale girl with a big nose.

Papa gave me a plastic Emerson radio with a gold clef on its face. I listened to it with my friends. Kati and I practised the

Watusi and the Strand in our bedroom. She wouldn't speak to me, she communicated by dancing the solo dances in front of me, and lying on the bed giggling at me.

I had plots in the night, because I knew I could do anything. Anything is possible. If you know that as a child, you are possessed. If you know that despite poverty and obscurity, it is yours to the core. I knew that the air itself could be spun into a mood. I nurtured such fabulous plots, in my room in Chesapeake, Kati unevenly snoring beside me, because beyond Papa's strictures and Mammi's disappointment – tears and fights and intransigence – I knew that I could become my own creation. The substance was my own to mould.

You only have you, Papa said. You have yourself. That is your gift. He didn't need to tell us that if you are immigrant, you are Ellis Island detritus. Sex and physical strength are the immigrant's way out. Or beyond that, beauty and determination. He told us how to be; he gave us a notion of self.

Then my father, the handsome European, left us for a woman who lived a few streets away. I never saw him again. And to the neighbours my Mammi must have personified every immigrant Hausfrau who ever cut her eyes away from their welcome to wrap herself in a veil of shyness or pride. The shame of desertion was ingrained in her generation, so that she never recovered. She befriended the neighbour Gloria, her only companion, beside her dog, during all those years, their absent men their joint private sorrow.

We hardly knew each other by the time I was fifteen, my mother and I. She had given up on me. She gave up on me when my father left. She was a dead Austrian widow. She barely barely lived her days. She was a high season bug drugged for winter in a corner. She was disappointed by me in ways that were profound and unvoiced and predicated upon the most secretive mourning for some long lost ideal of a kleines

Mäderl. We hardly knew how to talk. We had buried the wound my father caused when it was still suppurating, and now it was mummified, it would never be aired.

I loved her at such depth, the love I'd had as a very small child, rooted to the filaments of my body, so that I couldn't consciously think about her. She was there, untouched. I wanted her to be my Little Mama, like a girl from a book, like Miss Jo March with her Marmee. She stayed in her house with the jalousie shut; all summer the bugs buzzed, she stayed in there with her dog, and hooting convertibles backed into her street on the way to the ocean, to remind her of summer skies and a life where you shouted and swam, but she stayed in there, and she only talked to her neighbour Gloria and to her dog.

Our poverty was stagnant, lacking the redemption of intimacy or invention. It was a family in which the man was missing, and the hole he left was gaping and shameful, the woman with her brood of four, her crop-haired boys, her pale scruffy girls. We were never knitted together. We were moths, weighted down with secrets and inertia.

Mammi made an inadequate pioneer. She cauterised emotion for us until her own will was dead, and she slumped, and she never fought the immigrant's battle of night shifts and perfect grades. Her children flapped around her. Karli caught the bus to school alone aged five; my sister Kathrin grew morose and sturdy, a white slug girl with a faint brown moustache she bleached every week, sitting in our roof-bedroom tearing at the skin of her heels. And John, the oldest, was slender and inept. He did not help our Mammi as he was meant to, he renounced that role. He married a girl from Norfolk when he was nineteen, and left our mother to her attenuated debts and her stubborn rituals.

My mother thought her girl Adèle was a tart. Yet some little folded chamber of her mind admired me for being unlike herself, for being volatile in the most sequestered of ways, an underground spring of intoxication, and I was shabby and silent like Kati, but there was something agitated and divisive that they knew lay there, cat leashed, secret of sex unfathomable and distasteful.

I dyed my hair. I used subtle make-up. I never had the hair clips and rose reds of little girls with their white satin vanities and American mothers. I bit my lips until they looked swollen, and I coloured them and kissed off the colour so they were stained dark fruit, and I used tiny puffs of white-pink powder, and I made my brows very dark so they were inky and arched, severe on a young girl. My mother noticed with fleeting disgust and tiredness, and then she let me go, and I bought high-heeled sandals at garage sales out in the parking lot behind the high school; I bought second-hand brassieres, the button bras that the bratty girls owned, when I had no chest, in preparation, and wore them wrinkled and bleached under my petticoat. I was allowed 4711 because my mother used it on her wrists; it smelled of the Rhine, it smelled of men; it saddened me. I wanted the choked close scents of tea rose and musk, of raw nerved women shut in the bedroom late afternoons.

I pencilled on a beauty spot. Uncle Ed's wife, Aunt Ginger, said once, casting an eye over me, that I looked like a movie star. I ran to Karli's metal swing in the back yard, I swung till sunset, the chains bulleting me to the dark sky, and I became immaculate and stellar.

The only discipline that Mammi exercised was disappointment. It kept us at home, dampening the feral twitchings that would have sprung into rebellion under my Papa's authority. If he had stayed with us, I would have gone to college, since he wanted a tertiary education for his girls. With Mammi, there was not even a question, as though paying for school were paying for ball gowns or for polar expeditions.

So my father left, and I could not go to college; it wasn't even discussed. Mammi decided, with grim intractability, that I should learn to type and cook. We shouted, German words snaring with a shuddering atavism against the long new vowels of Virginia like crustaceans stranded on sand bars.

She made me take all the commercial courses over the academic ones in high school. I had classes in typing, sewing, pastry-making, child care, and I made out with the heating engineer in the boiler room underneath the cooking room. Those classes I took placed me in a shining prison scented with cake mix. There were boys there learning to be mechanics. They would work one day at auto repair shops in Norfolk, have some nice kids and cheat on their wives when the kids were at Junior High. I insisted that I was going to leave. And then I left.

Until I was nineteen I believed with absolute certainty that another *Snow White* would happen to me. I thought that *Snow White* was at once my passport to the arcane territory of adulthood, and a childhood confection preserved. When I was chosen for the play from a bunch of high school kids, my final year in Virginia, I thought that my life was at last a regular life, and a spectacular life, and it would alter from that very day. Me, my girlhood, on stage. It was Adèle Meier up there on the stage, her year book photograph in the *Chesapeake Bay Chronicle*. I was a *Mitteleuropäische* cherub, a man said in the paper. I was a cute honey, a white kitten. Then my breasts grew larger, and I didn't know how to act, and I didn't know about agents, and I never was chosen for a movie or another play.

I looked like a flower on a stalk in that play. I looked like a child-woman. It made me pretty. It was the first time I had ever moved as though I were simply pretty. I wore a tight bodice with a scooped neck, and my hair was dyed temporarily darker and crimped like shiny wood shavings. I missed some classes, and a woman did my make-up for every performance. And the mix of the laborious, the routine of a school or a club or a home where you belonged, snared me like a love affair, and the heady disbelief that painted all that was comforting and prosaic, remained with me. I couldn't shake it off. I loved that play. Its flavour coursed in weaker and weaker solutions through my bloodstream throughout the years, as though I had caught a raging tropical fever that finally exhausted itself on my blood cells, my body's chemistry altered for life.

It stayed with me, through my twenties. You know when you look back and you cannot say what you did with your life: you remember details of carpet and plaster stared at from a bed, and certain people, and certain feelings of fatness or inadequacy, but the structure of that life is not there, it slides into false floors and mud flats, and you are left with only a sense of vague shame. Such were my early twenties. I was waylaid by men. I was driven by huge but formless plans that drained into nothing: I wanted to be clever and exalted and sublime, but I got it all slightly off-key.

Men wanted to love and bruise my body's slightness. I knew it, subconsciously I knew it. They wanted to make the whiteness bleed. And yet rarely would I spend the entire night with a man, I would return at three o'clock in the morning, to wake up with my typewriter and my own quilt and my fresh underwear, to walk out free in the morning and buy breakfast.

There were too many men. I felt bilious in the mornings. There were flowers just beginning to slime in vases in my room, and my stomach was gaseous with dinners and sleep deprivation. Laurence never knew, when he met me, how there was a quiet despair, a little foetus inside me of shame and unhappiness. He said I manipulated men.

SIX

I lay on a hospital trolley in Paris. When I began to understand where I was, I struggled with the confusion of emerging from a morning dream after heavy sleep. Time had been blanket-stitched and tucked. It was like a little death.

I had been coughing and spluttering, fighting for air while half asleep. I had no feeling in my face. I couldn't move my neck, because my head had been wedged in blocks of hard foam. I lay in a hospital room with bright lights and taps and hand towels, and nurses busied themselves around me as if I wasn't there. They arranged instruments, they sorted through cupboards, and made markings on clipboards, and they chattered to each other, chatter chirrup chatter like muffled starlings.

I could not let my brain understand what had happened in that black glitch. Thoughts formed and then squiggled into holes like worms. I wanted to speak to the nurses, but I was, perhaps, still asleep, because I couldn't open my mouth.

I was reminded of Laurence's daughter Melina, and what she might be living through. The last time I saw her, it was in a bright white hospital, and she wore a bathrobe all day, through that endless false daylight of the hospital. She was only thirteen when she was hospitalised for trying to whittle down her body. She was a small child, who thought she was too fat – 'You don't understand, I've gained weight. I've really gained some,' she always said, and the robe clung in a dip to the space above her hips.

The last time I saw her, we held each other. We sat on the sofa in the patients' TV room and didn't let go of each other for several minutes, and when she lifted her head I realised my shoulder was hot and soaked. I drew her to me again, her bones like a poor dead crow's, and we cried mutely, not admitting our tears to each other. I think she had begun to know that she might be in that place indefinitely. I grieved for Melina and for her father, and she cried for what she had done to herself. We cried together for the loss.

Her hair seemed to be drained of its original colour. She could only walk like an old person.

She was always the squirrel, Melina. When she was a young child, I called her a squirrel, because she was like the squirrels in Gramercy Park, and they were her playmates. Then Laurence referred to her as the squirrel, and it became her name, Melina the pet squirrel with her plumped-out cheeks and darting run.

She had milkshake-pink cheeks then. Healthy limbs, a running-about body, and bright red hair. Melina's hair was a part of Gramercy Park, like the acorns and the gardeners. The neighbours would always comment on it. I gave her a dress in a Lanz print, like an apron, and she ran about in that blue and red cotton shift, flashing about through the grass and the trees. The gardeners in the Park knew her. We could even leave her under their care, following them around with her watering can.

I know the feel of that hand now. I remember exactly the sensation of holding that plump four-year-old hand, exploring the garden with eyes that were knee level and microscoped everything, focusing on a section of a leaf skeleton or a shadow under a leaning tree that half resembled a child-sized dwelling. Her hand was warm, damp, curled in mine like a milk and sugar snail. Or sticky and naily as a squirrel paw. She had light hazel eyes and a scattering of rosiness to her skin and stringy elastic curls of hair.

She grew tall later. She never was fat. She had a twelve-year-old's passing sturdiness, that last boyish phase of scabbed knees and boxiness. She starved herself when her curves were a faint sketch.

Dr Kreitzman came through the bright room where I was lying just once. He was so familiar to me, as if he were a movie star from another era of my life, a large-limbed male in a tuxedo. I felt my heart thumping and raised my eyes, but he looked down at me as if he was checking a dressing, he didn't smile at me, and passed on by. I wanted him to look at me so much.

'I need more swabs than the regular bunch for the rhino,' he said, and walked out of the room.

'My ear,' I said to the nurse.

She didn't hear me.

'My ear.' I could hardly speak.

She turned. 'What was that, Madame?' She gave me a bright motherly smile. 'Are you rested?'

'My ear – it – ' My lips were hard and swollen.

'You have some discomfort? We can give you a painkiller.' She nodded.

The nurses lifted my head very gently, very gently and slowly – I seemed to be wearing a large hood, swaddled and muffed like an infant's snowsuit – and she tipped a glass to my lips. I drank the minty liquid. My tongue cracked up like a creek bottom, its dehydration disturbed.

'Some water?' I said.

'Just a little,' said the nurse, and leaned a fresh glass against my lips. 'You must drink properly later.'

'How . . . Is it . . . all right?' I said.

'It went fine, no problems at all. You're going to look

beautiful,' said the nurse. She checked something by my ear. 'In a minute, we'd like you to rest.'

They wheeled me on a stretcher into the private elevator at the back of the building, they put me in my room, the blue and purple one, and then three nurses, one supporting my head, lifted me very slowly onto the bed. There was a pillow designed to brace the head, prohibiting neck movement, and a button on the phone so I could call a nurse. I was given some frozen jellified masks to reduce eye swelling, and an ice-filled bandage, heavy as a horse collar, was wound around my neck.

There seemed to be liquid in my ear. I swallowed, trying to exorcise it, like after the swimming pool. My head was wadded and ballooned. I was deaf when the nurses spoke. I could not turn and let the fluid escape in a plug of pressurised relief like I wanted to. I lay and drifted.

Before my features settled into themselves, before their proportions were cast, they were mutable with the fleshy fitfulness of youth, their rounder lines proffering the conciliatory pleasure of true prettiness like a plate of cookies. The classic notion of beauty which holds terror is predicated upon the simplest structures. The poetic proportions of my face emerged later. For a long time, I looked like a girl, the face a cat shape or heart shape, wide at brow and narrow at chin. The lines were later refined, the structure more disciplined, and I knew, at one point, a symphony had been born, that the Homecoming Queen harmony had reached its pleasing conclusion, and I had been blessed, in womanhood, with a symphony of a face.

My prettiness was never inert: it was taken by people like a change of light or mood, its refractions played back to me, so the air was cast differently. There was a certain wholesomeness which underlined the pallor that people wanted to fuck.

So, surely, if I wait here, the man, Dr Kreitzman, might come to my room. He'll come armed with a reason. Am I happy, am I quite well?

Men unpeel my legs from their pantyhose, their hands deft at the top of thigh, their fingers creeping and tickling between cloth and flesh. They unwrap my breasts from their support and caress the relaxing mound. Dr Kreitzman will come, unwrap my pretty new face, we'll unwrap the present together, we will unpeel it and he will want to fuck that round sweet thing, unwrap that candy. I am born like a baby.

For the moment, though, I begin to feel pain. When pain starts to come, it's just a sly rumour that dribbles through your mind quite comfortably. It's an interesting distraction. But almost imperceptibly the frequency changes. Pain rises and rises to become a high-pitched acid scream.

When the pain kicked in, it was too huge and overwhelming to understand. I couldn't locate it. It rung in a halo round my body. I wanted to call for a nurse, but I couldn't move my head to see the telephone. My head was a bullet of soreness.

I lay very quietly in a daze of pain, my cheeks swollen with false youth.

SEVEN

There were stories that shaped the nights when Laurence and I lived on Gramercy Park. They became a ritual, waiting for us, like darkness and sleep.

Our bedroom was at the back of the building, where an artificial city silence – composed of a thrum or a consistency of sound – fell in the early hours of the morning over Third Avenue, and there we talked, and kept the windows open and told strands of story between sleep and touch.

There was a story that lasted through weeks. It was the story of the girl being sent away to school, to learn the grammar of seduction, the art of Sapphism, the function of the nerve endings.

The legendary old woman in our apartment building initiated the girl's departure. She was the actress who had played the Wicked Witch of the West in *The Wizard of Oz*, and she had lived in the building on Gramercy Park before Laurence and I moved there.

One day she caught me hitching up my dress in the elevator, and she reported me to my parents.

'It is time that your girl was sent away,' she said. 'She is provocative. She jeopardises the mental well-being of our residents.'

I kissed my parents goodbye with all the fervour of a young girl going to a nunnery.

'Will her father miss her?' I asked Laurence.

'Very much,' he said. 'Deeply. As if he's torn inside.'

Laurence stroked my hair, lifting it at the roots with his fingertips so it was cool and sleep tickled. I thought in my night vision that he was making curls like the glassy sprouts of brine that lap against little Victorian water babies. He stroked me idly, his hand drifting, barely perceptibly, meandering as it went until there was the faintest suggestion of his skin against my breast; he talked to me and his nail skimmed my nipple casually, intermittently, his voice remaining at an even pitch.

My breathing shallowed.

'Did she kiss her father goodbye?'

'Of course she did. She loved him very much.'

'Of course.'

'I'm going to show you.'

'What was I wearing when the witch found me?'

'Well . . . ' said Laurence. He was silent for a moment, his voice coming from across the pillow. 'A black pinafore – you were hitching it up in the lift and showing your beautiful, incredible legs – with a starched white Peter Pan collar – '

'I am amazed you know about Peter Pan collars.'

'But you know all about entablatures. And she's wearing black silk stockings. So this is how her father kisses her.'

He placed a soft round kiss on one cheek.

'Another.'

He leaned over and kissed my other cheek, very slightly closer to my mouth.

I raised myself so my lips were near his, but never touched them, and I looked straight into his eyes for a long time, the darkness momentarily inking out my vision, then I kissed him, many times, on his forehead and his cheeks, grazing the corner of his lips. I could see the outline of the solemn mouth in the dark.

We lay together for hours, half sleeping. We talked, we drifted into sleep entwined, the vibrations of his speech travelling through my throat and making me think in the night that I could speak in his voice. 'I'm you,' I murmured, but never loudly enough for him to hear; he thought I was muttering the dislocated syllables of sleepers into his hair.

I tucked him in, tightly, under the quilt, stroked him, kissed him, and sometimes the back of my hand bobbed against the soft skin at the top of his thigh as if accidentally. And the girl had different arts to learn; sometimes rigorous, sometimes subtle.

I went on the Pill when I was seventeen, and it changed my shape. My breasts became full and alert, I put on weight and looked like a little woman. At that time, you were supposed to be flat-chested, then undergo a metamorphosis in the bedroom to reveal secretly large breasts. The hormonal doses were heavy: I floated around Chesapeake permanently pregnant on equine oestrogen, faintly sick, my breasts bearing a new heaviness.

I went on the Pill as a ticket out of Virginia. It was like bleaching one's hair or taking a stenographers' class. I had to leave my home, because there was no money anywhere, because my mother and I had no more to say to each other, her wounds too painful and her mistrust of me too deep yet unspecified. Mammi got a part-time factory job after my father left. I never asked her about it. She never told me. I never once asked her what it was like, though I worried about her. I always wondered later why I hadn't asked her how soul-destroying that work was, and whether she had friends there, how bad her exhaustion was, but with Mammi no one asked.

We couldn't talk about my father, either. Once, he visited our town. I arrived home from school too late, because I had been in a drama class, and he had been there, he had been inside our house, and Karli was shrivelled into a new form of pallor, and our mother was distraught as I had never seen before.

It was the only subject in our family. But it was the proscribed subject.

I was too old at seventeen to live in that house. Mammi was angry with me for many reasons, but her distress lay beyond logic, in a realm in which speech was impossible. We must have felt the same sorrow over a man who hurt us, yet we never shared it; the most private of wounds, jealously held, in competition with each other, and in love and despair.

I wanted to protect her, I loved her so much for all that was careworn, frightened, insular about her; I loved her even for her disgust with me.

There had always been trouble at home. John and I fought, as though John was preparing me for my father by emulating his anger in a softened form. My father punished me. He said he had to punish me because I was beyond his rational control. Then we talked into the evening, my father and I, in a slow tense reconciliation, about literature and the nuances of language, about my future, and how I would one day make him proud of me.

When he left our house, there was emptiness.

I always had a plan to go to New York. Chesapeake was built up around us, like a subdivision, a concrete tailing-off in the midst of the Old Country with all its historical obsessions and its spurious southern complacency. I thought that one day I would go to Paris, but before that I would live in New York and have good times, be brilliant and much loved. I would find a man who almost killed me with love.

I took the bus on my own, all the way to Port Authority. I was crying. I wrapped myself in a corner, to hide from the people who were looking at me. I pined for what was left of my family in Virginia, my mother and brother Karli and sister Kathrin, who was engaged to a Texan. I was sick with nerves.

I called a dull girl from my class in high school, Lorna, who had told me to contact her, and for two weeks, I stayed on the couch of her uncle and aunt all the way out in Paramus, New Jersey.

Leaving Virginia for New York City was the most frightening thing I ever did. I didn't even have the money to get back home. Every night I lay on the narrow couch in Paramus and heard the trucks thunder past on the freeway and dreamt clotted dreams about the commuter train into Manhattan and money and my mother, and I sometimes woke up with my heart crashing, the sound of Lorna's insomniac uncle pacing about between the bathroom and the kitchen trickling into my nightmare. Lorna's extreme dullness was my analgesic. I clung to it when I woke in the mornings, the predictable routine of Lorna and her conversation, Lorna simply a girl I had spoken to a few times at high school, with her attenuated links to New York City. I had to pretend to be very quiet in that house, so I could stay for a while.

After that Lorna and I got a two month sublet on a Formica-dominated apartment just near the bridge in Fort Lee, and we found bitty, ditsy jobs to keep up our apartment, mornings in dry-cleaning outfits where young mothers working the tills disappeared into the storage room to get high on the chemicals, and waitressing, Lorna on a Howard Johnson's shift, me in a fake French restaurant, all glass and palms, in Leonia. We were exhausted all the time.

I went to bed early and wrote in my diary. The shuddering contrast with all my ideas about the city – slapped by the cold and the commuter train – was a shock that silenced me. I thought of my mother every day. I focused on her rituals in Virginia, recalling the hours of her factory roster, and when we would eat, and what novels Karli and I would test each other on. I wanted to be back there.

I'd never thought I could be normal in the way of American girls. I thought I'd be a strange Austrian who came from a house without a father, and had some sort of an accent, and whose family was far removed from the cabala of summer camp, of Ivy Leagues, even Brooklyn tenements, that insistent round of native references that embraced all social boundaries but side-stepped us. Such American lives seemed as distant and complete as white sailing boats on duck-blue seas. Even a dull kind of routine with a job at Schrafft's and a rental in Bayonne seemed too normal, too American for me. I could picture myself only as housebound immigrant freak or as unspecified star: I was unable to fill in the details between. That we had jobs, we had frilly waitress uniforms and talked about the girls at Ho Jo's, seemed to contain the delirium of romance in its humdrum assurance of my own normality. Fear only got to me in the gaps between elation.

We kept finding jobs on the Jersey side but I became quietly inadequate the moment I travelled over the bridge, and began to think about my mother every night, and every time something went wrong, I wondered if it was possible for me to move back home.

When the sublet ran out in Fort Lee – Lorna now sporting a perm and a mover boyfriend and taking hairdressing classes at the Hollywood Beauty School – I moved on two weeks' worth of saved money into the Martha Washington, a depressive hotel for women on East 30th Street, where the guys at reception sat behind a grille, and the lobby had the sick plant feel of light deprivation and cruise ships. Old alcoholics in leopard skin sat shaking on the steps, dipping into the garbage cans. Later I wished that I'd known about the Barbizon and been a Grace Kelly–Sylvia Plath starlet, a high stepping girl about town from another era with fine typing speeds and a flair for the dramatic.

The connecting doors at the Martha Washington were lightly constructed, and sometimes in sleep I incorporated the hollow wood into a nightmare. It was there that an aspect of Loulou came to me, though I didn't know she was a character who would live in a book. She was a brushed abstraction of who I might be with wine in my brain and the confidence of privilege: she was unfettered, bewitching. I thought of her sometimes in the sleeplessness of black nights with the garbage truck booming into 30th Street at five in the morning; I filled those stretched spaces with thoughts of a girl who was me and who wasn't me, in the early hours when you can plane with the waxed ease of orgasm. I was given fluent inks in the nights, dreams in mediaeval stains. She was me – I was sleepless with excitement at what I would say, what I would do the next morning – and she was someone else, her rebellion outrageous but instinctive.

In the morning, I was exhausted; the roaches ran into the walls as I pulled up the shades, and inhibition arrived with the daylight.

I rarely went out at the Martha Washington except to find work. Among the down-and-outs and rouged harridans there were young girls in town, like me, who hung around the bar. We talked in passing in the early evening, but mostly I stayed in my room to dream and read, to cry slightly, wrapping privacy around me within the comfort of walls that were temporarily mine and seemed to be unique because they were mine, they soaked up my breath and my system of superstitions and auguries, the hieroglyphic termites that scuttle through the brain in solitude. New York City was on my doorstep, and I barely looked at it. I warded it off until I was healthy, or because it was too great for me. The loneliness was so extreme, it was like a companion. I missed my mother still.

I met Helen Kaufman three weeks after I came to New York because one of the girls at the Martha Washington knew her boyfriend. I met her in the graveyard gloom of the Martha Washington lobby, and I went out with the group, the first time I had ever been out for a drink in New York, and I talked to Helen all night. She called me the next day, and became my closest friend within a matter of weeks. She was like the best friends you have earlier in your life, sticky with private codes and hysteria. I moved out of the Martha Washington and stayed with Helen. She let me stay in her apartment, on cushions on her floor.

I emulated Helen's street smart disinterest with my own brand of understatement, and yet the street names embedded in the paragraphs of my diary stood out to me black-bulbed and melodic as the notes of a symphony: that bar on Ninth and 18th, so casually noted among the happenings of the day, the walk through the Upper West Side, the visit to a friend of Helen's on Spring, seemed couched in italics, in fakery and fame. Helen showed me all the good places, the cheapest Szechwan restaurants, the clubs and bars.

I arrived in New York when LBJ was still president and the anti-war movement had become a popular force. We joined the Vietnam rallies; we were there at the very beginning of the second women's movement. There was still a sense of the old New York, of New York before the Garbage Strike, a particular thin-air scent of euphoria, leaves in the Park, an existence on the streets at night. It became dirtier and meaner a few years later, the burnt out buildings and bums of the seventies altering the city in front of my eyes.

Helen grew up in Manhattan; she grew up in a rent-controlled apartment on West End Avenue, just Helen, her sister and their mother. So Helen knew New York with the mundane intimacy that I knew an unknown market town near Graz, a small Virginian sprawl. That New York City was overlaid for her with the workaday geography of park and school and laundromat challenged all my infatuated perceptions. That Broadway was simply a main street to Helen filled me with love for her, with simplistic adoration.

Helen was small, and thin, with hips that were bigger than the rest of her. She had very thick light brown hair, almost blonde, and she had it cut rigorously and frequently into a severe block of chopped curls that reached her shoulders, and never grew beyond. Her movements were different from mine. She walked like a black girl, a forced fluency of the haunch, a fast small step. She had black boyfriends at that time, nearly always, and she made friends with their mothers and got petted as a daughter, and I think she started to believe she was black, but it passed. Her sudden enthusiasms – for Czech movies, Nina Simone, the Mets – filled her apartment in an explosion of posters and songs and tickets. We followed obscure trails in search of such obsessions, Helen, her body wiry with nervous energy, veering between manic hope and despondency. We had fun those nights. We said very early on that we were soul mates, and that we knew we would have found each other somewhere, if not in the lobby of the Martha Washington.

Helen was in film school at NYU. She worked evenings, and I used to go and visit her at work when I couldn't sleep or on the way back from some boyfriend's house at two in the morning. It was dangerous; Helen always said it was too dangerous for me. She worked in an Irish bar on Avenue A where men stood in the doorway pissing straight onto the sidewalk, and where folksingers came to play and could barely be heard.

We found an apartment together finally, a rotting studio next to some music students in Chelsea, and then I stopped thinking my existence in New York was temporary, a sick joke on a fraudulent provincial; if I was very cool, if I didn't twirl around and stare at the skyscrapers, I would be allowed to stay.

I could not believe that New York was so dirty, so crumbled when I had imagined it a thrusting monument to modernity. I had pictured Chicago on Mars, then stumbled upon a decaying Dutch island whose spirit was closer to Styria than to Chesapeake. And I found, on days between high blue skies, that it was dull and vicious, with fogs and dripping store fronts, dogs on the sidewalk, and Abyssinian churches in Harlem, and artists living under the weak urine lights of the diners with their old stained silverware. The sediment of human existence was thick with roaches and air conditioning stains and broiling and steaming, and more dogs – too many dogs – inside the crusted, crenellated edifices. There were too many lives on top of each other, the shadows of old buildings and walls speaking a faded history of commerce, roof water tanks on precarious sticks like African huts, and sugar shakers already used by old men with lox on their fingers, and bleach on floors, and used watch shops, and panhandlers.

Loneliness in childhood breeds polychromatic dreams, but in young adulthood, it is a driving force. I realised there was no mother to rein me in with disappointment, and that my father had abnegated his responsibilities long ago. I realised it one day, when I had a bed and a friend in New York, with a surge of delight like waking to a sunny morning.

I could be naughty and nasty. I could run my own course through the city. I could do what I wanted. I could be a brilliant creature, or a lazy one, lying in bed with men and violet chocolates. I could seduce married men, movie stars, construction workers – anyone I chose – and be fêted, and grow quite extraordinary. And underneath all that, I would be very good. I planned to be very pure and very good. At night, I wrote elaborate plots, lists, psychological goads. I constructed whole empires of achievement.

The shame of having no degree after high school made me flounder. It levelled me. I veered between humiliation and an obscure pride. The proofs of my survival – my rent payment, my name on a Con Ed bill, the absolute fluency of my English – were the tokens of a New York life, and yet the structure of my existence was haphazard, my work a tearful mess. I did every job, every scrubbing, waitressing, typing, clerking job that makes you feel as though you are cleaning the ground, and between those I had brief jobs in publishing houses, the kind of minor jobs in prestigious places that other people coveted but which I viewed only as a source of money, and that way I managed never to be on welfare.

People always gave me work then. I would meet someone and fresh employment would usually follow, but it was effortless mediocrity, a sad ragbag, and I feared that I was falling the way of the generation just before my own, a life of so many interesting little stopgap jobs in real estate offices and art galleries. For me there was nothing interesting in such variety: I was searching, in a hopeless private capsule, for *Snow White*, or for Aunt Ginger's words, or for the austere discipline of the degree that I would never have, and I couldn't tell anyone, not even Helen, because there was no justification for it. I would rather mark time and fail.

It was clinging to survival. It was me and Helen cleaving together through our precarious existence, because the panic of day-to-day poverty was the dominant subject.

We were always cold, quite simply severely cold. Our apartment whined soot through the air vents, cockroaches and gas leaks. In the winter, Helen and I lay under our quilts from the time we got home. Sometimes we slept together in one of the beds to keep warm. We took turns to cook, running from the stove to the bed. Knives seemed to cling to our fingers with the cold. The iron-clad door downstairs to the street was kicked in, so we had to thump our bodies against it to make it open. The steps smelled of piss, the windowsills smelled of tom cats, so we kept the windows closed and lit incense.

We spent nights at the Mercer Arts Center until the hotel next door collapsed onto it, and we went to see bands at Popeye's Spinach Factory in Brooklyn. Helen and her NYU friends spent their Sundays filming each other. I obeyed the conventions of the time only in their most basic tenets. I went to thrift stores and bought forties jackets and twenties drapes before they were expensive, and I knew they were thought odd by people as often as they were thought beautiful; I wore astrakhan jackets with harshly darted waists and glass rosebud buttons. I went out on Route 1 with Helen to the flea market and I bought enough stiff jackets and tear-thin twenties dresses, kimonos and poppy prints, to last me a few years. I couldn't take the hippie stuff. I would not wear orange and brown and thongs; the big hand-tooled leather belts that guys sold on the street disgusted me, the burlap bags, the people who went out to Vermont and then came back. We liked trashy stuff better, Helen and I, the tiger stripes and platforms.

Helen graduated from film school, her student film was runner-up for an award, and then she went back to school and transferred to law, and after all her struggles, the mornings she got up to go out to Pier #76 to make her film in the lot where the tow-truck cars were dumped, her nights at CBGB's filming the guys with their bikes, all the work she did, after all that, she became a law student and got an internship in a law firm. It never ceased to amaze me, because I had thought Helen was the funky one, I thought she would make films until she was a middle-aged doyenne of the art house, with her crises and her poverty and her camera. She wore suits and tied her hair back and went to work in a midtown office, and it pleased her mother.

We lived in a lot of apartments. Mostly we lived downtown, but once we got a sublet on a student place up near Columbia, then spent three weeks arguing in Inwood, then finally we moved back downtown to the apartment that became our home, on West 13th. Mimi Ceccato, who had despaired with me in a Murray Hill temp agency, came to live with us.

The apartment was in a brownstone in the dusty and

blossomed upper reaches of Greenwich Village, on West 13th Street, where the white church struck bells and Sixth Avenue was a clutter of shoe repairers and discount shops.

It was a walk-up with a damaged parquet floor in the entrance hall and nightmare brown and purple wallpaper, briefly fashionable. It had small railings around the front, garbage cans, trees. We lived almost opposite the Village Presbyterian Church, and the trees would blossom, the bells sound, and the male couple next door would fix their tiny bit of garden. Crowds would drift in from further down in the Village, people on rollerskates, and hippie fathers with their kids on their shoulders, and guys you knew were on acid and played in bands, and guys in leather walking past at all times during the afternoon and night.

Our apartment had a closed train station feel, chokey and brown. But it had carpets in some of the rooms, and no draughts pouring in from the roof. We had become accustomed to random air currents twisting knee height, and showers slidey with vegetation. We moved into that apartment with dazed delight, as though it were a high day and we had been set free, and I declared it a public holiday, and we spent our first night there sleepless with talk.

We could hear the dog next door scuttering and sliding on its claws like a rat. In our bored moments we diverted the mundane irritations we felt towards each other as room mates by plotting to kill it, using various methods involving fire escapes or substances employed by the dry cleaners along the street. The dog's octogenarian owner, Katharine Holden, walked it the forty blocks uptown to Central Park every morning, and then neglected it for the rest of the day, so it barked in yapping arpeggios of excitement the moment Helen or Mimi or I unlocked the door to our apartment.

I felt like an immigrant in that city still, but I wrapped my foreignness to me and petted it, and it became a calling card.

When something is your curse – your accent, say, your poverty, your nose – it can, in time, transform itself into the aspect that elevates you, alchemised by loneliness and tenacity. So my European origins separated me from the Hispanics, but allied me with the Czechs, the Hungarians, the Russians even, in a city that absorbed all as it ignored it, the dysphoria of Virginia replaced by the short-fused indifference of New York City. And finally, by force of will, I made the alien exotic.

I found a new job because I spoke German. The wife of a German banker living on the Upper East Side, Sophy Gruber, wanted a personal secretary and assistant. She lived on 69th and Park. I rarely went uptown. To me, the Upper East Side was like Paris, a place I had never been, with its strange looming hush, its hurtling avenues. The elevator opened straight into the Grubers' private foyer in their apartment house. Expanses of pale carpet, falls of foliage, led to Sophy's own rooms, her walk-in closet, her miniature writing desk. Her office was blue and scented; there were uniformed staff; the telephone rang every few minutes. I had never been in such a place.

I started working for Sophy Gruber three days a week. She paid me in cash, and it saved me from financial desperation, from the insecurity of temporary jobs that held me suspended in a state of exhaustion and humiliation. Sophy Gruber gave me a salary, she gave me a haven, she gave me a sweet strange stability that I had never experienced.

She had two children, and she ran the household on 69th Street like a mechanical box, its every aspect interdependent and melodious. Sophy Gruber was very pretty, with a Scandinavian symmetry to her face, her blonde straight hair, her brown eyes, but there was a beige-pink fragile flavour to her, with her neat little body and short black dresses, her pinned and collared blouses, a faint intimation of something tragic behind that muted kewpie doll demeanor.

Sophy was not many years older than me, but she had

married an older man, Heinrich, a banker, precociously adopting the features of groomed wifehood, and in her awning-hung square mile, Bergdorf Goodman marking its southernmost end, she lived a life that was perfumed and confined. She called me her downtown friend, because she knew no one else who lived downtown.

'Adèle's from downtown,' Sophy always said, as though it were novel.

A horticulturist serviced their apartment; there were deliveries of food, art, kids, dry-cleaning. It was a different life from any I had ever seen. I had to write up all the cheques to pay the staff, mail Sophy's mother's rent upstate, organise her charity donations. I was sent to Bergdorf's, to Adolfo, to exchange clothes and scarves and bags. In every store, there was an assistant who knew Sophy. I reserved Sophy's theatre tickets, ordered her stationery, arranged for her husband's sports kit to be dropped off at his club, and I wrote little thank-you letters in German to his colleagues, endless notes in German signed 'Sophy'. I realised that my German was colloquial, it was kitchen German, adolescent Austrian argot; I made mistakes and had to look up spellings.

She was sad in her marriage, I thought, and she clung to me as I depended on her. We had long involved discussions in the afternoons as she wandered about her office in her bathrobe and I answered her phone and wrote her letters, speaking to her between calls. Sometimes she withdrew from me, she thought she was being disloyal to her husband by discussing him, and I became her paid assistant once more.

'Honey,' she always said, 'you're too pale.'

She tried to get me to go on the sunbed at her health club. I was known by her friends as Sophy's pale pet. They gave me clothes that I could never have afforded but would never wear. Sophy thought I was the key to some version of the real world, of drugs and parties and run-down rentals and the sordid youth she imagined to be teeming downtown.

I sometimes went there on weekends even when I wasn't working. Sophy stopped me from falling at a time when I had to weave new strands to hold me. She was part of the family I imagined: if Helen and Mimi were my sisters, Sophy was my godmother. She saved me from poverty, from having no anchor; just as later, in a strange way, Laurence saved me from other men.

EIGHT

I went to the hospital for an operation on my face which would make me appear to be something I was not.

I had thought it would be an extension of going to the hairdresser's or having my legs waxed, but it turned out to be different. It was a hospital operation. It involved cutting and recovery, blood and pain. It required stretchers, staples and bandages.

I lay in my private room at l'Hôpital des Cevennes. My head itched because my hair was full of blood, and Paris became some Arctic region in which life is very still, and only strange black species of birds fly past.

Nurses arrived silently. There was a siren of pain in my face, but it sounded into emptiness.

I lived in a larval stage between snow and pain. The snow was thick-packed, deadening sound and sealing sensation, long drifts of chemical comfort in which I couldn't separate the hours and features of the landscape. I slept under snow. I was muffed, and I was drugged, and I had long sleeps in the burrow I had dug. There was no one there. My head rubbed a crater in the pillow wedges, and soaked them. Nurses came up sometimes to check on my dressings, change my ice packs, or help me to the bathroom. They gave me soup and yoghurt through a straw. They told me never to lie on one side as the crumpling of a cheek could have a permanent effect. They didn't stay long. They were different nurses, yet they seemed to be the same, those small French women with dark eyes. Dr Kreitzman never came to my room.

The light was very beautiful. The shaft that penetrated the courtyard between the hospital walls was polar. I thought that when I had recovered I could go out with Laurence trotting on ponies round the Bois.

I mused then over the little Eric with his jersey grey irises, and wondered whether he'd notice, during his unaccountable perambulations around the Cinquième, that I had disappeared. In the night I was woken by the heart-crashing panic that propels you from nightmare to consciousness: I remembered that Laurence wasn't here, he lived in England. He wasn't here.

They were very solicitous at the hospital. There were copies of *Femme Actuelle* for the housewives from Vanves who'd had their facial flesh trimmed, *Vanity Fair* for Dr Kreitzman's American ladies, and this month's *Vogue*. The nurses treated me as though I was sick and in recovery from a serious operation; they monitored my temperature, my pulse rate, asked me questions and showed me the position in which I must sleep. They checked the tube that emerged from the bandages at my neck, and they wiped my eyelids with salt water. It stung. My eyes were nearly closed into slits between puffs of swelling. There was a constant itching in my ears. I was given colour-coded pills: pills to prevent infection, pills to dampen pain, pills to induce sleep. The nurses barely talked to me beyond a routine greeting, beyond professional concern, and I lived with the lights and the bricks, the sky changes. I couldn't detect activity outside my ear bandages and the double glazing: all that *metro-bûlot-dodo* round of life on a Paris weekday seemed a theoretical concept.

In the night I shifted between snow fields, the glittering sore stars of pain blanked by morphine and dark.

*

By the second afternoon, the pain in my facial flesh was like a child screaming behind a door.

I phoned Helen Kaufman. It was morning in New York.

'Adèle!' said Helen. 'How *are* you?'

'I'm fine,' I said. 'How are you, Helen?'

'I'm good. They've just brought me coffee. Uh . . . But I was fenced into Washington Square with the students while they did a drug sweep on my way home. The stupid Mayor was there talking to the TV cameras. Dean and I were just talking about you yesterday. How are you, honey?'

'I'm kind of sick, actually. I'm in the hospital for a couple of nights.'

'Adèle! Jesus. What is it?'

'Nothing. You know – just a . . . gynae . . . ' I began to cry.

'Adèle! What's wrong?'

'It hurts.'

'A lot?'

'It really hurts.'

I began to sob. The tears emerged fast because my eyes were thin slits. Liquid seeped into the bandages. I thought it might soften my stitches. I didn't know what would happen to my face then.

'Are they looking after you there?'

I sobbed. I made a sound of assent. It hurt to move my head. I winced. I tried to speak. It was hard to open my mouth, so my voice sounded thin and clamped.

'Adèle?'

'No. Helen, don't worry. It's just – the pain. Is bad.'

'There's something you don't want to tell me. Tell me . . . how can I help?'

'You can't,' I said. 'Helen. What's the weather like?'

'It's a fine day. Small clouds.'

'What's it like – in the Park?'

'Oh, the Sheep Meadow's a little parched.'

'No, I mean my – Gramercy?'

'Oh, I haven't been through there in a long time. I have a client on Park Avenue South. Shall I go look at it for you?'

I nodded.

'I never hear any more – about. The goddamn – '

'Laurence,' I said.

'Yeah.'

'Helen, I have to go. I'm going to sleep now.'

My lips were sticking together as I talked.

The pain was unlike anything I had ever known. It required a new level of perception and understanding.

I breathed fast. I thought I might vomit. I asked for more painkillers.

There was a numbness in my face contiguous with the pain, like bacon and fat. The antibiotics caused an itching sensation.

I could not believe this. Dr Kreitzman had told me that procedures are very simple these days. Muscles pulled in all directions, and my hair was crawling with ants. My ears were tightly pressed with bandages. There were small blood spots like strawberry stains on the gauze beside my eye. I felt so nauseous. The nurse said not to worry, it was the anaesthetic that caused the nausea.

When I saw my face in the mirror, I knew what I had done. I stared; I could barely absorb it. I searched momentarily for myself. All your life, you look in a mirror and that familiar reflection is there, like a member of your family, like the shape of your own fingernails. I looked in the mirror, and my vision slid and fell into a blank between thought frames.

A poor cartoon picture of a car crash victim, the head mummified in bandages. She had been split open by a truck, her flesh crushed. Bruise blankets extended over her face. Her eyes were slits in deep pink rings of wounded tissue, the flesh puffed and shining, blood crusts lining the sutures. The skin looked jaundiced: it was pulled taut, but it was raw beneath the bruising. Only the centre of the face was visible, a freakish swollen child. I was not there. It was as though a man had beaten me out of all recognition. The reference points were not there.

Is ageing flesh an illness, then?

Face lifts can cause skin death, nerve paralysis, infections, ulceration and scar overgrowth. Some women died of their face lifts. So many thousands of operations are performed every year, there are metres of women's faces incinerated for growing older.

When I was in my late teens and early twenties in New York, shonky guys said I should be a model; a woman came up to me in the street, she gave me her card, some midtown address, but I was not tall enough to model, and there was a part of me that I wanted to keep wrapped up and sacrosanct, not packaged as a fine pale brunette to advertise cosmetics.

At l'Hôpital des Cevennes, a woman in a peach coloured dress came up to advise me about cosmetics, about which foundation to use to conceal my scars during the first weeks of recovery. She told me to bathe my eyelids in salt water, and not to wear earrings for several months. She had a catalogue of wigs available for women with shorter hair, to disguise the scars around the ears. Perhaps this same woman went around the hospital with a catalogue of prostheses for patients who had had a breast removed.

Dr Kreitzman came to see me very briefly. He was charming. He showed no alarm at the extent of my injuries.

'You're going to be pleased with the results,' he said.

I looked at him.

'Smile for me,' he said.

I moved my mouth as much as I could. The muscles seemed to belong to someone else.

'Fine. Good girl,' he said. 'I'll look forward to seeing you again later. I think you're going to be pleased.'

'I'm in a lot of pain,' I said.

'Some discomfort is normal,' he said. 'We can keep you on painkillers for a few days.'

'It's pretty bad.'

'Just try to relax, Miss Lee. The discomfort with this operation is only moderate. Some of my patients have no problems at all.' He spoke calmly in his leatherette voice. 'Try to relax, and you'll give yourself a much easier time.'

Later, I had to sit in an angled seat resembling a dentist's chair while the doctor removed my bandages. He inched them off as they came away in a crust, lying beside him in discarded shards. There were sections that were attached to my skin with blood, clinging with little needle pricks of resistance like a Band Aid. Dr Kreitzman was very gentle.

My hair was now greasy and clumped; it itched when movement stirred it. The skin at the side of my face felt as though it had never known the cool new air.

My face was a fungal growth. A pale black bruise extended down my neck. I could hardly look in a mirror. It was not me.

On the third afternoon after my operation, they took me through a side entrance and helped me into a car that was waiting in the courtyard. I looked at the bedroom as we left, a prison of pain in pastel wallpaper. We drove past the refuse bins and out along rue Vaugirard to a hotel Dr Kreitzman's surgery had recommended. I could not enter my own apartment building with my face a puffball.

I stayed in the hotel for a week. I watched MTV. The surgery delivered a new prescription of painkillers when I requested it, and changed my antibiotics since they had caused a rash over my body. The hotel staff brought me meals; I kept the blinds closed; they never commented, but I was humiliated.

I used to alter little facets of myself for men. And then, after *Loulou*, something happened to me. My Loulou and her after-effects gave me strength. I was autonomous; I was a rocket ship. A quiet omnipotence was distilled in my blood after *Loulou*. It infected my system as it had when I was on a stage, in a small town in Virginia. Though life had tempered it, I would still understand, on a street, on a transcendent night, that anything is possible. Anything, anything. You can make a legend of your life if you are intensely and extravagantly determined.

My field of vision widened at the end of my twenties, and the men who had distressed me became dwarves peopling the periphery, my essence coming from a different source. And then of course they wanted me anew, but I really didn't want them, I only wanted Laurence.

Journalists said later that I had gotten radicalised at a particular point. But it wasn't like that. There was no apocalyptic moment; rather my life and my political vision merged until they ignited, fuelled by a time and a place. Helen and I used to say that the feminist movement saved us, but we couldn't tolerate the kvetching sisters in their overalls, so we avoided them, and we fashioned our own devices, launched our own battles; we marched and we campaigned, but we never once looked at our own cervixes or sat cross-legged complaining about men. We operated more subtly and elegantly and explosively, and when I became public, I continued in that vein.

So I lay in bed and the MTV VJs jangled through the remnants of caked blood in my ears, and my scalp prickled with dirt, since I could not wash it. I couldn't take a shower. I had to lower myself gently into a shallow bath, my naked body topped by a balloon of a face.

I gouged into the crown of my scalp for something to do. The snowflakes of skin that came away had their own perfume of sweat and sweetness. It is the most human of scents.

It reminded me of what was mine. I'd owned something very beautiful, and I'd had it tampered with. I cried for my face. There is a point after a face lift operation at which it is standard for women, upon seeing their battered features, to cry uncontrollably.

My heart thumped quite violently when I thought of what I had done. Dr Kreitzman never told me it would be like this. And then he left me, looking like a truck had hit me. This is what his scalpel did to me. I let this man do this thing to me, and then he didn't come to see me.

He left me.

It's not reversible. Not at all. The most poignant moments of pain in life are those when you shudder and wince in regret for something that is entirely your own fault. You can't lob a ball of poison at someone else. You feel sick because you made the wrong choice. You play it over and over in your head like a crazy home movie on a loop of sunshine and mundane human life, and you can hardly believe that you can't turn the clock back, you can't leap to that time before the fatal decision; you let yourself dream awhile, the child sucking a candy, for minutes, and oh it's a relief, a hand stroking the fever in your head, the sunshine again, and God's in his place.

The reality is a fight on a pillow. You grapple with it. I wanted my face back. I mourned it.

I had my stitches in for just over a week, then I took a car from the hotel to Dr Kreitzman's own practice in the Fifteenth.

I was on painkillers, but I winced as the stitches were pulled.

'Take a look,' said Dr Kreitzman. 'But remember, you're still a little swollen.'

NINE

The Gramercy Park stories become more structurally elaborate. We wove in pets and grandmothers and subplots.

Light soaked the dark furniture, as though our bedroom were a castle in a moat. Laurence liked the old bulk of colonial design. He was New England, I said, his time at the Massachusetts Institute of Technology had clearly drummed a folksy aesthetic into his head. I wanted drifting drapes and light patterns, the flimsy shimmer of layers of thin fabric, satin and embroidered cotton, and Oriental corners. So we married them, light against dark. There were solid chests on pale rugs, and angled shots of morning light came through the blinds, our private haze of sky above the neighbouring buildings. The marriage of light and dark was harmonious.

'If I wasn't here,' Laurence said, yawning, 'you would sleep in a meringue. A whipped white thing. With brothelish undertones. Luckily for you, you live with me.'

'Yes, sweetheart, why don't we turn our apartment into a big old sombre old *manse*? We could have thundering bureaux, and grandmother rocking chairs in mahogany. We could weave a few rag rugs in our spare time and block out the light with creaking shutters like something out of Hawthorne.'

'I thought I was meant to be the greatest living exponent of

Bauhaus?' he said. The dark brown of his eyes was intensified with sleep.

'Well, this is where all your troubles lie. You want a British version of a Bostonian clergyman's parlour on Back Bay here in our bedroom. Then it's Le Corbusier reclining chairs.'

I kissed his ear.

'You'd look pretty sexy on one of those, actually,' he said. 'Our heroine stretched out on the chrome and leather chair, her abrupt introduction to modernism. The broad necked janitor had been watching everything on a video monitor in his basement room, surrounded by photos of Britt Ekland in her younger days.'

The calm precision of his enunciation reminded me of old British movies.

'Who?' I said.

'Oh, some blonde Swede-type actress.'

'I think,' I said, 'that you should lie down. We will continue this story only if you're lying comfortably, and propped on cushions, just so. We will consider the janitor. Lift. Did you know that sperm can last five days in the body? So I have Mahon DNA entwined with me, inside me. I love to think about that as I walk alone along the street. So . . . the nymphic girl liked the sensation of the seat beneath her. The leather became hot in the sunshine, and she rubbed her calves up and down the grain, and eventually she became so hot she pulled off the dark pink stockings, all leafy and squirrelled, and her legs were milk white, and she tested them against the leather, rubbing them up and down, up and down. The afternoon slumbered on. She became a little bored then, half drowsing in the sunlight, so she played with the hem of her dress, and the air idling between her legs was like cool water. It feels like this, Laurence; a small breeze like a tickle, like a whisper, stirring around the tops of your thighs, like this, and then it covers you, covers your skin in a bath of air. Only the lightest, lightest fingertips can show you, you see . . .'

Those puffs of laundered heat that came through the window on June afternoons. Though the air was gritted with metal, there was some hot washed smell, perhaps a prelapsarian Virginian memory, an idea of bakeries and laundry. We lay in those buffered gusts in the afternoons.

When Laurence became more successful, he started coming home in the afternoons.

He called me from work. He sounded businesslike. 'Miss Meier, did you realise you have the name of a prominent architect?' I could hear the office all around him. 'Miss Meier, I'm calling to confirm our appointment for . . . an hour's time. Make it fifty minutes. Expect me at ten to four to fuck you.'

I was monstrously distracted by him. I worked hard all day. I unplugged the telephone, but the answering machine clicked and vibrated with his regular calls. Sometimes I left the volume up and his voice reached me through the hallway. He called five, eight times a day from work, even when we had lived together for some years. Eventually I rented a studio in which to work during the day. He always perceived that as a breed of betrayal. It made him furious when I was not at the end of a telephone.

So we went to bed in the afternoons in the summer, and then he returned to his office. He'd jump into a cab on Third Avenue, and I was left to write, but my head was always full of falling sand after orgasm, and sometimes I gave in. He tucked me up in bed before he left, he kissed me goodbye, and I slept until he returned later that night.

Occasionally a little strand of night-time story wove itself into my book. Laurence said he was going to denounce me as Willy to his Colette. He detected the subtlest linguistic echo. He had an uncanny recollection of the precise phraseology of our sleep-dazed sagas, an ability to locate it in novels he hinted he had never read. 'I'm thinking of going public,' he said. 'Confess that I write your books tied to a bed post. Tell them that you only lend your marketable face to my oeuvres. I'll accompany you on screen next time and tell them like it is. I may call a live debate on authorship and plagiarism. *"Loulou is a man"*.'

'What can I give you to continue the deceit?'

'Your body. Your mind, and your wealth.'

'OK,' I said.

'So perhaps we can marry soon, and then you will.'

'I will only marry you if your behaviour improves,' I said.

When I was first in New York City, before I had ever met Laurence, I was a girl, a pupa of me. I was not quite developed. It took me some time to crawl out of my family's semidarkness. When I did, there were men there waiting.

The moment I met Heinrich Gruber, a few weeks after his wife Sophy hired me, the atmosphere in that apartment on 69th Street changed. It had seemed a feminine hothouse until then. Heinrich was small and fleshy-faced and gave off an impression of grey. He had impenetrable eyes, dark and slightly narrow, so it was impossible to guess his thoughts, but the mood he emanated switched between wounded and domineering. He was brusque when we were introduced; he smiled briefly, he shook my hand, but the intensity behind his blank scrutiny caught me off guard.

He was a short German banker in his early forties, private with the codes that make men unreadable. He was set-mouthed, like a child who has been hurt until it shows no emotion, but inhabits a middle ground between the cruel and the hangdog.

The pale palace on the Upper East Side now contained a gamey masculine essence. It was winter. I fought through the frozen falls of sky around the park to get home that evening. I walked part of the way, then caught the bus, looking into the lit windows of À La Vieille Russie.

On those rare nights when we were all at home together, without boyfriends or parties or evening jobs, it was like a college: the walls ballooned with candles, and the sounds of music and voices drifted in from other apartments. I loved them then, I loved Mimi as well as Helen, and mentally I clung to them in case they should ever leave me.

But I had to watch out for Mimi, and be very polite to her. She complained when I turned one of the bedrooms pink with reject bolts of satin and rose curtains, even though it was usually me who slept in there. She was humiliated when I replied to Katharine Holden's carping asides on the stairway. She suspected me of over-use of bathroom lotions, of shirking responsibilities, and of getting her to run errands. She complained that Helen indulged me while she kept us in order.

Our apartment there on 13th Street was cosy. All the activities of the New School with its particular breed of radicalism permeated the neighbourhood, and it was young, with its bars, paella and pimento at Spain, our restaurant for rich days and celebrations, the old women's prison down the road, and the Village Vanguard where Helen met men. The train station fustiness of our apartment had been transformed, but there was reassurance in its ghosts. Helen lined the kitchen with movie stills, then studied her legal texts in there. I thought such juxtapositions tragic, but she seemed immune to her old passions.

My family was scattered by then, the legacy of a father who shot us apart. We had never been an entity: we folded secrets and cut ourselves off. There was a diaspora. My brother John, the eldest, hardly visited Mammi and Karli though he still lived in Virginia. Kati had moved to Wichita Falls, where her husband ran motels; there were little Meier-Wilsons now crawling about near the Texas Panhandle, nephews I had never met.

I hadn't wanted to leave Karli behind when I went to New York. I missed his dull blond crop, his sniggering behind his hands, and the novels he and I both read and fought over. I wrote postcards to him, drawing arrows on the pictures to indicate places he would like. He never wrote back, but I knew he would enjoy receiving them.

I couldn't talk about my family, not even to Helen.

'Ask your mother if she wants to stay one time,' said Helen. 'She can have my bed.'

I laughed. 'Oh, Helen! Thank you . . . My mother doesn't go anywhere.'

'Why not?'

'She's – She covers herself up. She has my brother to look after. I don't know.'

I couldn't explain to Helen that Mammi had buried herself long ago, in blinds and pans and late blooming religion – an eclectic faith, hardly related to the exigencies of her childhood Catholicism – in which she read hagiographies, she would not go to church, and she retained a steely indifference towards her children's and her grandchildren's religious lives. I couldn't tell Helen how she hated us as she loved us and how she greeted all attempts at dialogue with implied and toneless surprise.

I used to try to hold us together. Then, like my father, at a certain point I left. I had to get out.

I was happy living on West 13th Street and working for Sophy Gruber when it happened. I came home on a Friday evening, and my mother had died.

Mimi told me. She had taken the message from Aunt Ginger.

I went back to Virginia. I went on the bus to see Karli. I told Karli he could live with me, he could finish school in New York and I would look after him. I could find another apartment, Sophy would help me, and we'd move there together. But Ed and Ginger had asked him to live with them, so he could finish his final year at Indian River High School in Chesapeake. John never went to visit Karli, even though he had moved into our mother's house with his wife.

Karli was an American boy, far more American than I would ever be, and he seemed happy at Ginger and Ed's. Later, they looked after him during vacations while he was in school, at UVA up in the mountains. I went to see him. We hugged each other. He had grown much taller than me. His mouse hair had turned brown. It stuck up like Velcro. We waved goodbye when I left, and I could see that he was crying, and he was acutely embarrassed by it.

I went to see Gloria before the bus left the terminal. She never talked much to me; she hefted herself round her condo on her bad hip, and made us some coffee in her special coffee machine. She showed me a picture that had belonged to my mother. It was a photo I had sent her of me and Helen together on our fire escape in our favourite clothes. Gloria said Mammi had kept it on the vanity in her bedroom.

I cried on the bus on the way home. My face, my nose, my clothes, became a swamp. I had to take a cab from Port Authority because I was swollen with crying.

It was because Gloria had found her. She had had a heart attack, and Gloria had found her later on the floor.

That was what I always cried about. It was that thought that made me cry: that Gloria had found her while Karli was at school. Because she must have been so alone. It still made me cry much later, over the years.

When I got home after Virginia, there was no one in the apartment, so I propped myself on pillows in bed and watched the early night sky and the newly lit windows of neighbouring buildings, and listened to myself breathe, the astonishing, rhythmic assurance that I was alive, and healthy, almost as though I were a being other than myself; I was agitated just below the surface of numbness, incipient ideas travelling up my body and rooting in my forehead, while sleep lagged in the wake of exhaustion.

The small half-room at the back of the apartment was

146

dark-skied and wooden like a ski cabin at night. When I was not in my pink room, I could lie by the big sheet of uncurtained glass on that side of the building and watch the dusk fall, and hear shouts from the apartment buildings across the way, and the sirens down Sixth Avenue, and I was in a tent, or I was sailing, inky night seas, the dog's claws next door jolting at distant noises, and eternal life beyond the fire escapes.

And I decided that Mammi's had been a half-wasted life. She had tamped two decades down under mothballs. And I determined that mine would never be like that. I would make something of my life, and become famous. It did not benefit you to subjugate yourself. It did not exalt you to manacle yourself to one man.

I grew stronger after my Mammi died, because there was no one left. My father had not died, rather ceased to live; he existed nowhere that I knew of, spiritually or geographically. Even the uncles didn't know where he had gone, whether he was alive, or whether he had a girlfriend or more children. He had gone long ago, and I was on my own.

At that time, I had a face on which everything moved upwards: eyes, mouth, brows, only the nose forming a straight line. It was fine at the bridge, a straight nose, but emphatic. I never plucked my eyebrows to the thin line of the time; I resisted it; they formed dark arches, the curve slight but defined in a questioning trajectory, just as everything was tilted, the outer edges of my eyes, the lids in profile perhaps faintly semitic. My eyelids and brows met my nose in an interplay of lines that became more precise as I progressed through my twenties.

The brows were a little darker than the hair, defined against the paler skin. I dyed my hair often, or tinted it with a suggestion of auburn on the brown, a new definition of darkness to hit the pallor. There were two moles below my right eyebrow, which seemed to mark the source of the cheekbone, in further contrast, like the brown hair, to the skin.

I took youth as a given, because that is what you do when you are a girl. The soap-washed quality of young skin, you take for granted. You fail to see the shock of its clarity.

At high school, I had been perceived for so long as foreign, though my English was fast and fluent, that I became comfortable within that enforced strangeness, hugging it as one doggedly treasures loneliness or disability, because no one else will love that runty child. My features were over-drawn, their largeness flirting with beauty, flirting with ugliness. I was a dark pale girl in black and white foreign print.

I had assumed I was off-pitch, or flagrant and perfumed like the spiky shabby whore my mother saw even in child-hood, but in my secret mind, somewhere, in the smells of my hair, at night, I knew. And then, in New York, people said I was pretty, and that word was a gift of fat roses. Helen and Mimi said I was the pretty one; they told me once that they kept their boyfriends away from me. Sophy called me her alabaster pet. She told me one day, brushing my hair as I had brushed hers and dictating a letter for translation, that Heinrich had said I had a classic beauty. I rarely spoke to Heinrich; he appeared not to notice me. It filled me with disbelief, and then later little beads of exaltation ran through my head in the most glorious of revelations.

You are you, Papa had said. *You* are your own possession. And so I grew at a certain point, so I bloomed, and finally it enabled me to write *Loulou* and to spin romance in candy floss complication around me.

One evening when I was twenty-two or so, Heinrich Gruber arrived home early from work. He looked me up and down. I was wearing a small dark pink dress with old pearl earrings. I had washed my hair in Sophy's shower while she was out shopping, and it hung in damp strands. I could smell soap about me. The afternoon was drawing to a close.

'Have you written out my wife's invitations yet?' he asked me.

'Most of them,' I said.

He threw demands at me, abruptly angled enquiries. I walked about the room, answering him vaguely, while he spoke to me in the tone he used with paid staff. Then I answered him in German, and he smiled at me for the first time. He paused, and his smile broke through his grey defences. He dressed in execrable leisure wear when he was home from work, as though perpetually en route to his sports club. His baggy pants that day were a pale grey with orange detailing. Sophy reined in her beauty beside him, she made it polite. I wanted to dress her up and make her radiate beside him. I wanted to give her a lover.

I was a little nervous in his presence.

'Do you know my children?' he asked eventually.

'Of course,' I said. 'The nanny looks after them, but I play with them. They're adorable.'

'Do you like them?'

'Jack is very bad, but he suffers for it, so sadly and sweetly. Anna-Sofia is a little pet, and Jack is a wild bitey one.'

'Thank you,' he said. And Sophy came through the door. She had bought me a scarf that day.

When I returned to West 13th Street that night, I imagined, in a vague way, that Heinrich might try to seduce me. Then I thought of Sophy's trust and her damaged symmetrical beauty, and knew that I could not be seduced.

Heinrich's German friends liked to talk to me because I could speak their language, it made them smile in a particular touched way, as though their boyhood were there in a sudden brief haze over a hill they had not seen for a long time. Heinrich began to make a point of talking to me in the early evenings when he was home from work. He was sober and subdued, but he teased me about my Austrian accent.

Our father had not wanted men in the house in Chesapeake. John was permitted his corn-fed mistresses, while Kati and I were to study. Boys barely set foot in that rubbed and shuttered house. I completed my assignments and looked at uncles through my hair. I waved at the neighbours from the bedroom. I flirted in my bed, and felt my body, running one hand over the hypnotic line of my hips.

Men were new, to be discovered when I left home. I had known their flavour a long time, but I didn't know their exact substance.

In New York City, I met a man called Peter McAllister, and I loved him like a beloved brother, like Karli almost, a boy in a book with a feral cat and a tree-house, his pale-skin look, his rough and tumble sensitivities, and we cleaved together very fast with the calm inevitability of propinquity. Peter McAllister claimed he still loved me for several years, though he thought I was powdered and alarming; he wanted to take me upstate, because he feared that I would run off with a richer man, or a more extrovert man. He wanted me to have sex every night with him, to use my vagina as an athletic muscle around him.

I used to go and stay at his apartment on Thompson Street for three nights at a time, going to work at Sophy's from there, and talking to Heinrich Gruber in the evening, with his strange questions, his subdued intensity.

Then I met Ron Birle. I loved Peter McAllister with calm deep affection, like Karli and like my girls at West 13th, but Ron Birle was extravagant, stubbled. He wanted me to live in his apartment, he gave me a ring I wouldn't wear on my second finger, and we ran round town on dates. We had shouting matches, he was given to frenzied fits of recrimination: I would not give myself to him, he claimed, I didn't love him, I drove him to insane behaviour.

I started to meet Heinrich Gruber for lunch.

I had two boyfriends and a clique of German admirers, because some of Heinrich's friends had begun to call me without telling him.

It was as though I were veiled, and I lived through veils, the walls between seduction semi-opaque but interconnected, and men never quite got to me.

I was exalted by men as I was injured by men. It's commonplace. It is only an everyday occurrence. I inhabited, temporarily, different rooms, the worlds of men I met, a life I adopted so I could walk on Park Avenue South at three in the morning with peonies and the empty stomach of hunger.

Men make you feel so terrible, so high, you are their circus animal, pretty pelt and leash. You starve yourself. You strip all the hairs on your body until you are chicken pimpled and sore, and then soften yourself with creams for sex. They have you in a drug's high hold.

I was addicted. A bead rubbed my crotch in a small capsule of lust, a mercury ball that I fingered. It exhausted me. I was addicted as I was bruised.

I touched them as I spoke. I seemed to be given a new elegance by God in the presence of men. The touch was light, it appeared to madden them. Different men wanted to be with me. It amazed me. Older and richer, and married men, the men I'd never anticipated at first, yet as a child had presupposed as life's due. They asked me out. They gave me things. Helen went crazy. She said it was like being my maid, receiving the calls, pressing the door release, taking in my mail. She wasn't jealous because she had her black boyfriends, but she felt like a maid to me, or a madam, a duenna. Mimi refused to take my messages any longer.

What people don't understand is that if you make the rules yourself, you are lawless, and others mould themselves without knowing it around your peccadilloes. It is quite simple.

'I will not scrub and slave any more,' I said one day to Helen.

'Not so long ago you really *were* scrubbing,' she said.

'So? Now I'm sick of writing invites in pretty German. Same thing.'

'I think it sounds like a breeze,' she said. 'Trust you.'

'Trust me – not.' I tugged at the blind and stared at the night sky. 'There are ways . . . ' I said. I laughed.

Helen laughed. 'Oh, no,' she said.

In the morning, the street was already stirred with sirens and shouts. I fell asleep once more. It was nearly noon by the time I awoke, and my voice was dull with sleep when I called Sophy to tell her how sick I was.

I took a shower. The sounds of the neighbourhood were rising in a lunch-time clamour when I stepped out of the water. The streets had spawned a more extreme form of life that year: displays of sex, and the buzzing wasted residue of people out all night, that Quaalude exhaustion that marked the afternoons.

The phone rang. It was Heinrich Gruber.

'Why aren't you with my wife?' he said.

'Oh, Heinrich. Hello. I'm sick today,' I said.

'No, you're not. I'd like you to have lunch with me.'

'Would Sophy like it?'

'I don't know.'

There was a shot of spring to the day. Buds grew in stray snow. I wore violet-framed sunglasses and a narrow grey dress. I suddenly decided I wanted to see the Woolworth Building in the new light, so I left the subway early, and there it was in a terracotta mirage above me. I crossed to Nassau Street and walked, and I felt lawless and free, a breeze tugging my hair and I ran, and arrived breathless on Pine Street.

'I decided last night I might not work for you any longer,' I said to Heinrich. I nearly laughed.

'You might not?' he said. 'And where might you work?'

'I don't know. Some place dull and then I'll do something fabulous.'

'Like what?'

'I don't know. I see only a glimpse of it, and then it disappears. Like catching the ocean for one dreaming second over the horizon.'

'How will you finance this – project?'

'It's not a project now. It's a tiny abstraction. A fabulosity.'

'How will you finance it?'

'Herr bull and bear. I told you. Some dull old job.'

'What exactly is the trouble with your current employment?'

'I'm a servant,' I said. 'Aren't I?'

'Are you?'

'I scrub and slave and run to Bergdorf Goodman.'

He laughed one of his rare and abrupt laughs.

'My wife appears to treat you like a house pet,' he said. 'I know no other employee who is invited out with her friends to lunch.'

'Can you imagine the *horticulturist* at 21?' I said.

'You're treated as an honoured guest.'

I shrugged. I tried not to smile. I felt happy. There was a sunny breeze on Wall Street, and I was surrounded by dull bankers on leather chairs. My legs felt restless under the table.

'Aren't they sad?' I said cheerfully, surveying the room. 'They probably dream of getting high at Max's, when really the poor boys are swallowing sleeping pills and nurturing baby ulcers.'

He stared at me with his undisguised and arrogant curiosity.

'Where are you from?' he said.

'Styria – Steiermark. Small town.'

'I thought you were a young Viennese. Did you have Jause at Demel?'

'Oh, no. We were too poor. You don't understand – rich businessman. I only went to Vienna once.'

He nodded. 'I would like you to continue to work for us,' he said. 'What pay would you like?'

I tried to hide my smiles. I nearly laughed. I picked up my sunglasses. 'I'll think about it,' I said. 'May I have a week's vacation?'

I knew there were easier ways in this life than being paid by the hour. There were more intense, momentous solutions. You had to be clever; you had to know the shibboleth.

At that time, when the women's movement was still young, there were few paradigms. I might dream the life of Amelia Earhart, but my mother would dedicate novenae to my early marriage. The vaulting mind turned to men.

And yet I did not consciously plan it. Men think we conspire to torture them, when we only plot to keep them. We first know our own power when others give it to us. Sexual power is like fame, a gift bestowed. I didn't know I could exert an influence over men until it happened. I thought, sometimes, it was like making perfume: the sweet scents and the hooks and the subliminal effects all had their time and their place, their precise combination a honey trap, yet their logic a mystery. I didn't know how it worked.

The staff at the Gruber apartment had to wear uniforms. They ran about in white house-coats. I always forgot that I was paid staff, and turned up in the poppy prints I had bought at markets, and, on days I woke late, the most weary of clothes, and at other times, tight dresses. Heinrich occasionally frowned at me, but Sophy was happy for me to fulfil her colourful misconceptions about life downtown.

That spring, I noticed that I was working less. I arrived just as the breakfast table was being cleared by the cook's helper and the nanny was scooping the kids off to school, I was poured coffee, and there were leisurely mornings, the light like silk in the pale rooms, when I read Sophy passages from German novels and poetry, because I was beginning to teach her the language. Heinrich was too impatient and too busy.

The air on West 13th Street was gritty pale green in the mornings. I took the buses to work. Sometimes, on afternoons off, I sat in diners and I wrote small things. Loulou started to come alive in a diner. I scribbled notes, and larger passages, and divine plots for myself, and began to sew them together in places. If Loulou was conceived at the Martha Washington, she was nurtured in a diner, a girl who was at home in the streets and public places of New York. There was a particular quality she took on a divine and preposterous carelessness; there was a momentum I associated afterwards with notepaper and coffee.

As the spring became streaked with heat, the pigeons gargled earlier on the steps and weighted the skinny trees outside the window. I began to get up later and later. On warm nights, Helen and I went out to sit on the stoop, and smoked with the neighbours. We talked about sex. We were always tired. I called Sophy in the morning in a daze, but Sophy imagined I would arrive later in the day trailing the debauched scent of my downtown existence, and amuse her. I sensed Heinrich watching me when he came home early from work, as though I were a fascinating animal his wife had brought in.

I knew how to play old Heinrich. And while Sophy's set gave me their unwearable clothes and fussed over my unfashionable pallor, Heinrich's colleagues noticed me, watched me, bullied me with their attentions.

When you are eighteen, twenty, twenty-two, you inhabit a rosy little isle of unformed goddesses. You are insulting and thin-armed. You don't know the power of it. That delicate clavicle and ball of shoulder, that slight yielding roundness to the face, the rib cage as much a feature as the breasts, they capture men without thought. And it maddens them to bellowing distaste that this cute little ass, so tight drawn and insolent, is not theirs, their own property to cherish and abuse.

Your walk is not smooth: it's kicky, loitering. It's slender hipped, *faux* downtrodden, but the eyes are luminous even as the gait is shrugged.

If boundaries are pliable, perversity conspires with boredom. I started to play just a little. I knew the spirit of what I wanted, if not its exact form, and though certainty had to be disguised by the demands of femininity, I could lose my temper with Heinrich Gruber, with the most eminent of his friends, and still I was courted by them, and still I could laugh with them and rebuff them. Sometimes, later, I was hit with sinking shame at my own behaviour, and pity for Heinrich's fleshy grey features.

I simply couldn't organise my life. My laundry, my groceries, my dates, the novels to be read, all slipped and fused into a chaos that Mimi attempted to order. She organised me with dazzling kindness and efficiency. Then, without warning or explanation, she stopped waking me for a few days so I stumbled bullish and bruised out of bed into a pour of noon light.

When the streets were wide with yellow warmth, I took to leaving the subway early and walking in the Park, meandering through the spaces and dells and out onto Fifth Avenue so my forehead was stippled cool by the awnings. There were plump little birds on the Upper East Side, and some of the doormen started to recognise me and nod at me when I took the same route, and I looked into the glassy gloom of their lobbies, all dull red and crystal, and I was happy to be outside, the patterns of the leaves accompanying me, printing the walls of the mighty apartment houses. I sometimes lingered to drink coffee in the mornings, and Heinrich asked to meet me if I was very early. He smelled of aftershave in dark expensive coffee-shops, or he was vulnerable in the light of the day.

I felt so long-legged then, slim in heels or fast in ballet slippers, the Park waking up, Fifth Avenue honking, the striped awnings ricocheting with air like the idea of Paris. I didn't want to work: I went for walks with Peter McAllister, my pale and nominal boyfriend, or called Ron Birle, or talked to people with their dogs and looked at the sculpted birds on the Bethesda Fountain. A couple of times, Sophy spotted me walking late up Park from her car, and I blushed as I waved.

I had become very happy. Sophy looked after me. She sent school books up to UVA for Karli, though they had never met, and had flowers delivered when I was sick. The apartment on 69th Street was a home to me: play-pen and refuge. I gave Sophy her German lessons, flawed and haphazard though they were, teaching her the poems my father had insisted we read. Every day was a dance between sensitivities: Sophy's and Heinrich's and Heinrich's friends', those boring bankers who thought I was exciting, who squired me to weird clubs around town, and playfully asked me to marry them though they had wives at home. The early summer was filled with unwise dates. I had to hide behind corners to avoid Heinrich Gruber. My boyfriends downtown started making rules.

Inconsistency is the source of all fascination. You blow hot, you blow cold, and you have them.

I dared, then, to follow the path of my moods. You have to dare to be selfish, because others will censor you. I was bored, ultimately, by the men I met, and despite doubts in the night – the sudden sick fear of abandonment – I usually did what I wanted to do. I loved my lovers for months at a time. I was charmed until their essence became part of me, but the charm unaccountably swung to repulsion, they seemed mundane or physically sickening, and I had to be alone. And then they began to show signs of adoration, and I had to test them as they ran around me. I wanted to be good, like my mother, like Sophy or Karli, but a devil inside me sometimes pushed through my skin, just as youth granted omnipotence.

If you become bored before they do, you derange men's lives, they think you are poison as they think you are dipped in heaven, and you are plastered with notions: heartless smiles and sudden departures and havoc wreaked. While Mimi imagined I dedicated my life to the pursuit of men, I was energetic in my avoidance of them. It is an evasive eroticism. You mix light with shade, and sex with sweet sorrow. You are imperious and worrying and hard to please: 'A thirst for life tempered by a shade of satiety . . . ' said Baudelaire. It is dazzling duality: the child-woman, the tormented tormentor.

I had turned from a cleaner and typist to a dilettante German teacher. I woke at eleven, disrupted Heinrich's day, wrote strange paragraphs without direction, and went walking in the afternoons with Sophy, reciting *Hermann und Dorothea* along Madison Avenue.

TEN

I am a woman who has chosen to undergo a certain procedure, and now suffers for it.

My face was very bruised when I returned home after the operation. I pulled a light chiffon scarf around my head, over my chin, and walked past the *loge* in sunglasses, ignoring M Rouillier, the head gardien, though I knew that packages would have piled up in my absence. Papa said I should always wear sunglasses, because even as a girl they had suited me: green glass, pearly frames.

Laurence Mahon's raincoat, his petrol blue London businessman's coat, was hanging in my closet. It was the first thing I saw when I reached into the back to find a pile of scarves. He had lent it to me once, during a rainfall on Bedford Street, and somehow it unofficially became mine. I never got around to returning it; it travelled to Paris with me, and one day I might remember to ask him if he wants it back. It no longer smells of his hair and the streets.

If the face is a record of our histories, Dr Kreitzman razed mine from me. My cheeks were left child tight, gently swollen like baby flesh. The sore half-moons beneath my eyes where Dr Kreitzman removed the loose skin were surrounded by bruising. I couldn't yet judge the effects of my operation, because the swelling had distorted the placement of my features, my cheeks prodding them into new alignments. Sore red lines traced the area in front of my ears, and my ears themselves seemed unevenly positioned.

All day I looked in the mirror. I lifted hanks of hair to examine the crusts on the scalp. I stared at myself. My proper face emerged sickeningly in my memory, panning into my mind to merge with the image in the glass, and then I lost it again, and there was only the sore bloated child.

The pain in my face nauseated me.

I tried on my lipstick and turned the lights down low, and a tiny tab of excitement fizzed.

I caught a blurred glimpse of youth.

ELEVEN

I had never done so little at the Grubers'. The new laundress thought I was a Gruber daughter. Sometimes I dreamed I was indeed the slender and wayward oldest Gruber child home on college vacation, bought Day-Glo Fiorucci pants by my mother, taken to the park for brunch by my banker father.

I had begun visiting the public library regularly, a midway point between the Village and the Grubers' apartment. Heinrich gave me a fountain pen. I used brown and purple inks, then Mimi found me a fluorescent pink: I alternated the colours to keep myself awake, my notes a flashing variegated scrawl glanced at by the pompous scratchers who sat around me gouging paper with their microscopic writing.

In the morning, I would send a superstitious wish slanting through the window into the sunlight, and set off uptown. I had baskets and sprigged clothes, as befitted the time, like a country girl incongruous on Sixth Avenue, to be replaced by glittering stuff at night.

'I think you are – slightly *creepy*,' said Heinrich, who bullied me after he had courted me for a couple of years.

'Why?'

'You're like a shining white *child*. You gleam. You should have albino's hair, but you're dark.'

'I shouldn't. It's the contrast. It's like Snow White, you see.'

'Is it? That's *it* – you're a child with a woman's face. You'll go too far, Adèle. I'm telling you.'

I shuddered. 'Wherever too far is, Herr Gruber, I'm sure you'll be there before me.'

I didn't meet Laurence Mahon for some time after I had seen him at the Russian Tea Room. He was barely part of the circle I knew. I wasn't even sure of his surname then. The disco era had started. Helen and I had taken to sequins. Mimi stayed at home, then veered into alarming and unexpected sexual excursions. Laurence Mahon was not likely to be sighted on a disco floor. I imagined, idly, that I might run into him somewhere, the idea planted by his exaggerated claims.

Then he called me. His voice down a telephone line after some time was surprising and yet familiar.

'We'd – Carolyn and I, we'd like you to come to supper – dinner, I mean,' he said.

'Well, thank you,' I said. 'I work late . . . I may arrive a little late. Am I to be accompanied by room mates?'

'How many of them are there?' he said. 'Yes, yes. Bring hordes of them. Bring the whole bloody Tea Room crowd if you want. Ask the one with the irritating name.'

'Mimi?'

'*Mimi!* So North American, so diminutive – Missy, Prissy.'

'You have been reading too much *Gone With The Wind*. It's short for Miriam. I *won't* tell her what you said.'

'I like your name,' he said. 'It's poetic.'

'I like yours,' I said. 'Laurence Mahon. I have to go.'

'You always say that – "I have to go". With a little sharp twist at the end. Will you come on Friday?'

'I'll try to.'

Laurence's and his wife Carolyn's apartment was high up in a new building on 65th and Broadway, their balcony looking down on Lincoln Center. It blasted out too much heat or too much cold air, and they had flung the windows open. Mimi and I heard a muffled thud of music from their apartment as the elevator doors opened. Inside, it was all noise and confusion. Laurence and Carolyn were arguing in the kitchen. 'The kitchen's a no-go zone,' Mimi's friend Chris told everyone who came in, disjointed recriminations and the sounds of protest slamming into the spaces between music, before Laurence and Carolyn emerged, by then laughing; or he was laughing, she was hiccoughing between laughter and tension.

Laurence came over to us, and kissed me. I had forgotten his darkness. There was a berry coloured roughness to his skin.

'Hello,' he said. He put one hand on my shoulder. He seemed abstracted. The doorbell rang, and he went to answer it.

'Hi. Adèle?' said Carolyn.

We shook hands, and her hand felt very thin. She wore a tight top in blue and white stripes, which revealed the outline of small circular breasts and the shape of her nipples. She was nervous.

'I guess we didn't really meet last time,' she said.

'No,' I said. 'So I'm happy – to be invited.'

The dark shadows under her eyes were moody; they seemed to flicker and wince. She wore bold silver jewellery that presented an abrupt contrast to her nerves.

I hardly saw Laurence that evening. He positioned himself at the end of the table and then rarely sat, moving energetically between kitchen and chairs, addressing people at once. He was abrasive with an impatient, high-flown confidence that made him tiring; it stepped into the brutal. I was shocked by what he said, comments caught between other conversations, charm dicing with pure rudeness. His attention leapt between people and tasks, but he was socially at ease in a way that was foreign to me, as though he had been trained to it. And then later he fell into sudden fluent tranquillity, and I felt the edges of it from a distance, it lapped and touched me, but he didn't catch my eye, we rarely addressed words to each other. He seemed to control the mood. He was all tanned and slightly unkempt and over-confident.

I dismissed him. I didn't know him. He irked me. I walked over to the window and looked at the Hudson. It was hot. I watched the ghosts of sun waving in the water, I stretched and followed the boats passing by on the far side, and I could hear English cadences rising above the rounder sounds of the Americans behind me in the room.

'It is the most adorable accent,' I murmured.

He sat near me. He heard me.

There was a small silence.

'You're fading away against the window,' he said eventually. 'The butterfly net you're wearing – will carry you if you fly.'

I looked at him through the dusk. The lights had not yet been turned up. His mouth was downward turned at the corners, set that way in relaxation: a European look, like the Yugoslavian and Polish men with their large noses above a shadow of stubble and their unexpectedly intense eyes.

'Adèle, come and sit,' said Chris's friend.

'The evening is so beautiful,' I said.

'We want you here.'

'I want to go out in a boat. We should have a boat take us downstream to wherever it leads – "The shallop flitteth silken sailed" – to the Atlantic, or to Ireland. And then . . .'

'Your chair is getting cold,' said Chris.

'Let it get cold,' I said.

Carolyn was in the kitchen. Laurence was piling up plates, quickly and noisily. I wandered to the other window, and then to the room next door to look at it. It seemed to be an office, leading to the bedroom. There was too much to observe, too many large stacked art histories. It appeared to contain the trappings of an old English rectory: an antique black wood desk, Victorian paintings on glass enclosed in patchy lichen velvet and ornately carved frames. The walls were a dark military green. It was inappropriately heavy and confined, as though it belonged to a different country in a different era. The scarred severity of architectural drawings hung in sudden contrast on one wall.

'I didn't know whether this was the right thing to do – to ask you to supper,' said Laurence from the doorway.

'How can it be right or not right?'

He was silent.

'I have never known who is supposed to make the big rule book in the sky,' I said. 'Show me where the architraves are.'

'Non-architects always know about architraves – and flying buttresses,' he said. He smiled. He walked across the room and traced a line on one of the plans. 'There you have an architrave. No flying buttresses.'

'I see.' I studied the architectural plans. My hair fell over one cheek and I hooked it back behind my ear. My gauze skirt rustled and resettled when I moved.

I heard him behind me.

'There are so many darling little parachute string formations on this drawing.' I ran my fingernail over the glass.

He was still silent, but he shifted around, he transferred his weight to a different foot.

Later he said that he wanted to see her there, in his apartment, so he could simply be with her again, and listen to the faint strange mixed accents of her speech. Yet when they were alone in a room, he didn't know what to say. Her self-containment intimidated him, as though she knew a world slightly more exciting than the one she found herself in at that moment, as though she held a promise of it, just beyond reach. She was quite happy with silences, disregarding his presence while she studied the pictures. She was one of those women seemingly accustomed to seducing or to being seduced, so she was composed within seduction's overwrought rituals; she could almost parody them.

She had dressed herself in an impossible gauze or tissue confection so one stared to see if it was transparent and found that it was not quite, there was a confusion between the colours of flesh and cloth. She wore the simplest white round-necked top above it, and there were seed pearls in places – wrist, neck – and other pale stones. She smelled of something darker and sweeter. She looked disconcertingly young, her skin very clear and pale, as though she were a girl dressing up as a woman.

He wanted to anchor her and make her more definable.

'You're *presumptuous* to say I have an accent,' he said at last. 'Pronouncing your judgement in faintest Euro-mix. Is it . . . German?'

'Austrian.'

'I see.'

'I *hate* people thinking I'm German. Wouldn't you hate it if people thought you were an obnoxious, rainy *Welsh* person?'

'Oh, but here they think Wales is part of London, part of the Hebrides. They're only obsessed with Ireland.

'Do you have a sense of exile?' she said.

'Oh, yes. Do you?'

She nodded. 'But I don't exactly know where from. My brother became an American. My mother was never anything but Austrian. I don't think I'm either now.'

'Perhaps you're French. Adèle is French. It's very – it's very lovely. Perhaps you come from somewhere where they moon bathe.'

She paused and smiled slightly to herself. There was a distant gathering of sirens.

'Are you mocking? Or are you being quite sweet? I hardly can tell in that strange accent.'

She walked the length of the room. She took large steps

under her floating skirt. He watched her move about. He saw the dark lines that scored her pallor in the gloom of the evening, her precise dark eyebrows and the line of her hair.

'I'm just being Mr Polite Host, and getting to know you, and getting it fabulously wrong. No doubt. I don't really know you, do I?'

'No. You don't know me.'

'I want to. So . . . '

She moved, she looked at books.

'. . . Are you comfortable and happy here this evening?'

'Oh. Very very comfortable and happy here this evening. Thank you, Laurence.'

There was a crash of falling plates, a burst of laughter, from next door. The room was becoming darker.

'Where did you travel from this evening?'

'We came direct from 14th Street.'

'So – ' He cleared his throat. 'Are you involved, to coin a phrase, with anyone?'

She paused.

'Yes,' she said clearly. 'Are you involved with your wife?'

Laurence was silent. The voices next door rose to fill the gap. He looked down, his mouth closed and unmoving.

'Of course you are!' she said cheerfully. 'You will be happy forever and have pretty children – they will be so beautiful, and clever, and just a bit bad tempered. You have such a solemn mouth now. Relax your grim old face.'

He smiled. They could barely see each other; the night had fallen. Light shone from next door, suspending a moment, greying the dark green walls.

'I don't want to leave this room,' he said.

'Nor do I. But we must, mustn't we?'

'It's like lying in bed on a cold morning,' he said, 'and you'd pay anything to stay there in the warmth.'

'Like when you're talking in the middle of the night,' I said, 'and it takes on that transcendent quality – everything all at once ironed out – so compelling. All dark and warm. And you know you'll hate yourself, each other, in the morning, driven mad with tiredness all day.'

They hesitated still, they were motionless in that room.

'We should go back in,' she said casually. She looked at him directly, her eyes intense, the mouth held still and quite passive.

'I know,' he said. 'I – '

'Come on,' she said, and she suddenly walked through the door alone.

Carolyn looked up from the table.

'You missed dessert,' she said.

Laurence couldn't get me in the marble reaches of the 42nd Street Public Library. I would run up the steps between the lions and enter the place of false winter in the heat of early Manhattan summer, my afternoons off. But sometimes his voice would reach me there, the rich cold purity of his British accent seeping over the edges of Loulou, who was forming.

It was after two in the morning when Mimi and I left Laurence's apartment. The lights were buzzing out by the elevator, the doorman taciturn.

'Can we go somewhere?' Laurence asked me in matter-of-fact tones by the door.

'Somewhere? Now where would you want to go?' I said.

People were talking by the elevator. He hesitated beside the door.

'Somewhere with you. Anywhere.'

Mimi looked up. I turned to go. I smiled at him as I left.

'I'll call you,' he said, the level of his voice conversational.

Carolyn came over, and I kissed her goodbye, and my head was light with deceit and sadness, with subdued excitement.

I didn't see him again for some time.

I would sit at Sophy's desk in those days and look at the sparse leaves on Park Avenue. The warm industrial scent of the dishwasher was as familiar as the smell of Mammi's soup. The Grubers' pale haven of foliage and telephones was insulated from life as if refrigerated, the grease and cinder air a rumour outside the double glazing, and yet their existence was sordid.

I began to guess that Heinrich had already seduced staff: younger nannies, a Danish au pair. There was talk, over the years, of the doorman's wife. I pictured Heinrich's spilled seed rooting in the wool carpet. I thought of his choppy bangs and little glasses. His penis a pale tuber. His seed spilled. Then he would shock me by calling. I'd put down the telephone and I'd be shaking. Sophy colluded in hazy knowledge, dressed in collared blouses. I wanted to leave, but the fear of abandonment in my mid-twenties with no work or qualifications made me freeze.

Sitting at Sophy's desk alone on early afternoons, the cleaner's Cuban love songs winding in from next door, the place that had once been my refuge, with its familiar views, trees, buttermilk linen, now had a rotten undercurrent. Heinrich and his businessmen with their red flesh, their fat chests, leaked a meat whiff beneath their aftershave. They touched me as though it was their due.

I had never come home with so many different people's names in my bag, numbers scribbled on my hand. And yet I feared I couldn't keep men. I feared they would glimpse my soul and leave me. I thought about my existence, though I could barely probe it. I had escaped real poverty, but security was not security, and all my progress now resembled stasis. I wanted to be clever, to know the flavour of accomplishment: I wanted a greater life. My father had said his Adèle was an intelligent girl, and when later I learned Sophy's German poetry by heart so fast it disturbed her, I knew my brain had been dying for five years, and that disrupting men's lives was not a worthy occupation.

One Saturday morning I went with Mimi to Washington

Square, to meet some people, have coffee, and hang out. There was a flea market that morning, a man with a parrot, cactus pots, tarnished rings. Among the junk, in the sun, in the distance, was Laurence Mahon with Mimi's group of friends. He looked taller than I remembered. He was kicking a ball about with the scuffing, disconsolate motions of a young boy, talking between kicks to a couple of men. The shouting, the whistle blowing kids, the dogs in the Dog Run, obscured him from me. Mimi, a friend and I sat on a bench talking, I looked up occasionally and saw him as if in the disjointed frames of a French movie – boules, a market, the criminal filmed among the crowd.

I didn't want to be caught looking at him. I talked with abstract energy to the woman beside me, and then the group began to converge, and I was aware, without looking up, in sounds and senses, that Laurence was near me.

He carried his air of health and warm brownness which made me think of fields and tennis, yet he didn't match my image of the English. There was an ethnic narrowing of his eyes' inner corners, his hair was wavy, curling in places, frizzing; his nose was emphatic. I realised that he was potentially ugly within an impression of good looks, he was all height and brownness and stride, he created a stirring of energy, of skin tone and colour, but his features, when lingered upon, were less giving.

'Adèle Meier,' said Laurence, turning to me suddenly. A friend knocked against his shoulder, and then they were off, pushed back into a group of boys on bicycles. I felt a small freeze of disappointment.

The day was so bright with small turrets of breeze. I saw Laurence's wife, Carolyn. She was all in black, with narrow pants, the look that was suddenly replacing flares at that time. She was fashionable, nervous and very thin. She was laughing. She seemed to avoid me, looking directly at Mimi without catching my eye. I glimpsed her narrow pelvis and thought about her having sex with Laurence, and the idea of sleeping with him occurred to me graphically for the first time, and I shivered.

'Someone just walked over Miss Meier's grave,' said Laurence, coming up from behind me, and he walked away to join Carolyn. He put his arm casually around her waist so she seemed thinner and more brittle. I looked away. We bought pretzels from a vendor and ate them, and I realised I had to keep away from this man, because the fact of his existence and his marriage already hurt me.

He avoided me. We wandered among stalls, dispersing and merging. We drank coffee in the sun. We examined gold mules and large Afghan coats. I wanted to wash my hands of imagined fleas.

'Will you come over to Bleecker Bob's with me?' said Laurence, suddenly beside me.

We walked a few steps. I looked at the litter trampled beneath me. It seemed surreal in its ordinariness.

We walked on with the others, a little further, Carolyn was talking to a friend, and then Laurence and I were on our own, we fell in with the crowds, he moved ahead of me, pushing a path through the people, seemingly forgetting me again. He waited for me, and walked on once more. We turned into 3rd Street.

We went into the record store, and I stood to one side while he spoke to the man working there. Thoughts surfed across my vision in the cool gloom; I didn't hear his conversation.

'Come on,' he said, and we walked out with his arm across my back onto MacDougal Street.

'I think we'll be spending a lot of time together now,' he said, his voice loud above the traffic. 'Do you?'

'But you're married,' I said.

'So I am,' he said. He wandered ahead. 'However much I may fancy you.' His face creased into a nervous frown. Then he suddenly laughed. 'I'd better get back to Carolyn and the others.'

He walked ahead without saying very much. We held hands to race through the traffic on 3rd Street, and then he pushed through the crowds on the square, glancing to see that I was following, and joined his wife.

So I had a small secret, irrational as a dope habit or a florid fantasy, since I was not about to have an affair with a married man.

When I was little, I had fallen in love with whole families. They entranced me by not being my own, the strange and inadequate Meiers. Laurence interested me by not being Ron Birle or Peter McAllister, or any of the other men I slept with who eventually clung to my words for their poison or sorcery. As a child, there was always a fantasy figure, like a talisman or worry bead, a bright little hope rubbed under a pillow. Laurence and Loulou were such fragments of hope. I summoned them to ward off Heinrich, but he stroked my arms and shoulders, edging towards my neck, as he discussed the daily mechanics of the Gruber household. My tendons stiffened, and I contracted as if sobs went through my body. Then later in the day, some perverse spirit gripped me with a new radiance and on the buses home, I was still grit-headed with laughter, and it was only later, cold in that house at one in the morning, that I was restless.

There was the spilled blood of show and sexual threat. Heinrich brushed past me in doorways so my nipples were jolted, my tears and rages underscored by the knowledge that he could fire me. And yet later some divine insouciance infected me again: I thought my life might be short, I no longer cared, I rode the sweaty dramas of that household, sex tugging at me.

After some weeks, Laurence Mahon called me. His voice was different from how I remembered it, more professional. He took a veering path between joke-strewn rudeness and formality, in a pure briny race of speech. He called me during the following days without apology, to make and alter arrangements. 'Hello,' he would say when I picked up the phone, never bothering to mention his name, and there was a marked casualness to his calls, as though his only purpose was practical.

He wanted to meet me for lunch. I met him one hot day when I wasn't working, and I had alternated clothes and powders and earrings until I could no longer judge their effect and my lipstick had the blurred uncertainty of effort.

I found the restaurant, a tasteful midtown hush of glass and shivering foliage. My skin was clammy with the sudden cold of air conditioning; my vision darkened as I looked for Laurence.

He sat by himself, waiting for me, by a window.

'You're late,' he said.

'I am,' I said. The ceiling fans pumped cold through my temples.

He seemed irritated. He looked at me dispassionately, without smiling. Then after a moment, he lifted my hand. I thought he was going to kiss it, but he held it, looked at it, bent my fingers into a careless curve, and placed it on the table. I didn't move. The ghost of his touch stayed there.

'Thank you for meeting me,' he said.

'I thought maybe Caro— your wife would be here too.'

'You didn't,' he said.

His sun-warmed air of health formed a kind of spilled glow in front of me, and I could barely look at him because I was embarrassed, because he was brown and prodigal and yet not to be sampled.

He pulled his chair closer to the table, and I watched him obliquely. He couldn't sit still. He asked for bread, he moved salt around the table, he mimicked accents. He ordered champagne and water, not consulting me until afterwards. He checked my silverware, frowned, and asked for my knife to be replaced.

I sat and watched him.

'Do you have a nervous complaint?' I said.

'Only one I developed half an hour ago.'

'I see.'

'Do we – Do we have to be *normal*?' he said. 'You know, all small talk-ish? Do we have to get to know each other properly?'

'Yes.'

He was silent.

'All right, then,' he said. His eyes were very slightly uneven, adding to his impression of dark irises, of different origins. He lifted a fork and waved it vaguely in my direction. 'Where were you born?'

'In Graz, in Styria – the south east of Austria. You?'

'In a small hospital in Canterbury in England. Siblings?' He nodded at a waiter.

'Older brother, older sister, a younger brother.'

'The same.'

'Really?'

'Yes, I think so,' he said. 'Yes. Except I'm male, I think, so that makes three boys altogether.'

The waiter arrived with a bottle, and he poured champagne. Its icy pepper vibrated up my nose. I felt the stem of the glass. I rocked it and made the liquid flatten. I smiled at him.

'Now we know each other,' he said.

He glanced at me. We looked at each other for a moment, caught in the hesitancy of an undefined occasion, its codes flickering, embarrassing. He was self-conscious despite his charm school confidence.

'When did you leave England?' I asked him.

'When I was twenty-one. But I'd always known I would. I went to Cambridge, and then I went to study architecture in Massachusetts, and then at Columbia. A sad eternal student.'

'Then?'

'Then I was taken on by a couple of cunts working on housing projects on the Lower East Side. Then I ran away. Then I talked my way into the job I'm in now, which more or less resembles an architect's job.'

'Where did you meet your wife?'

'At Columbia. She was an art history major. I was in the architecture school, living on Stuyvesant Square with some rats and some student drop-outs. Met Carolyn. Got married. Moved to 65th Street.'

He nodded at a waiter.

'She works at the Modern now,' he said.

'She works at the Modern,' I said idly.

He mentioned her casually. My heart beat altered. His hair fell to one side, its knitted darkness flopping and loosening in the cool air. We caught each other's eye and we said nothing for a while, silenced. I could see the details of his skin in the hard light of the window. There was a red darkening of wind or rough sun or exposed veins.

He looked across at me and smiled. He combined irony with flirtation, and then his elevated mood turned serious, and I caught him looking at me intently, or his dark eyes made him look more intense than he was.

'Isn't it funny,' I said, champagne bubbles shivering my vision, 'that we're both sitting here privately thinking things all the time about each other, and yet, and yet – we hardly know each other, and we have to be polite. So there's an internal monologue going on in both of us that's quite different from anything we've said . . . Isn't there . . .? What were you thinking?'

'I was thinking,' said Laurence, 'I'm slightly cross with you for being late, and I want to go to bed with you.'

I looked to one side, out of the window.

'I was thinking,' I said, 'here I am yet again with a businessman who's probably bored with his wife.'

'It's not quite *right*,' he said. 'One, architects like to think they're virtually *artistes*. Two, am I bored? Or am I distracted? Or am I just a total fuckwit?'

The restaurant filled. We watched people arriving, mirage-like behind the glass doors, knocked by a blast of cold air when they walked in from the heat. His forearm rested on the table, near mine. The tendons moved minutely. We sat in our bright chill recess by the window. Some black nuns sailed past. A little dog lifted its leg at the street lamp outside. Smoke spilled over from the smoking section, carried on the laundered air, and I rearranged my napkin and looked again out of the window, because I was very aware of Laurence, his emphatically, almost disconcertingly male presence, sitting opposite me at the table.

'I want to know about being single,' he said. 'I have an existence that – Because I want to know all about your rosy single life, room mates, your life down in the Village. Your parties and your revolting levels of freedom, your boyfriends, dogs, friends, those earrings from Tiffany's worn so casually.'

'You're the first man I ever met who could recognise anything from Tiffany's. Then I want to know how often you smoke pipes in front of the TV, and how many wedding anniversary parties you host for the in-laws, and whether you have your baby fund started.'

'Oh, God,' he said.

I examined his irises. 'How do married people not *die* of terrible boredom?'

'I'm not the expert on that.'

'Are they embarrassed for their wives to see their used underwear?'

'Yes – no.'

'Do they feel loved, cooked for? Ego bolstered? Virile?'

'Sometimes very. Sometimes not.'

'Do they have little fantasies about running all over town and eating breakfast from a vendor as the dawn breaks over Brooklyn Bridge, and know they can't unless it's all prearranged?'

'Absolutely.'

'It sounds fabulously boring,' I said.

'What about you?' he said.

'I just want – adventures. Not experiences for the sake of it, but to know when I am older that I had youth and spent it well. Not to regret what I didn't do. So . . . I wouldn't stop myself doing something because really I must get some sleep, or it costs much too much money, or my mother would disapprove.'

'Would she disapprove?'

'Actually, she – she died,' I said. 'I don't know why I said that, I said it by rote.'

'Oh, I'm sorry,' said Laurence.

The leaves of my salad seemed ice glazed in the solid chill in which we were suspended. I stared at the window. My eyeballs hurt.

I tried to speak. My voice was tense.

'Where is your family?' I said.

'In England. They're all there, brother's even a doctor in the local village. They live in Kent, in the south; it's where I was brought up before I went away to school. My father's a retired priest.'

'"He was the sweet sweet son of a preacher man",' I murmured.

He looked uncertain. He smiled at me. Briefly, instinctively, he touched my hand. My heart was thumping in a sudden effort not to cry; its beat became jagged. Mammi's face was appearing in front of my eyes. I made my throat relax.

'Do you see them?' I said at last.

'I try to fly back every couple of years. They live in a dozy, balmy part of the country full of tight little fields, and a marsh. It's nice in the summer. My father and I don't get on, but I like seeing my mother and my herd of nieces. I do find the whole thing claustrophobic.'

'Why?'

'Because my family's so self-congratulatory. They've always had this "Aren't we bloody marvellous?" attitude. They're this big clannish pain in the ass when it comes to the subject of themselves. *Our* rituals, our bloody buggering family history, our class, our eccentricities. As if it's all so very interesting for everyone else. I don't think. I love seeing them in small doses, but I can't stand the claustrophobia, and I disapprove of never questioning oneself, of assuming this collective *marvellousness*.'

I nodded. 'It's – it's interesting,' I said. 'Very different from . . .' My throat was tight. My heart was beating hard with acute embarrassment. I knew I was going to topple into tears because the image of Mammi would not leave me. I focused very hard on not crying, on thinking happy thoughts, and I managed. I sat and stared and made my mind still, and the panic ebbed back in relief. Then it hit me from a different direction: my mother had died, and I would never see her again.

'Adèle!' said Laurence suddenly. He reached out and held my arm.

I shook my head. Tears slid over my cheeks and down my chin in a sudden release.

'I'm sorry,' I said.

The skin between my fingers became wet. He pulled my hand away from my face and held it.

'Is this because – You said your mother died. Oh, I'm so sorry, so sorry – me rabbiting on about my stupid family like I'm as obsessed as they are. Oh, darling, don't. Come here. Tell me.'

I started shaking. 'She died,' I said. Fresh shameful tears pooled over my face. 'I can't talk to anyone about it. My brother, he's not that old. The neighbour — '

'Did you love her?' he said.

I nodded.

My Mammi, I loved her, for all her grey-skinned disappointment, for all the strength in her. She bore four children, and she wasn't thanked for it. She was kind to us. She withdrew from us, but she was kind, and she was my Mammi, my mother, she was herself. She was left by her husband. She had very little, she made it do, and she was kind in hidden ways, and she taught Karli German because he was not fluent, and she let me use her 4711, and she read her saint books on her own at the breakfast nook.

'Come here, Adèle, come here,' he said. He pulled his chair next to mine so we were facing the wall, he pushed my plate away, and he enclosed me, he put his arm on my shoulder so that we became a huddle facing the wall.

'It hurts me so much to see you like this,' he said. 'You need looking after too – for all your strong thing – all the independence you have.'

He was very warm, a cocoon of shirt and comfort, his chin grazing my hair, pulling wet strands from my forehead.

'Adèle,' he said. 'Don't . . .'

We sat in silence. He held me against his shirt.

'You make me sad too,' he said.

'Why?'

'For – everything. I suppose we shouldn't meet.' He was silent. He looked out of the window. 'I'm very sad about the girl on Fifth Avenue. I just let her go. Why the hell didn't I try to talk to her? Why didn't I follow her in a cab? It was seven or eight years ago. I just went home in the bus, it was raining, and then – so my life went on as it did. How are you now?'

'I'm OK.'

He pressed his hand against my arm. 'You looked very beautiful among the crowds on Washington Square. You looked like a pale – not quite a ghost, a –'

'An eidolon.'

'What? How do you know these words?'

179

'My father. We've talked about my mother. Don't talk about him,' I said quickly.

'All right,' said Laurence, pressing my arm again, 'OK.'

We sat there. Some boys on skateboards coasted past the window. There was a commotion of policemen further up the street. The restaurant emptied, but we sat in silence, I was framed by the warmth of his shirt, his strange unknown register of flesh and soap smells, and we talked in sudden intense pockets.

The sky was thinning. We walked through the restaurant together, locked with certainty, fluent. On the street he seemed taller and more rigid. He tucked his briefcase under his arm. He kissed me formally on both cheeks.

'I very much wanted to see you,' he said. 'Thank you.'

I saw his back disappear down the street, and my heart beat with that sense of disappointment that is primeval: the flavour of a childhood grief returning.

TWELVE

There were some problems with my eyelids after I had them operated on. My eyes were frequently irritated. Tears formed in the corners; I dried them, they repooled, and my skin became sore.

With eyelid surgery, the eyelid to eyeball ratio is altered, so the tear distribution can be affected. The lower rims of my eyes became a dark bright pink. I could not wear sunglasses for long, because the arms pressed into my face, the flesh still swollen, and the uneven pressure could affect the healing process.

Dr Kreitzman put me under intravenous sedation and tidied up my eyes a little. Revision surgery is sometimes necessary after the main operation.

He gave me a brighter look, an approximation of innocence.

THIRTEEN

Laurence had entered my house by disappearing. None of my boyfriends – Ron Birle, Peter McAllister, the excursions and flirtations – had ever found the private part of my head. Now a hope sealed my morning, but I killed it with logic. He had loved me in the restaurant, and drawn me to him, my crying had made grey streaks on his shirt, and we had walked out light-headed, and then he had bent over from his straight-backed height to kiss me on both cheeks, the married man with manners. And I had felt like a foolish child.

My mind drifted out of the window to the leaves of Park Avenue.

'Have you left us, Miss Meier?' asked Heinrich.

I shook my head.

He ran a hand along my shoulder, down my arm, and guided my pen across Sophy's desk. I rammed my elbow into his stomach.

I saw a woman in the Museum of Modern Art. She had short dark hair, she was square-shouldered and moved too fast. I was sure she was Carolyn, but I didn't want her to see me. I left the lobby very quickly, and I realised then that I had gone there only for that reason, as though to punish myself with the thought that Laurence had someone else, who knew his birthday and his handwriting and slept with him. I knew the stupid kind of people who worked at the Modern, rich kids who imagined themselves artists.

There were days of neutral chill that were a relief from summer's heat. I looked out of the window one weekend afternoon, and he was there on the street.

I opened the window, and he looked up and saw me, he saw the woman, Adèle, her face white in the window, the sky white above her. He was let into the house, its garish wallpaper, the barking of a dog, and he thought the apartment a rosy muddle of freedom, delicate and almost adolescent after the restrictions of his life. He wanted to laugh at the femaleness of that place. There were pictures of brooding art house movie stars on the kitchen walls, and frothing twists of clutter, and a glimpse of ballet dancer material in a pinkish bedroom. He felt large limbed and heavy there. The dog scratched the wall next door. The room mates were there, and all alert, the presence of a man rumpling their Saturday. Mimi wore tight nylon stripes, glistening synthetically. Helen had little on.

Laurence turned to Adèle. 'I haven't seen you for some time,' he said stiffly.

'No,' said Adèle.

'I've been terribly busy.' He tailed off. She looked into him and beyond him as though he were an irrelevance. 'But I wanted to – '

He was almost repelled by her upon seeing her again, her beauty so present, it snared him and annoyed him, because she sported with convention – the heels, the hair – and then twisted it with dressing-up box oddity, with chalk whites and wines, a manner of dressing that was blatantly sexual yet parodic to the point of kitsch. It irritated him by soothing and then confounding his expectations.

'Perhaps we could walk?' he said at last, but Mimi and Helen had drifted away, and they were left in that room with its girl things and its pastel history streaked with candle wax.

He was all sun and energy in contrast to her. She thought he looked like a young man from Europe about to go to the Spanish Civil War.

'I've been thinking about you,' he said. He hesitated. He shrugged. 'My home life's a little . . . Well . . .'

She contemplated him in a leisurely fashion. Her lips parted. 'I think you almost enjoy that situation,' she said.

'God, no – '

'It makes you very powerful, after all.'

'I can't think of anything I'd like less,' he said. 'Completely ghastly. Really. Fucking terrible. I haven't come round here to discuss my marriage.'

'Good,' she said.

'I've often thought about you.'

'Me too,' she said simply.

'I want to spend more time with you,' he said.

'I only want to be with people who want to be with me,' she said coldly.

'Point taken,' he said. He waited.

'Perhaps we could walk?' he asked again.

She didn't move. She studied him in the strange way she had – strangeness and sweetness mixed, so she seemed distant yet utterly defenceless, simply kind – and then the corners of her mouth moved upwards with their own independent movement, and he shuddered: it was the particular formation of her smile that hooked him, and worried him because it hooked him.

'I want to stay in my house,' she said.

They seemed to have little to say that day. The oiled intensity of her tears in a restaurant, of a dusk room in his apartment, had thinned so their words began to float in the air, unconnected, borne by the helium of nerves.

He turned to her. 'I suspect you of collecting men,' he said, abruptly attempting to break the strain.

Her eyebrow arched minutely. 'If they're worth collecting,' she said.

She was silent.

'Are you cross with me?' said Laurence after some time.

'Not at all.'

'I think you have a life I don't know about,' he said.

'Since you know almost nothing about my life, that's probably true.'

'But – so – it makes me jealous,' he said.

She laughed slightly, a spill of light inside her, and she was muzzy and wholesome, and he wanted to bite her inner arm where the flesh was very white and young.

'Why would you be jealous?' she asked teasingly.

'Oh, God, because I'm sure you have a bus load of boyfriends.'

The church clock struck unexpectedly in the still sky. She smiled radiantly at him.

'And of course,' she said, 'you have every right to be jealous?'

'Oh,' he said impatiently. He dismissed the subject with his hand, and she caught again the sense of disturbance she had perceived in him early on, his lack of reason and blusterings of anger. She could see it in his eyes, how they became uneven, the darkness skewed and intense. His tranquillity was then restored with equal abruptness.

'Run away with me!' he said, standing up, so his size, in an apartment whose proportions were scored by female height, was a physical surprise.

'Let's get out of here,' he said, 'go to Coney Island or something, or drive upstate. Let's go to Dutchess County and look out properties! Let's become an old married couple and settle in White Plains. Come on, Adèle, we're eloping.'

She stood up.

'We'll wander through the Park,' she said. 'We'll look at the angel on the Bethesda Fountain.'

'Yes, yes, whatever you want.'

Mimi was hovering in the doorway.

'Your flatmate is quite *ghastly*, isn't she?' whispered Laurence outside the door.

'She's out of the Addams Family.'

Their fingers knocked on the stairs, he pulled her hand and they ran out into the street.

A secret affair confines you to a room, to the ringing of a telephone and the counting of hours. The movement of shadows across a wall marks progress: the melancholy, excited relief in early evening of another day spent. And yet this affair was only in my head.

Laurence shocked me at the beginning There was a certain ragged brutality obscured by his trained charm, a shouting lack of reason set off by drivers and bank tellers and Mimi Ceccato, as though his spontaneity had a troubled source. I thought I saw a little bit of madness there. I lost it again. His outdoorsy stride made me drunk. He grabbed my hand and I ran. I could smell the washing detergent he used, its spring and tennis. I listened to the cold currents of his accent. He turned up in his car and I ignored the signs of his marriage: maps, tapes, museum bags. He tried to kiss me and I turned away.

Laurence said he thought he saw me all that summer, the year I met him in New York. He told me he saw slim girls in the park, girls in crêpey summer dresses, walking with a fast straight walk, still at the waist so the hips subtly swung. It was a rhythm he got to know. The girls were always quite different to me, but they contained my flavour for a brief moment, he said, like the smell of a seashell or a school book sends your whole childhood unravelling in one speeded spool of memory.

Almost a week went by without Laurence and I calling one another. I stilled my mind with work, and entering the sterile hush of the lobby on 69th Street, I thought that the Grubers' was barely a life, vacuum-packed on their inhuman avenue, and I pitied them for living without church bells and detritus, and for being beyond love. In spite of the staff and private lobby, the bug exterminator still visited the building weekly, and Heinrich displayed his sexual needs like a hormonal pubescent.

Heinrich nuzzled my neck. I freeze-dried my mind.

Laurence went home every evening to see his wife. The hurt was sharp and animal, all rejection pitching into a past we don't understand. He in turn accused me of indifference, and the intensity stealthily returned, as though what we had was established, that sinuous underground urgency. Yet I had never even kissed him.

Such courtship was like a story in a child's book. Once, when I was in high school, there was this girl, Cathy, and she and I loved each other like passionate sisters. We used to leave each other daily notes: every lunch hour I would find a letter from my Cathy, and I would drop one off for her. We used the teachers' mail boxes. She was Mr Gates and I was Miss Canelake. We wrote our notes in mouse handwriting on scraps of paper, screwed them up and put them in the back left hand corner of the mail boxes, so Miss Canelake and Mr Gates would never find them. Sometimes there were two notes. Occasionally there were mouse-sized presents: a seed pearl, a Raisinet. All morning I invented sentences in my head for Cathy, and as I approached Miss Canelake's mail box, my pulse quickened in anticipation.

It was like that with Laurence. His communications to me were sidelong. He built a box of anticipation, and then revealed inventive trapdoors, so each day was circumscribed by expectation. Then he left blanks in between. Days of nothing and disappointment.

He often called me from work, but he preferred circumspect routes, unrelated to extra-marital subterfuge, which caught me by surprise. He signed erotic notes 'Katharine Holden', and had them delivered to our house. I found a letter addressed to me one morning on a row of desks at the front of the general reading room. It shocked me, that he had been there already, and taken the chance that I would find it. He sent postcards with the most mundane of enquiries. We had impossibly early breakfasts in diners near the river; we had supper at 21. We took the A-train to the Cloisters so we could talk; we walked, weaving away from the dealers on Bryant Park on days I was working at the library.

The presence then of Laurence in my life, the sad crumbs of a relationship that I accepted made my mind light-headed. He was a tumour of distraction pressing against the functioning part of my brain.

I wanted to imbibe particles of his flesh. I loved the essence of him, the brown cleanness, the different scents of his hair. I watched the way he couldn't sit still, beat a drum tattoo on any hard object, turned on electrical appliances, played with Mimi's popcorn cooker, bent Venetian blinds to look distractedly out at the street. It was charming only because his smell and his voice and his oddities of speech were compelling to me; in anyone else, it would have irritated me to nervous exhaustion.

But I would have crumbs. I would have crumbs of him. Bitty cake crumbs. Rabbit's droppings. I buried my head in a gauze filter of forgetfulness. I would not think about it. I lived day to day, scratched up the crumbs that were pushed through my door. I would think about it in the fall. I would forget him in the fall.

'I think you're highly exotic,' he said.
    'Thank you.'
    'Kiss me,' he said.
    'No,' I said.
    'Why not?'
    'Because you kiss someone else.'
    'You don't?'
    'Only sometimes.'

'Don't you want to kiss me?' he said.

'I don't know,' I said, and I leaned over and touched his lips with mine, just brushed the flesh to taste it. He quivered. My mouth opened, and my heart was beating fast. I pulled away, and sank my head on his shoulder, and we hugged, we clung to each other. My breathing changed.

'You're the most erotic thing I ever saw,' he said.

'Thank you. What do you imagine us doing together?'

'I'd like to have you behind the trees at the Cloisters.'

'Uh huh,' I said. We were walking around the park one free lunch time. 'Anything else?'

'I'd like – ' said Laurence. He walked a little ahead of me, by the old Wollman Rink. 'I'd like to fuck you stupid in broad daylight by that rather quaint zoo just up there.'

'More,' I said.

'You would be wearing that skirt, the black one, skimpy thing, and those tie-up shoes, and . . .'

'Would we have a polite type of blanket or would there be thorns and wild grasses?'

'Latter.'

'Would we whisper and melt into our surroundings, or would we be discovered by a buggy load of tourists?'

'Some adolescent children would be spying upon us, and they'd be affected by that moment always, their – what do you call it? – their sexual identities formed by the primal scene they witnessed on Central Park.'

'Would you kiss my neck, perhaps?'

We walked around the dilapidated rink.

'For infinite hours.'

'I think a policeman might surprise us.'

'That's right,' he said. 'Just as we were hurrying back into our clothes – '

'Grass-strewn tights stray on the grass – a plodding policeman lumbers up with a gun and gives us a mild but exciting caution. And then as the policeman's broad back disappears behind the – the sea lion enclosure, I begin to breathe on your neck, and opening up your shirt, and lingering above your belt, I pull you down on me and we become hidden in the grass behind that wall, and the dusk wraps us, and we're oblivious to everything but the sounds and the scents of each other.'

'Yes, yes. Can we go and do it now?' he said.

'No.'

'Why not? There's time. The zoo is this side.'

'Because I'm not going to fuck you, my darling,' I said. 'Remember.'

I thought that this was what madness was, the slow chemical corrosion of the brain by lust. I sat in the library and I plotted further adventures for Loulou, of an increasingly fabulous sexual nature. I made patterns on the metal shades in the reading room, my finger pads pressing on the surface; I sat in a daze; I looked at the clock and saw that I had been dreaming for twenty-three minutes. I had written no words in that time. My mouth hadn't moved: it was slack. My eyes were cow blank. I was almost dribbling. I was a dullard, dulled with desire.

I sat there, on the chair, the cloistered shifting of readers around me, and my vulva was a sliding clot of liquid, a queasy hormonal roll, as though on a ship on a mercury wave.

By the middle of the month, if Laurence had walked in there, if he had run up through Astor Hall, and just casually walked through the door, I would have stacked my papers, marked my place and drifted over to him. Moving tacitly together, we'd go to the bathroom.

I was so wet, I needed flesh inside me. Fingers, his penis, hard inside me. I needed it to roll and tease and tamp that fluid I had created. He would pull my panties off in a wringing wet strip in the bathroom, and test my vulva with a finger, pulling the tip along it so I was tickled and cat-stroked and my nerves flared into bloom. My breathing would be thin, light with impatience, and the feeling, when it came, would fill me, the forgotten bulk edged with the pain of the angle, a ring of tightness near the cervix, and then the fucking, his cock inside me, flush against me, fucking.

I murmured in the library, emitting just the tip of the groan that was inside me. A few times I went to the bathroom and sat on the toilet and made myself come. My finger slid and skittered. I feared people seeing my feet arching and vibrating under the door so I pulled them up. I rammed two fingers inside myself, biting my scarf. I wafted my fingers around later, the smell of my own lust echoing that of the old books: subtle parchment thick, a cream-coloured scent.

Loulou became a raging nymphet, her activities sketched with the insect scratchings of distraction.

I was permanently glassy-eyed and jittery. If I did not see Laurence, I thought of him, and so I was plump full of him, and seemed to bestow some sexual gift of which I was largely unaware, the response surprising and extreme.

It was like being a child with new shoes: all day the leather's waxen sheen is a glossy reminder of happiness, and then the shoes are placed by the bed to be within reach during the night. I thought that such dream-like happiness was only possible in childhood, diluted by adulthood, and that I had lost it when I was seventeen. Then I tasted it again.

Walking through Central Park, before the humidity rose, we were at our most peaceful, because that was our garden then, our hour's eden. I saw his tangled elfin bloom of skin at those times, or weather rough, and he was at home among the foliage and the mulch of dells. I would have meandered along the same paths – the Flintstone boulders at the southern end, the Mall, the boat house – but he had energetic visions of new and complicated routes away from set paths, ignoring danger, and so we snatched our existence.

'Don't you think,' I said, 'that when you're happy, you

hardly know it – or you *mistrust* it? But in retrospect, you know it intimately.'

'Oh, yes,' he said. 'But – it's like grief – better than being bored. At least it's *interesting*.'

We loitered under the trees, absorbing the shade, anchored there against the sun. The leaves made rippling patterns on our clothes.

'It contains its own shadowy insurance policy,' I said. 'If you worry like hell that you'll lose it, then you secretly trust you'll keep it. You know – it's thought the only people who know how to be truly happy are children, people in love, and the terminally ill, because they all live in the present.'

'We're happy, aren't we?' said Laurence, encircling my waist suddenly.

'Yes . . . Yes,' I smiled at him. 'Maybe we shouldn't even think about it,' I mused. 'It's just our century's preoccupation. And . . . you're married.'

'You take me back to the past,' said Laurence. 'It's odd, makes me feel very young, because I remember when I saw you. I was about twenty-three, and just in New York, and I had that feeling you have when you first really take in those streets – that was happiness – and I saw you, I saw the glorious girl getting into a taxi in a blue coat, I remember that dusk on the Upper East Side, the grandeur of the buildings, and the girl, and how differently I thought about my surroundings and how my life would be. So you remind me. You have a something – I think you'll become somehow famous.'

'Do you? Oh, I hope so. Then I can take my revenge on Heinrich Gruber. Leave his house and have him up on a sexual harassment charge. I'll talk about him on television. And then, one day, I'll be too rich to remember him any more. Do you think that's mean?'

'Yes,' said Laurence, shrugging. 'I love it. I love you.'

He said it casually. We walked along the dells between the Flintstone rocks; we didn't touch each other at all. I could not speak because of what he had said. I glanced at the shape of his hips, his neck, the way all the parts of him were linked in motion as he walked – so clever, the body's mechanisms – and I knew that later I would recreate this in my memory in the night.

We walked all the way up to the fountain, keeping to the shade of trees, emerging to heat. We ploughed along, barely talking. I searched for words. My skin was damp.

'I can't even say it,' said Laurence at last. 'There is no point.'

'No.'

We kissed each other. We were talking, and our lips touched each other's, seemingly accidentally as they formed words, among the trees by the pond. The knowledge that I was kissing him came to me with a time lag. The flat alkaline chill of his saliva contained a shock of intimacy in the hot weather. We sipped kisses, we pressed our lips against each other, open and still in patterns and angles, a new flavour and unknown register.

I could not quite believe it was him I was kissing. It was strange underwater kissing, hidden in trees. People were emerging from the Mall, but no one seemed to see us. I skimmed his top lip with my tongue, I pressed its tip against the centre of the lip, and slowly met his teeth, soft against pearl. My tongue moved inside. He pressed against me. I made him stay there, held him still with one hand. I explored the corners of his mouth; I made him remain motionless while my tongue brushed the outer edges of his lips. Our tongues met, that blank meld of blindness that turns slowly to heat, and we opened our mouths wider, harder, and we couldn't stop.

And then, in a restaurant, some hand, some shoulder, was always pressed against the other's, the evening slipping into darkness – a purple darkness – and I knew the inevitability of us being together. It was only a matter of time. He rarely spoke of his wife. At night, I was sickened by my attempts to think about them, jealousy a pussing mastodon crashing through my brain.

It was a hallucinatory time. I couldn't keep away from him. I tried to. We couldn't leave each other alone. He took time off work. We met in strange places. The sky was overheated. I felt drunk, my body light and tense.

My longing to see him became a sickness. I was oxygen-blown, I was barely functioning. The euphoria was sewn with nerves, my stomach nauseous over delayed phone calls or detected hesitation. I loved him in a way that I had never known.

You spend the rest of your life trying to recreate such madness, such richness.

I tore around the city catching cabs I couldn't afford, running along the street to pay phones, strung with sleeplessness and perpetual anticipation. I would abandon food, work. I would run for a cab in fear of minor subway delays, the relief of securing one, finding locations after snatched instructions, seeing him pacing ahead of me on the sidewalk. I buzzed with tiredness, leaping from bolted food to assignations, lust just in front of the brain, every move lined by sex.

It is horrible. You pine for sleep and stability. There is acid in the chest cavity, a race horse of a heart. And yet you know, then, that you are living.

And later, you're glad you had that time, for all its pain and adrenaline, at least once in your life. You had that time, returning home as the birds are singing in the early hours of the morning, and waking when everyone has long since gone to work. Your skin is bad; your flesh is transient, pounds tumbling off.

I didn't do that when I was younger, when I was sixteen. I was a girl who worked. I was a girl who pulled herself in under a sheet of hair, and concealed herself there, in the private scents and whispered codes of her own body, writing plots and notions, and whose boyfriends were distant flirtations and ravished her only in her mind.

With Laurence, I was an adolescent reborn. I stopped everything.

One morning in late July, he called.

'Can I see you?' he said. His voice was like a physical presence.

'When?' I said.

'Oh – this morning,' he said. 'Could we meet this morning?'

'I have to meet Sophy on Central Park South at one,' I said.

'So let's meet now, soon. I'll meet you in half an hour, forty minutes.'

We suddenly couldn't think of anywhere geographically logical to meet. We came up with hazy locations, blanks.

'Oh, look,' said Laurence. He was speaking fast. 'There's a deli on Union Square. I don't know what it's called, but it's on its own on the east side, just a horrible standard deli, browny coloured. We can have coffee there.'

'OK,' I said. 'I'm all dressed up – I have a work lunch with Sophy.'

'I don't care if you're in your pyjamas. Just meet me.'

I ran onto Sixth Avenue. The heat was humid and lead gritted. And so we met at a brown and speckled place of gravy lighting, and I was dressed for lunch uptown, I wore a white crêpe blouse that ruffled limply at the neck and at the cuffs, like a flimsy French poodle. I had to wear a bodice underneath its near transparent fabric. I was faintly sweating by the time I reached the deli. As I arrived, I could see Laurence's features in the tobacco gloom behind the windows.

We hugged each other for a long time. I smelled his body. My chin was pressed to his neck.

We sat down and I looked at him. I thought that I loved this man. The skin under his eyes when he smiled at me. The particular manner in which he said hello to me. It was complete. It was precisely pleasing to me. We smiled at each other, and I had a stirring of premonition, a knowledge of something I might feel for the rest of my life. It made me calm. So I moved, I sat down, with the ease of dream movement, when you can run down a hill as though the air were butter, and travel blood warm passages in your sleep.

We smiled again. We kept smiling at each other as if in agreement, this calmest of knowledge mutual. We called for coffee, and I waited for him to speak. I was primed. When deep calm is shot through with arousal – the certainty of coming to orgasm, the warm laps stacking to fever – you can do anything, you can play with the moment, there is only certainty.

The ceiling fans stirred the muddy air, but it pumped in rhythm with the subterranean gurglings of my mood.

'I dreamed of you,' said Laurence.

'When?'

'Last night. That's why I called in the morning.'

'I'm glad you did.'

'You were in my dream. I think of you. I try not to.'

'I think of you while I'm in the library,' I said. The ceiling fan stirred the neck of my blouse. The sweat on the back of my neck, at my hairline, was made cold, in patches, bars of sweat and chill. 'In the reading room. And as my pen forms lines, scribbles, your voice laps over the edges of the pages. I hear all its cool British.'

'I'm glad,' he said.

'You distract me.'

Brown mugs, ice water. I moved my fingers over the cup's rim. He lifted my fingertips and flexed the hand, the pads of his fingers meeting mine. Nerves sliced the calm.

'This ring,' he said, 'It's very nice. A rosebud.'

Our hands played, fingertips, like dabbling water.

There was a grease-smeared menu. Around us, old folk ate gefilte fish, cheese on pumpernickel, eggs and pancakes, such huge greased mounds. The sunshine was a flat blind on the windows.

'We have an hour,' I said. I glanced at the clock.

'And then you have to go uptown.'

'I wish I could get away from the city,' I said. 'I'd pay dollars and dollars to dive into cold oceans.'

He was silent.

'Well . . .' I said.

'I can't leave the city.'

His hand was twitching, as though it was straining to reach for a cigarette. He was wearing a blue shirt that day, muted sailor colour, he had loosened his tie, but he was clearly dressed for work.

'You seem to be able to leave work – frequently,' I murmured.

His gaze appeared to hang sightlessly around my midriff. He seemed nervous. There was that endearing quality he possessed of which he was probably unaware, the solemnity of the mouth that reminded me of an East European youth, an apparatchik etiolated with political passion, yet hurt, yet vulnerable, the poetry beneath the call to arms. His forehead and eyebrows were older. He was expressive, rude, he made me laugh. But when he was quieter, I knew all his vulnerabilities and I wanted to vanquish his enemies, tell him I was on his side for ever.

'Why can't you leave the city?' I said. I made a groove in a paper napkin with my nail.

'My wife. Carolyn, she – can't get more time off this summer. She's pregnant,' he said.

Blood pumped into my ears, deafening me.

I opened my mouth.

Time seemed to be pinned against a wall. 'Pregnant?' I said after a moment.

'Yes,' he said. He didn't meet my eye. 'Quite – a lot.'

Realisation spread through my scalp in a hot stain and down through my head and neck.

My lips slackened. I couldn't disguise it. I looked away from him. The restaurant turned white. It moved around me in fast motion, a speeding blank sky.

'I – ' I said. 'Well, I didn't – I didn't know you were going to have children. You never said.' I looked down. The grain of my silk sleeve click-framed itself on my mind with surreal clarity.

He looked like a snake. Shifty. His brutal male mouth. All male, male, snake in the grass.

I couldn't believe it. The blood in my head still pumped sickly. I felt like a child. I felt an utter fool, such a fucking fool.

'I didn't ever not say.'

He made one pathetic attempt only, like a bullying boy caught pants down at the scene of the crime. He had the staring blank eyes of the accused.

He shrugged.

'I'm sorry,' he said. 'Look. God, I'm so sorry about this. You see – '

I was silent. The tiredness of my dead-end work and of fighting to Park Avenue through that weather came over me; I fought a contraction in my throat.

'You have no obligations to me,' I said. 'Why should you tell me that? We don't even really know each other.'

I stood up. I gathered my work case and my little black pocket book that my father gave me when I was a girl, and I left the deli.

FOURTEEN

The skin is quite plastic now. You can shape a woman in many ways. The flesh is a building block.

If you insert a scalpel, puncture, sew, you can enlarge the breasts, expunge signs of ageing, create a false spring of blood and anaesthetic.

I only had one time in my life when I cut myself. There are features in women's magazines about it, so others do it too: it is a syndrome. I drew the knife across the back of my arms, it scored white lines on the skin, but it didn't penetrate. I jabbed and skewered. The pain was so good, so sharp, ooh là là. It pranged and rang against the pain in my head, wrapping a fire blanket over it. My eyes winced.

Now the pain in my face has subsided. There is a fatty numbness. I feel as though I have flu. I walk around Paris and my face does not quite belong to me, a senseless bulb upon a stalk. You go to the dentist, and afterwards you feel like a halfwit with one bloated jaw, but no one notices the difference, the squeezed-out voice, the paralysed nerves. Same. The gardiens look at me, see nothing much out of the ordinary. On the street, I can sail towards the most populous of tourist corners, the workers' junctions, and no one notices the woman with no feeling in her mouth.

So perhaps I fail to notice there are women beaten by their husbands, their bruise patterns cosmetically disguised.

I stayed in the apartment for some weeks. I tried on skirts. I didn't work for a while, though publishers' messages ran in sequence on my answering machine. The press agent fixed up an interview for me which I missed.

I was beginning to dream a new strand of feminism. The ideas trickled vague but luminous, like Signor Gramsci in his prison.

All losses are restored and sorrows end.

Spindrift of new ideas. A sweet sense of mañana in the air. I looked out on the airport haze over the city and longed to go to the suburbs.

There is after all a world of mopeds and Turkish bars here that is beyond me. I am too rich now. There is the Red Belt: Bagnolet, the gloomy problem townlets which nurtured the French Communist Party. And a life beyond the obvious Sarcellism and sprawling suburbia outside the southern Portes of Citroën garages and DIY outlets and the rougher inner areas north. Boys in bars and Arab corner shops and rabbly Portuguese restaurants. I know so little of it all, because I live by the Luxembourg in scarves and cabs.

I wondered whether the young photography student would like to take me out to the suburbs on a moped. His pals would be equipped with mopeds, if not him. He could dream up some social reportage project in gritty monochrome for his degree – graffitied warehouses, deprived babies, blank eyes, no doubt – and drink engine oil coffee with me in a shuttered RER outpost.

I saw him finally, the photography boy. He was emerging from Gibert Jeune with a bag of books.

My face was still somewhat swollen, but it lent me an air of plumped-up youth, I felt. The bruises were wraiths in harsh light: I had stepped up my foundation. Eric looked uncomprehendingly at me for a moment as though I were a stranger, but he had not seen me in a while. He hesitated and reddened, just faintly, with realisation; he looked like a butterfly in blue wool. We went to a bar. He had been with his friends, but he left them, to cut his lectures and visit a bar with me mid-morning.

The buses came up from Porte de Vitry and Gare de l'Est. So much chatter, the leaves and rain on the glass section of the roof. We sat at a table by a pillar, so it was more enclosed and sealed from the light. The shape of his skull was fine and blunt. The slightly Oriental curve of his cheekbones, his long grey eyes, his grubby fingers, made me think of little Tibetan children.

'I feel we haven't met in a while,' I said.

'Where did you go?' he said.

He wore chinos with the navy wool, and battered sneakers. He sounded faintly accusatory.

I raised my eyebrow at him.

'I haven't seen you since May,' he said, as if in explanation.

'You haven't?'

'No.'

I was silent.

'I had a little rest,' I said. 'I needed a little vacation.'

'You look very well,' he said politely.

I laughed. 'You have good manners. Does *Maman* insist upon them?'

He reddened and frowned.

'No scowls in the morning!' I said. 'Not allowed until early evening.' I took his hand, and played with it on the table for a moment. He was good-looking, in an intense and enclosed way, French, shadowed. He looked darker than he was with his defensive play of shade and mood. He had the Gallic thinness of youth and cigarettes, but his muscle tone was pleasing.

'How have you been?' I asked lightly. 'Who have you followed?'

He grinned slightly. The lips were dark red and still a little uncertain with youth. I wanted to make him smile so his face would slip into radiance. I wanted to unknot his eyebrows and lift his mouth.

The bullet rattle of the fruit machines behind us rose to a clamour.

'The *Rentrée* is upon us,' I said, glancing out of the window. 'All the little students back, going about their business. They look happy. It's exciting for them.'

I ordered a Terrine Quercynoise. He ordered an espresso and inhaled his cigarette.

I smiled. Sun was coating the rain on the trees. He became more beautiful, Eric, there was a perverse beauty to his overgrown eyebrows and stubbled shadows in the sunlight. He looked tired, as though he had been drinking. I wondered whether he was a small part Algerian.

I was suddenly happy. My face felt tight. I brushed my jaw in passing, and I couldn't feel the jowls that had formed in recent years. My heartbeat was conflated. If Eric looked closely, he would see where I had been stitched up, the porcelain doll's face attached to cloth and stuffing. The stitches were recent; the sutures still pulled my cheeks a little too tight.

I caught a sense of another time. I was reminded of being in my twenties in New York, and sitting in bars, and Laurence Mahon teasing me, and other men looking at me.

I turned back to Eric. He was watching me, as though he could decode the thoughts behind my pause. I smiled at him. I caught his eye. He was moody, intelligent, and infected by high ideas.

'I finished *Loulou*,' he said.

'What are you reading now?'

'The second – '

'Your studies are progressing well?'

'You mean, in your work, or . . .?'

'Your *Loulou* doctorate.'

'Yes! I love them. I think of her as you.'

'Well – you're not the first to say that. But thank you.'

There was a pause.

'I'm going to invite you to my apartment,' he said suddenly.

'Are you?' I said.

Unaccountably, I felt a slight lightness between my legs.

'Yes,' he said. 'I'd like to take your portrait. And – And I'd like to invite you to my apartment.'

'Where do you live?' I said.

'Rue Xavier Privas.'

'Where?'

'Off rue de la Huchette.'

I nodded. 'Near the dear, adorable little Ionesco theatre.'

He tapped his cigarette. He looked me straight in the eye. He projected the strange grey of his irises. 'I can't wait to photograph you,' he said. He looked at me again. 'I can photograph you on the roof. The towers of Notre Dame are behind, the domes of the Panthéon and the Sorbonne.'

'We must hear the same bell sounds, and you are way down the boulevard. You must sense the river, where you are.'

'I only just moved there,' said Eric. 'I used to live in a dump on rue Monge. With a friend. I have this to myself. Me and the cat.'

'What's the cat called?'

'Minette.'

'Of course.'

'So . . . Madame Meier – '

'Adèle.'

'Adèle. Yes. Do you feel well enough to have your portrait taken?'

He sounded faintly sarcastic. I looked at him without smiling.

'Do you?' he said insistently.

I looked out of the window.

'Give me two weeks,' I said. 'And then I'll visit you on rue Xavier Privas.'

He nodded. He paused. 'Good,' he said. His features took on the glow of his smile.

As I walked home, there was an unfamiliar nerve plucking my cheekbone, as though a nestling creature was in there, just waking from hibernation. It went. My heart beat as I walked down the boul' Saint-Mich'. My walk was sprung. My hair blew back. I caught glimpses of sculpted angel wings sprouting among the leaves and railings of the Luxembourg.

FIFTEEN

I knew after Laurence and I stopped seeing each other that my life wasn't normal. I sleepwalked through my days. I lay in bed all morning, and I knew that regular marriages and happiness were for other people, and that however many men had claimed to be in love with me, their feelings were a forgery.

I was loose-jawed after that. My face went to marble, then to putty. I walked along the street, my mouth hanging open with the weight of grief and exhaustion like a halfwit child.

The heat was soupy. August, and everyone was out of the city. There was a muffled punch of air at ground level, no shade under the skinny trees that lined the sidewalk on West 13th. The city had reached the point of steam bath, eruption, when everyone is close to actual craziness. The Grubers were in the Caribbean, Helen left to go to the beach for two weeks, and Mimi was in Rhode Island. I stayed on alone in the apartment. I decided to ignore Katharine Holden, not even to greet her on the stairs. I slept in all the beds, and I dropped my clothes all over the apartment so I had to weave through bathrobes and underwear and scarves to cross the room.

I stayed on all that August. I rose early to dress in the shade. The air conditioning units rattled. The dog clawed faintly next door. To me, alone in the apartment, the garlic string wallpaper in the kitchen looked shabby and sinister, no longer quaintly fifties like a cake bake ad. I let Helen's and Mimi's mail build up downstairs. Katharine Holden put a note through my door, and I stuck it on hers face outwards without even reading it. I caught cabs instead of taking the subway the few times I went out, so I could dive from my doorway into an air-cooled box.

I lost it after Laurence said he and his wife were expecting a baby. It set off echoes into chambers that I couldn't follow. An awful symmetry loomed at me, too overcast and neurasthenic to absorb. I thought of all the men, and how I was supposed to torment them, but how they were ultimately in control. They wanted me in the beginning for certain flavours, they said, for the extremes and oddities, for all that was volatile or charming or disturbing, and then within a month they wanted to dampen it all down. They hinted that I looked trashy. The very clothes that had once intrigued them they wanted left at home.

Ron Birle gave me a ring I refused to wear, and then he slept with a freshman from law school, and I forgave him. Then he slept with his sister's best friend, and he blamed it on me in a squall of accusations: I didn't love him, I abused him, I drove him to such actions. I never talked to him again. Then Peter McAllister claimed he loved me for several years though he wanted me reined and scrubbed and cotton dressed, and so I tired of him. Men said I wasn't available, and that my attention was elsewhere. And so we parted, and I was left on my own. I shouted, I walked out on them, and punished them. I always fought back, because I would never become a victim.

Then Laurence Mahon: I met him, he seemed to pursue me, he gave me intimations of love, and he was married and about to be a father. I was as naive as a child who has been coddled and hit.

I started to work.

The heat rose in a tropical fog. I stayed inside. I sat there watching the minutes on Helen's alarm clock, and didn't leave the apartment. My heart thumped in anticipation of the buzzer – I was a sick woman, a lunatic from the mental hospital awaiting food through the slot – but it never rang. All day, I imagined Laurence might turn up.

I went out and walked up to the next floor, creeping past Katharine Holden's, and pinned my head against the window on the landing. The glass was sooted. I pressed my head against it, my eyes rolled liked a calf's trying to watch the sidewalk below without being discovered, but I could only see a wide angled slice of tree tops and cars parked along the street.

I wrote notes, strange inconsequential scratchings that may have contained hidden flavours, the way such notes do, and would be decoded in sobriety.

I reconstructed *Loulou*. I wrote it out of despair.

When Loulou was formed in my mind, it was as though she was a character already born, my early nurturing of her so vague. Someone else had seen her through the messy stages of her development, and she came to me in the space of minutes, it seemed, gloriously accomplished, growing sharper edged and more complete with erotic possibility in the weeks that followed. I always thought that it was like stumbling upon an invention while thinking along different lines, an accident of electricity or aerodynamics for which you were only partly responsible and could never recreate, and which grinding effort only served to prohibit. I knew later that you are only given one Loulou in a lifetime, if you are lucky. Or perhaps you are luckier still if your progress is slow and organic, and frustrating, and old age sees a late blooming. Loulou was a blue rose who grew in a hothouse.

When I finally wrote *Loulou*, I completed it very fast. I wrote it in despair at being left by Laurence, at being twenty-six, with none of my chaotically fabulous plans fulfilled. I wrote it in drugged excitement, because Loulou could not stop, because she put a rush of ideas in my head, expressed a dynamic that was purely mine, my invention, and yet Loulou was my America, my new found land. I wrote for weeks, and I hardly went out, and I shuddered to think of how other people had always sustained me.

The Grubers returned tan from their vacation. The apartment on Park Avenue was uniformly icy.

'The beautiful Adèle,' said Heinrich, portly and relaxed, as he slapped through a cupboard for his sports kit.

I looked down at Sophy's desk, and I was ashamed. My face was white and uneven. Its milk bath texture had gone, like the nacreous coating on a false pearl peeled to expose grey plastic. I was the other white, of pasty dull girls, earth grubbing and unpleasant.

'You're very beautiful,' said Heinrich, by rote.

'Am I?' I said.

My body was slack. I turned just as he emerged holding his sweat shirt. 'The music has gone from my Adèle's voice,' he said, and then he kissed me for the first time. My mind in free fall, I tasted the whiskey edge of mature masculinity, and after that, the bland plumpness of his lips. I hesitated before I pulled away. I turned my back on him until he left.

Laurence was in the very same city somewhere, and a foetus became his child.

Doom smells rotten. I caught its scent in my daily life, the shadows that seep behind the conscious brain. I knew that something was changing. Heinrich and his fleshy cohorts swarmed like fruit flies. When Laurence left, I resisted them less, in my ugliness and uselessness.

Heinrich felt entitled to stroke my buttocks through my skirt when I rose from a chair. I looked out of the window, thinking about Loulou, at the rich emulation of humdrum life on 69th, its brownstones and strolling people; I sat at Sophy's desk the other side to calm myself with the volleying uniformity of Park Avenue.

'Are you busy, Miss Meier?' said Heinrich.

Sophy was out of town with her mother. Heinrich came home early, as I had half known he would.

'I'm writing out the fall pay rolls,' I said.

'What a peaceful afternoon.' He paced behind me. I focused steadily on my paper. 'I closed an – an important deal today. I awarded myself this afternoon. The weather is fine.'

'I'm happy for you, Heinrich.'

'You're not yourself,' he said. I heard him scratching his head behind me. My heartbeat immobilised me. 'Who is making my wife's little friend sad?' he said.

'I have to finish these lists,' I said.

He brushed the top of my hair. My scalp tightened.

'I've always wondered – *who?*' he said.

The door's double locks clicked as the weekday maid let herself out.

'Who's your real – love?' said Heinrich.

I was silent.

'Who – who cares for you? In all this time, it's *men*. Not a man . . .'

'I don't know who cares for me,' I said. 'I'll be all right on my own.'

I caught his eye. His shortness gave him the air of a rubber doll. His boy's bangs contrasted with the maturity of his skin.

'There'll be no one who – Who else feels for you like I do?'

He caught my shoulder and drew me gently back against him. I rested there a while, my chin tilted up, the traffic rising from Park Avenue, and his thumbs sank into the tense hollows below my shoulder blades. My body slumped in warmth.

'I really love you, you see,' he said behind me.

'Do you?' My eyes winced with tears. I leaned back against him again momentarily.

He kneaded my collar bone, working his way down, methodically, rhythmically, over my ribs until his fingertips just skimmed the border of my right breast. I trembled in slow panic. Perversely, the lower half of my body lightened, I became aware of my breathing, as though it were controlled outside my body, and his movements grew more persuasive, insistent in their path downwards before he pulled back. And I knew then that I wasn't good enough for anyone else, and I was almost aroused, and almost nauseated, and in my panic, in the alien cologne smell of him, I looked forward to it, as one looks forward with dread to duty.

He guided me into one of the children's bedrooms. He removed his spectacles. He moved down my neck, wetting me with a firm tongue, kissing me roughly on the mouth, palming my breast. He breathed in sharp spasms, the whiskey hormones dredging further depths. His breath blew heat into my hair. He had my panties off in two movements. I focused on the candy-coloured drapes of the bedroom, the saliva below his lip blown up wide screen in front of my eyes, my body tense. I started to panic, turned and tried to push him away, but he was steel-sprung in his absorption, his eyes dark points never catching mine, his penis glimpsed in its white rearing, and I said no, the skin of his neck sealing my words, and as he was about to enter me, my body slackened, I turned my head from him, I sobbed and sobbed.

I left the Grubers' that evening, and Mimi wrote to Sophy saying that I wasn't going back. I stayed in bed.

The crowds returned to the city in September. It was hot, but the heat was high sky heat that didn't punch you into a foetal ball.

The new season had started, the TV and theatre premières,

the academic year, and everyone back in town. I asked Helen and Mimi to answer the phone. When our father left our home, it was like that. My body was dead.

'This is a sickness,' I said to Helen when we talked for the first time. 'It's a stupid little virus. Just treat it like that. Don't worry.'

Laurence went to Europe. My favourite waiter at the Russian Tea Room told me. I was furious that Laurence had been in the Tea Room without me, contaminating the place with his presence.

'Who was he with?' I asked.

'Pardon me?'

'Who did he come in here with?'

'He was alone, Ma'am,' said the waiter. 'He came here on a Friday afternoon.'

Laurence was in Europe. He would be on a night train, passing through Belgrade, Zurich, Paris. There would be dark blue windows and small tables. I sent him love on the night train: the moon on his window was love.

I hoped the train would be skewered on its tracks between Graz and Prague. He would die in the cold. I would wear a black pillbox hat with a net veil at the funeral; I would look much better than 'Carolyn'.

Cathy from high school was probably married by now. Lorna had stayed in Paramus where her relatives lived, and married a man from the Fire Department. She had two baby girls. She and her husband talked in the evenings and took their little girls on shopping trips. They were rarely grey on Sundays. Whereas I had scads of men loving me like monsters and hating me for not giving them my life and my face and my focus, and then marrying someone else.

I knew the way in which Laurence loved me. It was not entirely healthy. I glimpsed it in men. I sewed hooks and springs in their bloodstreams. I saw Laurence wrapped in those snares, but he shot me from inside them, he caught me too. So he loved me for what I stood for or for how I seemed, the way other men did, but beyond that, beyond all that, I thought he understood a sedimented layer of history that I hardly remembered myself. He knew me in an uncanny way: my tricks didn't work on him. The simple devices that reeled in most men charmed him as a child charms an adult but they didn't work on him. I had no weapons, only myself.

He was going to stick with his wife Carolyn. The things he had said to me, the love he had told me, nudged at the nausea that always rocked inside me. I grew thinner. The spiders of hope that used to crawl up my scalp – he loved me, one day he would leave his wife – had died. Only one little baby, almost an egg – he had gone to the Russian Tea Room on a Friday – stirred minutely in unguarded moments in the night.

One day I ran into Laurence Mahon outside the public library.

He was coming along the street from the 42nd Street entrance, walking with that particular sprung stride of his that suggested he had too much to do.

I was strangely calm. There was Laurence. There he was, as I had seen him many times before. He looked up, he looked about, and then he saw me.

'Adèle!' he called from a distance. People in front of him turned round to look at him. He waved at me fiercely; I was on the steps; he waved again, and ran up to me.

'Hello, Laurence,' I said.

'I was looking for you. God, I've found you!' he said.

'Were you?' I said. I was utterly calm; he couldn't get me any more.

'You were in Europe,' I said. My voice seemed dull. Marbled clouds were scudding over the sun.

'Yes,' he said. 'You knew? While I was there, I . . . Let's go somewhere where we can talk.'

'Not again,' I said. I felt tired. 'What's the point? Were you on a night train?'

'Yes . . . Two. Why, Adèle?'

'Oh, I don't know,' I said. 'I thought you might be.'

I looked down the street, confused with cloud shadow.

'I'm so *glad* to see you,' said Laurence.

I looked down again. The shadows streamed over the steps.

'I'd – I'd like to talk,' said Laurence. He sounded nervous. 'Just for a while.'

'Is there any point?' I said.

'Yes,' he said. He linked his arm with mine. My arm felt dead. We were walking through the crowds on 42nd Street, towards the bridge by the station. He guided me into a coffee shop, one of the overpriced travellers' traps by the station; or we guided each other. My body was indifferent. I was with Laurence.

'I wanted to talk alone – and we end up at Grand Central Station!' said Laurence. His voice was croaky; he spoke quietly.

There was a moment of silence.

'I wanted to ask you, Adèle,' he said. 'I wanted to ask you to come away with me.'

'Away?' I said.

'Yes. I want us – I want to be with you. I want to be together. With you, I mean. Please. I'm sorry.'

I hardly heard him. He still couldn't get me, couldn't hurt me again, because that part was dead.

I didn't answer him. I just looked at him, and it was like staring at a picture. There was Laurence Mahon's mouth, there was Laurence Mahon's hair, all in the right place. The face that had hung in my mind, just in front of my day-to-day vision, superimposed on everything else, and there it was, a cardboard cut-out. It didn't affect me any more.

'Did you have a good time in Europe?' I said.

'Yes,' he said impatiently. 'I thought of you. I had business – Germany. I went through Austria. I looked out at the fields, and I thought, this is amazing, this is where Adèle Meier was born, this is where she lived, a little girl, Adela. She played in this country.'

I made a small laughing sound.

'What are we going to do, Adèle?' He put his fingers through his hair. He lowered his head, looking at the table.

'Nothing,' I said.

'I want you to be with me.' He sounded desperate, like an adolescent boy. Or perhaps he was merely demanding: a spoilt rich child.

We were silent again. The sounds of the station bubbled behind the glass, a blur of voices rising solidly. 'What do you mean?' I said.

'I went mad in Europe. I've been thinking about what to do.'

'You're with your wife,' I said. I felt calm. 'You told me your wife was pregnant. Then we stopped seeing each other. Is there anything else to tell me? Anything else I don't know about?'

'I've got a daughter,' he said. He looked down at the table again. 'She was born last month.'

I suddenly thought that he was going to cry. He had lost his certainty, and therefore his charm.

'Uh huh,' I said. 'Congratulations.'

He looked up at me. His mouth opened. He looked ugly, as though twisted with pain, unable to control his features. He looked like a melodramatic old movie actor.

'She's called Melina,' he said.

Some rumpus of hooting and shouting started up on 42nd Street. It seemed laughable, suddenly, to be sitting in a sordid hole on 42nd Street while Laurence told me about his new daughter.

I ordered a coffee. 'Laurence,' I said. 'I'm sick of the crises your life seems to be composed of. They're nothing to do with me. I'm *not* your confidante.'

'Oh,' he said.

'These minor passions of yours . . .'

'They're not bloody minor,' he said. 'For God's sake! I've been looking for you since I came back. I knew if I walked by the library or along 57th or 13th I'd see you at some point. I stopped by your house a couple of times.'

'You lost my phone number?'

'You never answer the damn phone these days.'

I looked at my watch. I kept needing to take a deep breath.

'What are we going to do?' he said. 'I'd like it – I'd like us to escape from the city for a while.'

'Take a little vacation?' I said.

He half nodded. I laughed.

'What a cool idea, honey,' I said.

He laughed. We both laughed. I felt a shock of tears suddenly coat my eyes.

'You mean, you want to wind this all up again and have an affair with me?' I said. 'I've already told you what I think about that,' I said. I was distanced from the tone of my own voice. The calm had broken, and I was trembling.

'It's not what I mean,' he said. He shook his head.

I was silent.

'I don't mean that,' he said.

I looked at him.

'If I hadn't met you, I'd have probably stayed with her,' he said. He sighed.

He seemed reluctant to talk. He talked slowly, he stopped. 'I probably would. I don't truly love her. Carolyn, my wife. But – anyway. I met you. Anyway, I – you know, I *love* you,' he said.

He sounded embarrassed. He seemed like a boy again. He looked at me pleadingly. He was still ugly, distorted. I thought how ugly he was sometimes. His stubble stood out, darker than his hair, and there were shaving spots near his chin, and he looked glassy as though manic or morning tired, his eyes narrow and uneven.

'You want me to have an affair with you, don't you?' I said. I flicked some ash off the table. 'You want us to fuck our brains out, don't you, honey, as a little excursion from the dull nuptials?'

'No I don't. Come away with me,' he said. 'Let's go up the coast.'

'No.'

'OK. OK, I probably would have had an affair with you,' he said. 'I'd have done that until about a month ago, and stayed with her – and had it – both. I've got Mel – I've got a *daughter*. But then I knew – I completely knew what would happen. I knew, when you didn't call me any more, and I felt so completely bereft – '

'You didn't call *me*.'

' – And then when the train went into Austria, I felt as if I was losing my bloody mind. If I could have sent you a telegram from the train right then I would have. I thought of jumping off at the nearest one-horse station and ringing you, but I knew you wouldn't pick up the damn phone even if I did.'

He paused. He looked down. His voice was quiet, as if suddenly aware that there were people around us, people reading newspapers or just sitting there idly looking about. 'I couldn't just have an affair with you,' said Laurence. 'That'd be – impossible. I'd have to leave her, because I'd be too jealous.'

'Excuse me? Jealous?'

'Of you.'

'*Me? I'm* not the one with a lover.'

'No.'

'You are outrageous. You truly are.'

He was silent.

'Have you had affairs?' I said eventually. I sounded tired still. 'I mean, since – you married.'

'Yes. One.'

I looked at him. I raised my eyebrows.

'There was no question – I'd never have left for it,' he said. 'I mean, I'd never have left Carolyn.'

'But she maybe thought – '

'No.' He paused. 'Maybe.'

'Is that all?'

'Yes. And a one night, one night with somebody.' He paused. He looked grey. 'The one night thing, it was quite near the beginning. It was unforgivable. I was away. I told her about it, much later. It was unthinkable. Awful.'

'The affair?'

'Last year. Last year . . . the end, end of the year, October, November. For a month or five weeks. I already knew things weren't right.'

'And that's it?'

'Yes.'

We sat there. He said nothing. A waitress came and wiped our table.

'What are we going to do?' he said.

'I really don't know,' I said vaguely.

'God,' he said. 'You could make "Pass the salt" sound provocative.'

'Why?'

'Everything you say sounds like an invitation. And then a little veil comes down at the end of your sentences.'

'So you say.'

'So come away,' he said.

My stomach seemed to be separating from its walls.

'Where?' I said eventually.

He shrugged. 'Where? Up the coast. We'll go to the sea and swim somewhere.'

'That's all? We leave town and wife and book and *child* and, and – goddamn architraves, and swim?'

'Yes. Doesn't that sound the most wonderful thing? You and I swimming.' He looked tired. He looked at me through a haze of tiredness, and the cigarette smoke in the coffee shop, and smiled at me directly for the first time. He hadn't looked into my eyes. He had been oblique, embarrassed.

'Let's just buy some tickets and go,' he said.

'What are we going to do?' I said at last.

'I'm going to leave her,' said Laurence.

My stomach plummeted sickly. He looked serious. I dragged my mind beyond disbelief.

'What can I say to you?' said Laurence. 'I owe you such terrible sorries. I owe you – I'm so sorry not to have told you everything. She was pregnant. I tried. Let's go away.'

'I'm going to have to think about this, Laurence.'

'Are you?'

'Yes.'

'Why?'

'Because – Of course.'

'I mean this,' said Laurence. 'I'm going to leave my wife.'

'Are you sure?' I said.

'Oh, yes,' he said. He looked inexpressibly weary. 'Look, whatever – whatever happens, I'm going to have to leave. Whether we're together or not, I shouldn't be with her. I know that now, because I met you. I'm going to leave – you know. Now. I have to. So I'm going to leave, tonight, tomorrow, I don't know, the end of the week – we have to talk. But it's you . . .'

'What?'

'I'm leaving her. This is beside . . . I'm asking you – to come away with me, you know, be with me. I love you so much –' he reached out and touched my hand. 'Please, Adèle. I love you. I can't be without you. I really tried.' He put his head down on the table. He looked pathetic, reduced, pleading.

I looked down at him coldly. I touched his sleeve. I stroked the hairs emerging from his cuff. Hope rose, surfed and pumped air through my head.

'All right,' I said.

SIXTEEN

The light in Paris was sharp and high enough for my portrait on a roof in the Cinquième. And so I went to the young Eric's house. We drank coffee and spirits high up on the roof. He had some foul beer called 1664. He showed me his portfolios, his aggressively trendy monochrome wisps and distortions. We argued about my portrait after I saw those.

He lived on the fifth floor, with no elevator, on a pedestrian street of couscous joints and piss-wet gullies. It was cobbled there and medieval, the chicken and sediment of Paris before Haussmann. You had to walk past a huge slumberous dog on the steps of his house, the stairwell swelling and contracting before it narrowed to the roof. The apartment belonged to Eric's uncle's wealthy boyfriend, and so it was in the tourist area where no one in their right minds would live, suspended above clamour and cooking vents and students, louche things wanting sex, hardly the descendants of the young monks who once scuttled there. Eric was house-sitting the apartment with his cat for the academic year while the boyfriend was out of town.

'You are a beneficiary, Eric,' I said. 'This is a miniature palace – a student palace in the very centre of the student area, so they will all come to visit you. You can throw parties on the roof.'

When I arrived, he smiled, he jerked his hair off his forehead where it habitually loitered, took my hand on the stairwell and led me up the steps to his sitting room with its skylights cut in an unevenly sloping ceiling and its exposed joints and wind chimes. His hand was hot and rough. The bedroom was a mezzanine up a ladder with a futon, some beer bottles, an abandoned lens. We climbed past it, out of a window onto the roof.

There was a breeze up there, though the day was hotter than the days had been, the restless air of height.

'Look, you can see right over to the Bois.'

I pointed to the west, beyond the river's snake glint. 'The courtesans used to walk there, and meet their friends. Some of them used each other as literary muses,' I said.

'I could borrow my friend's car – drive over there,' said Eric.

'That would be adorable.'

Seagulls dive-bombed the river. The door buzzer kept sounding. Various people came up to the roof. His friends Vincent and Philippe, and Monique and Mariette, who was beautiful, a *poupée*, Mariette. I looked at her and admired her.

'You see. They all come to visit you. You have the palace.'

Eric smiled at me across the roof. More young men turned up. I looked at them all, but I preferred Eric. My Eric probably traded Ecstasy pills and any number of misogynist vulgarities with his teen friends, but beyond that, he was sensitive, and he was a fantasist, and he was just a little arrogant.

When the crowds had finally left and there were bottles stacked by the dried-out plants on the roof, and the light was still fine, we played with shots. I hid and emerged and half shadowed myself. He panned into the horizon and came close up to my face. There was only a tinge of a bruise colour under one eye, and the scars by my ears had turned girl pink before they dulled to white.

'You are so beautiful,' he said once, from behind his camera. He sounded as though he hadn't meant to say it out loud.

'Thank you, Eric,' I said.

He reached out and held my hand to steady me down the last steps of the ladder, and his hand clung to mine quite hard, blood warm.

I looked out of the skylight at the metal-clad chimneys.

'Can we take more?' said Eric. 'A different – you know – series. A new theme.'

'For your college course? "Today's theme is woman as natural object against backdrop of urban alienation . . ."?'

'No no! For – itself. For you.'

He looked at me. Self-consciousness flitted across his show of boldness.

'Yes – Darling,' I said. I was thinking about a new book I might write. Strands of invention twitched silver filament behind my eyelids. They disappeared.

'Good,' he said. 'I'll devise it. I'll compose some shots. Thank you.'

He reached out as if to shake my hand, but we held hands, and he was trembling very slightly.

I hadn't been listening to him. I looked up and registered him and smiled at him. His wool grey eyes had gathered intensity. I suddenly knew that he wanted to kiss me.

I caught his eye and my mouth opened.

He leaned towards me.

'Eric.' I ran my hand across his face with its supple skin, the odd spot a crater of surprise in its perfection. 'I don't play with children.'

I kissed him goodbye on both cheeks.

I could do anything with my face, anything at all. If my lips parted in quarter profile, my vision angling down as he shot me close to, the chin did not pouch in counterpoint. It pulled in new places, but it was fresh and tight, a little swollen, the tightness and the swelling blending together in a new palette of youthful characteristics.

SEVENTEEN

A bunch of lavender hung just inside the closet in our room in Cape Cod. I saw my skirt beside it, my black net skirt like a Spanish dancer's, and it looked Moorish and crushed against the chalk white, the lavender. Laurence's clothes spilled over a bottom drawer, not yet properly folded, all those natural fabrics he favoured, the faded sea grass cottons, sheep-coloured wool, stripes. We had merged in the room, the first time, married.

The old paint colours were coming through later coats, blue beneath the grey on the guest house's outer sills. We ate and the sun disappeared and left only a suspension of day in gold and then grey in the room, and our words were disconnected, our voices slurred and thinned as though we were drunk, that drowsy evening talk when relaxation is as close to arousal as it is to coma.

We washed our hands together in the sink in our room. I sat down on a little flower-painted stool, and I almost slept for strange linked moments, coasting a wave of exhaustion. Laurence put his arm around me, and I came to suddenly against his shoulder. He was stroking the area behind my ear, round and round with the slightest touch, following the outline of my ear and dipping below it into the hollow behind the bone to linger on the skin.

I quivered.

He played on and on. He said nothing. He knelt on the floor beside me. I leant against his shoulder, and his fingers moved steadily, lightly, his tendons flexing only faintly against my back.

'Just stay here. Rest,' he said.

His touch became lighter, disappearing then returning to trace the elaborate paths where my ear met my face. He explored the outer tendrils of my hair, and trailed his finger to the top of my spine, ran it along the downy nape of the neck and below, to the swell of my vertebrae. I shivered. It was the lightest touch, his middle finger running up and down my neck for minutes on end, dipping to the top of my spine. My skin tingled in a ghost trail after it.

I thought of Heinrich Gruber suddenly, and I froze. Laurence hesitated, but I leaned harder against him, for safety, pressing my face into his shirt, my neck arched and bared towards him, and I gripped him tighter to me, enclosing his back in my arm as he skimmed that same path until my scalp was netted in a sneezing contraction. It was light with the frenzy of one tickled.

He held my head and looked at me. His head dropped slightly, he glanced at my chest above my dress, where it was white and hinted at the swelling of the breasts. We were aware of the faint voices of guests on the pathway outside, the blue-black sky. The flag was fluttering out on the deck. I heard the wooden pole easing in its socket in the breeze.

I wound my hand up his sleeve, to touch the hairs of his arm. He looked at me again, as though observing me from a distance. I couldn't smile: it would tear the surface tension.

He undid the top button of my dress.

'No,' I said.

'No?' he murmured.

'We must be very patient. Do you think the owner is on the deck?'

'What'd she be doing?'

'Whale watching. Looking for Moby Dick in the night.'

'Do you think she knows we're up here?' he said.

'Yes. I think she knows everything.'

We heard her words floating somewhere below, in the house with the front door open, or in the garden. She was talking to her girls, the women who lived in the basement and operated the washing machines in part payment of rent. I heard them replying to her. A light came on above the deck and marked our floor through the screen windows in points like bright sand.

Laurence shifted so the billow of warm air between us was compressed and laundered.

His towel hung on a hook on the door, carelessly draped. Our room was like a sailor cabin. The lamp light was low and tallow coloured. The paintings were all of shells and sea grasses and tide woods. A church steeple rose in a black slant to the west, through the small window by the bed. Years had worn the brown shellacked floorboards to soap ridges and hollows. It was our home, the storm windows raised, evening air fitful through the screens.

Our movements were careful and spidered. The room became darker, the people less present, the night drawing in and enclosing us. His mouth crept along my leg. I sat there, my limbs careless on the floor, like a calf's, and he dragged heat up my legs, he travelled so slowly, so slowly, insistently, as though he was water suspended, he would not deviate, the movement was buoyed. My legs eased to different angles. His hands moved slowly up the sides of my thighs, warming me and sending a ripple through me. He washed Heinrich away.

We kissed then. Our mouths met, by chance, in the dark, and our tongues crowded, we were ragged and wet. He prised my mouth open with his kissing. He flattened my mouth.

'Come to me,' I murmured. 'Come here now.' But he wouldn't, or he didn't hear me; he stroked me, he held me still on the little stool and composed trails of sensation on my thigh, radiating to my pelvis.

'Come here,' I said, louder. I made curls of his hair. I dug into his scalp, ran my nails along it. I dipped my palm under his shirt and moved over the hair of his chest and edged towards his nipple.

'Be patient,' he said.

I wanted to twist open my legs. I was moaning. I didn't know the noises I made, I heard them in fragments.

I planed from frustration to calm. A breed of slow ecstasy grew from such tension. We haunted each other in the dark. We twisted suggestion over each other's skin. There were cinders pricking us, but we couldn't see them.

I undid two buttons of his shirt. My nails rested on his belt, and slid beneath, and moved minutely within that space between belt and flesh.

He undressed me in glimpses, so when my dress wrapped the stool, I didn't know it had fallen, and he carefully unhooked my necklace, my skin hot on my chest against his fingers as he pressed the clasp and twitched the chain.

I let my hand drift over his crotch, my nail trailing over the weave of the cotton. The longer he pinned me to the stool, the more flutteringly and insistently my nails juddered over the cloth. I sensed the hardness compact. He tensed. He kissed my breasts where they swelled above my bra. I dabbled my fingertips in a pattern – a scale, a child's spider wave; he arched towards me so he would be enclosed in my hand, but I pulled back, I resisted, I tapped the same soft tattoo over and over, rain pats first on the window before it streams, and I wouldn't take it, though he strained, though I wanted his penis so badly, to encircle it with my hand, to have it as a living object I had never seen, never felt. I wanted his lips on mine, his tongue inside me, on me, travelling further down, further and further.

His hand was on my back. 'Let me see you,' he said. 'I want to admire you.'

Then we were on the bed, fluently and suddenly, his hands lifting me by my buttocks.

'I want to see her,' he said.

So she lay on the bed for the first time with her flesh exposed. The bleached wood ached in the sea wind, the fireflies butting the screens. His hand slipped and hooked beneath her underclothes. The alignment of her body on the bed changed; she seemed to be alone for a moment, in a still cradle of thought removed from him.

There was a pale yellow light, candle-coloured, that came in from the deck. It lifted her skin to a new transparency, as though a sheet of wax lay beneath it. Snail trails of sand scrolled her ears and the pink of her membranes.

When they both lay still, her nakedness was a milk-white shock.

'I've never seen you before.'

She glanced down at her breasts. She considered them as she had known men consider them, her eyes slanting in a shallow sweep down her body.

She looked young, spills of brown hair over her face. There was a blue-green translucency around the eyes like veining on pebbles. She didn't know her own youth.

She was like a postulant scrubbed and possessed, lying on a palliasse in contemplation. Her skin was the gift she couldn't give, the flush and liquefaction of the flesh denied to her. Her mouth was a serious pink petal placed just so on her cold complexion.

There was a disturbing suggestion beneath her porcelain precision. You wonder whether the silk she wears is crumpled; you look at it, and it is not after all. The question tails away, leaving only a void where the suspicion once lay.

The whorish undercurrent was but a ghost trail about her. She was a little dead. She pinched and ravished from behind her strange passivity, her *petite mort*. She sewed knowing

227

looks like dimpling smiles, as though she could play with abstractions in her insouciance, irony flirting with excess.

He took her to him so they lay together for a while. They were as slotted as shells. They kissed in a dry staccato fashion, the momentum briefly suspended. She stroked his chest, covering it, planting small kisses there. He lay very still, he watched her, their eyes meeting in the blurred blackness of babies' eyes, and slowly his hand moved. The trail of stroked nerves spread to a haze of sensation. They pulled each other closer, they lay hugged and entwined.

They talked in clusters of words mouthed into each other's ears, as though clarity of meaning would break the incantatory drift of movement. They kissed for minutes, their mouths frantic and open, and her breasts brushed ghost shapes past him, so he felt the swelling as she moved against his chest, and reached to still her and stroke the flesh. He told her she had seashell nipples.

He was erect against her thigh, she could feel the dampness and the excitement of his flesh. She sucked his nipples in small movements. She ran her nail down his back, returning, skimming further down; she scratched the dip at the base of his spine where it tapered to his buttocks, her finger focusing on that crest. He moaned almost silently, it emerged as a vibration against her neck, nuzzling the white flesh of her shoulder.

He could hardly think. He was thick with arousal. He could thrust or spill. She was like a scratching pliant girl. He was frantic with the desire to enter, to take, his lips and his chest and the lower part of his body on fire as if he could douse them in whiteness. He hesitated in the face of her fake passivity. She had such knowing stillness, it was almost remoteness. She was pink and white on the bed, her hair brown twists on the sheet, she was all shadow and glow and artery, not to be touched. The base of her pubic mound was narrow and yet quite prominent, so it rose in a small fleshy cushion, self-contained, her thighs white and sculpted beneath.

She kissed him. She tasted sweet, she tasted neutral as saliva; the richer strands of sex she preserved and revealed much later.

They entered another plane. The steady bulk of the landlady mounting the stairs, the flush of the toilet, were absorbed into a world that was skewed, in which they were uncertain of their orientation on the bed, or beyond it, among the trees of the deck and untethered by sex.

He was different, in the way that men are when they are erect and as vulnerable as boys with sticks, and sinewed and Biblical and alarming. She absorbed his tonal darkness, how his head hair graded into his neck.

'We are different races, look,' she said.

He glanced down at their legs. He laughed, planted the laugh on her shoulder and ran his tongue down to her nipple, sucking it hard. She jolted. She took his penis suddenly in her hand and caressed it, ran her fingertips up and down its length and held it firmly, and her row of nails shone as pearls in the light through the window. He pushed further into her hand. She felt his penis firmly, rhythmically; she dallied and teased the tip.

There was a release of sweat on his forehead and his chest. 'Please,' he said.

She trailed her nail lightly around his foreskin. He moaned, his tongue rough and fast over her nipple. He jammed his penis against her hip bone, his back tense, his mouth moving fast over her face, her lips, her neck.

She wanted him inside her, but she resisted. The bead of liquid inside her had broken and spread, edging her thighs. The shaft of his penis was pressed between her hip and her pubic bone.

He teased her in return, taking slow detours, he opened her legs and examined her vulva, his face so close to her that his breath stirred her pubic hair, she felt its warmth cover her. She was aware, momentarily, that there would be sand left over from the day on the beach, but he was breathing over her, letting the tip of his tongue move so near her, so slowly, she was unsure whether he had touched her or whether it was his breath that covered her. She opened further. Her head moved to one side, rocked against the sheet.

He tickled. He inched the lips of her vulva very slightly apart with his fingers, and his tongue tip explored, whispering and rough like a cat, it lingered there in spasms of contact; she drew in her breath, she uttered small pink sounds; his tongue tip flitted over her flesh, and he wouldn't go closer to her, though she pulled his head towards her. He sank into her intermittently, his tongue widening and sliding over her, so the sounds she murmured rose and thinned, and her vulva moved to meet his mouth, sand hidden there in particles of friction, and he moved closer, finally, bathing her membranes with his mouth, moving inside her to taste the flat metallic liquid that lined the passage.

'Come here,' she said.

She licked inside his ear, she ran her tongue light but thunderous inside, talking to him in distortions while her hand drifted almost imperceptibly downwards.

She lifted her pelvis. The head of his penis was hard against her vulva. It moved almost clumsily, to press against her in staggered steps, that moment suspended, hardness, merge of pain and pleasure; she barely remembered it could be so hard. Stretch and a release, a momentary dazed shock that something so large and alien could be inside, pressing the rectum, more extreme than in the memory, the tensed membranes, the dull bulk that fills and stretches as it blanks sensation.

They moved, they moved and twisted, and sensation took on a planetary ease again, lost to hours and darkness, in which they heard only the sounds of their movements.

She thought of him beside her so many times on a New York street, and here he was, on a bed inside her, and she flexed against him and embraced him, tightening her muscles around him to draw him inside her body, and she found new strengths, dark and surprising in all that slow pallor. She eased him over, she seemed abstract but she was persuasive, she took him inside her more deeply in new and acute angles that caught her breath. Images of him on 13th Street, of him leaving her, returning to her, came to her elliptically when she planed and paused, and then her mind was scattered with thrusting, and sweat covered her chest and made strings of her hair, and they moved in a frenzy, they could smell each other, they brought the salt of sweat to the other's lips, they bit and tensed and arched.

She was liquid and changeable under his hands, then she would spread her net of wiles to combat him with sudden assertiveness. The reality was shocking to him too, in its urgency. They said they loved, loved. She would speak between frenzy, her words punched and swaying, her breath becoming thin, and they were aware, on some outer level of hearing, of the sounds they made in that tent-like room, of how they built heat and noise and movement to a frenzy. She pressed his anus, hard, with her nail and he strained further inside her with his penis and cried out, he reached inside her until she was partly numbed, tendrils of orgasm threading the numbness. He told her to lie on her stomach and he entered her from behind, he probed her with his fingers, tapping against the vaginal wall. She moaned in dribbled cries onto the sheet.

They reached new boundaries. She trailed her fingertips over her legs and married his juices with hers. He moved slowly towards her vulva. She was swollen, exhausted, but each touch was a rash of friction, releasing liquid heat to seep through her, crawling and receding and teasing. She cried out from somewhere outside herself, from behind her head in a spatial plane of spasm and trance, and it engulfed her in its dark sore ecstasy.

EIGHTEEN

'You know, I'll always think of you when I wear this,' I said to Laurence Mahon, when he gave me one of his old T-shirts once for a nightdress, and I did, I do.

I woke up in it on my bed in Paris, it fell in folds over my nipples as I lay there, and the notion of Laurence made the skin leap. I thought I might see him soon.

It was a sunny morning. I felt I was the same, nearly the exact same person I had been when I woke in this T-shirt in rentals with Laurence all over town before we bought the apartment on Gramercy Park. You do not change inside. You are eighteen for ever, but you look through grimed glass that dulls your skin to the world outside. Lying still that morning, I felt the drowsiness and aroused limbs of late summer on the ocean.

Once, many years after I had been there, I saw Cape Cod from the air on a flight into Kennedy.

'Just below you to your left, you can see Cape Cod on the Massachusetts coast,' came the pilot's voice, official and casual, and I saw it laid out like a map, a freak of brilliant sunshine, blue and white and sand. It looked as though that whole peninsula was sand, not grass and streets and houses, and I saw the exact places we'd been. I couldn't bear to see it, to know that once I was young and very much in love on that coast. Looking down on Cape Cod from an airplane, the waves rolling oblivious, like a travel brochure of white and vivid blue, was one of the hardest things I did. It weakened me, flying over Rhode Island, shuttling across Jamaica Plains, and left me with a knowledge of what sadness is: family and death and wasted years.

At home in Paris, the pigeons mechanically rotated their wings as they chuckled and gobbled, tails wedged against my windows in paintbrush silhouettes. I watched them from my day bed, like an old black and white art house movie without meaning or sound, a dull farrago of repetitive motifs. My face relaxed in the morning light.

My apartment had fallen into clutter drifts since I returned from the hospital. I saw iridescent dust slants pour onto my clothes. Breakfast cereal was glued to dishes. I wandered through my apartment in my underwear: a new bra of grey velvet with small soft tassels, like a lampshade; I wore it as a bikini in the sun angling off the Luxembourg; I ate olives and mixed small drinks, sweet condensed peach juices, dessert wines, shots of grenadine, I who rarely drank, and I took another vacation there in my apartment above the leaves and stone deities of the public gardens.

I plotted some adventures. I was not working. I never listened to my press agents' messages, never called the Danish journalists back nor opened the charity requests and cheques made out to me. My pen was still. The same slow dust falls coated it; it remained motionless, while my brain was a glinting thing. Young Loulou, that temptress, had grown up in my mind until she was rope-veined and mundane, and had walked away into some suburban house party where the outré is tried and tested and scandals are fashioned in a catalogue. She had gone: it made me happy. I could no more resuscitate her than could some syndication agency, some cartoonist or ghost writer. As I sat there in the high solemn light of Paris, conceits hallucinated: sunbursts and lanterns and green green grass.

I wondered then where my Papa was. He could be anywhere, or dead. How can you become a separate entity from the man whose sperm you once were? How is that possible? It makes me want to scream in despair. The man who donated me his DNA walks this world, oblivious to his daughter, Adèle, here in Paris. He must have seen my name sometimes; he must have wanted me back, but known it was too late. Or perhaps not, the handsome older man, the dark haired European in America, with his arrogant nose and his General's chin, he knew it was too late and he didn't care, furnished as he was with his women, always the same age as he grew older, his pride, his soft pressed grey pants, his piano, his grammatical stringency, his three languages, the uptight chalk-dust parochialism that tinged all his urbanity.

His daughter Adèle is trilingual, like him. Three languages, and a face that snares.

The phone rang. It was the boy photographer.

'Mlle Meier – Mlle Adèle, I'm trying a new monochrome paper – high contrast, dramatic. It's a fibre paper.'

'Yes, honey,' I said.

'So,' he said. 'Could I – How are you?'

'I'm fine, Eric. How are you this week? Are you working hard?'

A pigeon backed away from another, its rump pressing into my glass with a dull plump.

'Quite hard. Yes. Could I – '

'But this is interesting. Who gave you my number?'

'Didn't you? I think . . . Didn't you?'

I scraped some polish off my nail. I made a jagged track in the middle of the red and smoothed out the serrated shaving.

'What do you want to ask me, Eric?'

'I'd like to photograph you.' His low boyish tones were hesitant.

'That might be OK. In a couple of weeks. But no boring old regular old portraits – we don't want that, do we? Life is about constructing themes, and symphonies. Artifice! You can create trompe l'oeils with your Nikon. Do you agree, Eric? A series needs to be broken into themes.'

My themes are Oriental. I think we need to go out to the famed bridge at Giverny and sport with cliché, or build a catena of paper. With his ink and snow paper we can print the contrasts of skin and hair and brow in severe apposition. Veils will provide the middle grey. You have to unwrap the subject with your imagination, so there is suggestion even in starkness, confabulation in clarity. A double take, a visual slip.

I am becoming accustomed to this new face of mine. It stabilises in my incubator of private sunshine. Its essence is quite different.

I wonder if I ever will see Laurence Mahon again. I suspect, without the ballast of reasoning, that I will. I sense his presence.

But my Laurence was a long time ago. My Laurence, my Laurence. People called him that: 'your Laurence'. For a long time people asked me about him, as if we had been irrevocably joined, and I was pathetically proud that we had been associated together so strongly, that it was not a product of my imagination. This was proof after all. The pride was a kick in the teeth of sadness. I hated Laurence then, and wanted him to die.

It was a long time ago, after all. I have met different people since then. And sometimes everything is all right, there are rich flavours out there, surprising my dulled mind, washing their colour over me temporarily before receding again, and I sit there and I pine. Inevitably the others fade, and there is this space again, where Laurence once sat, becoming a ghost, hard to retain. If someone says his name casually – like the title of a book or a household object – I am amazed, as though they have seen my ghost.

The fact that he hasn't gotten in touch with me fills me with blind amazement. So when people refer to Laurence I am shocked. Why would they be asking me? Did they really see us walking together, he and I, did they see us from the outside? A regular couple, walking together? If that is so, then why doesn't he call? Other people can see what I can see. He invalidates everything, as though I dreamed it all, I was a hysterical child clinging to him and he never loved me, just tolerated me, then abandoned me as soon as he had a chance.

Sometimes I think it is normal. Laurence does not call me because we both know it's all past, we are both adults, we have gone on to different lives. But how can he do this? That time was richer than anything he can know now.

The film is turning grey. The print is an old one, it has scratches and areas of fading.

So I saw the young student, with his thinness, his grey eyes and heavy brows.

My face was shiny. There was not much experience there. It was a shiny egg face. Flesh draped over a wig stand with a store front stare.

I went to Eric's apartment again, roosting above the absurdities of the Latin Quarter. I climbed the dipping stone stairs and stepped over the St Bernard. A fly hung near its tail.

The apartment was more tawdry than I had remembered, tablecloths and quilt covers sporting the cheap dulled primaries of the supermarché. I went to use the bathroom. A cockroach scuttled behind the sink stand. I noticed Eric's shaving cream, its wet canister suggesting recent use.

He was sitting cross-legged on the floor frowning over a lens bayonet. He had some music on, a drum heavy something with a demented beat.

'Will we use the roof today?' I asked.

'Uh uh.' He shook his head and pointed to the corner, below one of the skylights. 'I've set up all the lighting. I've been using other models to experiment.' He smiled. 'It's all ready for you.'

'You'll need to make minor adjustments for me?'

He nodded. 'Of course.' His squatting hips were narrow. He wore faded bluejeans, with patches on the sides and knees reduced to a trellis of white thread.

He took out some tobacco and expertly rolled a cigarette, still twisting the lens. He seemed more at ease. He spoke while focusing on his camera equipment in a fluent and inconsequential monologue, glancing up occasionally to smile at me. There were two little Erics: smiling radiance; nervous intensity.

He repositioned a tripod. He rolled up his right sleeve. His arm floated under the light and became golden.

'How old are you, Eric?' I asked.

He paused. He looked at me, frowned. He hesitated again. 'Nineteen. The week after next,' he said.

'So you are eighteen.' A smile bubbled through my chest. I wanted to laugh. 'You must dodge your military service.'

'Would you – ' He shrugged. 'I was just wondering if you'd like to come – if I have a party.'

'To a nineteenth birthday party! What should I bring you as a present? Would you like a new lens – wrapped up in a bow? But Eric, I hope you . . . have other hobbies. It is your youth, after all, and though it's admirable to be passionate about something – I *despise* dilettantes – I hope you have nice times too. Girls and drinks and new adventures. Jumping on trains with skis and backpacks, and – and ransacking this city for all that's not apparent to the lazy eye.

'Where do you want me to sit? Do you think that paper looks Oriental?' I frowned.

'Yes, I think so.'

'It looks like a pure product of the Occident to me! It won't have the delicate shape-shifting qualities we require. Are you trying to emulate the great Madame Yevonde, by any chance? Because if so, you need to do it more convincingly. She is something of a genius.'

'But, Mlle Adèle – '

'"Mademoiselle Adèle" – it has poetry built into it! You know how to do it. This is a goddamn mess – if you don't mind my saying.'

I went into his bathroom. I asked him for extra light, and I made myself up. I dressed myself in an expensive student's garret in the Cinquième. Little Esmeralda and her dancing slippers.

I mixed an impasto of kabuki base: stage powder thickened with a touch of glycerine. I moisturised my face with a heavy duty cream, and then I layered the powder very precisely. My hair I sleeked back and combed with gel and moisturising solution until it possessed the heavy straightness I desired: it was classical, centrally parted into two ebony wings. My face returned to a heart, Snow White. Mute cherries, black lacquer, salmon silk. I spent forty minutes on the mouth. I could always paint my face. I was taught, and then I enhanced the lessons by trial and experiment, and I never required the make-up artists the TV companies foist upon one. I painted my nails a dark petroleum blue with metallic depths: they had grown long in my greenhouse, protected from my keyboard.

I walked into the main room. The light had fallen.

'Eric!' I called. 'How strange it is in here. How lovely . . .'

He stared at me. He looked for a long time, and then he was all smiles. He had changed his shirt, I noted. He smelled of an unusual aftershave, something dark and woody like bark or church incense.

'Look!' he said.

'You have transformed it all! An Oriental transformation. I want to sit there now, in the little glade.'

He seemed excited, the child. There was a jerky fluency to his movements.

He had added blown-up lanterns, and draped surfaces of paper of a finer grade. He had slightly adjusted the lighting.

He relaxed. His shoulders softened.

He put the Allegri *Miserere* on his CD player.

He reached out and held my hand. He pushed himself beyond his nerves into boldness; the mental process behind his actions was quite apparent to me. He placed me gently on the seat he had fashioned me. I smelled his skin heated by the photographic lights. He was agile as he moved around, crouching, mobile on one knee. He could slip between lights as he could occlude himself between cars and buildings.

'May I see your Polaroid?' I said.

He handed it to me. I was shocked. Geisha doll, cherry blossom details and china stamp of mouth. The shade and light was a stark punch, even behind the Polaroid's grey dulling. It was suggestion, the landmarks of a face, Loulou grown.

'*Les Enfants du Paradis*,' I said.

'Baptiste or Garance?' he said.

He swathed me in more light from a reflector. He had never seen me so white, so strange.

'You look so . . . Absolute,' he said.

He took four or five shots consecutively. He seemed to be able to say such things from behind the camera; it lent him power and refuge.

'Have you ever modelled?' he asked dispassionately.

'No!' I said. 'But I'm used to the camera.'

He was eighteen. A boy! A tender sly youth! It seemed beyond the realms of the probable that he would notice me.

I skimmed my hair with my nail, loosening a strand, just to see.

He reached over from where he stood. He put it back in its place calmly, without hesitation, the touch of his finger echoed in the gel's cold settling. He positioned more paper, in sequence, and as he leaned back he redraped the silk on the shoulder section of my wrap. He was becoming bolder.

'Eric . . .' I said.

'. . . Yes?' he said.

'What do you want to do with me?'

He blushed a painful red and pinned his face against his viewfinder.

'Oh,' he said. His voice took on a humiliating echo of the castrato.

'Mmm?'

'I'd like – I'd like to take you out.' His voice now stumbled drily into gruffness.

My heart softened.

'Oh, Eric,' I said. 'I meant, how do you wish to take my photo now?'

He froze. The flickering red of his face became steady, like frostbite.

'But – sweetheart, of course we can meet for a petite crème after your classes,' I said.

His rigid frame relaxed minutely. He started shooting photographs, very swiftly and abruptly. I moved, I responded.

'Come here,' I said. I took his hand for a moment. 'Don't take things so seriously, Eric. You're young. You're meant to be wild and unconcerned!' I trailed my thumb over the back of his knuckles briefly.

He looked at me then. His hair flopped; his mouth was slightly parted; there was a light release of perspiration on his upper lip and forehead.

'Will you go out with me, then – to the cafés?' he said in a low and considered voice.

'Oh, yes,' I said.

He reached out and touched my knee, just softly, where it

was covered in layers of silk. I sat there. I didn't move. His hand rested on my knee with a surprising firmness of intent. My blood pumped in confusion.

He looked down. His brown fringe flopped and obscured one of the stern bas-relief eyebrows. He glanced up at me. He reddened again, the febrile young teenager. 'You're the most . . .' He tailed away. 'I ever saw.'

'You have to fill in the gaps, Eric. I'm not clairvoyant, after all.'

'I mean . . .' His voice was hurdling octaves again.

'No,' I said. 'I think I know what you mean.'

He lifted his hand slowly from my knee and repositioned it precisely, as if every movement were choreographed. He placed both hands on my seat, his wrists lightly tensed against the cloth that fell over my thighs. His touch was firmer than expected, just as his voice sent low vibrations through a thin frame.

'Eric, darling, don't do this, don't be so serious all of a sudden. You can't come this close to me with this make-up on. In any case. Can you?'

He raised his head, and as he did so, our lips brushed, just the outer edges of his skin catching my lipstick. It sent a small fan of warmth through me.

He hesitated. His grey eyes seemed to lose their focus; he came towards me again.

I stroked his arm. 'We must finish our photos,' I said. My voice was light honey.

When I returned home that night, Laurence was on my answering machine. It sent cold tapping up my spine and into my scalp. He and I were always a little psychic with each other. He was bluff, gruff. How are you? He would call again.

My life surprises me. My life has always surprised me. I never had a ten-year period of sameness. Others have that gift: family, home, dog, love, child, boredom. Even the inert periods – mental phlegm and head cold – finally heave their tails and flick.

In the night, I suddenly remembered the women of the Upper East Side who had had their faces lifted. I had forgotten about them. They had been a passing image in my youth, without emotional resonance as I ran past them for Sophy Gruber. The iron-faced matrons flashing calculated crimson animation: shark grins of effort stretching their features.

Such faces are strangely torpid, the flesh half paralysed into puppet skin. I remember it now. The hair sits uneasily atop like a teased and tufted wig. It no longer seems to fit, the strands by the ears dead transvestite locks. I remember. Progressive operations have a strangely masculinising effect, female curves tugged into androgynous planes of flesh.

It is the eyes above all that come to me now. They are widened with simulated youth and yet precisely blank, a dull dead glitter. And eventually the surgical interventions create a homogenised tribe: women who resemble each other, sisters under the skin.

I never thought to question those looks.

Is this, then, what I have done to myself?

In the early hours, I thought I heard the phone ringing, but as I walked out of the bedroom, there was no sound.

There was something thrumming behind my cheek, as though I had been numbed and become accustomed to it, and had forgotten I would ever feel again. It bled into my dreams. It was five in the morning. My skin was stirring. There was a harsh prickling.

I called the doctor's offices at eight o'clock. I went to see Dr Kreitzman about the pain.

The pain was my face in recovery. Dr Kreitzman and I

decided I would have some skin resurfacing. There were a few problem areas that needed clearing up.

Resurfacing the skin erases wrinkles. The patient is sedated and anaesthetised while the surgeon sands down the top layers of skin with a diamond fraise, a pad covered in diamond dust attached to a rotating motor.

After dermabrasion, the face is covered with a dressing for twenty-four hours, the area then dried with an air dryer.

The process leaves the treated facial areas raw and shining, bright red. The sides of the mouth and eyes, or individual problem areas, are flayed. Ice packs lined by lint must be applied to the wounds. Antibiotic ointment can be applied locally, and antibiotics taken orally.

The patient must then take painkillers before scrubbing the dermabraded areas herself whenever they begin to heal. At regular intervals in the day she stands in a hot shower for twenty minutes, allowing the flow of water to soften the scabs, which are then removed with a rough face flannel. The face bleeds. It is washed gently with a soft cloth and covered in a thin layer of petroleum jelly.

The scabs reform at regular intervals. The flesh around the eyes swells and can cause temporary restriction of vision, and the patient experiences the sensations associated with severe burning. The mouth cannot be opened as the skin will crack. The patient takes in liquid food through a straw. Painkillers and sleeping pills are prescribed.

The removal of scabs is gradually reduced to twice a day, leaving uneven patches on the face which usually continue to bleed.

The severe facial itching continues for some weeks. The skin will carry a sensation of over-heating. Small white spots may affect the dermabraded areas, but these can be punctured and wiped with a sterilised needle.

If the skin is exposed to sun or wind within the following

year, there is a risk of permanent keloid scarring.

The exposed skin usually varies in colour from the old: the new skin is baby pink and smooth and hairless.

NINETEEN

I hated men sometimes. They took their fill and they left you. My father dressed me in linen and drilled me in verbs. He left me there, on my own, in the wind of Chesapeake. Heinrich Gruber took the areas of flesh he wished for. Laurence also did this to a woman. He left a nerve-thinned twenty-nine-year-old woman with a month-old baby; he left his family for a strange European he hadn't slept with.

Men twisted my intestines with anger.

There was a purity to Loulou: I wiped away her after-birth so carefully. She was conceived in the dreams of poverty, and written in love and grief for someone else, and she was clean.

The monochrome images created for the *Loulou* covers were cropped and figurative details of a woman. The photographer infused suggestion or uncertainty with a delayed erotic shock. The arterial marbling of the skin's whiteness was almost palpable, while the image in its entirety was ambiguous: the cropped outline of a profile deliberately misleading; a single breast suggested in hollows and shadows of flesh. Then the press began surmising that the body was that of the author herself, and so it went on.

And I understood a form of magic, when my private notes, grown in diners and on the kitchen table and on desk 582 of the 42nd Street library, became public, became so public. Life changes with a stroke, when someone unknown to you is offered your soul in polished form, and signs the contract that turns it into black black print.

I hated men because Heinrich had troughed in my vagina like a pig with his excited flesh, then wiped his limp penis dry on a sheet, and still he had power. He could employ me, sample me, fire me, yet I had been blind to it. I'd thought I could entrance men and control them, but it had all turned out to be a pretty game, to be aborted when they wished. I had marched with Helen, we had joined women's movement protests and anti-Vietnam demonstrations. Now I wrote, sometimes in anger, in fury, my ink pure toxin. Loulou floated above men and laughed down on them.

I hated the strands of such power detected in Laurence Mahon: the outrageous assumption of one's place in the world, the drum tattoo on every object, the cheerful coughs and belches. But one loves what one hates, that otherness, that rape.

Did Laurence and I cleave to each other with a mutual neurotic need at that time or did we love as one loves a child, simply and well? Did the first underline the second? I thought about it often, but just as the past's secrets are revealed awry, it was obscured to me then. It only occurred to me after some time – when we had lived in borrowed apartments all over town, and I looked at him, lying in a single bed beside me, and I thought: how odd, it is mine, as though I had given birth to a baby or a lamb, an autonomous curly miracle – it occurred to me then that we were passionate lovers and terrible partners. The quasi marriage we formed, with property, dogs and borrowed child, always strained under the weight of our affair, unable to contain its excess.

But at the beginning, we ran like children all over town. Mimi had thrown me out of West 13th Street, and we stayed on friends' couches in Connecticut, Williamsburg, Chelsea. I looked after Laurence and made palaces of floors for him. We stayed out all night in restaurants, to escape roaches and generous friends, and we met in every halfway safe corner of that island, and I realised that Laurence was running away from his guilt. If he kept moving, it wouldn't catch him: the baby head sweet with vomit, the wife's shadowed eyes, his colleagues' distrust of the Prussian mistress.

Opportunity conspired with invention, and we met on street corners to talk for fifteen minutes when he was on his way to a client's, the traffic honking by, crowds nudging us from the crossings. I could pick him out, my heart speeding, from several blocks, and I was often late, and he was angry. Then we found other places to meet. Our favoured location was the 69th Regiment building on 26th and Lexington, its incongruity a joke as I would be forced to loiter there by that barrel of a building with soldier boys lounging on the steps. We began gabbling addresses: 'Meet me at 283 Lex, seven o'clock,' I'd instruct him. 'Wear your blue stripe shirt.' And when he got there, it was the Soldiers', Sailors' and Airmen's club, and I'd stand under the sign saying 'Welcome to enlisted personnel of the Armed Forces', as a variation on the Armory tradition.

We barked out locations by street number before cutting the line. We'd turn up at the Flushing Savings Bank or the Lipstick Building, or St George's Episcopal on Stuyvesant Square where old Hell's Angels hung out and the flowers were caked in dog excrement. The meeting places became more obscure: a business school that had closed down and become a steak-house, so the old sign in faded paint ghosted on a higher floor above the neon, surgical supply stores, stove repair businesses, old-fashioned hat shops. The gabbled address would approximate to a construction site or a newsstand, and just as Laurence was giving up, he'd spot me waiting there, reading a magazine. He'd give me an odd number on a street side of even numbers, the number invented by him for a hotdog stand. It led to confusion, panic, rain, bus stops, and still we carried on.

Once I had to wait for him in Dunkin' Donuts on Broadway, and I pulled off my jacket and sat there, my arms air ruffled, I cupped my face in my hands, the breeze coloured with spring sunshine, little sand storms of grit twirling up from the sidewalk. I sat facing the photo shops and tanning parlours, the Black Belt martial arts academy above, and the wind became so strong, people were laughing at it in the street, it punched trash in the air, it threw raindrops against the glass door, and then it was an electric storm, dark, dark, the neon running, people bolting, gusts from the doorway kicking paper cups off tables.

Laurence came in. He looked slightly older than his age. He had that distracted, impatient air that came from abundant energy and which pooled to sudden concentration. He was late. He was wet, he brought a cool stream of air in with him, it felt clean, like the suburbs, and I knew at that moment, as you know with premonition and fear and exquisite excitement, that I would always love him more than anyone else. I was condemned to it, or blessed with it.

We found rented apartments that merged in my mind until I only remembered certain lobbies and certain feelings they gave off, cookie-cutter apartments with heating systems that banged beside our heads at night, and Melina, a tangled bundle of griefs emerging from elevators hand in hand with Laurence.

Laurence's height seemed discordant in those apartments; he was tethered by them. His frank troubles and wilder notions were thrown into somehow embarrassing proximity as though I had cast for a fish and landed a seal. The realities of specked shaving cream on a sink and conversations over dinner and large shirts and sudden tempers were magnified.

I was sometimes a little nervous of him, of the contrast

between his irritability at home and his charm when he was at large in the world. His tangled disturbed darkness, its berries, flourished outside. I tapped into some deep hurt of his, in the fleeting, obscuring irregularity of his focus, and I stood by him and protected him. His mind was a fast thing that torrented to self-despair. He wanted to control each day of our lives together, but there was kindness in it, as though I were a precious girl to be protected. I thought, despite his haphazard quest for adventure, he was bound by a strange adolescent land of leather-covered books and cricket bats and high romance.

'I don't know if I can live with myself,' said Laurence one evening.

'Why, darling?'

'You know why.'

I hesitated. 'If I were the woman you left, I would never get over it either,' I said.

He threw his upper body towards me and we lay together until my arm was pricking numb, and I saw that he was crying.

Loulou was unaccountably selling – a joking miracle, a lantern show. My Loulou was people's naughty daughter, or their alter ego, or their model for dazzling impropriety. She sailed upon the zeitgeist, and the magic worked through the decade and into the next before it started to thin.

Part Scarlett O'Hara, part call to arms, so the journalists wrote of *Loulou*. It was perceived as a novel that changed lives at a time when such a concept was considered possible.

I used to think, when *Loulou* first came out and started to sell, and went into reprint, and became a little notorious, that this was the definition of success. It was like the foreigners in Austria learning to ski: the first day they are a stooped scrawl of indignation; within a week they can glide along a speeding angel, while their bored exuberant minds vault to glaciers and Olympic pistes. And it's only with progress that their shortcomings thump them in the face with ice and shame. I thought I was famous before I was.

When the second book was published, the money started coming. Laurence became a partner in his firm, we laughed at all the money we made, and after so many friends' beds and rentals and hotels, we decided to buy an apartment together. We were rejected by the condo board of the Parc Vendome, who seemed to know my name. It secretly made me very happy, as I dragged Laurence back downtown. Our battle over where to live continued.

One Saturday, we went down to Gramercy Park. We emerged from Lexington into its industrious silence, and there were squirrels in the private gardens, lattice work and town houses. I wore a twenties dress, blossoms and oriental bridges on brown-black crêpe. I had just recorded a radio interview, and my face had then reached its classic form, the way it remained for many years.

We saw the building rising, stained lace, gryphons, through the trees. We put our arms around each other and looked at it.

'It's a monstrosity,' he said.

'Let's ask the doorman,' I said. 'Ask who the agent is.'

'It's a urinal, isn't it? Surely it's not a block of flats.'

There was delight in his derision. I suspected then that I would make him live there.

'There is no logic,' said Laurence. 'Just a set of rules invented on the Planet Meier.'

It was a foaming, neo-gothic terracotta clad creation, a white-crested chateau with awnings and silver guards in that city oasis of red brick town houses with echoes of Wharton, of Melville and James.

So we bought our co-op there, overlooking the square. It had ceiling roses and large fireplaces and tiled floors. The neighbourhood cars became familiar, the dogs, the kids from the Washington Irving High School, the Palm Sunday

Procession, the Jewish weddings, the doormen from the hotel.

In the residents' garden, we ran about with Melina. We named the trees with her. The willows floated pale green across the shade and ivy of the park. Melina fed the squirrels. There was a world of trees: Oriental cherry and Norway maple and London plane; a Chinese magnolia; an Ohio Buckeye and a Tree of Heaven.

Happiness lies early in the curve of progress. In retrospect, you see that the most exquisite experiences occur when promise still outweighs achievement. The thrust upwards is feathered and muscular. The ground is left behind, the peak is an uncertainty, and the air is very pure. Success has not yet gripped you and left you in fear of its own volatility.

We were a little family. Melina came on weekends and Wednesday nights. My books trailed strange shock waves.

TWENTY

It has been so long. I haven't heard from Laurence. I haven't seen the photography boy.

I take walks about the dog cemetery, out by the Pont de Clichy near St-Ouen. I am scarcely recognised. I wear my astrakhan jackets, my dark grey pencil skirts and heels. Perhaps after all I resemble a dead poodle. My heart rarely stirs at the Assyrian gin palaces housing the canine remains. I hate all dogs; I hate their smell, their gums, their tails. The dog cemetery reminds me of Laurence, the dog enthusiast, and it is a fine place to walk between afternoon and dusk when the sky is pale pond water behind the trees. There is a Muscovite bear buried there, a wolf and a lioness.

If I construct a fantasy about Laurence, I begin to believe in it. I start to think he might be strolling here, on this island in the Paris suburbs on a Wedesnday afternoon – and not in his Chalk Farm, London, not in his Appledore, Kent, the quaintly named map of the Mahon family. After all, he is so very fond of dogs, and Paris is so very close to London. I catch coats, solitary figures, arms, between the trees, in the darkening spaces that knit to form forest. I jump, and I examine the parking places outside. The last car I saw him in, an angular black Saab, bears only a momentary resemblance to some of the darker cars parked in a row, the delayed stab of heartbeat a damp fizz.

*

Laurence Mahon is married. I keep forgetting this fact. He divorced his first wife, Carolyn, and now he lives with some English woman in England. What a surprise. The adventurer is not with an American or an Austro-American in New York. No, he married an English woman in his home town. *Quelle surprise énorme.*

So he lives in London, with his wifelet Suzy, Suzannah, Crêpe Suzette – I forget – and his two children, two boys. The boys go to a private school, and Laurence buys them dogs and cricket bats. They go to the country on weekends.

I'm sure that Laurence still retains his blustering charm despite Crêpe Suzette. I can almost be certain of her function in his life: he will love her, and protect her, and think that he was somehow honourable – the little warrior – in marrying her rather than me; she will be coloured the faded blonde of the British upper middle classes, and wear those long British A-line cuts in peaches and beige-browns, adopting a surprising touch of the cocotte of an evening. Crêpe will not fuck Laurence in the way I do: their fucking will be less muscular and precise; he will not bite open her skin, she will not provoke him and rinse him and have him washed up beside her, beached bodies that had tasted and preserved ecstasy for loop after loop of time.

It took me some months to recover from the dermabrasion Dr Kreitzman performed on me.

A woman came up to me at a party recently, a little drinks party held by a friend of mine in Les Halles. 'You're very beautiful. Who are you?' she said by way of introduction. She was one of those red-haired French women whose cheekbones ball when they smile.

I suppose I am beautiful. I suppose that is the gift God decided to give me. It influenced things, I think.

I was used to having the men I liked. Why, then, was Laurence able to resist me? The after-effects of love are an illness. There are days when the ulcer leaks. There are times of remission.

He didn't call me after he left the message on my answering machine.

I plot elaborate plans, the love ruses of adolescence. I cannot call him in England because a wife is there. Helen could call: 'Have you seen Adèle? We're worried – she doesn't seem to be any place at all. Her life is so spectacular just now, she must be kind of busy, but – You'll let me know if you hear something?'

When I am not plotting to irritate Laurence, to impress him or kill him, I wonder how he is. I know the minutiae of the strangely conservative regimes he adheres to in the midst of his excesses. It makes my heart loose to think of those. It's the details that get to you. Even his spontaneity is a peculiar, Laurence-style spontaneity. I wonder if someone is taking care of him. I hope he is being loved and understood and respected. I do respect him still. I think he is very wonderful. After all this, I think he is remarkable, and I wish him well. It makes me cry to wish him well.

I was asked on a television programme to debate the new feminism: the ideology of the younger feminists, those miracles of marketing with their big hair and their taunting of sacred cows for personal gain. I prefer the revolutionaries of the sixties and seventies, for all their suspicious admiration of me, for all their bemusement at my personal style.

I had much to say, but my skin could not tolerate the raw heat of the television lights or the scrutiny of three cameras.

Laurence did not call me back. I dialled his number in England – the codes had all changed – and I let it ring, then I replaced the receiver before Crêpe Suzette could come running.

A couple of days later there was a high young voice, the child's helium tones of sickness and self-consciousness on my answering machine, and it was Melina. It was like finding a kitten on your doorstep. I wanted to kiss her and look after her. She was in her early twenties, and she was speaking in the voice of a ten-year-old.

I called Melina. We spoke for three hours in the night. Her father had let her have my number, though he hadn't called me back. She had been let out of hospital. They still monitored her, and hauled her in when her weight dipped. Her hair had turned from red to brown. She was fine, she said. She was stronger now. Only her teeth had been damaged, eroded by the acid of her vomit. There was a possibility of impaired fertility. But she was fine. She was starting a college course. She did not have a boyfriend. She missed me; she had always missed me.

One day, I will visit Melina in San Francisco, or she will come to me here in Paris. I would offer her a home.

I remember that Melina finally grew light hair on her skin, a yellow-white down over her face, the anorexic body's attempt to keep itself warm. Melina grew her own blanket, the primeval hair of the baby in the womb. There was an old man and a monkey in her little girl's features. All this she did to herself.

I remember not eating once after a flu when nourishment was nausea, and I grew thin and visionary, and it was addictive, my body a testament to my will. I wrote and thought on a hallucinatory high, half intoxicated, half dulled, and I understood the dark starved flights of the wildest Brontë, and I understood, for a week, the fevered distortions of Melina.

Self-discipline is immortality, self-immolation ecstasy. The flesh is a form of evil. Purge yourself, and angels fly. Cut yourself, starve yourself, grow beyond the flesh, and you are sainted.

Sex as you starve, the man's weight pressing upon the bony outcrops of hips, the head light with hunger, punishment, orgasm. Oh oh oh, and harder, harder, the pain bleeding to exaltation.

I always loved what was feminine. Even as a young child, I was no tomboy. I liked dresses and lightness of flesh; a fluttering hand, a small sweet punishment.

I went to see Dr Kreitzman. He tidied me up a little.

When the skin around my eyes was thin and new, I blended its tone into the rest of my face with cosmetics, and I tried myself out on the Bois de Boulogne. I had needed a little more lipo under the chin. The scar I could hide with collars and scarves. The short anaesthetic left me a little shaky, but it was a delicate deer's shakiness upon high heels.

I passed some boys training in a concrete games ground in the Sixteenth. They run around, these suburban French youths, emerge from their yellow concrete apartment buildings, all chrome grilles and dark glass doors, wearing their nylon track clothes with sneakers, whether they are training on the athletics field or merely thrusting their groins at the pinball machines. The boys stared insolently and unemotionally at me.

The Victorians used to take their furred and hooded little daughters in carriages pulled by goats through the Bois de Boulogne, for novelty. Goats like Djali, pet beastie of la Esmeralda. Odette de Crécy, Renée Vivienne, all the ghosts of the Bois.

Rain iced the leaves on the paths.

I wore a big fur hat and a light wine mouth. The black fur made a Russian icon of my face, the mouth a berry stain in snow.

Some men looked at me. I thought of picking one up for his hot breath against the winter. But I did not desire a tawdry two hours with a stranger. There were stitches under my chin, six days old.

Adèle Meier. Adèle Meier. Not so many recognise me now, though I get half-curious looks, the mind struggling to place a long-ago friend. I used to hear fragments of my name sometimes in my wake.

Men looked at me. The wolf flicker, the old moment of sex was there. I wore sheer black stockings, creating Degas sculpture legs, and a flowing burgundy coat like riding dress.

I passed the boys at their practice session on my return, and thought of Eric Dérioz, the young photography student, for the first time in many months. I felt happy. Laurence hadn't called again, but my jaw didn't soften in relaxation, the hinted crêpe of my eyelids was an uncertain memory. Dr Kreitzman objectively pronounces me beautiful. The Greeks used a standard of aesthetics and composition that was later named the Golden Section. In beauty, the ratio of one to one-point-six is dominant. So the Doctor appraises my looks: clearly and professionally, with his mathematical instruments and his perfect aesthetic pitch.

I think my existence was in storage for a long time. The exodus from the United States back to Europe muffled me in dead history. It was a dumb thing to do, to run away as a man had done before me. But it begins to change. I see the sky is coloured and mobile. It used to be static storm pressure.

I remember, before I went back to my doctor and the seasons passed, there was a young man who seemed to want to seduce me. An intense, intelligent and uppity mannikin, barely more than a boy, and, extraordinary fact, he seemed to take an interest in me though I am two or three decades his senior.

So the memory of Eric suddenly ruffles my brain cells. He takes life very seriously. He has high expectations of himself, he suffers for his loves and art. With his rural upbringing in the Lot, he romanticises all that is urban and tinged with artifice. He is handsome in a strained, nocturnal manner. He cleaves to the baroque and the kitsch, for all his personal understatement. He is surprisingly conversant with current trends: as well as his Proust, his Bosch and Bellmer, he has his life of

257

Minitel and E-Mail and Internet, his clubs and Absolut Citron and drop-out's clothes. He knows the American beers and the 'trance' music and the Brazilian martial arts. Thus he swigs and jigs as he writes his no doubt Rimbaudesque journals and types his quote-heavy assignments.

I found his telephone number. He was gruff and taciturn to the point of rudeness. I bid him adieu virtually mid-sentence.

A few days later, he came knocking. I was in my bathrobe, my hair was wet: I shouted a conversation through the door.

That Friday, I met him in a Chinese horror on rue du Sommerard, the address of which he had scribbled on a note pushed through my door. He liked it there. It was one of his regular haunts. They served wine in sturdy tumblers, and you could buy a meal laced with MSG and sweet animal fat for the price of a subsidised student dinner.

He was very angry with me, it seemed. He would not quite delineate my crimes, but swung instead between sulks and reluctant charm. I let him have his moods. I told him of my life. I checked that he was getting sufficient food and rest at that college of his. The sweet sweet boy insisted on paying for our meal, counting out his bank bills carefully, though I protested. I worried about it.

I cannot be seduced by a schoolboy. I shiver at the thought.

I should leave him to play with his CD-Roms and his lenses, experiment with his sexual urges, see if he prefers girls or boys. He should pay homage to Lartigue, imitate Mapplethorpe, pick up girls in the bars and *banlieues*, and talk baby politics on trans-European trains. These college boys are gauche or honeyed, acned or silken, but they are not quite formed; one must handle their malleable young sensibilities with care.

But to my surprise, the idea of Eric makes me a little excited. My tender neighbour is quite delectable. I have become accustomed to his presence over all this time. I shouldn't.

Certainly I should not. I find there are unexpected softenings to my body when I think about him. A combination of boredom and regeneration distils the components of desire.

So he visited me a few weeks later. I wouldn't let him visit until my facial flesh was calmer. He came to visit. We would have a photo shoot, we decided.

He showed me his prints, finally, the shots from many months ago. He had printed them very large, the paper matt and fibre-bobbled, the blacks like oil slicks. They must have cost him a lot. His crops were brutal: one pen-lined eye, one wing of hair; the chin tilted down, the mouth and eyes filling the frame. It was the beauty of blankness.

The ideal of beauty is death. Models stare at the camera, to one side, with no expression, without fire or animation. The rejuvenation processes of the surgeon perhaps achieve that: manufacture a shop-soiled tabula rasa, a mock virgin holding nothing in her eyes and face, to be imprinted upon by a man.

'Come here, Eric,' I said. 'Make yourself at home while I prepare myself.'

I made him wait.

'Are these a conscious echo of the *Loulou* pictures?' I asked him.

'Oh, yes,' he said. He smiled. 'A different take on that idea. Intentionally.'

'Thank you,' I said. 'Thank you for doing that. I think they're very lovely. You're going to be a fine photographer. I truly think so.'

I fetched him a drink. I sat him on one of the sofas in the living room. He resembled an animal princeling, some sleek woodland creature of haunch and nerve on his brocade throne, crowned by a candelabra and framed by curtains.

'Stay there,' I said.

I put on my tea gown over my linen petticoat bought in the south, in Arles or Avignon, in an extortionate emporium of antique lace and silk. I had some old ivory pins, to which the infant ecologist would probably object, and a peacock feather shawl embroidered in the twenties, jewellery, gloves, my ballet dancer stockings.

'Eric!' I called. 'Location scout time! Which room?'

I showed him the rest of my apartment: each room a jewel box. He had never seen the other rooms. I had made the spare bedrooms a shock of saturated colour: ochre, turquoise, emerald and rose, the study violet with a burgundy Persian rug. The emerald bedroom was lit only with tiny white lights. I had cabbage rose cushions, damask, net, gold-painted ceilings. I always loved this apartment. Gramercy Park, my favourite home, was tamed by that old fogey Laurence, adherent of military green, parchment and thundering good taste.

Eric selected the rose-coloured bedroom with a heap of cushions on its kasbah bed, and I left him to his lights, let him trail his cables and his battery packs, and I was suddenly nervous. The phone rang: some old friend from New York. I let the machine take the message.

I returned when Eric called me. I was more composed.

Some of my dresses spilled out of the closet door in the pink room. I showed them to him, I tucked them in and pressed the door against their bulk. 'I have to keep my clothes in all the bedrooms now,' I told him. I showed him the signed *Loulou* cover prints.

My hips felt thin and narrow. I walked around and picked at cushions. 'Where?' I said.

'There,' he said. He jerked his head, forgetting his social graces, at the pile of cushions piled against the wall end of the bed.

'These will be less stylised than the others,' he said. 'Less rigidly thematic.'

'You are so grown up,' I said.

I was not dressed as formally as before. My themes were only allusive: love in the afternoon, the comtesse and lover, the hair casually twisted in a chignon so the profile is naked. Pale face and dark eyes.

I arranged the tea gown. I placed my hand on my knee. I laughed when I looked at him. I couldn't quite be serious for the student's camera.

He seemed irritable.

I posed. I laughed again.

'I can't photograph you,' he said dully.

'What are these new severe tones?' I said.

'How can I photograph you?' he said. He raised his voice.

'Eric!' I said. 'You have to show some understanding of how – How my life is! How busy I am! Now don't be so demanding. Please.' I pressed my thighs together and nudged the folds of my dress into a regular sequence. I shifted on the purple-pink stack of cushions. I frowned, rearranging myself. I forgot to look up at his camera.

'I had to get used to you not being there,' he said suddenly, blurting out a tumble of recriminations.

'Eric, Eric,' I said calmly.

'Yes?' he said.

'I might have to teach you a lesson.'

My head was lowered. I tried to catch a glimpse of him. I looked up from under my eyelashes and saw him obliquely: a blushing bullishness, sexual realisation just beginning to spread across his features. I lay back on the bed slightly. One of the elephant pins pressed into a cushion and slid out. I laughed again. 'Do I resemble a *fin de siècle* courtesan, Eric?' I said. 'Is that my theme?'

I stretched out my arm to him, and he took it coldly and stiffly. He was still wrapped in a stormy sulk of plosives and frowns.

'Your beetling brows have a life all their own,' I said, fondling his stiff hand on the bed.

I unbuttoned his shirt slowly with one hand as I talked. His narrow frame was more defined than I had anticipated: smooth, without hair, except the shadows that graded into his taut tense stomach. I breathed slowly. He froze. Then his lips loosened and I saw the primitive glaze of longing – it looks the same in all men – through the sullen cast of his features.

My tea gown fell open, lingering against one leg.

'So, I thought I might teach you a lesson,' I said. I breathed rhythmically so my tone was in harmony with my words.

The subtle firmness of his muscles, the smooth skin and exposed pink nipples made my heart thump. He wore an endearing little thong around his neck. I wanted to press a kiss on his torso.

'Lie down, Eric,' I said. I touched his chest with the tip of a finger and guided him back against the cushions.

I kissed him softly, just below his neck, then the tip of my tongue trailed down to his nipple, and I nested my lips gently there. His skin smelt of silk, of winter.

He sucked in air harshly through his nostrils. I circled his nipple persistently with my mouth. He emitted the husky outer notes of a groan.

I lifted my head. A rosette of lipstick bloomed around his nipple.

I looked at the boy in my bed, his head rigid and slack-mouthed against a cushion. He who strolls among nymphets might observe the tarnished surface of my skin.

'I can't corrupt a minor in full daylight,' I said. I nearly laughed.

He shook himself. His fringe flopped and tangled. He muttered something. He stumbled off the bed to unplug the studio lights. I looked at the shoulder blades, the silken tension of the stomach.

He returned and sat without moving. He looked stupid and inebriated with good fortune. Idly I played with him. I stroked his earlobe. I flicked my eyes to his crotch and saw the rigid outline of his penis.

'Do you want to play?' I said.

He nodded. He stared straight at me without embarrassment, his lips slightly parted, like a young child. My shawl was slipping off my shoulder, revealing bluish shadows where my breasts began to rise.

He turned to me suddenly, pulling my head to him and planting his lips roughly and wetly on mine. We kissed fast and hard. He tasted sweet, only his nicotine flavour emulating maturity. We parted. His lips were wet. I wanted to taste the tawny, peach flavour of his youth.

'I love you. I love you so much,' he said quickly in his gruff voice.

'Oh, Eric. That is a sweet thing to say. But thank you. Thank you.'

'I do love you.'

'Thank you,' I said. 'Darling. Sit comfortably.'

He looked like a schoolboy. I quivered with an involuntary reaction. He was forbidden and intense, differing subtly from those I had sampled. When Eric was but a foetus, I was already a sexually experienced adult woman.

I stroked his head. He should have had nubs of antlers, a stubborn little tail.

I bent over him, I smelt my perfume follow me and drift into a hollow created by us. My hand brushed the outline of his penis, barely touching, my nail skimming over him, and he jerked. My fingers were knowing.

I pulled his shirt off. I ran my hands down both his well-formed arms.

'You are quite grown,' I said idly. I kissed him. 'Are you a virgin?'

He moaned. He didn't answer.

'Have you had sexual intercourse with a woman before, Eric?' I said.

I planted a short warm kiss on his chest, and I felt his heart vibrate through my lips. I sucked in the clean sweet silk of his chest.

263

He jerked his head as though shaking away an insect. He reddened faintly. 'I – '

'Yes, Eric?'

'Kind of – I . . .'

'You have "kind of" done this,' I said softly. 'So you have . . . made out with girls on sofas. Yes? How pretty that would be.' There was a sudden series of throbs inside me.

I kissed Eric again, dipping down to skim my tongue's tip over his wet lips. My crotch was ticking and swollen. I was a little light-headed. I wanted to play with him as clay, savour that honey-skinned young torso. I wanted his mouth hot on my crotch. I wanted him to enter me.

'How beautiful you are, after all,' I said. 'You should always be undressed. Please lift. I wish to relieve you of your pants. Thank you.'

'You are the most beautiful thing . . .' he said.

Blood filled my head, my groin.

His penis reared and bobbed against his stomach. It was young and smooth, so very erect. It was quite large, as I had suspected it might be for all his thin strength. His breathing was hoarse and light. I bent over him, my chignon still secure, my beads falling in slow clusters over his thighs and abdomen. Laurence had been like this, uniformed and dizzy with vast new horizons at an English public school, so long ago. He smelled my pheromones: hormones still throb through my pores after all. It is not just the garlic and perfumed blankness of old skin.

'Now wipe your mind,' I said. 'It is only me and you, my mouth and your pleasure, that's all that exists.'

I took the French boy's penis into my mouth and explored its rigid smoothness with my tongue, and bathed it, safe and warm. He bit his lower lip; a trail of saliva ran from the corner of his mouth to make a dark mark on the cushion. He strained. He began to rock his hips. His eyes rolled like a trapped animal's. He hardly knew what to do with himself.

'Calm, Eric. Be calm. Go into a little trance.' My voice played its lightest ascension of notes.

He moaned. I stilled his hips with my hand. Gently, I stroked his hip bone.

I could do anything with him. I had a different generation snared. I hushed his hips once more. I took his penis out of my mouth, stroked its wet shaft, held it and skimmed my eyelashes down its length, tickling, returning, tickling. He emitted his gruff broken groan. I flexed my nails, gently, persistently, evenly, against its root. His breathing was jagged. 'Now you're learning to enjoy yourself,' I said.

He reached down and tried to grab his penis. I pulled his hand away and pinned it down on the bed.

'You must wait,' I said. 'Relax into that peak. Don't move at all.'

I sat up, my lips parted, I felt the heat of my cheeks under the wisp of rouge I had used, and I watched his penis against his hip bone, swaying haphazardly from the root with a life of its own.

'Please,' he murmured. 'Adèle . . . Please.'

'Timing. So much to learn!' I said lightly.

My tea gown slipped off one arm. I shrugged the other shoulder, and the cloth slid to my waist. He watched me, the sly young boy, out of half-closed eyes. I watched him watching me. My lips were open in an echo of his.

'Turn over,' I said.

He looked at me with the blank confusion of arousal, murmured questioning sounds.

'Turn over.'

He did so, and I leaned over him, and whispered into the light down at the base of his spine. I lingered there, breathing in small circles, then I parted his buttocks gently, and blew a path down to the hair of his testicles, making caverns of warm air. He writhed. He ground himself onto the bed. His buttocks were paler than his legs' smooth caramel.

I pulled the pins out of my chignon, and my hair untwisted to fall on my shoulders and over the straps of my petticoat. It was a simple linen square-necked petticoat. I had been a grande dame practising fellatio on a neophyte, and then in a moment I became a girl, a French colonial schoolgirl perhaps, an English child as Laurence had been, faintly shabby in her innocence, with her dull pink coryphée hose, her spilled hair.

'Now you can look at me,' I said. 'Eric.'

He turned his head slightly. He rolled onto his back. I stroked his penis lightly; I took its straining shaft in one hand and knelt over him, my knees on either side.

I looked down at him. His face was contorted. In a leisurely manner, my nerves light despite such control, I parted my pubic hair. I touched myself. Slowly, I pulled his penis into place, it strained against my guidance, I unravelled a condom, kneading it swiftly down the shaft of his penis; I quivered in a trail of tiny spasms; I opened my legs; and then I took him inside me. I winced as his penis reached high up inside me.

His moan became light, his expression ugly in the ecstasy of realisation. He thrust his hips upwards, I cried out a little at the tight pain, and then he took hold of me, he gripped my waist, and he wrenched me onto my back, using more strength than dexterity. He tensed inside me; I cried out in a punctured gasp, shocked at the unexpected movement, and he would not let me go: he was strong, suddenly, and determined. I was numb on the base of my back, folded beneath him. We kissed, our mouths banging, my teeth cutting against my inner lip, and we struggled, we wrestled on the bed, we cried out, he bit my nipples, and we shook and tensed, he arched inside me, and I was amazed at such strength, his face changed by the distorted grimace of sex.

My petticoat twisted, bunched under my breasts. His penis seemed to strain against my bowels, all sensations merging into one dense chamber of pain and pleasure. He drove his mouth against mine, the blunt banging of teeth making me wince, the urgency of his tongue exciting me.

'Eric . . . Eric.' Our thrusting sliced my voice. And then he plunged inside me one final time, he could not control himself, he came in a series of whiplash spasms, his spinal column shuddering.

My petticoat was under my chin. My hair was disordered. I caught sight of my own breasts, white girl's breasts in the early night. The teenager observed me with the crossed eyes of orgasm. Subtly I trailed my finger around my clitoris, the shuddering muted but sprung.

We took small draughts of sleep wrapped in each other's arms on the bed. My body was pure and relaxed as a girl's.

TWENTY-ONE

One of the *Loulou* covers resembled tightly packed petals. After a moment's study, it seemed to suggest delicate folds of flesh. It was the most abstract of the series. The journalists questioned me obliquely about that photograph, once they had softened me.

The home grew around me. Laurence's dark furniture, such gloomy French wallpaper (burgundy turrets, muted gold); shaded corners, brocades and writing desks; a Manhattan duplex became a gothic growth, elevated by light on the top floor. My desk spawned books, became a library; his architectural plans snow-leaved a room.

Melina grew to be a little girl. With her gentle sombre spirit, she child-dreamed a princess in a castle of twin-towered 36 Gramercy Park. She was my tame squirrel walking in the gardens, talking to me at night in her squirrel nest upstairs. If Laurence was working late, I let her sleep in our bed curled in my arms. Her red hair lay in flimsy springs. Her breathing was fast and pink. Sometimes I found it hard to accept she was not my own daughter.

We lived in old New York, where the Con Ed building had been an opera house; the private garden with its keys and carping residents, the druggy old Kenmore Hotel, that moment of evening when Madison Square becomes moody and restless, all merged into a village, removed from the anonymity of the famed apartment buildings uptown. The garden opened to the public on Yom Kippur; squirrels rooted in the ivy; *I count none but sunny hours* read the sun dial, and our building caught the last sun on the top of its towers, while the garden was dark and ivy-flooded beneath, only the anaemic willow braiding the wind. The blast of hot air from the dry-cleaners' on 21st kept me warm among the strollers and sneakers and beauty parlours.

Our house was filled with Hundertwasser and John Philip Souza and two repulsive dogs imprisoned in the kitchen: the passions of Laurence. That I lived with a man who played dull and pompous marching music was a surprise to me. It drummed through the apartment. The dogs moaned and slavered. It seeped to gothic there from the building itself: the lobby's tobacco tiles and horse frieze, the terracotta outcrops of the façade. My white ballerina panty hose, my scarves, would slide and crust the furniture. I bought too many clothes; they spread to other rooms, and shimmered and crushed. The fire places and ceiling roses made it seem like a theatre in the apartment, with the drapes, the grisaille of my *Loulou* photos.

I faked passivity for Laurence. I lay in a bed and I said, what will you do to me? His nearly-black furniture stormed above me. He got caught in silk on the floor. I opened my legs, and he wouldn't enter me until I asked and asked. My face dropped to one side on the pillow, my lips parted, I barely moved, and then harder, harder, harder; I winced and the pleasure crept.

I pretended to be dead. He went to the bathrom after fucking with me, and when he returned, I was spread out, comatose, marble in the night. I didn't move at all. It made him anxious; it made him excited and half-crazy. I was pumped and jerked.

The only muscles I used were inside me, clamped suddenly tight around him in all my fake pliability, so he groaned, like his dogs.

We went shopping together, the entrance to my vagina a ring of soreness as I fingered clothes in Bergdorf's, flexing my pelvic muscles to test them. He showed me items that might please me. I wrote into the night. He called me to come to bed, but I slept in the early hours and woke for radio broadcasts, and he was irritated. We were sexless, then he came home from work, in the middle of the day. I was wet when he announced he was going to fuck me at noon.

I sometimes thought that Laurence wanted to sleep with me more often because he was irritated that people gave me a different brand of attention after the second *Loulou*, so he wanted to possess me. Those famous photographs lifted me to an iconographic level. Such attention was effortlessly gained; I protected myself in a manner of ways. There were strange ramifications: I inspired amateur songwriters and the love-stricken and lonely and the half-crazy. Letters of hyperbole with a dull taste of threat found their way to me.

I could not believe I had become so beautiful.

In my late twenties or early thirties, I came across my looks. I had not truly known them before; I hadn't known the power of beauty enhanced by perfect knowledge of its own temperament. I became acquainted with what to overplay and what to underplay, forsaking softness for definition. It was like an exultant mathematical solution, the placing of the cheek and jaw bones so carelessly soaringly parallel. Beauty is a matter of split millimetres.

When a face is celebrated, it almost caricatures itself: it barely knows where flesh meets reputation. I had to protect my body. I learnt all the tricks I needed from the make-up artists, and then I refused to have them work on me.

I could afford maids and cleaners. They fixed my hair, they

made me small drinks, they left the apartment half tempesty. I had my hair set as I wrote and the prose became staccato and intense as they curlicued my scalp. I thought I might travel to Paris to meet a couple of journalists, take Melina and buy her tailored French dresses with bows. I dreamed of creating a room for Karli next to the squirrel nest at the top of our apartment. I wondered most days whether my father saw my name. I received notes from barely remembered contemporaries at high school, and so my father must have absorbed my name, floating on the airwaves.

I made pleasure domes for Laurence of our home, with hooked emotions, sweetness nearing decay. I created a world, he complained, then withdrew from it, and by then the drug had taken hold, scattering its highs and lows. But I cared for Laurence in those places.

'Are you jealous of me?' I asked him once. 'Of – you know – ?'

'That French hottentot you write about? Should I be?'

'A little, perhaps.'

He hurt me in bed that night, a game taken too far.

I bit him as a punishment.

He sucked my skin on a Sunday afternoon, and my shoulder oozed. Afterwards, there were blurred teeth marks. I knew it would go a little further. He lifted my whole body off the bed with his fingers inside me and the next day, my membranes were reptile dry. There was a small fire inside me; I could barely walk.

Then he bit me too hard. A bite on the shoulder to start. The shock of a bite on the breast.

Men colonise the body.

I thought, sometimes, writing at my desk, staring half cross-eyed at the tree tops, I wanted to kill Heinrich Gruber for having entered my body when I had been stiff and slack with resistance. He had taken his pleasure as though I were rubber, as soldiers do, throwing the skirt over the woman's head to conceal the terror in her eyes. I never saw him again: I refused to see him, despite the phone calls, his secretary's and his lawyer's letters. I wouldn't see Sophy either, for all our love. She suspected that her husband had violated me, and she melted back into her surroundings like pinkest jello, pinned, mute and pretty, and there she stayed on the Upper East Side and sent me typed congratulations cards via my publisher.

Men kill, they eradicate. My father with his hard penis in his grey pants sighting the neighbour, poking, poking, coughing, putting it away. He left his Adèle though he had created her, a perfect daughter on a Chinese rug. The mother had slack dugs, so he sought his flesh along the block.

I wished I could love women like that, but where is the hurt, where is the divine otherness?

I spoke in sound bites. I polished them very well to form little explosions, and they were used by the media.

Once I couldn't go on television because Laurence Mahon had scratched my neck at night. They took my comment down the telephone line.

'You,' said Laurence, 'are too vicious.'

'No.'

'You'll go too far.'

'Someone else said that to me. I can hear the rhythm of that sentence already in my head. Who?'

'Your mother, perhaps?' said Laurence. 'Or your own guilty conscience?'

Laurence called me at home all day, he faxed me love notes, he left queries and recriminations on the answering machine. He wanted to know where I had been. He tracked me down to the offices and the photographers' studios at which I had appointments, floating around their telephone systems until he discovered the relevant extension. He didn't shave well enough. His breath smelled in the morning. I hired a studio. I needed to be pure to write.

It was a large studio on West 27th, with an installation artist for a neighbour, and burnt out warehouses across the street, the hollow of air ducts.

Loulou developed more sweetly there. She was a little surreal. I hung my covers on the walls, and I looped beads about the frames in passing, made velvet corners, so that the studio became a shrine to a strange French girl in New York. I ran around to the classical music programmes on the early night radio, performing haphazard *jetées*, glimpsing myself in the Loulou covers as they streaked past.

The image of Loulou coloured my day like a bright drug pattern. It kept radiating through my limbs in chemical surges. I had been blessed in a secret ceremony. She was mine. I had thought that such glimpsed satisfaction was only possible in childhood, when a pattern of shells and sea horses against bright paint blue on a purse or a dress or a beach ball was delectable in an almost edible form.

I was myself. I was my own theme. You have yourself, my father said. You have your beauty, and whatever you create with your own mind. The theme was myself; I was liberation packaged, a series of photographs, aspects of femininity exposed.

I had been a poor girl, and all I possessed was myself, and I became this creature. Loulou gave me economic power for the first time in my life, and the hit was almost greater than love, or comparable with love in its first moments. She was a little bohemian, perhaps. She was not a British wife, and Laurence Mahon was unable to understand that.

*

I propped my chin on my hand, I watched the ghosts of bodies behind the glass of the dance studio across the way as I wrote. Laurence worked, and waited for me late evening. I spoke to journalists in my office, no longer in our apartment, where they made a socio-economic analysis of every decorative choice. There were dull arguments because Laurence failed to understand the reasons for my lateness.

I started staying in my studio nights. The artist held parties frequently interrupted by the police. I could hear the anomalous sweat shops of that Flower District in the sounds of the sewing machines starting early in the morning, Korean women arriving on the street at dawn.

I took little Melina to my studio to make her a doll's corner. We sang nursery rhymes in French. I thought she was a sugar mouse, her face flushed porcelain, her hair in scrawls. She was a sensitive girl, her fingers gentle with my pens. I told her she must be courageous and tenacious and much, much loved; I let her use my lipstick, and she drank a tumbler of watered alcohol at the neighbour's parties. He made a sculpture of Melina of mirrors and reflectors. It showed at John Weber. I didn't tell Laurence. The mother, Carolyn, had nervous problems, she was taking crazy pills, so we could have Melina to ourselves. I brought her home late, or tucked her up, a sleep-warmed cherub in velvet and cushions while I worked, and Laurence was in a towering rage by the time I came back home. He threw objects across the room. I laughed.

'Tell me about your preacher man father and your mother in the meadow,' I said to him the next day, more gently.

'Tell me your childhood first,' said Laurence. 'Then I can. Tell it in instalments. First instalment. Nought to five. You were born in Graz. You were such a beautiful baby that the good burghers of Leibnitz all wanted to come and touch you . . .'

He kissed my neck in the sun. We were sitting in the gardens at Gramercy Park. Children played by the fence. There was a dog, its tail feathering in the distance along Irving Place.

'I was born in Graz,' I said, 'and my parents loved me when I was born, because I was the baby for a long time. The third child is always the baby in the family scheme, it seems. Karli, my younger brother, was *my* baby when he was born, he was my pet like an adorable rabbit in a hutch. I became a fat-faced little *Mäderl*. If you saw photos, Laurence darling, you would laugh.'

'Do you look like a stuffed Apple Strudel?'

'I look like an exploding plum dumpling. There are photos my father took of my Mammi and I together. She looks kind and weather-worn, I really can't look at those photos now – and I'm just braids and fat cheeks, and I look like I might bite someone.'

'My Adèle, the fat little baby with her Mutter.' He stroked my arm. The hairs caught flat gold lights.

'I wish I could tell you that I was a wild child who ran riot through the town,' I said, 'and invent tales for you involving skis and licentious priests. But I only rebelled in my head.'

'How, darling?'

'I was an adult in my head. I wanted to be a woman when I was five. It's as if . . . an awareness that Paris is there. Do you understand what I mean? You don't have to be a fat housewife in a small town in the mountains. There is perfume, there are women who . . . I wore perfume a lot when I was five, six, I hoarded, took Mammi's, breathed the incense in the church. My father gave me a bottle once – *Je Reviens*, such an expensive scent for a little girl. He went on a trip to Berlin and he brought it back for me. I plotted. All my childhood, I think I plotted. I knew how to pretend to be demure while my head was fraught and soaring, because such expression is forbidden.

'You, Laurence, zero to five. Then move on to age fifteen so you can tell me all about your young passions. But anyway, age zero you were a kicking bundle of boy with bark coloured irises – and baby scented curls of hair.'

'Except white babies have blue eyes,' said Laurence. 'So, I was a boy in shorts. You know, standard boy in shorts, red setter doggy, large house in Kentish countryside. No internal life whatsoever. I thought of nothing but rowing boats and football and butterflies. My sister liked cats. I was the butterfly freak. You know – we lived among the hops and the orchards in a brick-and-pub village. It's a bit like France down there. Want you to come. I was disruptive at the village school. It was an experiment – put young Laurie in the village school with the dyslexic locals, see if he gets an accent and has his head stoved in. But I was a young tyrant. They packed me off to the same frightful prep school as my older brothers, and so the path was set.'

'You are baked by five.'

'Do you think that's true?'

'Sort of,' I said. 'I kind of do.'

'You were baked an angel cake.'

'Thank you.'

'I'm so glad they made you that way. They spun you like a perfumed cat. Come here.'

If Laurence did not adore me, I became frantic, panicking and shouting like a child because I was frightened he might leave. I spent some nights in my studio in a pre-emptive protective gesture. Miss Loulou-Adèle with velvet studio and fresh-minted royalties and poem of a face.

If you appear on television, you are seen on the street. I could hardly help it.

I seemed to come home late when I meant to be early. Laurence busied himself with our apartment while I was out. He threw away a large pile of my clothes, because there were too many, he said, because moths were beginning to eat them. He threw away some of the oldest silk, stuffing it crushed down the garbage chute. I didn't come home for a few days after that.

We drew our fights into sex, they metamorphosed at night in an osmosis of themes. My brain shifted to grain; I rose to a different level, where pain couldn't hurt, it was all pleasure, blows to the membranes felt only behind numbness. After we had come, I had vagina dentata, the soul's resistance manifest even as the body is aroused. I bit his fingertip with a circle of flesh teeth.

I kissed an artist in my studio one day. I couldn't quite help it.

Loulou was so delicious, so very nasty, you see. They all thought her me, and where others conjectured, the painters in my building could quite easily see that it was my face and my body in the *Loulou* photos.

You can create yourself. Carolyn gave birth to Melina, and I gave birth to myself, in my late twenties in New York City. And I was aware that I had elevated men as they had subjugated me: men had been my focus, yet I had hardly known it at the time. I dissected my spirit prettily for them, and they ate it. I had cut myself down as I polished myself up, and they complained that I never compromised, that I was impossible and elusive and volatile, and so I performed illusions of the mind and body, and still they required more. And when I had economic power and my vision became a wide shocking vista, I knew that if I had protected myself as I had nurtured men, if I had not cut my spirit into chunks, I would be invincible. Love and art are a self-sustaining contradiction: love feeds art, and then it eats its own product. The creator enacts a paradox with every passion.

Journalists came to interview me in the studio. The conversations lasted three hours, and we became closer, as my soul was revealed little by little to a stranger. There were girl interviewers

277

sometimes. In the eighties, they were always aged twenty-four, dressed in a Lycra mini-skirt. Always. I was older than them: how strange, women younger than myself imbibing my wisdom, tarnishing my skin with the contrast of their surprising presence.

But my strange notoriety gave me a patina of which they were quite devoid. Fame is a substance. You can dress in it, you can taste its chemical rapture. It emulates the high of love in synthetic form. It feeds you as men leach you, and it is infinitely less treacherous.

The arguments with Laurence were baroque, as though that elaborate apartment gave us licence to ransack excess. We were bound by unspoken jealousy, its blood leaking hot until it began to smell. He was jealous of my work, as money was minted exponentially, multiplied on statements, spawning foreign editions and lecture offers. I was jealous of his privileged, insolent, crowd-pleasing charm, while at home he was unshaven and moody, he called me cunt, mad woman, hell bitch, he hurt my breasts, he crushed my features.

I lay on top of him, pressing into his wrists with my nails to pin them to the floor, little white half-moons like sleet on his skin. He bathed my vulva with his open mouth, sucking and biting; I pressed harder, so we were like two mouths kissing. I dipped my head and bit him on his inner thigh, tasting the grapey bunching of arteries. He cried out in surprise, not pain.

You make minefields of love. Where once you sewed flower seeds, you sew small bombs, to injure, not to kill, for the shock effect and for the repair of so much damage afterwards.

Every time he hit me, the bruising occurred inside.

TWENTY-TWO

A teenager is my lover. I keep the lights low. He likes to run errands to please me. He likes to dominate my body.

My face begins changing again. The effects of age take it differently now, the centre of gravity seemingly altered as though there is a reverse gravitational pull upwards at the ears. The panel of skin that traverses my cheekbone is still smooth, while my jaw combines taut flesh with slack, the folds falling abruptly in its tightness like small crumbles on marble. I notice now the dough-soft pliability of my neck, my stomach, my shoulders: the restored areas throw their imperfections into relief. I hate it; I hate it. It makes me nauseous. How could a younger man ever caress this body? The older woman starts growing a store of flesh across her shoulders, like camel fat. The shoulders fall to rounder mounds, the arms flabby yet capable, pointy potato knuckles for elbows.

Legendary beauty contains its own time bomb of cruelty.

I am felled by this. I blot it out. I stare at myself with a double mirror under full lights and I'm drenched in a fall of understanding: I play and I flirt like an attractive woman, all my facial expressions long ago formulated with that assumption. How, then, does one adapt them? Assume the self-effacing, minimal gestures of the homely, to whom facial expression is merely functional?

My eyes, particularly, betray age's humiliation. A crêpe twitch marks the left lid in the morning, smoothed out by raising my eyebrow.

'Blepharoplasty can be performed independently,' says Dr Kreitzman. 'You can complete the effect with a secondary lift when you're ready for it. But you shouldn't let the eyes go for too long.'

'Will it help me?'

'The eyelid procedure is one of the most successful operations we've developed,' he says. '*The eye is the mirror of the soul*, Adèle! If the surgery is relatively conservative, there won't be a dramatic change – but the patient achieves a more wide-eyed, youthful appearance.'

I am to visit Dr Kreitzman's own small theatre, in the basement of the building that houses his consultation rooms. His fees have risen. He is friendly – a valedictory arm around a waist, a small private joke – but his ease comes gift-wrapped in formality.

He cuts away the ravages of age so carefully.

'Make a tight fist for me,' says the doctor, stroking my hairline, settling the muscular leaping of my nerves.

The patient lies awake. She has a still, dead beauty to her, her profile passive on the pillow. Two nurses move about the surgeon.

He marks her eyelids, closed to the circle of bright lights above her, her nerves rising and subsiding under intravenous sedation. He measures her eyelids with a calliper and makes his decision about how much of her skin to remove. He draws a crescent moon shape in red along the upper eyelid, and marks it with black points in which to inject anaesthetic.

A piano concerto plays softly.

He marks the skin below her eyes. He strokes back her hair, nudging stray strands inside her surgical cap.

'Feel calmer?'

'Yes, thank you.' She drifts. 'Such lovely, lovely music.'

The most intimate of experiences. The nurses are blind handmaidens insecting the periphery. The music softens. The doctor sits looking down at her, waiting so sweetly for her to sleep. He is patience and softness.

'OK, close your eyes again,' he says in a murmur, strokes her, and the music swells. She closes her eyes to have them cut. It is dawn or evening in her head.

They wait.

The piano gathers itself. The pianist is young and excited at the Concertgebouw.

He holds her head for minutes and minutes.

He injects local anaesthetic. The whole lid swells to soft fruit. He waits. It becomes a gourd, a pouch of its own making, marked with its cheerful red-black tracks. The nurses put on gowns, hats and masks, and assist the doctor with his clothes. Tools are arrayed on green paper. Nurses open swabs, and wipe down the patient's face. The doctor has two magnifying glasses attached just above his eyes.

Green paper is draped over the patient's body, a section cut out for her face, so her features alone are visible, neckless and headless as a death mask.

The skin is cut. Blood weeps down her face. A white thin crescent of skin is scored and stretched with forceps. The doctor cauterises the flesh revealed beneath it with a hiss of burning. The monitor beeps. There is a raw area on the upper lid where skin no longer exists. A string of fat is then cut away from the lid and removed along with muscle fibres. The strips of skin and eye fat lie like palest sand worms side by side on paper that is left upon the patient's chest. The doctor sews and twists thread into a knot; he cauterises the bleeding; tiny needles are dug into the crater of flesh to sew the skin seams from the inside. The eye is sewn up so delicately, the white of the eye is revealed in dead blinks as he pulls the thread and closes the new seams of flesh. There is a little protruding matter at the end of the seam which he removes in tiny particles of flesh, wiped upon the nurse's proffered swab.

The doctor cuts below the eyelid, following the line of the eyelashes. A half-moon of skin is cut open with scalpel and scissors to form a pouch, held open by a nurse with a retractor while the surgeon digs deeper, creating a blooded hood of exposed flesh under the eye. He finds the yellow lump of fat nestling there, soft but rubber-tough as a mussel on a fork. The nurse holds it with forceps while he cuts it away, and discovers a second fat store to remove from its pocket. He cauterises. Smoke emerges from inside the eye bag. The eye's harvest is wiped on a square of paper.

The doctor stretches the eye bag to decide how much skin he will remove. A tiny strip is cut with scissors, then the two flesh edges are attached with a single stitch. They will knit themselves together. A little piece of fat is stuck to the nurse's hand.

The other eye is cut, emptied and sewn up. Fine strips of plaster are placed over the wounds.

'All done. All fine,' says the doctor.

The patient stirs.

'Try to relax your eyes and keep them closed,' says the nurse.

They lift her to her room.

Smooth skin swells beneath her stitches.

TWENTY-THREE

We lived in a gothic castle in Manhattan that enclosed Laurence's strangeness.

After six years, we bought a smaller apartment next door, with cornering rooms to warren our home: a squirrel nest and ballet attic for Melina, a little suite of new wardrobes for me.

Melina and I lay in her room in the evening, and I played with her hair; she played with mine; we braided and curled. Her body, she said, was too big, her thigh flesh chunking, her stomach a small pot. Her voice rose thin to mania as I caressed that average-sized child and hushed her and taught her. We made our French fluent together, and I remembered my mother teaching Karli German in the kitchen because he was so young he had forgotten it; I remembered the dishwater tow of his cropped head beside her, his knees bare and scratched on a stool, and it made my chest bubble to imagine it, so long ago, in a forgotten kitchen, the woman's flesh now seeped from her in a grave by the Tidewater. I wished I had talked to her more. I loved Melina as I had loved that younger brother, their gentleness and strange thought processes uniting them in my mind.

I spent days and nights in my studio when I was not travelling – to France, Germany, Atlanta. At home, we became a little reclusive, hiding ourselves behind brocade drapes, in semen and darkness. I was jealous of him in the world, I wanted him enclosed by the walls of 36 Gramercy Park, but he had become broad faced and angry, he had changed over the years and I had barely noticed. He swore and kicked objects, lost his temper with the doormen, shouted at drivers and argued with his colleagues in his rash conviction that architecture now failed to interest him, so he would write about it instead. That sprawling ceiling-rosed apartment gave us licence to rage, his jealousy unashamed. He hated Loulou or the Loulou industry with a passion, mocking and parodying it, claiming I had become what he had always anticipated I would become: spoilt, vicious, vain.

Hype is a flashflood, fame a sea change. With the third book, I was Loulou, a pretty freak for the newspapers to play with. The attention was rough and relentless. It tore open my life and presented its intestines neatly in a pre-set pattern that the public could access. I became thinner during it. Slow panic lay under the moments of excitement. I was like a child having her clothes pulled off. It cut this wound, and the wound itched, but once I was exposed, I needed further exposure. Capillaries fizzed in the shock of air, and everything seemed dull afterwards.

You get caught in the crossfire. The lies make you seize up with anger. You feel nauseated. But you are powerless: you can never control the direction the exposure might take. That is the mistake you make. You can't choreograph the buzz bomb, but you imagine you can. It ricochets and rips you as it goes.

And that became a way of life. It always hurt a part of me, where I was vulnerable, but it had become a way of life. I dipped myself in their myths.

So the woman arrived home a little springy stepped, because she had been scrutinised by journalists that day. She was dressed in dull gold cloth, a short skirt, clusters of antique pearls. She took little notice of the man as she put down her work case and edged past his dogs, arching her legs to avoid their fur. She kissed him suddenly, a wet rose planted on his mouth, then walked into a different room.

He sat heavily, his limbs older, and her movements in contrast were gold and light.

'How is the charming suffragette today?' he asked, following her into the main room.

'Loulou is *très heureuse*,' she said, examining a book.

'And yourself?'

'I'm tired, exhausted, overstretched. Otherwise . . .'

'And how are your fans from *Newsweek*?'

She turned to him blankly.

'A little sick of the story, perhaps?' he said.

'Probably.'

'How are the boys from the *Village Voice*?'

'Hard at work, I imagine. How are you?' she said patiently. Her dark gold cloth took on the fall shadows from the window.

'I'm bored, if you really want to know,' said Laurence abruptly. '*Bored*. Tired of you never being at home.'

'I'm sorry, Monsieur M. If you had any idea how busy I am . . .'

She turned from him and walked to the window.

'I know very well. I've heard it a million times,' he said. He coughed. 'It just strikes me as a bit ironic – that some pimple-ridden junior hack on the *Village Voice* sees more of you than I do.'

'Perhaps the reporter boys like me more than you do,' she said. The corners of her mouth moved upwards.

'Don't do your cat smile.'

'I don't even know what I'm doing. What is a cat smile?'

'What you shine on a herd of newspaper men.'

She raised one eyebrow. It skewed the sculpted regularity of her features. The leaves were yellowing in the park; she

285

watched the sky darken between the trees, the willow paling with night light.

'What am I supposed to do for you?' she said. Her shoulders sank. Then she composed herself and stretched out her hand, testing her nails against each other. A small vague smile played on her lips.

'I knew – ' said Laurence. 'I knew you'd be bloody impossible to live with.'

'So he says nearly ten years later.'

'Even my colleagues ask me how I deal with you. Oh-so-subtly enquiring.'

'Your colleagues are snivelling little frustrated take- home salary office workers – mostly men – who're most likely threatened by me.'

There was silence.

'Thank you, Adèle,' he said.

She paused.

'Oh,' she said. 'I don't mean that's what *you* are, you dumb thing.'

She walked over and kissed his sleeve, leaving a lipstick mark, then sucked his arm, wetting the cloth. 'Do we have these fights just to have something to say to each other?' she said in his ear.

'Do you think we have nothing to say any more?'

'Not when you're angry. When you look like a crazy old bull.'

She laughed. Car headlights moved slowly around the square, yellow-staining the sky.

His eyes shifted, so his thoughts became invisible behind his anger. His hair was longer, the spring grown to wiriness in its neglect. His eyebrows formed a line of distress.

'Oh,' she said, 'Laurence,' and held him.

'You speak of men,' he said. 'It's ironic – you treat Melina as a man would be accused of treating her.'

She glanced at him dispassionately. 'How?'

'Let her stay out all night, charm her, spoil her. Buy her

every precocious piece of clothing she thinks she wants. You don't discipline her – '

'You're too hard on her.'

'One of us has to be. You're not good for her.'

'Melina loves me.'

'Yes, I know. I know she does,' said Laurence.

He frowned, the hurt line of his eyebrows disintegrated, his face taking on the swollen uneven pressure of anger. He pulled at the upholstery of the chair he sat on, prised out a pin, scrabbled at the stuffing.

'For God's sake. Laurence!'

'Shut up, Adèle, shut up.'

'Don't talk to me like that, you ridiculous man.'

Her laugh was a bright clamber of notes.

He breathed slowly, his jaw rigid. 'I thought – I'd met my match. With you,' he said. 'But now – now I find your behaviour dull. The lateness. And – how you cut me out, limit my time with you. God knows who you're flirting with all day. God knows.'

She pressed her lips together in a faint parodic pout. 'You do not, Laurence Mahon! You don't find it *dull*. You find it angry-making and exciting like the mad preacher son thing you are. I do love your British accent when you tell me these things – however.'

She turned to him. She opened her strange coloured eyes close to his. 'Never forget – ' Her lips parted slightly, so they were large in front of his eyes. 'Never forget – you are – ' She spoke with a level, hypnotic certainty. 'You're – addicted. You and me. Smell that,' she said. She proffered her neck, warm and pale by his mouth.

He sank his mouth into the crook between shoulder and neck; he pulled her hair so her head snapped forward.

'Cunt,' he said.

Working in the evening, the photographers' strobes flashed

from the studios opposite, sometimes in sequence, planes flew low on night flights, and I was less alone than I was at Gramercy Park, my ear swollen, my hand moving over a page. My Papa, had he been there, would have stroked my head to comfort me.

I felt my body. I felt the slant between waist and hip, trailing my hand over my own flesh to feel its miraculous human curves. I made a mosaic on the desk of my press photos, their shade, their brows and mouth, the images exalting me as Laurence despised me. Then, one night, after I had been interviewed, I slept with a reporter there. It was very odd: his flesh hard in unfamiliar places, the smells disturbing in their contrast with Laurence's. He loved my Loulou, you see. He wanted to imbibe the fragrance of her skin, infatuated as he was by her photograph. He loved me while he was inside me, crying out his passion as stray strobes flared in the dark and the body of Loulou moved about him like water. He anaesthetised me briefly with his desire.

There was a columnist who came to visit me there, a rich middle-aged man smelling of perfumes that made me think of Tsarist Russia.

What an amazing life I have indeed. I travel; I am courted; I cut swathes for women.

I had a lover who was addicted to me but had stopped liking me. He was not even my husband. Laurence had divorced many years previously, but every time we thought of getting married, a fantastic disagreement would erupt that prevented us, and so there was endless postponement. I was in love with a man with whom I clashed, in jealousies and misunderstandings.

We had a fever for each other's bodies despite the years and injuries. Love, if boiled down to its fat, consists largely of pheromone. Our smells locked together very well. I wanted to go inside him to seek out his pretty kidney and dip myself in his blood as it flowed. I was frustrated by the body's limits. Sometimes we merely stroked one another for hours, pulling the skin's nerves to the surface. We went to different countries, and on trains and in hotels resembling barracks and palaces, we explored one another to the blood.

I could extend one nail to touch, lightly, the dip beside his pelvic bone, and his body would be primed with that one little scratch. He traced the crest-line on my upper lip, up and down, up and down, biting it and licking it, and through the cross-hatching of the dark, I glimpsed determined hatred such as I had seen before in Heinrich Gruber and in misremembered faces, rubber and scrabbling. I was sore inside.

We fought.

'You almost force me to abandon control,' he said.

My clitoris hurt in a television studio. It rang as I moved in my chair. I feared the blows of his body had dislodged it. It ticked like a poisonous insect as I mouthed the tenets of the liberation movement. I hated men for doing this to me. I wanted to elevate women to a level of exquisite supremacy: I wished to incite them as I excited them. We are so beautiful and so determined after all. Men are lumpen beasts milk-fed by their mothers. I threw bombs in ink and in our home.

So he is not charmed by me any more. The signs are as evasive as they are insistent: death knells ring so deep in the brain they can be half heard or ignored.

It's in his eyes: they've lost that dark liquefaction, like a chemical change that used to occur when he looked at me. He doesn't show me things in shops any more. He ignores the books I tell him to read. He makes me nervous and frightened in his presence. He doesn't linger to talk to me in the shower. He has few expectations: when I am late, he is cold and not angry. My enunciations, my odd night thoughts, my breathing patterns, are not streaked with magic. I fail to charm him.

*

And now: he has thumped the shelf that holds my books, hurting his hand. I am a woman who is hit at home and I have failed to notice the progress of violence. Injury is a diversion from boredom or jealousy: it jolts the sluggish flow, and the wound must later be mended with well-bred guilt, or the euphoria of new understanding, or with sobbing orgasm.

I made a speech at an international women's conference, and I was given an award. I slept with a man in the velvet corner of my studio, to ward off Laurence's infidelities.

The first indication was always in the eyes.

I came home very late after two days in Boston.

'Hello, how are you?' Laurence asked stiffly.

The irregularity of his focus made his gaze impenetrable. When he was angry, he retreated behind private school politeness, shouting only after asking how I was. He was full of unnecessary thanks and proffered drinks.

'How are you, Adèle?'

'I'm very well, my darling.' I put down my bags and hugged him. He was stiff. He gave me a small self-conscious smile. 'Give me a *proper* smile,' I said, 'a Laurence smile – not a badly behaved boy smile – son of a preacher man.'

His smile sickened, as though haggard with sleeplessness. I felt my heart ticking. He picked up my scarf where I had thrown it.

'I've decided,' he said abruptly, looking away from me, 'I've – and I have Carolyn's blessing – I think Melina shouldn't –Well, I don't want Melina seeing you any more.'

I was silent.

'Why not, Laurence?' The blood sank from my face.

'I've told you.'

'I – don't understand.'

'I've told you before. You're just not – I don't think you're good for her. She can be influenced at her age.'

'With my *bad* influence?'

He looked at me with his despairing expression. He shrugged. I glimpsed traces of disgust.

We were silent.

'You're jealous of me!' I said suddenly.

He stood there stolidly.

'You're jealous of me – and – you have been for years.'

Blood came to his cheeks. My own face echoed his with a dark blush.

'You're jealous of my career. You don't like it, do you? Because it shows up shortcomings – inadequate whatever. Frustrations of your own. Because you never built the Chrysler Building, for Christ's sake. And then you see me on some dumb stupid chat show. And now you're jealous of me and Melina, because we're a team. We exclude you. Because we're horrible, vicious females who *plot* against you – I know, I know that's what you think. Well, you can go to hell, Laurence.'

'I'm there already.'

'What?' I looked up at him. I wanted to knock his head against the wall, subdue him and make him love me. I suddenly noticed how old he was, the furrows on his forehead bleeding into drier fine lines.

'What do you mean, Laurence?'

'I'm – I – my life. I've fucked up.'

'No you haven't.'

'I have! This isn't what I thought it would . . .'

'Why do you say that, darling?'

'Because – '

I wrapped my arms around him. His torso was so stiff, it was like holding Melina in a spasm of self-disgust. I held my face against his shirt. We hugged. He was warm by my cheek. I pulled him harder towards me and kneaded his back. We made small moaning noises, nuzzling and butting like animals, pulling each other closer.

'I'm being punished,' said Laurence. 'For leaving a wife with a baby. It's only fate after all. Do you have any idea what my father said to me after I did that? You can't do those things in your life and get away with it. And now I have this – a daughter who won't eat. I have – you. My marriage – relationship – gone *rotten*.'

'No it's not. I love you.'

'It's *high*, for God's sakes, Adèle – crawling with horrors. Can't you smell it?'

'You're like a Jacobean dramatist. We have – We have problems. But you're my love.'

'And you're mine.'

'And you don't want me to see your daughter, who's become like my daughter. You want to take my daughter away from me?'

He was silent.

'You don't mean it, do you, Laurence?'

My scalp prickled.

I laughed. I kissed his face.

'Of course I'll see Melina,' I said.

He stiffened under my arm. He pulled himself away, my hold on him crumbling – hand, arm, shoulder – as he disengaged himself to stand up. His mouth was set, his focus again impermeable.

He caught my eye. He shrugged.

A wave of nausea hit me. I saw the colour of Melina's hair. I heard her light high American girl voice explaining a theory to me. I wanted to run to her and embrace her. It was a physical need for her, my own ghost arms hugging her in my mind.

'No!' I said. I laughed. 'You can't do this to me.'

'I don't want you to see her. I'm going to visit her at Carolyn's.'

'No, you asshole. I will see her. And I will not see you. I'll make sure *you* end up in hell.'

'I've told you – ' He shrugged again. 'I'm there.'

'And I'm supposed to feel sorry for you? So I accept your *outrageous* behaviour. You hit me, Laurence. Hit me! What is this? What have I – what have I sunk to? You *hit* me! For God's sake, what am I?' A sob blocked my throat and cut my speech.

He stared at me, a glint over his occluded gaze.

'Am I a thing to be hit?' I said.

'No.'

I tried to breathe.

'You know, you're – *depressed*,' I said. 'It's taken me so long to see it. You think you've failed and so you're depressed – but in your upper-middle class, whatever it is – Winchester choir boy – way, you can't express it. God forbid. That would mean more failure. You can't *tell* me you're goddamned lethargic, depressed, football kicking, so you listen to marching music and smash a picture. And you know what depression is, Laurence? Anger. It's anger.'

'Psychobabble.'

'Well, do normal people hit their wives? And slam out of cars to threaten drivers? Do they? Yes?'

'No, no, of course *I'm – a – total – asshole*,' said Laurence, drawing his words out in parody. 'And you – ' he took one step towards me and gripped my shoulders. 'And you, dear Adèle, are an angel, as the world and his wife knows.'

'You can't stand it, can you?'

'No.'

'It's just – male pride.'

'No it fucking well isn't. You haven't got the first bloody clue.'

'You sound so sweetly British when you raise your voice. Why haven't I got a clue, or whatever you said?'

'Because – for a start you're never here to know what's going on.'

'But my life is different now. I can't get in at six every evening to feed the fucking dogs. I can't change that now.'

'I don't want you to. Really, Adèle, I don't.'

'No?'

'No. But – it's not worth it – not worth discussing now.'

The warmth ran from my face again.

'Even if you were there to feed poor Tray and Appledore,' he said, 'you'd be two hours late and then discover that meat made you ill that day. But it doesn't matter.'

I sat down. I breathed deeply. I needed to flush my brain with oxygen.

'I understood it all recently,' I said. 'In a flash of clarity, I understood you, Laurence . . .'

'Really?' he said, abstracted.

'You think you've got to get over me. I'm there to be *got over* by the sensible man – you have an addiction to me you don't want, but beyond that, you don't really *like* me very much. You battle against being with me, as if it's against your better judgement. I think you feel – weak for being susceptible. To someone like me. You're waiting till you can be with someone sensible. That's what I think.'

'I've loved you so very much, every nerve, every vein of me.'

My heart thumped painfully. 'You have loved me?'

He nodded.

I turned away and cried wetly, in a sudden storm of crying. I glimpsed a future. I almost retched.

'I can't bear this,' I said.

He looked straight into my eyes with the darkness of his.

'I've really loved you,' he said. His eyebrows merged again into a line. Car headlights moved slowly around the ceiling. 'I love you too much. I can't . . .'

We were silent.

'Laurence,' I said. I sobbed. 'Every fibre and brain cell, atom of you – is a thing of love to me, every little beating part, every horrible smelling part – it's as if I'm in love with it. It's only you I want to be with. You were the first man I ever loved.'

'Huh.'

'True.'

He looked at me; he half turned away. His shoulders had sunk. He looked old, his back slumped.

He became restless, as though about to leave the room. 'I love you too much, I always have,' he said. His forehead crumpled. 'We've never been able to live together, have we?' he said.

'You've changed.'

'Shall we count the fights? Walk outs? Nights spent away?'

'Are you surprised? I hate you for having ever laid a finger on me. I *hate* you for that, Laurence, so much. I'll never forgive you – I let a man hit me without walking out. Oh, God.'

He stared at me blankly.

'We hate each other,' he said, almost casually. 'Haven't you noticed?'

I looked at him coldly.

'The myth,' he said. 'I *hate* all that fucking rubbish, that, that *mythology* that's whipped up around what you do. Making people think you're – some goddess. Available to them.'

'Jealousy, Laurence,' I said. 'It's not pleasant.'

'Shut the fuck up. God, what do you think it's like trying to live with a woman who's always exactly two hours late. Beyond reason. And a common flirt. Flirts with every child-man-woman-dog?'

'How *dare* you call me a common flirt in your constipated British Broadcasting Company voice?'

'Corporation.'

'I do not flirt with dogs.'

'Doormen. Women behind make-up counters. Audiences. You're never with me.'

He rose from his slumped position, gripped my shoulders and shook them. I recoiled.

'Get your hands off me.' I twisted away. My heart was beating hard. I walked towards the window. I saw his reflection moving in the glass. I could still feel the ripple of his grip on my shoulder.

'Come to bed with me,' he said.

I looked over to him standing by the fireplace, his gaze half lost in the dark.

'No,' I said.

'Why not?' he said quietly. He walked towards me. Panic drifted through me.

'Because you,' I said, backing towards the window, 'are a monster. You take my child from me and you expect me to fuck you.'

'How many times, dear one, infamous little Loulou,' he said, darting towards my waist and tickling me, prodding so I cried out, 'have you ended up in bed with me to make it all better?'

I backed into the glass. I tried to move from his grip.

'No!' I said.

'Cunt.'

'I'm going to leave you,' I said in panic, my voice unlike my own.

'I know you are. But don't you think we're rather energetic enemies – really?' His voice was macabre in its lightness, its enunciations so precise. 'How many fat little dicks do you fuck in that studio? In your tragic shrine – to your good self?'

I turned my head from him.

'And not me? Not good old shambling old Laurence Mahon, the moderately successful architect who's lost his touch. Not exciting or useful enough for Loulou.' He gripped my shoulders hard. His voice rose. 'You drive me mad.'

I twisted my shoulder, panic rising and making my heart beat fast. I heard myself whimper. He knocked my head a little, one cheek then the other, slapping the temple.

I could see the future, rolling on and on, dull as prairie. A shot of vomit hit my mouth, and I swallowed it, my own vomit an acid streak in my throat.

*

It was a hot summer. The metal car exhaust gritted my sinuses. Sleep deprivation left an almost chemical aftertaste, like the acrid trickle of cocaine down the back of the throat, a sensation of tiredness that was spangled and synthetic. There was black grit on my skin like pepper shot, and as I walked uptown along the bleached gridlocked avenues, cars five wide and the sirens a solid layer of sound, the city was a mirage shivering on the verge of combustion. I saw white spots of light in my head and my skin was instantly wet. It was as though I were in Qatar, Dubai, Bahrain. I was a nothingness in a trail of heat and sand and white air strips. The offices had a blind refrigerated look. The broiling heat gathered early, so by noon there was a tense volcanic hush.

I looked at my photo printed on a page, and I was soothed. I wondered what my father would think, and whether he would be proud of his Adèle, who took what she was given and created a small empire of it. Excess wards off men as it entices notoriety. Fame is a sexual flight beyond sex. If I worked, he did not hurt me. If I sank my head in a book, it became a senseless thing, my mechanical focus an analgesic.

I slept in the day in the studio. I dribbled like an old lady on my pillow the moment I fell asleep, viscous slicks of saliva pressing my ear when I woke. I slept through the bugling sun in the afternoon. I woke early evening, my hand clamped to my crotch like a child to a pacifier, and the sweat had dried in places, and I was panting, hallucinations and black headaches. I kept thinking of my mother and how she had been left by my father. I could barely examine it. I thought I saw their shapes in the shadows of the blinds. I twitched and slumped through the night. The sirens were company. The late night radio programmes were like voices from another time, like far distant shipping news.

The studio was hot in the early hours. I heard the sound of the artist next door grinding glass. My cover photographs were animated in the midsummer night, their blacks and whites so distinct they seemed to dilate and recede.

Returning home the next day, the sensation I felt when I opened the door was instantly recognisable. It had been imprinted upon me as a girl. When my father had left many years before, it had been the same. The echo of the apartment had changed. The hounds didn't thump against the kitchen door. The space left by missing objects altered the acoustics of my footsteps.

He came into the room quietly. I jumped.

'You're here,' he said.

The head turns to vegetable matter when hit.

He came towards me. I screamed, I heard it with a time delay, and I bit, I grabbed at objects near me, I kicked him, and my head made the window pane boom and shudder as soft as a sail.

The blows became addictive to him, they grew an elastic momentum of their own. I couldn't fight him. I clawed his face, I spat my own blood that caught his lower lip. A clot of pain hit my eye to darkness. Then the other. There was a punch-punch-punch like a punch bag. I watched it outside myself for long strung moments as though I was my own ghost, dazed after the first sear of pain. My terror haloed me, not touching me as I saw the animal madness in his eyes, like his dogs when rutting, and I heard my face pulp. The crushing of flesh resembles the fibrous compression of fruit.

The silence was as separate from me as the screams, all sound sealed, only the textures of beating palpable, and I was quiet as I slid, my spine jagging against the window seat to the floor, and our blood merged in a hot sweet bath, his and mine.

My head swelled in its decay. It sweated liquid that was

surprisingly thin. The eyes closed to slits smooth and slick as my own genitals. I had three stitches in my scalp and two neat little ones on my finger.

TWENTY-
FOUR

I couldn't see the photographer Dérioz for some time after my eyelid operation. My face had swollen in new ways. The swellings bloomed suddenly and delicately as though all the flesh of my face was now transient. The skin seemed raw and taut, as if I had been peeled. There were narrow strips of transparent tape around my eyes.

The boy Eric was frantic. His stormy protests were interspersed by calm. Later to be revealed as mock calm, designed to manipulate me. His urgent wish to establish communication was driven by sex, but he translated this into romance in his mind. He wanted to try out his newly used genitals again.

I had some rogue lines on my face – mouth, brow, eyes – filled in with collagen. Dr Kreitzman recommended one of his colleagues, Dr Urvoy, an impressive young practitioner in a white coat who injected collagen drops the length of my wrinkles. I winced as the skin was punctured. The forehead sent pain in a starburst through my scalp. A string of blood beads bloomed.

At first, the collagen pumped up the flesh, so I was unevenly swollen. Eventually, as with most surgical procedures, the swelling subsided into a pleasing surface plumpness. I sent my suitor, M Dérioz, on a little vacation while my collagen settled into its new home. I suggested it was about time he visited

Maman in the Lot, and bought him a new shirt for the occasion. I always have a sense that he is a boy cared for by his mother, with his sweet smelling wool and his fractious young mouth.

I am still beautiful, after all. Time has attacked me, but I have such bones, the face's stark rhythm, while blondes and small noses fade.

I think for some years I have been chilled in the shadow of Loulou. I've been attempting travesty, as though success were simply a mathematical solution, whereas in truth it marries laborious equation with purest inspiration. My pen is stilled by old shadows.

The journalists, I note, have begun to call me 'reclusive'. This amuses me. In recent years, I have received scatterings of attention for unwise comments, for a small car crash, for the AIDS-related death of the Loulou photographer, for the clothes I've worn on television, for tussles with the media, and for quotes I have given on pressing contemporary issues. Now I have become 'reclusive'. There will be a whole new set of angles for them to cull from that moniker, and perhaps a paparazzi value. I think I will only allow Eric to take my photograph, and have him step in as minder should there be a requirement.

Eric writes me cards from the Lot, displaying defensive nonchalance with floral outbursts. He wants to suffer for love, you see, though he thinks he rebels against the outrage of his suffering. I would not choose that way any longer.

If you are hurt by someone so the pain reaches the level of the bones, you cannot choose to suffer again, because a small part of you has been killed off. There is nerve death. I remember the suffering now in three stages: when Laurence changed towards me; when I went to hospital; and when he married Crêpe Suzette. I couldn't stay much longer in our

Gramercy Park. By the end, the pain saturated me, and I had to leave that city, I had to follow a chimera to blank a little of the pain with false hope.

Perhaps young Eric sees his love for Adèle Meier in stages, from absurd infatuation to sexual obsession, scored with anger and frustration. I suppose it is not so easy for poor Eric. I must make sure he is happy in his new job, and that he can afford extra developing solutions for his pictures.

Young men like Eric remind me of my Karli in their passions and their intelligence, those qualities the root of their pain. Karli joined anti-Vietnam rallies when he was only a little boy. He lost his mother in his early teens. He graduated *summa cum laude* from the University of Virginia, and I was so proud of him, so very proud of Karli, and our father would have been proud of him, too. Later, Karli moved to Washington DC for graduate school. I thought quite early that he was gay, but he never told me: it got lost somewhere in the diaspora that was our family, along with the nieces and nephews in Wichita Falls and Chesapeake, who knew about their Aunt Adèle but did not often see her. I tried to tell Karli I was happy for him, and I think he understood me, but he never directly told me about his life. I wanted to meet his boyfriend. But our family had done this for us, cut us off and scattered us and made us think such distance was not so very out of the ordinary. Karli and I were each other's love; he wrote me long letters, he fell silent, he wrote me shorter letters, then called in the middle of the night, and that was the way of our family. Our father left, and we never spent a Thanksgiving together after our mother died.

I went out with my face protected by cosmetics. I bought a frothing skirt in Auteuil, roses on dark pink net over layers of white net. It resembled the clothes Papa used to buy me very occasionally when he was away from home, just as he once bought me a bottle of *Je Reviens*, so precious and expensive for a child.

That day, I got home, carrying my shopping, and Laurence had called again. The voice held echoes of times that were as familiar as they were forgotten. He offered no excuse for his delay of some months. He said there was a possibility of him coming to Paris. He sounded cautious and formal, but friendly.

My surgeon, Dr Kreitzman, said to me that I have reached the optimum level of rejuvenation that is desirable, and that further procedures aren't necessary for a period of time. But once a face lift has been performed, it is customary for the patient to repeat the procedure. I may have my face discreetly lifted again when we are ready: the surgeon can use the same scars as on previous occasions to make his incision. The skin is more firmly attached to the muscle sheet beneath it now, since the severed connecting tissue scars and re-forms like glue.

I fear such pain like a fever, but then I blank it out.

There have been complaints lodged by Eric that he cannot do his work. He tells me so in an abstract and complicated manner, pacing my apartment with the loose-socket walk of the young. He has no idea of his own crumpled, iridescent youth. The concave area between his hips is vulnerable, the curvature of his shoulder blades at odds with his bloom. There is the church incense smell, the stale smoke, the grey eyes: the palette of my little suitor.

He grumbles.

'Well, so be it, Eric,' I tell him. 'Try a little harder, my sweet one.'

'But you distract me.'

'The image in your head distracts you.'

He is intense and solemn, that boy. He should be careless with young sap.

303

'Need you live your life with such blinding and articulate seriousness, Eric?' I ask him.

He loves to prepare surprises for me of an elaborate and flattering nature, but prone to failure. Then occasionally I send quaint packages on bikes to his work place: candy and belts and lens brushes just for him. Sometimes he deals with my publishers and accountants when my voice needs a rest. He rebels from time to time. It always takes me by surprise when one of his storms approaches, but I know it will pass. He grouches and bitches and punishes me until it becomes somewhat tiresome. He is all curled lip and explosive declarations. He simply fails to understand that my preoccupations lie elsewhere, that I am very busy.

I wear shades all the time, and every day, now, something happens: I ride a motorbike with a youth; I taste new intoxications in alarming hues, in tiny measures, in unknown bars; I eat grubby couscous; I dress as a geisha or a doll or a candled spectre to play out seduction in all its varieties; I suffer strange pains, and experiment with painkillers. I live with the albatross of Laurence, but Loulou is dead, and my thoughts fill notebooks with bright artifice and truths, as yet unstructured. There is an unfurling, like a warm baby fern nudging its casing. My celebrity seems to flicker. I think it is all but moribund, then it rears up in some alarming fresh metamorphosis. The later stages of fame travesty the original, the air so rarefied only strange plants grow: a life distilled to its extremes in rumour and quote and retouched image. I can barely quite think of it.

Eric is my manservant, rather better even than Jean-Pierre – surprisingly swift and assertive – and my beloved pet, like an orphan or a boy minion or a tom kitten. He arranges to have my windows fixed when I am busy; he cuts out articles from newspapers for my interest, to initiate college-style discussions; he tracks down chiropractors and courier services. He is infinitely patient and inventive in his assistance. He is determined and possessed in sex. The former virgin has had a taste of pleasures, and wants more, and more, and more. He has been guided into skills of consummate timing and the delicacy of pauses, of quivers and deliberate spaces, but beyond he is vigorous, more forward than ever I would have guessed. After his sly passions and intellectual circumlocutions of the daytime, he is almost angry in the night; he wants to possess and invade my body. I have to control him and command patience, and this he learns before the eruption. Such sex lends me a pale bloom.

Laurence Mahon is now some kind of a roving reporter with a professional speciality, who lives in England with his wife, La Crêpe Suzette herself, and their two sons, Seamus and Fabian. Seamus and Fabian! He never had children with me. He had a daughter with the neurotic wife in New York and then his double dose of sons with a dull Briton, with me as child-free intermezzo. Milk pumps and episiotomy stitches are a messy business.

I was not as kind to Laurence as I could have been. He didn't understand that sometimes I played with concepts, I spun moods for art and interest. He always thought I meant everything I said.

I didn't notice that my life had become extraordinary. I didn't notice it as it occurred, after years of living in the cold and working as a pretty servant on the Upper East Side. It crowded upon me, I was overstretched, and I was tired, and my life at home swung between extremes, and when I did notice what was happening to me, Laurence became unhappy. If one cuts one's life into stages retrospectively, that time was gothic and glorious, yet there was no purity there.

So mentally I prepared myself for my meeting with Laurence. All the sublime philosophies and urgent dialogue that had plumed through my mind over the years, as I soared about my apartment to music, washed the dishes, walked by the river, all that had gone. I was a shell.

I focused on my face with terror and elation, the poetry of a practised position studied in my triptych of mirrors, the sick shock of a slack expression caught unawares, and I used to be an angel, Laurence thought, I used to have a praline heart of a face scored with brown and red: the face, like the breast, a simple bloom of curves. He used to love this face with passion and obsession. He said he looked at this woman and he could not believe the face was in the same room as him, lying on a pillow, looking up at him, instead of glimpsed on the street or spied and treasured in the Russian Tea Room.

When my eyes were soft pale canvasses of skin, I went to see my doctor, Dr Kreitzman. For all his collagen-wielding colleagues, it is Dr Kretizman who knows me the best. He has an instinctive understanding of my needs. He kisses me hello, he praises my clothes (I play with conventions, diamonds on plastic, visual dares, especially for him) and then he retreats into the smoothest professionalism, the down-shift so calibrated my fears are paralysed.

A large new sculpture graced Dr Kreitzman's consultation room. The blue carpet had been replaced by one in grey-verdigris, once again its tufts mixing with faint medical scents, my nerves carried upon those strands of smell. I let my fingers drift beneath my jaw bone. The tightening achieved by the lift and liposuction had slackened over time so when I lowered my chin, age's frog pouch appeared.

We talked in the late afternoon, when favoured clients can relax.

'Of course, a face lift can be performed, though it's comparatively soon after the last,' he said. 'We can afford some slack. We could attend to the problem areas next year.'

'This has dropped a little,' I said. I brushed my jaw.

He leaned over. 'May I?' He placed both his hands softly on my cheeks, and nudged the flesh upwards. 'Of course – It will do that with time,' he said. 'Certainly, there's a little tidying up – call it good housekeeping if you like – that could be done.'

'You think so?'

'We can gently reposition. But the effects of the full face lift will be more apparent than last time. Are you sure you're happy with that?'

'Yes.' My voice was alien.

He observed me, then he smiled, and repositioned himself on his seat. His movements were heavy. His cufflinks were like small bullets of gold. His features had become weightier, his stomach filling his shirt.

'You know, Adèle, you have great visual awareness,' he said. 'The earlier we attend to potential problem areas, the less aggressive the surgery has to be, and then – then you can keep it up. We have a little time to spare. It won't be an emergency procedure, so to speak. We'll be catching things before they start to slip. You can congratulate yourself on your decision.'

'Thank you,' I said. My tones thinned in Dr Kreitzman's rooms.

'And your features. They remain very fine, Adèle,' he said. His voice emerged calm as oil.

I fear ugliness like loss of limb or cancer. I would starve or vacuum my flesh were it fat, as Melina vomits hers.

So the patient was dry mouthed and sedated, her knowledge of the pain to come glimpsed and chemically calmed.

Once more, the surgeon opened up her face. She slumped in the operating theatre. Her skin was tighter and thinner than before, falling to rumpled softness in some areas. The surgeon pierced and incised the old sutures. The face was reopened along the same scars. He inserted his scalpel deep underneath the facial skin, separating it from the underlying structure.

He sliced at the fascia, the fibrous connective tissue that forms in sheets below the surface of the skin and between muscle groups. The face was more firmly attached than it had been before its first separation, the flesh glued with scar tissue, but it fell and flopped when the surgeon pared it away from its roots. He suctioned the excess fatty tissue that had fallen into the neck with the ageing process. The surgeon tightened the muscular system of the face and neck with stitches. Blood leaked and ran. Nurses mopped it. He pulled at the sheets of loose skin on either side of her face, stretching, cutting sections of cheek and scalp near her ear, redraping and stitching. The patient's age was surgically removed and incinerated.

The face a nest of bruises.

I cannot go through it again.

The pain nearly defeated me this time. I was carried, limp, into the cab to take me to a new small hotel and clinic specifically catering to patients recovering from cosmetic procedures.

There were private elevators, neck rests, and nurses on call. The most intimate of suffering was lived out behind tulips and discretion.

I'm not sure whether days or weeks are passing. At home on the boulevard Saint Michel, I can alter my position only with small muscle movements, my face bound in a gauze web of pain.

I ignore Eric's calls. The poor child resorts to offers to complete my annual accounts, buy me dinner at Polidor, fetch and deliver my dry-cleaning. He is a butterfly battering at my window. He is brilliant with new beginnings, but I seal myself from him, and still he taps, amazing me and alienating me with his attentions.

'Please, darling, try to learn patience,' I tell him on the

telephone but the lack of movement in my mouth skims my voice of its tones, and he asks me if I am quite all right.

Laurence Mahon, you see, was the only love. On Cape Cod, when we ran away together, I thought someone had dropped me from the sky, and I had drifted sideways to a kind of heaven. I felt it in the plants and the coffee and the sky-blown air, walking up the crookedy throughways to the houses on their banks of last-bloom flowers and tortoise-coloured stones. We walked along the spits, long rambles out through the dunes and sea grasses, and we had sex, the wordless communication of bodies enclosed in each other, those secret hours, our bodies separate in the day, wandering together and apart to look at pools in the sand. How strange, our bodies separate, air between them blowing off the bluff, blowing my dress about, his T-shirt, the lighthouse there, the bodies that had been dark and enclosed only hours before.

There is another life, then. We think that when we've grown up, away from the sea-ringed fables of youth and adolescence, that life is a bitchy tragedy after all. We believe cynicism to be a component of intelligence, and happiness the province of the mentally inferior. The huge shock of disappointment when adulthood dawns on us, rings in our ears and resonates, a dull dark earache around the sunshine later. We have a knowledge of the world beneath this glossy vista and that funny moment, the awareness that we are ageing and mortal, of cancer and betrayal. There is a trail of little pebbles indicating all we once were, of all the terrible wrong choices. You can never possess the clear white field of sand of your childhood, running across it fresh after hotel breakfast with the adults, some vacation once, in Deauville. And people are dying in Africa. And there's a wheelchair.

And then later, as life's wonderful surprise gift, there comes a second bout of joy, all dazzles and small rainbows, a realisation that such black-clad youthful existentialism can be transcended. I think I was given it after I had been alone for so long and had learned how to struggle and how to live.

Now I wonder, here in Paris, and my vision widens again.

I am taking pills to fight off an infection. I've had a physician visit. I cannot think much about it. My analgesics calm me. There is some skin tension on the scars behind my ears, where the tugging on the seams is the greatest. The blood the surgeon draws seeps around the ears. It drifts slowly, balletically.

Dr Kreitzman is away at a conference. I told him before he left that I've been experiencing difficulty in keeping my eyes closed. I suspect they lie open a slit at night, because they're dusty in the mornings. More of the white is revealed since the lids have been surgically tightened, but this is a minor problem, and is not surprising to the surgeon.

'You're not produced – you're not quite who you are yet,' he tells me. 'The real Adèle is emerging.' He taps his pen on the table. 'It's a new beginning. We have a way to go.'

It is the face that is the locus of the pain. I have had the cuts re-dressed in bandages. The infection I've developed can occur as a side-effect of surgery, and I battle against it with medication. I can't quite move.

I don't know exactly when Laurence is due to arrive in Paris.

He met me in my twenties. I am a middle-aged woman now. Laurence is four years older than me, but men become rugged eagles, they wear the lines that fan from their eyes as simply as they shrug themselves into a jacket, with barely a thought, with an innate strut, the *droit du seigneur*. The man ages and he burnishes; the woman fades into oblivion, pity, faint revulsion.

Laurence is four years my senior, yet it is I who carry the burden of middle age.

*

He would meet me in the lobby of the Hôtel Montalembert. Of course.

I dressed in the skirt from Auteuil with a tiny cropped jacket: a miniature box of a jacket like a Chinese girl's or a doll's, in pure white velvet. I took out my father's pocket book. I wore candy-pink hose. I arranged myself all morning, wincing nimbly between the fires in my flesh. I sculpted the hair, and then shook it out into limping curls, dark whorls on a sugar velvet shoulder, and catching a glimpse, I thought perhaps I had never looked better. I had a suggestion of colour on my cheeks – the faintest blush of pink – Snow White, Laurence would call me. It seemed to me I looked quite young under my bedroom lamps. The bathroom spotlights I use only for fine detailing – the outer swoop of the eyeliner's curve, the painting of the cupid's bow – because they make me look unlike myself. The lipstick brush bobbed over my upper lip's distinctive crest. Men have liked to lick and bite that line. My cheeks felt tight. My mouth spans a different repertoire of movements from that of a few years ago, less expansive, but perhaps more elegant.

I took a handful of scarves. I ordered a limo, dark windows, blinds, for unlimited use. The driver came to collect me at the appointed time. He accompanied me through the lobby.

By the place St Thomas d'Aquin, my stomach was in spasm. Sweat clung coldly to my skin, and I needed the bathroom. I made the driver turn down the boulevard Raspail, circle, and chug slowly back towards rue de Montalembert. Trees were cold in the grey light. I breathed deeply. We stopped by the sidewalk in front of the hotel, and I paid off a strolling porter to keep him away. The hotel had been modernised, its windows now large paned but shadowed, obscuring the figures in the lobby, yet instinctively I knew that I would recognise him by the simplest movement.

When you see someone again after years, there is a falling into place. All the old mauled images shuffle into a different formation.

My heart sent small drums to my throat, I was so nervous.

I looked at the hotel through the window. I had slept with the man within those walls so many times. History dies. Porters emerged from the door.

I watched. My eyeballs dulled. I thought I saw him through the dark glass, just glimpsed him as he stood up and circled the lobby with an impatient movement, wearing a white shirt. A police siren came by, stretching down the boulevard. But perhaps it was not him after all. My heart beat with a light fast pace. I was not certain. I saw others in various incarnations and ghost trails: dark and motionless, sketched figures moving towards the door. They carried fragments of him. He could have been any of a number of men in the lobby.

My heart raced faintness through me. I stared through the shadows with such intensity that my temples seemed to contract in diamond splinters of vision, the bodies moved around their sea world behind the glass, and then I saw him. The figure stood, walked; it was Laurence.

He came out of the hotel. He looked impatiently around, then he noticed the car, long and discreet with its shades. I just saw him catch sight of me. He caught a glimpse, and it was like a snap shot of the past. He saw, fleetingly, a section of me as he had loved me, the skin so firm, the cheeks and eyes that were celebrated and loved. It was there on its stalk, a face growing independent of its body. It was coddled in lace, scarves, girls' things. He saw a clear pale flash of beauty, a memory of her features come to life; that was all he saw. His mouth opened.

He was walking towards me. Each step a year. Your life passes you by in slow motion when you fall from a height.

He was broader, the hair a little shorter. The height and stride and dark radiance were there. I tried to grasp them to savour, but I couldn't. They were too obvious, as though manufactured: these are the charms of Laurence Mahon that hook me. It was a play I had already been to. A knowledge came to me, a certainty. It was a slumping of organs that had been tense for two decades. It was a gift of neutrality. When I rooted for his smell in my mind, I recalled it only with the mechanics of description.

He was coming towards me, that fragmented moment of recognition on his face. The pedestrians moved along, dogs ran, Laurence came towards me, and I was free to leave. I left him, standing on a sidewalk, as he had once left me bleeding. I told the driver to go. I looked back once more, and saw him turn in surprise, the whiteness of his shirt bright in tree shadow. He caught, once more, the tiniest glimpse of familiar features in the centre of a face, the head balloon large with gauze, bandage, scarf.

I peeped from between the shades of the limo like a infant through her cradle, frothingest lace to protect her skin, laid as an eggshell upon a lamb fleece, and we drove away. My bandages sweated beneath the scarf.

I see a sun setting in its yolk behind the snow blossoms of the Luxembourg (suddenly Oriental, like the tall wands in Tiffany's or the blossomy trees about the 42nd Street library) and my face is egg fresh. An egg in its hood of bandages, resembling the ruffs they put around your boiled egg for Easter when you are a little girleen. The *Mauserl* Adela had an egg ruff. Melina had one, made of my Chantilly lace. Easter eggs and plastic grass.

The woman is perfected. She is incarcerated now in footbound perfection. The body is plastic after all. It has achieved new dimensions of suffering and mutability. We pierce, we cut, we vacuum to new shapes. It is our ultimate offering, beauty attained through sickness, the narcissistic exultation of the victim, bled and starved to perfection, as little Melina.

I know happiness, looking at such a spilled sun. The Dufy on the street moves. All its fine strokes and railings score the suspension of evening in the city. I am born swaddled, a swaddling babe. I can fall in love using my tight tight face and the infant roundness of surprise in the eyes: chocolate and love.

I always needed my Holy Grail, the male with his hormones and his gifts to me. But I will never find my father, I will never see Laurence.

Our beauty keeps us indoors: it keeps us very sweet and still. I will sit in my apartment on the boulevard Saint Michel with my recast flesh and write of punishment, self-hatred, starvation. There is no place for the totems of an earlier era, such as my flighty crusader, pretty Loulou, who rebelled against her men so naughtily and pleasingly. We created a revolution, and were punished for it, and started to enact the punishment upon ourselves.

Sometimes my skin hurts too much to write. Sometimes it punctures me, shoots me in suffering to cold heights of clarity. Through the decay, I see brilliance shining there.

The peeled skin of my face sends pain tensing in my fontanelles. I begin to think that there is paralysis in the left side of my face. The familiar prickling numbness performs its slow dance beneath my right cheek, but the left is dumb and weighted as a dentist's injection.

'You're experiencing some discomfort,' says the doctor, and he refers to nerve damage in his comforting parenthesis but his final prognosis has yet to be delivered.

I hope I helped women to see they can be strong, and they can be free. My bandages still hood me. My lace dress strokes my chin. I am numbed. I will sit here and sculpt beauty, liberation in imperfection. I write in a shaft of sunlight through the dust of my desk, and what I create is glittering and freakish.

*

The stitches removed, I look up, trying very hard to move my face. I see only the blank eyes of the nurses examining me, kind as little angels. A country-shaped stain dribbles onto the pillow, and forty years have now seeped away. The woman has the face of a girl.

TWENTY-FIVE

I was a girl with the face of a woman. I was thought strange as I was thought exquisite.

The townlet was pretty: Leibnitz, a small market town among the lakes, mountains, vines of western Styria.

Krampus the devil hits children if they are naughty, the Baron owns much of the land, and the roads are snowed under in winter. I am Puppi and I am *Mauserl* and I am little Adela Schatzerl.

My face was plump animal, round and soft as though fashioned with fur, but the first curves fell away by five, and by nine I was sculpted and severe, the eyebrows dark, cross, womanly, the bones pre-figuring the face to come. My nose was not pretty. It was faintly imperious, a strict line above the mouth's plump scroll.

The town made pink wine and pumpkin oil. We prayed in church on Sundays; we went to every Fest. The Priest ran Leibnitz with God's fear and God's benediction. He heard all sins, he blessed the Geselchtes at Easter.

This is where my parents lived, Hans Gerhardt and Maria Brigitta Doesinger Meier, with their John, their Kathrin, their Adelaide, their Karl. My Papa was a school teacher in Graz, and he spoke three languages, he played piano to us, he wanted us to be clever, extraordinary, impeccably mannered. He taught the children at school, and then he taught us, in the caught breath of our evenings, in the corners and darknesses. Discipline required self-denial, it led to glory.

I lay in bed every night, my knees to my chest, to dream for a while. I had a superstitious sequence for prayers, dolls, plans. When he visited me at night, we had another world. I was Papa's favourite, his secret favourite, so beautiful, so different from Mamma and ugly Kati. I wore the perfume he gave me, and I was the china doll, and I was the wife. So beautiful, so beautiful, so beautiful.

The scream was only a dream scream, and it flopped as a rigid object gone slack. And then he loved me, he caressed me to make it all better, because I vomited after the salt substance filled my mouth.

If it hurts, it is your duty, a punishment of pain that takes you heavenwards. You can't eat, and you fly higher. The Priest can make it kinder, the boys in the town can press it sore and better again.

You are your own gift, my father said.

All Orion/Phoenix titles are available at your local bookshop or from the following address:

Littlehampton Book Services
Cash Sales Department L
14 Eldon Way, Lineside Industrial Estate
Littlehampton
West Sussex BN17 7HE
telephone 01903 721596, *facsimile* 01903 730914

Payment can either be made by credit card (Visa and Mastercard accepted) or by sending a cheque or postal order made payable to *Littlehampton Book Services*.
DO NOT SEND CASH OR CURRENCY.

Please add the following to cover postage and packing

UK and BFPO:
£1.50 for the first book, and 50P for each additional book to a maximum of £3.50

Overseas and Eire:
£2.50 for the first book plus £1.00 for the second book and 50p for each additional book ordered

---

BLOCK CAPITALS PLEASE

name of cardholder ....

address of cardholder ....

....

....

postcode ....

delivery address
(if different from cardholder)

....

....

....

postcode ....

☐ I enclose my remittance for £............................

☐ please debit my Mastercard/Visa (delete as appropriate)

card number ☐☐☐☐☐☐☐☐☐☐☐☐☐☐☐☐☐☐

expiry date ☐☐☐☐

signature ....

prices and availability are subject to change without notice